NO PLACE FOR A LADY

Gill Paul is a London-based writer of historical novels and non-fiction books and articles. Her novels include *Women and Children First*, which tells the story of Reg Jones, a first-class steward on the *Titanic*, and *The Affair*, which takes place on the *Cleopatra* film set in Rome in 1962 as Elizabeth Taylor and Richard Burton fall in love. Her non-fiction includes a series of Love Stories which is published right around the globe: *World War I* and *World War II Love* Stories and *Royal Love Stories* are among the seven titles available. She is generally found at her computer all day, except at lunchtimes when she swims year-round in an outdoor pond.

To find out more about Gill Paul, please visit **gillpaul.com**, or on Twitter **@GillPaulAuthor**.

By the Same Author

Women and Children First
The Affair
We Sink or Swim Together

GILL PAUL

NO PLACE FOR A LADY

AVON

AVON

A division of HarperCollins*Publishers*
1 London Bridge Street,
London SE1 9GF

www.harpercollins.co.uk

A Paperback Original 2015

1

Copyright © Gill Paul 2015

A catalogue record for this book is
available from the British Library

ISBN-13: 978-0-00-827149-7

Set in Sabon by Born Group using Atomik ePublisher from Easypress

Printed and bound in the United States of America
by LSC Communications

Find out more about HarperCollins and the environment at
www.harpercollins.co.uk/green

For my brother Gray and sister Fo, who mean the world to me.

Odessa

Perekop

CRI

Eu

A

Sebastopol

ROMANIA

River Danube

BULGARIA

Varna

Bl

Constantinople

Scutari

Bosphorus

O T T O M A N   E M P I R E

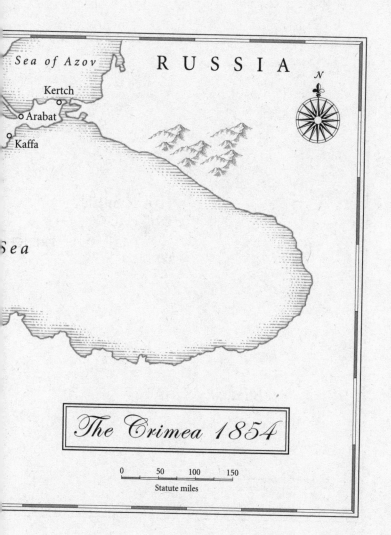

Sea of Azov

RUSSIA

Kertch

Arabat

Kaffa

Sea

The Crimea 1854

0   50   100   150

Statute miles

French Harbour

Sebastopol

Kamiesh

FRENCH

FRENCH

Black Sea

0   1   2   3
Statute miles

N

Malakov
Great Redan

SSIANS

Inkerman

R. Tchernaya

BRITISH

Fedoukine Heights

FRENCH

SARDINIANS

TURKISH

Kamara

BRITISH

Kadikoi

British Harbour

Balaklava

Prologue

25th October 1854

Mrs Lucy Harvington stands shivering on a hilltop near the coast of Crimea, watching armies massed for battle below, waiting to find out if her husband will die today. Charlie is somewhere in the group to the far left: she has overheard Lord Raglan pointing out the Light Brigade when giving an order and she peers in the direction he indicated to see indistinct figures on horseback, cold sunlight glinting on the steel of their bayonets. All around she can see lines of men standing poised, waiting for the order to rush forward and try to kill each other – men who are sons, nephews, husbands and fathers, even grandfathers. She can hear the impatient whinny of horses and the squawk of a bird high above. It sounds like a warning.

Suddenly it seems incomprehensible that she should find herself in such a situation. In less than a year her entire fortune has turned on its head: she's gone from being a young lady of just seventeen years who lived at home with her father and older sister, to being the wife of an army captain who has followed her husband to war in a remote, inhospitable land. She still can't quite believe the change in her circumstances. In London she has a wide circle of friends and is used to attending balls and soirées wearing fashionable new gowns and the latest hairstyles. Now she has been wearing the same gown for almost a week without the opportunity to wash, her cloak is smeared in mud and her hair hangs in matted coils. She spends most of her time alone while Charlie is out in the field. She is cold, her clothes are damp – they never seem to dry completely – and she is very, very scared.

But her fate has been sealed since that first unforgettable meeting with Charlie Harvington, the beginning of a chain of circumstances that had led her to this godforsaken hillside.

It was a dull November day in 1853, when London was thick with sooty fog and the stench of the Thames. Lucy had called upon the Pendleburys, old friends of her parents, in the hope of seeing their son Henry, whom she knew was home on leave from the army. They'd enjoyed a brief flirtation during his last leave and she was curious to see where it might lead. Unfortunately, Henry was absent and she had to make conversation with his mother and father, a rather staid couple. Once they had run through the usual topics – the weather, plans for the festive season, health of respective family members – Lucy offered to play the pianoforte and sing for them, simply to pass the time until she could decently make her excuses and leave.

She picked a Mozart *lied* that suited her first soprano voice. Her singing teacher was critical of her pronunciation of the German lyrics, but she was fond of the pretty melody. As she was singing, she heard the drawing-room door open and glanced up to see Henry Pendlebury standing in the doorway with a friend, a very handsome friend, kitted out in a royal blue tunic with gold braid draped over the chest, who was staring directly at her. The attention made her sing a little more sweetly, play a little more precisely, while she felt herself flush at the unexpected audience.

When she finished, all clapped heartily and Lucy bowed her head.

'Please don't stop. I could listen to you forever,' the stranger said. It appeared he couldn't take his eyes off her.

Henry Pendlebury laughed. 'Miss Gray, meet my army colleague, Captain Charlie Harvington. Charlie, this is Miss Lucy Gray.'

Charlie came forward to take her hand. He raised it to his lips, kissed it, then fell dramatically to his knees. 'I declare in front of all witnesses here present that I volunteer to be Miss Gray's willing slave and do her bidding for as long as she will tolerate me. Please, Miss Gray, tell me some service I might perform for you. I ask nothing in return but the honour of being allowed to remain in the presence of such breathtaking beauty.'

Lucy laughed, startled by his unconventional forwardness. 'Very well. I should like a cup of tea to wet my throat after its exertion.'

There was a pot of tea on a tray by the fire and Charlie bounded over to fetch her a cup, enquiring carefully about her taste for cream and sugar.

'Now I should like you to bring my shawl,' she said, enjoying the game with this lively stranger. She noticed a disapproving look pass between Mr and Mrs Pendlebury and knew she was pushing the boundaries of propriety but couldn't help herself.

Charlie fetched her shawl and as he held it towards her their eyes met. His were a startling blue, an unusual combination with his chestnut hair. He was smiling, but behind the smile she could sense something sad about him. She felt a tug at her heart and knew in an instant, all joking aside, that she was going to fall in love with him, and he with her. It was as simple as that.

When she rose to leave, as the hour was approaching when she must change for dinner, Charlie escorted her to her carriage and asked if he might call on her the following morning.

'What about me?' Henry called from the front door. 'Am I to be forgotten so readily, Miss Gray?'

'You must come too,' she insisted. 'Of course you must.'

But it was Charlie she had eyes for now. It was what the French called a *coup de foudre*, a deep-rooted, certain knowledge that they belonged together.

Now, eleven months later, she is standing on a hilltop in the Crimean peninsula, and realising she might never see Charlie alive again. She could even be killed herself, or taken prisoner by the Russians – and she's not sure which would be worse.

There is a bright flash down below, then a deafening explosion shakes the ground and she sinks to her knees in terror. 'Dear God,' she prays silently. 'Please save Charlie and please save me. I want to go home again. I want us to go back where we belong.'

PART ONE

Chapter One

11th January 1854

Dorothea Gray watched as Henderson walked slowly round the dining table dispensing devilled kidneys with a clatter of cutlery on a silver serving dish. Her sister Lucy waved him away but Dorothea accepted a modest portion, while their father licked his lips and directed the butler to heap his plate with spoonful after spoonful. The meaty, tangy smell mingled with that of freshly baked rolls and a certain mustiness that permeated the dining room, a mysterious odour no amount of spring-cleaning could shift. The girls' father lifted *The Times,* neatly folded into quarters, intending to peruse the front page as he ate, but was interrupted by Lucy, who lobbed a question across the breakfast table with studied casualness.

'Papa, would it be acceptable if Captain Harvington comes to call on you around eleven this morning? There's something he wishes to discuss with you.'

Dorothea looked up, instantly suspicious.

'What's that? Captain Harvington? Do I know him?' He frowned and peered over the rim of his glasses.

'Of the 8th Hussars. You've met him several times, Papa. He joined us for dinner the evening before last. Remember he

7

made you laugh with his witty impression of Lord Aberdeen?'

Still her father couldn't recollect the man and he screwed up his eyes with the effort.

Dorothea interrupted: 'What might Captain Harvington wish to see Father about?' As soon as she said the words, the answer came to her: 'You're not planning on getting engaged, are you? You've only known each other a matter of weeks. Besides, he may have to go to war soon if the Russians don't withdraw from the Turkish territories on the Danube.'

Lucy tilted her chin defiantly. 'No, we're not bothering to get engaged; we plan to marry straight away so that I can sail with him if he has to go to the Turkish lands. He says officers are allowed to take their wives along.'

Dorothea gasped and put down her fork. 'But that's ridiculous! What gentleman would ask his wife to go to war with him? It's an appalling idea.' She glanced at her father but he was savouring a bite of kidney, oblivious to the storm brewing between his daughters.

'We love each other with all our hearts. It's been nine whole weeks since we met and both of us agree we've never felt as sure of anything in our entire lives.' Lucy spoke passionately and in her words Dorothea could hear echoes of the romance novels she loved, full of chaste young girls and brooding heroes.

'What do Captain Harvington's family think of this idea? Surely they'll see that it's silly to rush into marriage while war looms? Everyone says it's inevitable after the Russians destroyed those Turkish ships at Sinope last November. Why not wait till he comes back? It's bound to be over quickly. The Russians are no match for us, especially when we are in alliance with the French. It would make much more sense to wait.' Dorothea cast around for further arguments that would carry weight with her flighty younger sister. 'We could plan a beautiful ceremony and there would be time to invite all the family members we haven't seen for years. You could have a dress especially made, and use Mother's Chantilly lace veil. Think of it, Lucy; a proper wedding, not something rushed and over-hasty ...' She tailed off at the determined glint in Lucy's eyes.

'Our minds are made up, Dorothea. Fortunately it's not up to you. It's between Papa and Charlie.' She turned to her father. 'Papa, you will listen favourably to his request, won't you? We are so much in love and he needs me to go with him and care for him. Besides, you don't want to be stuck with *two* old maids on your hands, do you?' She looked pointedly at her sister, unmarried at the age of thirty-one, who tutted at the rudeness of her jibe.

'What's that you say?' their father asked, exasperated that his poor hearing meant he had missed much of their conversation. 'What must I do?'

Lucy spoke slowly and clearly: 'Captain Harvington will come to see you at eleven. When you speak with him, just remember that I love him very much and want to be his bride.'

After breakfast, Dorothea followed her father down the hall to his study, where he liked to spend the morning snoozing over his newspaper. She waited till he was settled in his comfy leather armchair, with a view over the leafless trees of Russell Square, before speaking.

'Papa, I hope you agree that Lucy's ridiculous scheme to get married and go to war with the troops would be disastrous.'

'Quite.' Her father nodded in agreement.

Dorothea wasn't convinced that he understood the gravity of the situation, so she continued: 'She and Captain Harvington are both good-natured, happy-go-lucky characters, but neither has a practical bone in their bodies. And Lucy is far too young and giddy for marriage.'

'Yes, indeed.' He opened the newspaper.

'You have to stop them, Papa. I know it puts you in an awkward position, but I have a suggestion. Don't refuse permission outright, but play for time by telling them they can marry on Captain Harvington's return from war. Doubtless Lucy's head will have been turned by some other charming fellow by then and the marriage won't go ahead. Only a couple of months ago she was smitten with Henry Pendlebury, and before that it was Alexander Gwynn Jones. Make them wait and I'm sure this one won't last.'

'I expect you're right. Remind me: what is it that I am to do?'

Dorothea explained again, speaking slowly and clearly until it seemed the message had got through. The carriage clock on the mantel chimed ten, meaning she would be late for her work unless she got a move on. She was a member of the ladies' committee at a small charitable hospital in Pimlico and counted herself fortunate to have an occupation, unlike most ladies of her social class who spent their days sitting idly at home or calling upon friends for tea and gossip. If Chalmers had the carriage ready and traffic was not too heavy around Covent Garden, there was still a chance she could make it on time.

'Thank you, Father.' She leaned in to kiss his brow and he murmured his goodbyes before opening the newspaper and closing his eyes.

Looking back, Dorothea couldn't put her finger on a time when her father's mental acuity had begun to decline. In her youth he had run a thriving bespoke furniture business and was clearly an astute businessman who had earned enough to buy a large house and employ five members of staff, as well as keeping a carriage. Russell Square was not a fashionable area of London but it was convenient for the City, and therefore popular with merchants such as her father. He'd often been away from home during her childhood, but when he was there he used to regale his girls with tales of explorers such as Christopher Columbus and Captain Cook, a subject that held endless fascination for him. There was a globe in his study on which he showed them the countries to which these pioneers had sailed, some of them right on the other side of the sphere. But since he sold the business – there being no son to inherit – it seemed his brain had shrunk. When had that been? Maybe six or seven years ago, she thought. A couple of years before his wife – Lucy and Dorothea's mother – had lost her long battle with illness. Were these events linked, she wondered? It was hard to remember why he'd made the decision to stop working although still only in his early fifties. Maybe it was grief, or perhaps he already felt his abilities lessening and had bowed to the inevitable. Either way, the man who shuffled around the house, snoozing his days away and rarely receiving company, was a pale shadow of the fine gentleman he had once been.

When Dorothea returned, exhausted, from her work at the hospital, Lucy was sewing by the fireside in the drawing room with a half-smile on her lips.

Dorothea chose a chair closest to the flames so as to warm her frozen fingers.

'Did Captain Harvington call today?'

'Yes.' Lucy looked demure.

'Did he accept Father's decision?'

'He certainly did.' Lucy beamed in triumph, the smile lighting up her face. 'And he's delighted. We plan to be wed as soon as we can arrange it after the reading of the banns.'

'Father consented?' Dorothea felt a kick in the pit of her stomach.

'*Please* be happy for me,' Lucy entreated. 'I know you are opposed to the match, but you can't deny you like Charlie.

Everyone likes him! We're so happy together.' She threw down her sewing and clenched her fists in excitement.

Dorothea was momentarily lost for words. 'I'm not opposed to the match, Lucy. It's just too soon. You scarcely know each other.'

Lucy leapt from her chair and came to kneel at Dorothea's feet, head tilted, her clear blue eyes peering up, her pretty lips pursed with the same endearing expression that must have swayed their father earlier. It always made Dorothea want to kiss the flawless skin of her little sister's cheek and stroke that soft strawberry-blonde hair. Lucy's was a beauty that turned heads in the street and made it hard not to stare.

'Oh, but you're wrong! It's because you've never experienced that glorious feeling of falling in love and finding you already know everything about the other person because you are so perfectly matched. We laugh at the same things, cry at the same things, think the same way about simply *everything* … You're soon going to learn to love Charlie as I do. I *know* you will.'

Dorothea stood abruptly and stepped over her sister's legs, ignoring the disappointment that clouded her expression. 'Forgive me,' she murmured. 'I really must change for dinner. We'll talk more later.'

As she climbed the stairs with leaden feet, one thought was foremost in Dorothea's mind: the marriage must be prevented, one way or another. She was the only responsible guardian the girl possessed, since she could patently wrap their father around her little finger. It was up to Dorothea to take action and she felt the weight of the responsibility keenly. If Lucy wouldn't listen to her, who else could she appeal to?

Chapter Two

The following morning, Dorothea left early and asked Chalmers to take her via Lincoln's Inn, where a gentleman of her acquaintance was a barrister in chambers. Mr William Goodland was the brother of her friend Emily and around a year ago he had begun to call on them for tea every Sunday afternoon. He would ask after their father's health and Dorothea's work, comment on the weather, then Dorothea would struggle to maintain a conversation of sorts until he wished her good day and left after barely an hour.

Behind his back, Lucy made fun of him for his bushy side-whiskers and social awkwardness, and was rather good at imitating his tedious conversation: 'These scones seem to me the perfect combination of lightness and sweetness. It is quite some time since I have encountered such a sublime scone. You must compliment your cook on their sublimity.'

'Don't be so cruel, Lucy,' Dorothea had chided, unable to suppress a smile. 'We can't all have your conversational skills.'

Dorothea was unsure of the purpose for Mr Goodland's regular visits. Did he feel protective towards them as two women living under the roof of a father whose mental capacities were failing? Or did he consider himself a

13

potential suitor for one of them? If so, he had never made his intentions clear. However, she had decided to seek his advice about the legal position regarding Lucy's proposed marriage.

'She is still two weeks shy of eighteen,' she explained to him now, 'and I consider myself to be *in loco parentis*. Is there anything I can do?'

Mr Goodland pursed his lips. 'I'm afraid, Miss Gray, that if your father has given his consent, upon reaching her eighteenth birthday your sister may legally marry; unless there are any grounds for objecting, perhaps because of a prior engagement by either party. What impressions have you formed of this young man?'

Dorothea frowned. 'He seems very affable but Lucy is young and I am concerned by the speed with which they have made their decision.'

'Do you know much of the family?'

'Nothing at all. I believe they live in Dean Hall, Northampton, but there have been no introductions as yet.'

'Perhaps it would be worth writing to introduce yourself and to ascertain their views on this – may I say – precipitate courtship. If they support Captain Harvington, they can perhaps bring some financial pressure to bear and urge him to behave with less impetuosity.'

'Yes, that seems a sensible idea.' Dorothea was glad of the suggestion, which seemed likely to help.

'As for going to war, I can't believe the army would give permission for such a young girl to accompany them. Perhaps Captain Harvington has not told his superior officers quite how tender in years she is. If I might make a suggestion, you could write to his company – the 8th Hussars, was it not? – and make your objections plain.'

Dorothea hesitated. 'I don't want Lucy to hate me for my interference. She is such a passionate girl and feels things so strongly … I don't suppose I could ask you to write to them discreetly, as a friend of the family?'

He sat up straight, puffing his chest out: 'Indeed, I would be delighted to perform this service, Miss Gray. Do not concern yourself overmuch; I'm sure common sense will prevail.'

That evening, Dorothea wrote to Charlie's parents telling them of her fears for her sister if she went to war, and asking them to consider putting a restraining hand on their son's shoulder. Perhaps, she suggested, the families should meet to discuss what was best for the headstrong pair.

She gave the letter to Henderson to post straight away. There was no time to waste. With any luck Lucy would never find out it was she who had curtailed their nuptial plans – but even if she did, Dorothea didn't doubt she was acting for the right reasons.

A reply came from Mr Harvington of Dean Hall three days later and it struck alarm into Dorothea's heart.

'We have washed our hands of our erstwhile son Charles,' the letter read, 'and we sincerely advise you to prevent your sister from marrying him. He is a scoundrel of low morals, a wastrel who will never be sufficiently practical to look after a wife, and all in all a man who is not to be trusted.' Mr Harvington added that although they had bought Charlie his commission as a captain, he could expect no further support from his family but was quite alone in the world, with no one to blame but himself.

Dorothea read the letter several times, agonising over what to do next, and finally she decided she had no option but to show it to Lucy. She knocked on the door of her sister's room, and opened it to find Lucy engaged in brushing out her waist-length hair in front of her dressing table. It was a cosy room, with heavy drapes and a fire in the grate. Candles flickered by the bedside and on the dresser, making shadows dance on the walls.

'I wrote to introduce myself to Captain Harvington's family,' Dorothea confessed after a moment's hesitation, 'since we must soon be kin. This reply has recently arrived.'

Lucy grabbed the letter and her cheeks reddened as she perused it. When she reached the end she screwed the paper into a ball and flung it across the room. 'You had no right to contact them!' she hissed. 'I could have told you his family hate him! He explained to me all about it. They disinherited him over some stupid argument five years ago which was not his fault in *any* way and it is a source of *great* sadness to him. How *dare* you go behind my back and write to them!'

It was just the reaction Dorothea had feared but she tried to stay calm and reasonable. 'Of course I had the right. It is a serious matter if Captain Harvington has no family backing. I'm surprised Father didn't ask about his prospects. You are too young to know what it means to marry for love to a man without a secure income; you'd have six months of happiness followed by a lifetime of worry and petty resentments.'

Lucy was intractable. 'Charlie will make his own money. Major Dodds speaks highly of his prospects in the army and he's extremely well liked in the regiment. Extremely.' She swept her hairbrush off the dressing table, her temper clearly building by the minute.

'He can't advance up the ranks without family money to buy another commission. You know that, Lucy-loo.' Dorothea used the childhood pet name and reached out to touch her sister's shoulder in a conciliatory gesture but Lucy batted her hand away.

'This is my one chance to be happy and I will not have you spoil it. You're jealous and bitter and I hate you!' Tears sprang to her eyes. 'I wish Mama were here. She would love Charlie as I do, and she'd be happy for me.' Lucy turned her back but Dorothea could tell that she was crying.

She paused: their mother had been very similar in character to Lucy – lively, gregarious, but hopelessly impractical. No doubt she would have reacted with frenzied excitement to the marriage announcement and would already be planning dress fittings and floral arrangements. But that didn't make it the right thing to do.

Dorothea tried another tack: 'Have you thought about the danger you would be in overseas, with Russian guns aimed at your living quarters, wherever they might be? There would be none of the amenities you take for granted. Imagine – no running water, no clean, pressed clothing, no meals served at a dining table or servants to serve them. Lucy, do you even know where the Turkish lands are? They are fifteen hundred miles distant, across rough seas. And once there, perils lurk all around: vapours that rise from the land and cause fatal disease; snakes and scorpions that kill with one bite; not to mention the horrors of battle. It would not be some nursery game of soldiers.' She stopped, wanting to comfort the sobbing Lucy, but the set of her sister's shoulders did not invite affection.

Lucy's words were muffled by tears. 'Don't you think I've considered all that myself? Charlie will protect me now. I've had a lifetime of being patronised by you and I'm fed up with it.'

Dorothea tried once more: 'I'm not saying that you shouldn't ever marry Captain Harvington. I'm just saying wait till after the war ...'

'Don't you understand that I can't be happy for a single moment without him?'

Dorothea sighed. 'You know I have to show Father this letter, don't you? He will have to rethink his decision once he knows Captain Harvington's precarious situation.'

'I see you are determined to ruin my happiness. Well, get out of my room. Just leave me alone.' Lucy was shouting now, completely beside herself.

Dorothea paused in the doorway, but could think of nothing more to add and so she closed the door softly behind her. She could only hope that her father would see sense and, if not, that Mr Goodland's letter would have the desired effect and Major Dodds would talk some sense into Charlie. It seemed Lucy wouldn't listen to any point of view that didn't agree with her own.

The next afternoon, Dorothea returned from her work at the Pimlico hospital to find an agitated Henderson waiting by the door.

'Apologies, Miss Dorothea, but I didn't know how to contact you. Captain Harvington came around noon with a coach and four and Miss Lucy asked me to carry down her trunk and help the driver to load it on board. Your father did not seem to appreciate …' He paused, trying to find a tactful way of expressing himself.

'My father didn't try to stop them, you mean. Did she leave a letter?'

Henderson handed her an envelope and Dorothea hurried into the drawing room, threw herself into an armchair, and tore it open. Lucy's normally pretty handwriting scrawled all over the page with rage emanating from every line. 'I will never forgive you for trying to stop my marriage,' she wrote. 'Never. I am going to stay in lodgings with Charlie and as soon as I turn eighteen we will be wed without your presence since we are to be denied your blessing. I'm sorry that your jealousy led you to try and ruin our happiness but our feelings for each other are so strong that was never a possibility.' At the end, she wrote the most hateful words of all: 'I want nothing more to do with you. Charlie is my family now.'

Dorothea buried her face in her hands and curled forward into a ball. 'Oh God, no. What have I done?' She wanted to cry but all that came out was a keening sound. How could everything have gone so badly wrong? She'd only acted as she did because she loved Lucy more than any other human being on the planet. Now she had caused her to run off into goodness knows what kind of danger. Anything could happen. Her good name would be ruined, and her very life might be at risk. All she could hope was that war could be avoided, or that Major Dodds would forbid Lucy from accompanying the troops. While Charlie was away, she would surely have to come home again and that would give Dorothea a chance to repair the damage she had caused. Oh please, let that be the case.

An agonising four weeks later, Mr Woodland received a curt reply from Major Dodds and he called round that evening to share it with Dorothea. It read that Lucy and Charlie had been married on 20th February in Warwickshire and that the Major had been honoured to act as Charlie's best man. The regiment was still waiting to hear if they would sail for the Turkish lands – the decision was in the hands of politicians – but in the event they did, he would be happy for Mrs Lucy Harvington to accompany her husband.

'Your sister is a foolish young girl,' Mr Woodland began. 'I shall reply to Major Dodds in the sternest terms insisting ...'

'No, don't.' Dorothea rose to her feet, suddenly finding his pomposity unbearable. Whatever he had written to Major Dodds had clearly exacerbated the problem. Had he been more tactful in his letter, she was sure the reply would not have been so abrupt and unhelpful. 'You must forgive me, but I find myself quite overcome. I must be alone. Perhaps

'...' Tears were not far away and she was unable to finish the sentence. She turned and fled from the room.

'Of course,' Mr Woodland said. 'I'll see myself out.' Though by then there was no one to hear.

Chapter Three

During the winter months of 1853–1854, Dorothea had a particular favourite patient at the Pimlico hospital. Edward Peters had been a soldier at the Battle of Waterloo almost forty years before but had since fallen on hard times. He had no children and no family members came to visit but Dorothea enjoyed the company of this softly spoken old man whose health was slowly but surely failing. Every day she brought him her father's copy of *The Times* from the previous day because he liked to keep up with the news. He had trouble reading because his spectacles were not strong enough (she guessed he couldn't afford another pair), so she would sit and read aloud the articles that interested him most, namely those about the impending war in the Turkish territories – which were, naturally, of great concern to her as well. Mr Peters interjected his own comments as she read, fiercely critical of government procrastination: 'All this time we could be preparing for action and instead the politicians sit chin-wagging. They're yellow, I say.'

'We've given them an ultimatum and with any luck the Russians will comply,' Dorothea argued.

But they didn't, and on 28th March news broke that Britain and France had jointly declared war on Russia in support of the Turks.

Mr Peters was excited: 'About time,' he exclaimed. 'Now we'll stop those Russians invading their neighbours.' Dorothea could tell he wished he himself were going to fight, a young man once more.

'My sister's husband is a Captain in the 8th Hussars and bound to be sent to fight. She is hoping to accompany him.' She asked the question that was foremost in her mind: 'Do you think she will be safe?'

'Who can say? Wives have accompanied troops to battle for centuries past, and they had their uses in cooking and doing laundry for the men. But times are changing and it's damn foolishness that they still take them now the new longer-range guns are in use. Commanders' attention is diverted from the battlefield to providing suitable accommodation for ladies, and extra food is needed. I always thought it was madness.' He coughed with the effort of this speech. 'The 8th Hussars, you say? Part of the Light Brigade. Safer than the Heavy Brigade, at least. The Heavies lead the attacks but the Light are mostly used for reconnaissance. Who are your brother-in-law's family?'

'The Harvingtons of Northampton.'

'Are they a military family?'

'I'm afraid I do not know. I haven't made their acquaintance.' Dorothea coloured. 'I regret to say the marriage was somewhat hasty, arranged so that my sister might go with the army and remain at her husband's side.'

'You must be very concerned,' Mr Peters said in a hoarse whisper.

'I am.' Dorothea blinked back a tear. 'I'm terrified for Lucy but I cannot write to her as I don't know where they are lodging.'

'If you write on the envelope "Care of Captain Harvington, 8th Hussars" and send it to the regimental headquarters, they'll pass it on …' he rasped, then a tickle caught in his throat and he began to cough with a nasty hacking sound. He closed his eyes as his ribcage heaved with the effort. His lungs often became congested, causing him to choke and struggle for breath but he never complained. Dorothea thumped his back to dislodge the phlegm and held a bowl for him to spit into, noting that his sputum was an unhealthy greenish-yellow in colour. Earlier she'd noticed that his feet were turning black from lack of circulation. She hoped the principal physician would look in on him later.

When the hacking cough had at last subsided, Dorothea saw that Mr Peters' lips had a bluish tinge and his skin was pale. He seemed to summon every effort to say one more thing to Dorothea. 'If you'll excuse me saying, Sister, it's best to make peace while you still can,' he whispered, then closed his eyes to rest. Every coughing fit drained his remaining strength.

'Would you like me to fetch a vicar, or a priest?' Dorothea asked, wondering if that's what he was hinting, but he shook his head vehemently. In earlier conversations he had expressed a low opinion of religion but she often found patients changed their minds as death approached.

The physician who came to examine Mr Peters later told Dorothea that he thought the end was near. 'Can you contact his family?' he asked.

'There are no close relatives, I'm afraid. I asked him who I should contact if his condition worsened but he said there was no one.'

Perhaps that will be my situation one day, Dorothea mused – especially if this terrible rift with Lucy is not healed. At thirty-one, she was too old to marry and have children. The thought filled her with sadness, but she comforted herself that at least she had her work. She loved being useful to her patients and knew she was good at easing their suffering and making them feel they were not alone. Hospitals were terrifying places, where you were surrounded by strangers, with doctors whisking in to perform painful procedures before disappearing again. Dorothea tried to make patients feel she was a friend, someone on their side, and their heartfelt thanks were gratifying.

She decided to spend the day sitting with Mr Peters, whose breathing was now tortured and shallow. He clearly didn't have long to go and she couldn't let him pass away on his own. She made herself a cup of tea and pulled up a chair by his bed, then wiped his brow and offered him a sip of water but he shook his head. Each breath was an effort and before long he drifted into sleep. There was a rattling in his throat, the noise some called the death rattle, caused, she knew, by saliva gathering once he could no longer swallow. She kept wetting his lips so they didn't crack and holding a cool cloth on his brow. Although he was unconscious she hoped he could sense her presence.

At four-thirty he opened his eyes one last time, choking from the fluid in his lungs. His hands were freezing cold and she could smell the sharp chemical scent she often noted right at the end. Dorothea slipped the pillow from beneath his head because death would come quicker if he was lying flat. 'Goodbye,' she whispered. 'You are a good man and I'll miss our conversations.' She squeezed his shoulder as he took one last virtually undetectable breath, just as she had done five years earlier on the night her mother died.

That had been a cruel death. Her mother had been in hideous pain as the cancer gnawed through her insides. She could keep nothing down, not even the laudanum that could have offered some relief, and her opium enema seemed to do little good. Towards the end the disease had been in her spine, making it impossible to find a comfortable position whether sitting or lying. She was terrified, yet strove to muffle her cries of agony in the blankets so as not to waken thirteen-year-old Lucy, who was asleep in her bedroom down the corridor. Dorothea could see the fear etched in her mother's eyes, could hear her whispered pleas for help, and was powerless to do more than hold her hand, moisten her lips and soothe her with whispered endearments. The doctor came and went, leaving further useless supplies of laudanum; their vicar came to pray. Her father couldn't bear it and retreated to his study, leaving Dorothea to witness the final throes of the awful death struggle on her own. It was an experience that scarred her, something that would never leave her. Her mother's last breath when it came was a blessed release from acute torture and the expression caught at the moment of death was one of horror. Thankfully Lucy had not witnessed any of it. By the time she came to see the body the following morning, their mother's features had settled into a peaceful repose. Lucy complained of not being called to say goodbye but Dorothea knew she was too young for such a distressing sight.

Mr Peters, by contrast, had a peaceful death, the best he could have hoped for. Dorothea sat with his body for half an hour watching the tightening of his features, the blanching of his complexion, then she helped the orderly to wash and prepare him for the undertaker. It was five-thirty in the evening when she walked out into the street in her dark wool cloak and climbed into a Hansom cab the hospital porter had called to take her back to Russell Square.

Covent Garden was abuzz with costermongers dismantling their fruit and veg stalls under the metal and glass awning, and flower girls with a few remaining pink, white and yellow blooms in their baskets. Some ladies of the night hovered on street corners, hoping for an early piece of business. Nothing shocked Dorothea after her work in the hospital. She had seen all types pass through its doors.

Back in her bedroom, she started to change for dinner but she was too agitated to fiddle with all the buttons on her gown. Instead she sat at her dresser to compose a letter to Lucy. She told her she was sorry for her actions, that she hoped her marriage would be a very happy one. She was sad to have missed the ceremony but perhaps once they were reconciled she could host a celebration for them ... Suddenly Dorothea dropped the pen and a great sob tore from her chest. She gasped and tried to control herself but emotion took hold and she shook with intense grief.

'Please God, don't let any harm come to Lucy,' she prayed, squeezing her eyes tight shut. 'I've let her down and I will never forgive myself if anything bad happens to her.'

She laid her head on the dresser and fell asleep, waking an hour later when the bell rang for dinner to find her tears had soaked the writing paper and blurred the ink.

PART TWO

Chapter Four

24th April 1854

Plymouth Dockyard was teeming with people bustling between precarious stacks of luggage. Tall-masted ships stretched as far as the eye could see. The noise of ships' horns sounding, street traders crying their wares, and the anxious chatter of bystanders was overwhelming. Lucy worried that they would never find their way but when Charlie hailed a porter and asked him to take them to the *Shooting Star*, the man seemed confident about finding it. He loaded a trolley with their steamer trunk, all their bags stuffed to bursting, and their large tin bath, and set off. Charlie clutched Lucy's arm tightly and hurried them through the throng in pursuit of their luggage.

Before long, he spotted some comrades in royal blue and gold Hussars uniform and hailed them, pulling Lucy forwards to introduce her. She shook hands with several gentlemen and was pleased to note their appreciative glances. She had dressed with care in a wide-skirted soft wool gown with cascading ruffles in the skirt, and a warm fitted jacket, both of a deep blue very similar to that of the Hussars' colours. A prettily trimmed bonnet framed her face.

'I think you have new admirers,' Charlie winked, squeezing her hand.

As they approached the ship, she noticed several women sobbing, with young children clinging to their skirts, and asked Charlie what ailed them.

'These are the soldiers' wives who can't come along,' he told her. 'There was a ballot and only a few won a place. You're lucky to be the wife of an officer, as we can all bring our wives, if our commanders agree.'

'What will become of them while their husbands are away?' She felt alarmed for their plight. She had no idea what would have happened to her if she hadn't been allowed to accompany Charlie because his wages were not sufficient, after stoppages for uniform and so forth, for him to have supported her in lodgings like the boarding house where they had been living in Warwick for the last three months. She suspected from the haste with which he insisted they leave that he owed money to the landlady there. If a captain couldn't manage, how could the soldiers, who earned so much less?

'I expect their families will look after them,' Charlie said, as if the question hadn't occurred to him.

Some called out – 'Miss, can you help us?' 'Need a lady's maid, Miss?' – and Lucy cast her eyes down, feeling guilty that she had a place while they did not.

They walked up the gangway onto the ship and followed their porter down to the officers' deck, where Charlie located their cabin. Lucy swallowed her surprise at how small it was, barely six paces wide and ten long, with a bunk so narrow they would be crushed tight together. There was hardly any hanging space for her gowns, and only one tiny mirror above the washbowl.

'This is one of the better cabins I've seen on a military ship,' Charlie remarked cheerfully. 'It's very well appointed.'

Lucy kept her thoughts to herself. 'I'll just unpack a few things, dearest, to make it a little more homely.'

'In that case, I'll go and check on the horses on the deck below.' He kissed her full on the lips and grasped one of her breasts with a wink before he left.

Lucy felt her cheeks flush and she hummed as she arranged their possessions. She liked having someone to look after, loved the intimacy of sharing a bed and eating meals with Charlie. 'You see, Dorothea?' she thought. 'You were wrong!'

Before long, she heard women's voices in the corridor and popped her head out. The first woman she saw introduced herself as Mrs Fanny Duberly, wife of the 8th Hussars' Quartermaster. She seemed rather superior in attitude, and moved off after only the briefest 'hallo' but not before Lucy had noted that her gown was plain grey worsted and not remotely fashionable. The other woman, Adelaide Cresswell, had a kind face and shook Lucy's hand warmly.

'Charlie is a good friend of my husband Bill, so you and I must also be friends, my dear.'

'Yes, please,' Lucy cried. 'I would love that. We women must stick together. I need your advice on how I can support my husband. We are so recently wed I don't yet know what is expected of an officer's wife.'

Adelaide smiled and squeezed her hand. 'I was overjoyed to hear about your marriage. Charlie is a very lucky man. Look how pretty you are! Such lovely china blue eyes.' She glanced past Lucy into their cabin. 'Goodness, you've brought rather a lot of luggage.'

Lucy looked at the pile. 'In truth, it was hard knowing what to bring. I've had to leave many of my possessions in store,' she explained. 'Charlie told me I would need summer clothes, but I also tried to think of items we might need if we have to sleep in a tent.' She couldn't contemplate quite how she would manage to change her gowns and perform

31

her toilette in such a cramped space but she was prepared to give it a try if that's what being an army wife entailed. As well as the tin bath, she had brought some soft feather pillows and a pale gold silk bedspread that used to be her mother's, so they would have some home comforts.

'Of course you did – and I'm sure they'll come in very useful. It's just that we may have to carry our own luggage at times and your trunk looks rather heavy ...' Seeing Lucy's alarmed expression, Adelaide added quickly: 'I expect Charlie will find someone to help you. Now, I was on my way below deck to introduce myself to the women travelling with Bill's company, the 11th Hussars. Perhaps you would like to come and meet the wives of Charlie's men? There's plenty of time as the ship won't leave harbour till after dinner.'

Lucy's eyes widened. 'I'd love to!' It hadn't occurred to her that Charlie had men beneath him, men who obeyed his commands, but she supposed as a captain that he must. She was anxious to give the right impression and decided she would follow Adelaide's lead.

Two decks below their own, there was a strong smell of rotting vegetation, which Adelaide told her came from the bilge. The soldiers' wives were in a shared dormitory and Adelaide greeted them, explaining who she and Lucy were, and saying that they would be happy to offer assistance if any was required. The women looked doubtfully at Lucy, who was by far the youngest of the thirteen wives accompanying the 8th Hussars. Most were rough, sturdy women, with ruddy faces and cheap gowns; none looked a day under thirty.

'What an exquisite shawl,' Lucy commented to one woman, who was wearing a gaudy, paisley-patterned garment round her shoulders. 'Are your beds comfortable? Ours is so narrow I think my husband will knock me to the floor if he turns in his sleep.'

'Make sure you sleep by the wall so he's the one that falls out,' one suggested, and Lucy agreed that would be the sensible course. She asked about children left behind, about where the women normally lived, about their husbands' names and duties, and she felt by the time she and Adelaide left that she had made a good first impression.

'We will all be good friends after this adventure. I am sure of it,' she called back.

That evening she and Charlie shared a table in the officers' dining hall with the Cresswells. Lucy had changed into a blue and purple silk taffeta evening gown with smocked bodice, and dressed her own hair in the absence of any apparent ladies' maids, but she noticed that Adelaide wore the same plain serge gown as earlier. Looking around, all the officers' wives were in day dress; it seemed dinner was not a dressy occasion.

'Why didn't you warn me not to wear evening dress?' she whispered to Charlie, feeling embarrassed.

He grinned. 'I love to see you all dressed up. You are by far the most beautiful woman on the ship and I'm so proud to be with you.'

The food was plain cooking: soup, stew, pudding, with not even a fish course. The conversation was lively, though, with the men talking of war, and the belligerent stance of the Russian Tsar Nicholas I who dreamed of creating a huge empire in the East from the remains of the tottering Ottoman Empire.

'Do you have children?' Lucy asked Adelaide, and realised she had touched a raw nerve when tears sprang to Adelaide's eyes, which she blinked away before replying.

'We have a little girl called Martha, who is four, and a boy, Archie, who's just three. I'm sorry …' She closed her eyes briefly to regain control. 'It was a wrench leaving them

33

behind, although they are with my mother and will receive the best of care. I decided that Bill needed me more. I want to make sure he has a clean uniform and decent food as well as a woman's comfort while he is out fighting for us.'

'Well, of course,' Lucy agreed. 'All the same, I can imagine how difficult it must have been to leave your little darlings.' Adelaide must be in her twenties to have such young children, she guessed; she looked older, her face tanned and lined by the sun.

After dinner, Lucy and Charlie strolled out on deck to watch as the *Shooting Star* pulled out of harbour then promptly came to a halt while they waited for the wind to change. She felt a thrill run through her: it was the first time she had left English soil. She felt so lucky to be there, with the man she loved. In their cabin, Charlie poured glasses of some rum he had brought along and they toasted the voyage: 'We're on our way!' He raised his glass and she did the same. 'This is where the adventure begins! And I am the happiest man alive that you are here by my side.' He gazed at her and despite his words she could see the sadness in his eyes. She knew his loneliness after being cast off by his family still haunted him, although it had happened five years earlier. 'If you had been unable to come, I swear I would have deserted from the army. I couldn't bear to be without you now, Lucy.'

His words caught in his throat and Lucy knew how deeply they were felt. It was part of what made her love him so wholeheartedly: the sense that beneath his confident manner there was a vulnerable man who needed her in a way she had never been needed before.

'I know, darling, and I couldn't be without you either.' She stroked his dear face with the tips of her fingers.

'We are so lucky to have found each other,' he breathed. 'Before I met you, I was nothing, a hollow shell of a man. I had no family, just some friends who enjoy me larking

around: "Good old Charlie, he's always up for some fun."
But with you I can be myself and know you love me no
matter what.'

'I will always love you …' she began to say but Charlie
silenced her by covering her mouth with kisses so tender that
her heart almost stopped. They fell onto the bed and while
they made love she marvelled at his passion; she loved the
way he lost himself completely in her, loved the amazing secret
of married love into which she had now been initiated.

He fell asleep straight afterwards with his arm wrapped
around her neck. She would have to wake him later because
both were still half-clothed: her petticoats were twisted
beneath her while he still wore his dress shirt, but she would
let him rest awhile.

When she opened her eyes the next morning, Lucy could sense
from a gentle rolling motion that the ship was on the move
and she felt a quiver of excitement. That rolling became less
gentle as the day progressed, and she had to press a hand to
the corridor wall for support as she and Adelaide made their
way to luncheon. Charlie's day was spent trying to settle the
horses, who neighed and whinnied, terrified of their enclosure
in this rocking vessel, so Lucy and Adelaide strolled the deck
gazing at the grey-green seas that surrounded them and took
meals together. They went down to visit the soldiers' wives
again and Lucy was astonished to find some standing around
in drawers and stays without a hint of modesty but she chatted
as before, asking if their food was adequate and whether they
saw more of their husbands than she was seeing of hers. She
joked that Captain Harvington seemed to care more about
the horses than his new wife, but in fact she loved the caring
way he spoke of those magnificent creatures, particularly his
own horse, Merlin, and his determination that he would do
all he could to see they survived the journey unscathed.

On the second day, as they entered the Bay of Biscay, the sea became choppy. Loose objects fell from shelves and a little flower vase of Lucy's was smashed on the cabin floor, startling her. After dressing, she made her way to Adelaide's cabin to find her friend vomiting into a bedpan, her face bleached of colour and eyes sunken in their sockets. Lucy gave her a handkerchief to wipe her mouth, then went to find a steward who would empty the bedpan and bring a fresh pitcher of water.

'All the other ladies are sick as well, Ma'am,' the steward told her. 'You must have a strong constitution.'

Sure enough, she heard retching sounds from Mrs Duberly's cabin, although the quartermaster's wife came to dinner that evening and remarked to Lucy she thought it a poor show that Adelaide didn't make the effort to join them.

In fact, for the next three days poor Adelaide couldn't keep down more than a few sips of water and Lucy was concerned for her. There was no doctor on board but the steward found a supply of Tarrant's Seltzer so Lucy fed Adelaide teaspoonfuls of it, trying to keep her spirits up by telling her that the rough weather must pass soon; everyone said it must. She herself remained miraculously immune to the seasickness, and was able to go down to the soldiers' wives and dispense fizzing glasses of seltzer to them too. It was good to feel useful, and as Adelaide began to recover Lucy sat and read to her, growing fonder by the day of her sweet nature. She was the kind of woman who would never hear bad of another; a woman whose outlook was sunny even while she was feeling so ill.

On their fourth night at sea there was a horrendous storm. Waves crashed against the side of the ship, lightning crackled and lit up the entire sky, and the frightened whinnying of horses filled the air. Lucy couldn't sleep a wink but sat petrified by their porthole, watching the violence of the storm outside, while Charlie spent the night down below, sponging the horses' nostrils with vinegar in an attempt to calm them. At one stage there was a terrible cracking sound, like an explosion, and for a moment Lucy feared they had been attacked by the Russians. She wrapped the silk bedspread around her, rubbing it against her lip for comfort as she used to do as a child when she fled to her mother's bed after a nightmare. If only Charlie would come soon. There were a few terrifying hours before the worst was over, but as soon as dawn broke with a pale pink shimmer, the storm passed and the ship stopped rolling.

Charlie returned with some awful news: 'The mizzen top and the main top mast broke at the height of the storm and crushed a man's leg as they fell to deck.'

She was shocked. 'Will he be all right?'

He shook his head. 'He'll lose the leg, for sure. Two of our horses – Moondance and Greystokes – perished. I couldn't settle them and the poor creatures raved themselves to death.'

'Is Merlin all right?'

'Yes, thank goodness. Biscay is always rough but this is the worst storm I've experienced and it followed us right down the coast of Spain and Portugal. At least we're through it now.'

Spain and Portugal: names Lucy had previously only seen on her father's globe. She knew that Columbus had sailed from Portugal and imagined it as being very exotic. 'Will they be able to mend the ship?'

'Yes, the carpenters are hard at work.' He noticed Lucy's anxious expression and pulled her in for a hug. 'Everything will be fine, my love. And you have been extraordinarily strong in the face of adversity. I knew you would be.'

She was thrilled with the compliment. 'You must be exhausted. Why not lie down and rest awhile?'

'I think I will. Come lie with me.'

Lucy held him close until he fell asleep and then she rose, dressed quietly and slipped up on deck to gaze out at the millpond sea glittering in the early morning light. The ship was close enough to shore for land to be visible and she shivered at the thought they were getting ever-nearer to the mysterious Turkish lands.

'What is that huge black rock?' she asked a passing sailor, and he told her 'The Rock of Gibraltar, Ma'am.'

She stood watching as they pulled up beneath it then came to a halt, becalmed in the Straits. The Rock's sheer slopes towered high above the ship's main mast, like an ominous shadow against the sky.

On the 8th May, the *Shooting Star* docked at Valletta in Malta and all were allowed to go ashore. Adelaide had fully recovered and she and Lucy, along with Charlie and Bill, descended the gangway to the dock, the ladies sheltering beneath parasols from the heat of the sun. 'What larks!' Lucy cried, scarcely able to contain her excitement as she set foot on foreign soil. Locals flocked around trying to sell them hand-coloured cards, china knick-knacks and bonnets made out of scratchy straw. They sat in a café near the dock sipping tea and watching fishermen drag boxes of fresh fish up the slope. One man was pounding a freshly caught octopus against a rock – to tenderise its meat, Charlie said – and Lucy flinched at the blows. They dined well in a local hostelry, with fresh fish in a cream sauce, tender lamb chops, and delicate little custard puddings. A fiddler played in the corner and once they had eaten Charlie persuaded the waiters to clear some tables so there was room for dancing, which he led in high-kicking style, pulling Lucy up to join him in a lively polka. Bottles of jewel-coloured liqueurs were produced, made from fruits Lucy had never heard of: prickly pear, pomegranate and carob. The ladies tried delicate sips but found them over-strong.

They were joined by Major Dodds, who challenged Charlie to drink a shot of each spirit behind the bar and said he would do the same. Their aim was explained to the bartender who lined up glasses in a row, which they supped in carnival style. A game of cribbage was initiated and Lucy could tell from Charlie's excited whoops that he was winning.

'They call him Lucky Charlie,' Adelaide told her. 'No matter what the game, he seems to have a knack with cards.'

Lucy hadn't known that her husband liked gambling. Dorothea was very disapproving of gamblers and would have considered it a black mark against him, but Adelaide didn't seem to see any harm in it. Lucy was learning more about her husband all the time. It wasn't just his funny dancing style, and the fact that he was said to be lucky; she had never realised how popular he was with his fellows and it was heart-warming to watch. She had no regrets about coming away with him; she just wished it had been possible for her older sister to share her joy.

The next day she wrote to her father. Charlie had asked her not to write before they set sail in case Dorothea made one last attempt to stop them, but she missed her papa and now they were on their way she could see no harm in it.

'The soldiers' and officers' wives are one happy family,' she wrote, 'linked by a warm camaraderie and eagerness to explore our new surroundings. We are enjoying the foreign aspects of Malta, with its fragrant flowers trailing up the walls of houses and twining round balconies, the dark-eyed children who follow us in the street, and the uncannily bright blue of sea and sky sparkling in sunlight.' She sucked the end of her pen then continued: 'I hope that you are in good health, Papa, and that your back is not troubling you. I will write again when I can, but do not worry if you don't hear for a while as we may not be able to post our letters when in the field.' She signed the letter

'Your loving daughter'. She didn't ask after Dorothea, still cross whenever she thought of her meddling. Her sister had believed she was behaving as a mother to Lucy, but in fact their real mother, the irrepressibly gay woman who had died when Lucy was thirteen, would have been wildly enthusiastic about this trip. Lucy imagined her crying, 'My darling, what fun! Be sure to write and describe all the details. And bring me back a Russkie's helmet!'

Before they set sail from Malta, Lucy was astonished to hear that five out of the thirteen Hussars' wives had asked to be sent home to England. The rigours of the voyage had been too much for them and they did not want to continue further. She remonstrated with one woman.

'Won't you stay to support our brave troops? Think how much comfort it would bring your husband to have you with him. Please say you will reconsider.'

The woman shook her head, a little shamefaced but determined. 'It's too hard on the ship. You have a nice cabin but we've been stuck in that awful dormitory listening to the sounds of each other vomiting, and breathing smells the like of which I hope never to come across again, while being tossed around in an old wooden bucket.'

'But the war will not last long. With the British and French joining the Ottomans, it is three armies against one. The Russians can't possibly hold out.'

'All the same, I can't take the risk, Ma'am. I have four children. I have to get myself back to them in one piece.'

Lucy bit her lip, thinking of the sobbing women in Plymouth Dock who would have given anything to be there. It was incomprehensible to her that someone could decide to leave just as the adventure was commencing. Granted, the voyage had been unpleasant but now they were all together, exploring the island by day and throwing impromptu parties every night, she was filled with excitement at the prospect of the coming months. She was doing her duty to her country and to her new husband; who would have thought it would turn out to be such fun?

Chapter Five

After Malta, the *Shooting Star* sailed into another storm, so violent the ship keeled onto its side and the horses were hurled off their feet. It passed quickly, leaving a fierce heat like the inside of a bread oven, and an overpowering stench that resembled (and possibly was) rotting sewage. Lucy spent much of her time leaning out of her porthole to catch the breeze, gazing at the hazy contours of the islands and coastlines they passed and the fishing boats painted in vivid blues and turquoises like the colours of the sea.

At cooler times of day, she and Adelaide strolled on deck and exchanged confidences. One morning, Adelaide asked how Lucy and Charlie had met, and Lucy described it with animation, enjoying reliving the moment.

'Him declaring that he would be my slave was a bit of fun, but I knew from his eyes he was serious as well. He said he would give me his heart and I could do as I wished with it, even trample upon it.' She smiled fondly. 'When he called on me the following morning, we couldn't stop talking. He told me about being in the Hussars, about his love of horses … and then he asked about my family. And when I told him that my mother died when I was thirteen, I swear there were tears of sympathy in his eyes. I think that's when I truly began to fall in love with him. He was so compassionate.'

Adelaide took her hand and squeezed it. 'I'm so sorry to hear about your mother, my dear. Thirteen is very young to be without a mother's guidance. Do you have siblings with whom you can talk, perhaps an aunt to advise you?'

Lucy grimaced and turned to look out to sea. 'I have a sister, Dorothea, who is thirteen years my senior, but she is a stern old maid, who took against Charlie and tried to prevent our marriage. She said we hadn't known each other long enough – but we knew from the start we were perfect for each other. Both of us are outgoing on the surface but lonely underneath. We were instantly as close as close can be.'

'How long had you known each other before you got engaged?'

'Nine weeks.' Adelaide raised an eyebrow and Lucy hurried on. 'For some people that might not seem like much but when you are in love, why wait? I couldn't bear him to go off to war without me. Even an hour apart is difficult, a day unbearable. Don't you feel the same way about Captain Cresswell?'

Adelaide cocked her head to one side. 'My story is quite different because Bill and I grew up knowing each other. We lived nearby, our families were friends, and we played together as children. The realisation that we loved each other came gradually, and I think our families knew before we did. We married around your age – are you eighteen or nineteen, my dear?'

'Eighteen.'

'And it was blissful. But then we had some difficult years when I lost four babies in a row ...' She stared out towards the horizon, her voice flat. 'I felt terrible for Bill. Such a fine man should have a son, and it seemed I would not be able to give him one. I became very ill and almost wished I would die so he could be remarried to a woman who would be able to give him an heir. And then, at the age of twenty-eight, when I had long since given up hope, along came another pregnancy. I rested all the way through, never venturing out of the house, and my daughter Martha was born hale and hearty, followed a year later by little Archie.' She turned to Lucy, eyes glinting. 'Bill was beside himself with joy when he held his daughter for the first time. He was nervous as he cradled her tiny body in his big hands,' – she curved her own hands to demonstrate – 'and I have never loved him as much as I did at that moment. You see, love changes through the years. We had our childish love, when we played together as youngsters, then the love of sweethearts and the thrill when we were newlyweds, but going through adversity together deepens love and makes it more true. You'll find this with Charlie, my dear. You're only at the very beginning.'

Lucy was enthralled. 'What an inspiring story! You make me want to be a better wife to Charlie so as to earn this deeper love you talk about.'

'I'm sure you will. And in time you will prove to your sister Dorothea that Charlie is a worthy husband for you. She'll come round, I know she will. If nothing else, she is going to want to meet her nieces and nephews one day.'

Lucy blushed. 'That blessing, I hope, is a little way off.' Charlie had assured her he was taking precautions, although she wasn't entirely sure what these might be.

'Of course,' Adelaide teased, 'but babies have a way of surprising you, just as my two did.'

'I realise now why they are so precious to you, after such a long wait and so many disappointments.'

'Yes, indeed.' Adelaide blinked hard. Evidently it was difficult to talk of them. 'If only your children could one day help to heal Charlie's rift with his own family. I wish that could be so.'

'Do you know the Harvingtons?' Lucy was keen to hear about them. Charlie had painted them as heartless but surely they couldn't be all bad.

'Bill has met them and told me a little. It's such a tragedy.'

'They must be very harsh people to cast off their own son. Charlie told me it was over some debt or other. Why do his brothers not forgive him at least? I know he feels desperately sad about it.'

Adelaide's eyes widened, and she seemed lost for words. 'At least he has you,' she said finally. 'He told Bill he loves you so much he would do anything for you. Already we can see how much you have helped him to overcome his grief. Now I think it's time to prepare for luncheon, my dear. Shall we go down?' She offered her arm.

When Lucy reached the door of her cabin, one of the soldiers' wives, a Mrs Williams, was hurrying along the corridor towards her. 'May I come into your cabin for a moment, Mrs Harvington?' she asked, her tone urgent, and Lucy replied 'Yes, of course,' thinking that perhaps the woman wished to borrow some item she had forgotten to bring herself.

'Sorry to intrude, but Mrs Duberly is after me,' Mrs Williams whispered and put a finger to her lips.

Just then they heard Mrs Duberly charging along the corridor, calling for Mrs Williams. Lucy quickly pulled her cabin door closed and the two women stood quietly until her footsteps had passed.

Mrs Williams gave an indignant snort. 'I agreed to act as her lady's maid on the ship but I didn't think that meant I had to be her general skivvy. She wants me up all night laundering whatever lace handkerchief she might have blown her dainty nose into during the day, then woe betide me if it is not dry by morn when she wants to use it again. The woman's a battleaxe. Not a human bone in her body. She's only interested in her beloved horse.'

'Can't you resign from your position?'

'I tried, but she threatened to have me put off the ship. Says I only got a place on board because of her. So it seems best I just stay out of her way.' She cackled. 'I'm rather enjoying making her charge round huffing and puffing with ill temper.'

Mrs Williams winked at Lucy before opening the door a crack and peering out to check it was safe to leave.

'Thanks, Ma'am,' she said. 'I reckon as far as officers' wives go, you're one of the decent ones.' She slipped away and Lucy smiled to herself, while hoping that Mrs Duberly never found out about her complicity.

On the 18th May, the *Shooting Star* entered the Dardanelles, an enclosed channel with high rocky coast on either side, thickly covered in dark green trees running from just above the waterline to the top of its slopes. The ship was becalmed for two days while awaiting a steamer to tow them to Constantinople and the ladies had ample time to view the cattle and mules grazing wild in the forests. Lucy borrowed a pair of binoculars and peered with curiosity at a Turkish fort high on a rock, with some camels at the gate and soldiers in bright red uniform milling around.

They arrived in Constantinople at sunset on the 22nd and Lucy's first impression was of tall slender towers (Adelaide told her they were minarets) standing stark against the rosy-orange of the sky. As they admired the view, a melancholy chant echoed round the town, and Adelaide told Lucy it was the Muslim's call to prayer, an exhortation that was repeated five times a day. Lucy was thrilled at the exoticism of it. They hadn't even disembarked but already she could tell that this city was much more foreign than Malta. Once they were

46

at anchor, hawkers paddled out on boats that looked little more than large wicker trays, holding up goods for sale: bales of fabric, live chickens, and unfamiliar fruits. It was too dark to see but still they called out in English: 'Hello lady, beautiful things, very cheap.'

By daylight, Constantinople was impressive, with houses painted in pretty shades of mustard, terracotta, pale blue and mint green, surrounded by dark green trees and masses of purple flowers. Adelaide explained that the city was sliced in two by the Bosphorus, the wide strait in which they were at anchor. One side was Europe and the other Asia, making the city unique in straddling two continents.

It was a disappointment when they disembarked to find the quay was made of rotting planks on which they had to tread carefully for fear of falling into the foul water below, where a dead dog floated amidst some yellowish foam. The water in Malta had been clear turquoise, but this was murky brown.

For three nights they were to stay in the Selimiye barracks, a fine building from the outside, built of brick around a huge quadrangle with turrets on each corner. But as they entered they were assaulted by a fetid smell of unknown origin that had the ladies covering their noses with handkerchiefs. The rooms they were shown to were filthy, with a thick layer of dust on each surface and stains of an alarming nature on the walls. During the first night, Lucy provided sustenance for a number of insects who seemed to find a way to bite her skin even when she swathed herself from head to toe in her mother's bedspread. Next morning she had eighteen angry red lumps on her skin, which itched like the devil, including one on her cheek about which she was particularly self-conscious. For some reason they had left Charlie alone.

'Your blood is so much sweeter than mine,' he soothed. 'I'll find a net to cover the bed before night falls.'

Lucy attracted more bites during the day, and the itch became fiercer if she scratched them. Adelaide advised that she cover her skin with lemon juice to deter the creatures and went to the barracks' kitchen herself to procure some lemons. It made Lucy feel sticky but she didn't get any more bites and the itch in existing ones lessened a little.

The ladies were too nervous to venture outside the barracks by themselves, but in the late afternoon when Charlie returned from his duties they went exploring, taking a small boat known as a caïque across the water to the European side of town. They lay back on cushions, barely higher than the water level, while a dark-skinned sailor, in an open white shirt that showed off his chest, steered them around the huge ships traversing this international shipping channel. On arrival they hired a guide who took them by landau to a magnificent mosque, where gilded domes were balanced on top of each other like oranges in a bowl; to the Sultan's Topkapi Palace set in lush pleasure gardens; and to Lucy's favourite place of all, the Grand Bazaar, a maze of stalls under a wooden roof selling more goods than she could ever have dreamed of. The guide warned them that it was easy to get lost so they concentrated on keeping their sense of direction, but even so within ten minutes had to admit, giggling, that they were completely disorientated. The stallholders wore flowing robes and a head-dress, and many were smoking hookah pipes that gave off aromatic scents. Lucy saw a few women wearing loose-fitting gowns of Eastern colouring, their heads and faces covered in veils; they flitted into doorways and through archways like elegant tropical moths.

On one stall Charlie spotted an intricate ship in a bottle with a painted backdrop of the minarets of Constantinople and he picked it up. 'How much?' he asked the stallholder and when he heard the price, he mimed great shock. 'That's over a shilling,' he told Lucy. 'They must think me a fool.'

48

He put the trinket back, upon which the stallholder lifted it and pressed it into Lucy's hands, naming a figure that was about half of the original offer.

'Lucy, put it down,' Charlie instructed in a low voice. 'We're going to walk away and see what happens.' She did as he asked. Instantly the stallholder came after them, grabbing Charlie's arm and indicating in mime that he was a poor man, that he had children to feed. He caught Lucy's eye, making a sad face and miming the rocking of a cradle and she flushed. Charlie shrugged with open arms; it was none of his concern. The stallholder suggested another price. Charlie shook his head. It was a good-natured game and it seemed to Lucy that Charlie's gambling skills came in handy: he could keep a straight face and not give away his tactics. Eventually a price was agreed that was about a tenth of the original and Charlie counted out some coins and handed them over, whereupon the stallholder wrapped the ship in a bottle in fine tissue paper.

Lucy and Charlie chuckled as they walked away. When she turned back, the stallholder was watching them with an inscrutable expression. She got the feeling he didn't approve, whether of her or of both of them she couldn't tell, and it made her nervous. She knew that Muslim women covered their hair with veils, and wore high-necked, long-sleeved tunics to disguise their figures, yet here she was wearing a short-sleeved gown patterned with rosebuds, her blonde hair visible beneath her bonnet. Did the market stallholders look down on her? She didn't like all the stares she was attracting, sensing an element of hostility in them.

'I have some news, darling,' Charlie told her, 'and I don't want you to worry about it. Promise you won't?' He made her swear with hand on heart before he would continue. 'Lord Lucan wants to leave women behind in Constantinople when we sail to Varna.'

Her consternation registered on her face but all she could say was 'Oh.' She would be scared in this city without him. She was even nervous by his side. She couldn't bear to think of them being separated.

'However, I think he will face a mutiny if he tries to enforce it. Bill and I have discussed it and decided that if you and your lady friends board the ship tomorrow morning, take up residence in your cabins and refuse to leave, I can't believe he will dare to drag you off, petticoats flying.'

'Why does Lord Lucan not want us to come?'

'We're going to be camping at Varna and I suppose he imagines the conditions will not be suitable for ladies. But I think you have proved on the voyage out here that you are remarkably resilient.'

Lucy hesitated. She had never slept in a tent before and wondered whether it would be safe. Would they have to sleep on the ground? How would she manage her toilette in privacy? She did not want to lower his opinion of her resilience so she simply asked, 'Will Adelaide be coming?'

'Bill certainly hopes she will.'

She nodded. 'Then of course I will. I've brought many home comforts to turn our tent into a palace where you can relax after your duties. This is exactly what I came for. I'm not about to turn back now.'

Charlie grabbed her and pulled her to him for a kiss, his arm curled around her waist. She sensed rather than saw the disapproval of the Muslim stallholders who surrounded them. When she looked up, their expressions were blank but they were all watching in a way that definitely didn't seem friendly.

Chapter Six

The quayside at Varna was milling with soldiers of different nationalities – noisy Greeks in olive green, golden-skinned Ottomans in purply-blue tunics with a red fez cap, the French in red trousers with blue jackets, plus others whom Lucy couldn't identify – and everywhere there were piles of cannonballs and shells. The town itself was small and whitewashed, its pot-holed streets broiling in fierce heat. While Charlie oversaw the disembarkation of the horses, Lucy and Adelaide strolled along the main street purchasing supplies to supplement the army rations they would receive in camp later: a loaf of black bread, a side of ham, a bag of lemons. Lucy hesitated over a bottle of milk because Charlie didn't like tea without milk, but Adelaide warned her that in this heat it would surely turn before they could pitch camp.

A much-decorated officer scowled at them as he hurried past. He wasn't wearing a helmet and they could see that the top of his head was quite bald while hair grew profusely down the sides and around his chin in an elongated U-shape.

'That's Lord Lucan, commander of the cavalry,' Adelaide whispered. 'His plan to stop ladies accompanying the army has been sorely thwarted. I don't think any women stayed behind – certainly none of the Hussars' wives.'

'I hope he has more influence over his men than he does over us,' Lucy giggled.

Charlie ordered two of his men to bring their luggage ashore and load it onto a gun carriage, which was a relief to Lucy, who had a niggling worry about bringing too much, especially in comparison to Adelaide who had only a modest bag. That night they were to sleep outdoors on a large plain alongside a lake, before travelling north the following day. It was a pretty spot as the sun began to set, with flocks of graceful white birds swooping down to rest on the water then lifting off in a giant cloud. Some folk set about erecting tents but Charlie peered at the sky and decided there was no need for shelter that night.

'I don't expect you have ever slept under the stars, my dear. It's a glorious experience in a climate as temperate as this. Everyone should try it.' He began arranging their bedding underneath a sprawling bush.

'Will we be safe?' Lucy asked, all kinds of worries simultaneously crowding her brain: snakes, scorpions, Russian soldiers …

'We're surrounded by the bravest and best of the British army, my love. What could possibly happen?'

He built a little campfire on which to boil water for tea, and in lieu of milk he added a glug of rum to his cup.

'Anyone care to join our party?' he called to those round about. 'Bring your own hooch!'

Bill and Adelaide joined them, and several of the men, all passing round their bottles. Mrs Williams and her husband Stan perched on the edge of the group, and she and Lucy exchanged smiles.

'What about a sing-song?' Charlie suggested, and burst into a tenor rendition of the popular ballad, 'Thou art gone from my gaze, like a beautiful dream'. He sang the first verse, then turned to Lucy: 'I don't know any more of the words, my dear, but perhaps you do?'

She took over – 'In the stillness of night, when the stars mildly shine' – and the group fell silent as they listened to her pretty singing voice, quite the finest many of them had heard. For years she had been studying under an Italian singing master, hired by her mother so that there would always be music in the house. Lucy put her heart into it, wanting Charlie to be proud of her.

When she reached the end he cheered 'Bravo!', and the others joined his applause. One soldier piped up with the lively 'Cheer, boys, cheer!' and Charlie rose to his haunches and began a clumsy Cossack dance, hopping, kicking and falling over in a parody of the well-known Russian dance style. Everyone laughed until their sides hurt. It was clear he was the company jester and Lucy suddenly felt a pang of sadness that her mother never met him. Their characters were so similar she was sure they would have got along famously. Mama would never have allowed Dorothea to cause this horrid rift in the family. She would instantly have welcomed Charlie as one of them.

When Lucy crawled into her bedding later, Charlie was inebriated and keen to make love. He cupped her breast, squeezing it a little too hard, while trying to push up her skirts.

'We can't,' she shushed. 'Others will hear.' The nearest men were only ten paces distant and although they appeared to be asleep, Lucy didn't want to risk them seeing or hearing anything compromising. Charlie grumbled but soon gave up, fell back on his bedding and began to snore.

Lucy lay awake, alert for movements on the ground. Dorothea's words about scorpions and snakes echoed through her head, but all she saw in the moonlight was a large beetle with yellow markings and sharp black pincers. She watched it for a while, wondering if it might bite her in her sleep. And then she reminded herself that she was a captain's wife, who must be strong to survive this extraordinary experience. She picked up a rock and crushed the beetle, then settled down to sleep.

Bugles sounded at daybreak and everyone rose to pack any belongings that had been unpacked the night before. Lucy washed her face and rearranged her hair, smoothing down the creases in her pale blue silk gown as best she could. They were travelling eight miles north to a place called Silistria, where the Russian forces were under siege by the Ottomans, and Lucy felt a knot in her stomach when she thought about that. But for now, Charlie helped her and Adelaide to climb onto a gun carriage to ride with their luggage and they enjoyed the drive through the countryside while it was still early enough to escape the glare of the sun: the sky was cloudless but a light breeze made the temperature pleasant.

Adelaide transpired to be something of an expert on wild-flowers and plants and she identified the blooms they passed in fields and hedgerows: wild roses, larkspur, borage, even purple heather, which Lucy had always thought to be uniquely Scottish. 'I enjoy gardening,' she explained. 'We have a pretty garden at our house in Oxfordshire.'

When they arrived at Silistria, the French had already set up camp on one side of the plain, and Lucy caught sight of the red fezzes of the Turkish soldiers further off. The area left for the British troops lay on swampy ground near a river and black clouds of flies rose into the air as they stepped on it.

'We'll have our work cut out making this a home from home, but I'm sure we're up to it,' Adelaide called cheerfully.

They chose a patch that was slightly drier than the rest and some soldiers helped to unload Lucy's trunk and bags onto the ground. Charlie and Bill approached, joshing each other.

'I'll put a plug in your nose if you snore as you did last night,' Bill told Charlie, while Charlie insisted that Bill's socks must never be allowed in the tent.

'What's going on?' Adelaide smiled at them.

Charlie answered: 'They brought four-man tents. Bill and I have decided we'd rather share with you ladies than with any of our men – if that's acceptable to you, of course.' He bowed theatrically.

'I'll hang a sheet down the middle so we have a modicum of privacy,' Bill added.

Adelaide and Lucy looked at each other and agreed. In fact, Lucy felt greatly relieved that her friend would be so close at hand, even during the night. It would make her feel safer. She wondered what Dorothea would make of her sleeping under canvas. She would be forced to revise her low opinion of her younger sister if she saw how well she was coping with army life. Just the thought of Dorothea made her feel cross. Lucy shook her head, trying to erase the memory of their argument.

The men erected the tent in minutes then had to return to other duties, so Lucy and Adelaide began arranging their possessions, agreeing where the food store should be kept, where the washbowl should sit. There was nowhere to hang clothes so they had to stay folded in the trunk. Lucy's tin bath could be used for bathing and also for washing clothes.

'Isn't it strange to think the Russians are so close, perhaps just a mile away?' Lucy mused. 'I haven't heard any sound of their presence. Have you? I thought maybe there would be gunfire …'

They both stopped to listen but the only sound was the chirruping of insects in the long grass and the idle chatter of soldiers as they set up camp. The sun was a huge white orb and there was no shade from its unrelenting fire except inside the tent, where the air was stuffy and close. The ladies drank some tea, then loosened their corsets and lay down on their bedding rolls to snooze through the hottest hours of the day.

Chapter Seven

Two weeks after their arrival at camp, Charlie and Bill
returned from the front with news that the Russians had
abandoned Silistria and pulled back across the Danube. 'We
could be on the move again soon,' Charlie warned, but they
waited and no orders came. Meanwhile, the women had
slipped into the rhythm of camp life. Every morning, before
the heat grew too fierce, Lucy and Adelaide walked out to
nearby farms to try and purchase fresh food to augment the
chewy salt pork and tasteless dried biscuits distributed by
the army. They didn't speak the language, of course, but the
local men seemed receptive to Lucy's pretty face and Adelaide's
friendly smile and they were usually able to buy a loaf of
sour black bread, gritty with sand from the floor on which
the dough was kneaded, and perhaps some butter. Occasionally
they were offered a few eggs or a scrawny chicken, but the
only vegetables available seemed to be onions.

After a nap during the hottest hours, Lucy would venture
out to call on some of the other women and chat to them
as they washed clothes in the river or sat in the shade of a
stand of trees. She began to know several: Mrs Williams,
who had now resigned as lady's maid to Fanny Duberly – 'I

can't say I'm surprised,' Lucy told her with a conspiratorial twinkle – and Mrs Blaydes, who had taken her place; Mrs Jenkins, a forthright Welshwoman, and Mrs Higgins, who was said to have too much of a taste for alcohol but whom Lucy found shy and very companionable. She noticed that the women had shed their corsets and petticoats in an attempt to keep cool; in fact, she caught a glimpse of Mrs Williams' bare leg one day and realised she wasn't even wearing drawers. Lucy still wore all her layers in order to maintain a fashionably full skirt; she was determined not to let her standards slip, even though the intense heat meant her undergarments were often drenched in perspiration. In her head, she frequently argued with Dorothea: 'You see? I am sleeping in a tent, making tea on a campfire and, contrary to your expectations, I am perfectly capable of looking after myself.'

At night, they dined with the men on greasy communal stews doled out with slices of gritty bread, unless they had procured a chicken that day, in which case Adelaide roasted it over the fire with great competence. Lucy had never learned to cook and she watched carefully, eager to learn. After dinner, Charlie usually instigated the entertainment: sometimes it was a card game or a musical evening, but he also developed the raucous new sport of beetle racing. The men prowled the undergrowth collecting beetles then raced them along a length of sheet. They placed bets on the likely winners then cheered on their own creatures, to whom they gave names: Horatio the Horrible, Nimrod, Lucan and Raglan (the last two named after the cavalry commander and the army's elderly general).

Bill didn't care for gambling so he kept the ladies company on these evenings, conversing about books and music, or telling them what he had learned about the progress of the war: there were other fronts being fought in the Baltic, in the Eastern parts of Turkey and in Crimea, and it seemed possible they might be redeployed to one of them now the Russians had left Silistria.

'I wish they would make their decision soon so we can fight our battles and go home,' he told Lucy. 'I can't tell you how much I miss our little ones bouncing on my knee, or climbing all over me while pretending I am a big bear.' He chuckled. 'I love to hear them chattering in their serious little voices. Martha has an opinion on everything and is not shy of expressing it.'

'He can never deny her,' Adelaide smiled. 'If I have refused her anything, she will go to her father and extract his consent in an instant. He can't resist her.'

'It's true,' Bill grinned. 'You remind me of her, Mrs Harvington. I think you have steely determination beneath that pretty exterior.'

Lucy laughed. 'Thank you for the compliment, sir. I certainly hope I am more than merely decorative.'

At bedtime, Charlie returned to their tent and they made love quietly but Lucy blushed scarlet the next morning when Adelaide and Bill greeted her; she could hear when they had marital relations, just from a change in breathing pattern, a slight shifting of bodies, so she knew they must hear Charlie and her as well.

Weeks passed, June turned to July, and the men had little to do but tend their horses and race beetles. It felt like an anti-climax after all the excitement of the journey and Lucy wondered about the cause of the delay in getting new orders. Meantime, she was concerned that the horses drank from the river they used for their own drinking water, and she had been disgusted to see some soldiers urinating into it. She began to venture further afield to a spring where she collected buckets of water for drinking, enjoying the walk in the cooler hours of early morning. However, one day after she returned from such a trip she felt movement on her legs and lifted her petticoat to find a slimy black slug about two inches long stuck to her calf. She lifted the hem of her drawers to find another. She shrieked hysterically and couldn't stop shrieking.

'Get them off me! Get them off me!'

Adelaide came running at the sound of Lucy's terror: 'Those are leeches,' she quickly identified. 'Don't worry, they won't harm you.' She pulled a stick from their woodpile and used it to flick the creatures from Lucy's leg to the ground. A thin trickle of blood ran down from each of the bites. 'Perhaps you should check the other leg,' she suggested, and when Lucy rolled up her drawers she screeched anew to find four leeches attached there as well. Adelaide removed them then picked them up one by one on her stick and tossed them onto the fire, where they squirmed and crackled.

When she had done, Lucy burst into hysterical tears, still patting her legs in case she had missed one. 'I'm sorry ...' she sobbed. 'I didn't mean to make a fuss. I wanted to be brave.'

'You are extremely brave, my dear. For all you knew they could have been poisonous. In fact, they have long been used in medicine for bloodletting and their bites do not have any harmful effects but it's understandable you got a fright. Go lie in the tent and I'll bring you some tea.'

'Please don't tell Charlie. I don't want him to think I can't cope.'

Adelaide put an arm round her shoulder. 'Of course I won't tell him. And I think you are coping extraordinarily well, given your tender years and sheltered upbringing. Every morning you manage to look so spruce and well turned-out you put me to shame! And every day I find you chatting to someone new; you are one of the most popular women in the British camp and an inspiration to all. I'm proud to call myself your friend.'

Still Lucy was ashamed of her outburst and determined to be stronger when next she was challenged. She wanted Charlie to think her a worthy officer's wife. And although Dorothea wasn't there to witness it, she was determined to prove herself to her as well.

On the 19th July, Mrs Blaydes came to Lucy and Adelaide's tent with some alarming news: a soldier in the Royal Horse Artillery had died of low fever.

'Oh my goodness!' Lucy panicked. 'There must be poisonous vapours in the earth here. What can we do to avoid them?'

'Perhaps we should stay out of company until we can be sure there are no further cases,' Adelaide suggested. 'We could halt the beetle races and card games, just for now.'

'Seems a shame,' Mrs Blaydes said, 'but I 'spect you're right.'

Four days later sixteen men had died and it was confirmed as an outbreak of the deadly cholera. Lucy listened with shock to Charlie's description: 'I've heard a man can drop dead within hours of the first bout of diarrhoea, and his final hours are spent writhing on the floor with liquid spewing from both ends.'

Adelaide admonished him for scaring Lucy, but he continued: 'It's the truth. One captain in the Horse Artillery took an overdose of laudanum after his diagnosis as he couldn't face the horrors of such a death.'

'We must all keep out of harm's way,' Adelaide said firmly. 'If we are careful, I am sure we will avoid it.'

Lucy wondered if Dorothea had encountered any cholera sufferers in her hospital and might have some advice. If only she could write to ask! But even if her sister replied, the letter would take too long reaching them to be of use and Dorothea would probably just tell her to come home. She had not received a reply to the letter she sent her father from Malta. She knew some letters were getting through to the troops because in Constantinople Adelaide had been handed several, with coloured drawings made by her children, which had left her withdrawn and silent all afternoon.

In camp, there were whispers about those affected by fever, and Lucy steered well clear of sufferers' tents, anxious about vapours. She stopped wandering out to chat with other women at the cookhouse or down by the river, keeping close to the area around their tent in the hope that they had chosen an area of healthy soil. But her precautions were in vain. One evening, Bill was unable to eat his dinner but rose unsteadily and lurched towards the latrine trench where they emptied their bedpans. Shortly afterwards they heard him throwing up. Adelaide's face turned pale as she rushed to help him. His forehead was hot and his eyes glassy. The diagnosis seemed clear.

'Should I take him to the hospital tent?' she asked Charlie.

'Don't,' was his advice. 'No one who goes there comes out alive. I hear it's best to nurse patients in isolation. Lucy and I will move out of the tent to give you space, and will leave supplies for you outside.'

Lucy's throat was tight with fear – *what if their patch of land was poisoned? What if Charlie caught the cholera?* – but she was determined to be strong. 'Don't worry about anything but caring for your husband,' she told Adelaide. 'I'll bring water and food, and will empty bedpans if you leave them outside. Tell me whatever you need and I'll find it.'

Adelaide helped Bill to lie down in the tent and moistened a cloth to wipe his brow. 'A cure,' she said, her voice choked up. 'I need a cure.'

Charlie and Lucy retrieved their bedding and slept under the stars, as they had done on the first night in Varna. They clung together, both terrified but unwilling to put their fears into words. Lucy decided she would write to her father asking if he knew any remedies and presumably he would then ask Dorothea's advice. Perhaps she would send some miraculous medicine post-haste.

Next morning, Lucy called to Adelaide from outside the tent and was relieved to hear that Bill's condition was not any worse. She set off to get fresh water, the legs of her drawers tied tight to deter leeches. While she was filling her bucket, she saw one of the Sisters of Charity who accompanied the French army and in her best French asked for advice on treating cholera.

'The doctors give calomel for purging,' the Sister told her, 'but we believe it only increases the agony. Keep your friend's temperature down with cool cloths and feed him tiny sips of water and chicken broth. May God be with you all.' She made the sign of the cross.

Lucy took a bucket of fresh water back to their tent and called to Adelaide, telling her the advice she'd received and adding that she was setting out to beg for a chicken from one of the farmers. At the same time she would post the letter she had written.

'Don't take any risks on our account,' Adelaide called. 'Stay well clear of others. I couldn't forgive myself if anything happened to you ...'

Lucy had never made chicken broth before but with Adelaide calling instructions from inside the tent, she managed to produce a palatable brew and she left a large bowl of it by the tent flap, along with half a loaf of black bread.

For two days and two nights, neither Bill nor Adelaide emerged and there was little sound from inside the tent but Lucy could tell from the contents of the bedpans that the illness continued. She felt desperately lonely and scared during the day when Charlie went about his duties, and every evening she examined him for possible symptoms

– was his brow slightly warm, his complexion pale? – but he seemed fine. Fatalities multiplied and coffins had to be constructed from any materials that could be found: Lucy saw one that read 'Bass's Superior Pale Ale' on the side, which seemed horribly disrespectful to the dead. Was life really so cheap that a man could be full of life one day and buried in a beer crate the next?

On the third day of Bill's illness, Charlie went hunting and brought back four quail. He plucked them then Lucy roasted them, following Adelaide's method, and she was delighted to hear that Bill had managed to eat a small portion. He must be on the mend, and, thank God, Adelaide was showing no signs of having caught the disease.

Only when she and Charlie lay down to sleep that evening did Lucy dare to put into words the fearful thought that had been in her mind these last days, making her chest tight with nerves: 'Promise me you won't die out here,' she whispered.

'Of course I'm not going to die,' he replied, stroking her hair back from her face. 'I'm Lucky Charlie! I didn't catch the cholera and I've got you for a wife.'

They made love for the first time since Bill had fallen ill, and Lucy clung to him, feeling the warmth of his skin, the beating of his heart, the rise and fall of his chest, all the signs that his body remained healthy. He stroked her hair and kissed her eyes, her nose, her neck. 'You are extraordinary,' he whispered. 'Lord knows, I don't deserve you but somehow I am lucky enough to have you in my arms and nothing could make me let you go.' His voice cracked with emotion and Lucy had never loved him more; this must be what Adelaide meant when she said love deepens in times of adversity.

During the night she woke to hear Charlie mumbling in his sleep. She leaned in to listen and suddenly he grabbed her in a tight embrace and whispered 'Susanna' with such longing in his voice that her blood froze. The name had been clear, no question. Her insides twisted with jealousy. Who was Susanna and why did it sound as if Charlie felt so passionately about her? Was she a woman with whom he had been in love before he met her? If so, why had he not mentioned her? Perhaps he loved her still. She dismissed the thought – Charlie's love for her seemed beyond question – but all the same she found it hard to get back to sleep.

Chapter Eight

Once Bill had recovered sufficiently to emerge from the tent and rest in the nearby shade or go for gentle strolls to regain his strength, Adelaide was able to keep Lucy company once more, and the women became closer than ever. They were chatting together when Mrs Williams came by to ask after Bill.

'He is much better,' Adelaide replied. 'Thank you for your concern.'

'The 8th has been hit bad,' Mrs Williams told them. 'We've lost several men, and poor Mrs Blaydes has perished.'

'Mrs Blaydes? Oh no!' Lucy was distraught to hear of the loss of someone she had known, albeit slightly. 'And some of our men? Which ones?'

Mrs Williams rattled off a list of names, and tears filled Lucy's eyes. 'Their poor wives. What will they do now? I must visit them.'

Adelaide extended a restraining hand. 'Perhaps you had best not visit. I'm sure Mrs Williams will extend your heartfelt sympathies and let you know if there are any services you can perform for them.'

'Of course,' Mrs Williams agreed, her head bent.

After she left, Lucy told Adelaide about her letter to her father and her secret hope that Dorothea would write with advice that would help all cholera sufferers in the camp.

Adelaide poked the fire with a stick to stir the embers. 'My dear, if it is a painful subject then you needn't answer, but I am curious to know more about the argument with your sister. Was it simply because of Charlie or were you never particularly close?'

Lucy tried to answer truthfully. 'I think we were close once but it changed after my mother fell ill when I was seven years old. Dorothea appointed herself chief nurse and I was only allowed to see Mama when *she* said it was convenient. She often scolded me for making noise while Mama was trying to sleep and I suppose I began to resent her for keeping me away. Whenever I visited, Mama seemed cheerful and pleased to see me so it didn't appear I was doing any harm. She always liked me to play and sing for her, right up to the end ...'

'How many years was she bedridden?' Adelaide touched Lucy's arm with empathy.

Lucy tried to remember. 'Six years, more or less. Sometimes she came down to the parlour but such occasions were rare. They scared me because she looked so frail that I worried she would slip on the staircase. She seemed safer in bed, propped up on her pillows, and that's where she spent most of her time until she died. Dorothea didn't waken me that night but told me in the morning.'

Fresh tears came to her eyes, even five years on. 'I had no chance to be there as she passed away, to hold her hand and tell her how much I loved her, but Dorothea thought I wasn't old enough, that it would be too distressing for me. She made that decision on my behalf.' Lucy was surprised how angry she felt talking about it, even now.

'I expect she did what she thought was best.' Adelaide pursed her lips.

'No doubt she would say she did what she thought was best when she wrote to Charlie's family trying to prevent our wedding, and got a barrister friend of hers to write to Major Dodds.'

An intake of breath signalled Adelaide's surprise at this disclosure. 'Goodness! I can understand her trying to persuade you that eighteen is rather young to come to war, but perhaps she went too far. I'm sure she only did it because she loves you.'

Lucy shook her head. 'She has to be in charge. After Mama died, she was constantly scolding and correcting me. I was always in trouble for taking my gloves off when etiquette said I should not, or wearing a coat she thought was not warm enough, or talking too much in company. But although she may be thirteen years older, she is not my parent and does not have the right. So I often disobeyed, knowing Papa would take my side.'

'And he consented to your wedding?'

'Of course! He likes Charlie. Why wouldn't he?' Lucy felt defensive.

'I suppose he too must have worried about you coming out here with a man you haven't known for terribly long ...' Adelaide's voice trailed off.

Lucy looked at her. Was she taking Dorothea's side? 'Papa simply wants me to be happy.'

'So Dorothea was twenty-six when your mother died? I suppose devoting herself to nursing her meant she had missed her opportunity to marry. Such a shame.'

'I'm not sure Dorothea was ever interested in men.' Lucy picked up a stick and began to trace a pattern in the dusty ground. 'She's too domineering. She volunteered to work at the Pimlico Charitable Hospital after Mama died, where I imagine she is very bossy. She has no time for anyone who doesn't agree with her.'

'It's good that she lives a useful life. I hope she enjoys her work?'

Lucy pondered this. 'I suppose she wouldn't do it if she didn't enjoy it. She talks about it a lot. I only hope she writes soon, and maybe she will be able to send us some medicine to cure cholera. I expect it will be accompanied by long lists of instructions about what to do, what to avoid; you can count on that.'

'A family rift is such a sadness. I worry about you and Charlie both being estranged from your kin. Promise me you will make peace with Dorothea after the war.'

'Only if she will respect our marriage and treat me as an adult.' Lucy folded her arms, determined that any apology should come from her sister since she had done nothing wrong.

That evening, Charlie and Lucy went for a stroll in the moonlight, arms linked, and she mentioned that she had written to her father and very much hoped that Dorothea would send advice on preventing cholera.

Charlie seemed hurt. 'Why did you write to them? We have each other now. Dorothea only ever caused trouble for us and, to be frank, your father doesn't know the day of the week. You and I don't need anyone else.'

Lucy squeezed his arm. 'Of course we don't, darling. I only wrote because of the cholera. Don't be cross with me.'

He fell silent and she could tell from the way he stiffened and peered into the distance that he *was* cross about it. He wanted her all to himself. Perhaps he was worried that Dorothea would try to persuade her to return home again – as no doubt she would. But nothing would make Lucy leave now. How would Bill have survived cholera without Adelaide's tender care? If anything should happen to Charlie, she wanted to be there to offer the same comfort.

*

69

The summer passed slowly and Lucy grew increasingly frustrated with the delay in any fresh orders coming through. She missed her home, her friends and her father, and the novelty of living in a tent had long since grown tiresome. Towards the end of August, rumours began to spread that the troops were set to sail for Crimea but that officers' wives must be left behind in Varna, since there would be no decent accommodation for them once the army was on the move.

'I am not staying behind,' Adelaide declared firmly. Although Bill had returned to his duties he was still weakened by his illness and she could not contemplate waving goodbye to him. 'I will go along by hook or by crook.'

'And I'll come too,' cried Lucy. She could think of nothing worse than being left alone in this land of cholera and leeches.

Charlie told them that Lord Lucan intended to patrol the quayside watching every person boarding the ship, and they tried to think of ways to avoid his eagle gaze. Lucy suggested she could hide in her trunk, but Charlie pointed out that she would soon suffocate.

'Why don't we dress as soldiers?' Adelaide suggested. 'We could borrow some trousers and tunics and hide our hair under busbies.'

Lucy laughed at first but her friend was serious. She rushed into their tent and emerged some minutes later wearing Bill's spare uniform. While the blue tunic was baggy on her, and the red trousers with a yellow stripe threatened to fall down at any moment, she could have passed for a man if you didn't look too closely.

'Charlie's would be far too big for me. Perhaps I can borrow a spare uniform from Mrs Williams' husband Stan, who is slighter,' Lucy suggested, feeling a surge of excitement. 'I'll ask her. It doesn't seem fair that soldiers' wives are allowed to go along while we are not.'

'They plan on putting the soldiers' wives to work, cooking and laundering clothes,' Adelaide explained, 'but we can do that just as well.'

At daybreak on the 31st August, when the Hussars struck camp, Adelaide and Lucy were already dressed in their borrowed uniforms. It meant they couldn't beg a lift on a gun carriage for the eight-mile march to Varna and even had to carry a bag apiece (although Charlie managed to arrange transport for Lucy's trunk, the bath and her heaviest bags). Their feet blistered in army boots several sizes too large, stuffed with socks so they didn't fall off, but both marched with determination and kept up with the others, chatting along the way.

'By the by, there is something I wanted to ask you,' Lucy said. 'Did Charlie ever mention a girl called Susanna? He called that name in his sleep. I don't want to embarrass him by asking about her, but wondered if she was perhaps a lady he used to be enamoured with before he met me? He is a man of seven and twenty years and must have courted other ladies before we met. Perhaps Bill knew her?' Sensing Adelaide's discomfort with the line of questioning she continued hurriedly, 'Don't worry; I am not a jealous type of woman.'

'I ... I think I have heard the name,' Adelaide told her, hesitantly. 'I believe there may have been ladies before you, but you must know you have nothing to worry about. Charlie dotes on you.'

'I'm not worried. It's just that he seemed to feel so passion-ately about her.'

'I'm sure one day he will tell you about her.'

'Won't you tell me?' Lucy pleaded.

'It's not my place ...' Adelaide began, then cried, 'Look! I see the ships ahead. We are almost there.' None of Lucy's questions could induce her to say any more.

On the quayside at Varna, crowds were milling and amongst them Lucy recognised Lord Lucan standing by the gangplank watching those boarding. Shoulder to shoulder, she and Adelaide pushed forwards, trying to adopt a masculine style of walking, keeping their heads down, and the Major General barely glanced at them as they hurried on board. They asked directions to the officers' quarters, and were momentarily surprised to find Fanny Duberly there, already having commandeered the best cabin. She glared at them in their uniforms.

'Hardly dignified, ladies,' she remarked, making them burst into fits of giggles.

'How did you get past Lord Lucan?' Lucy snorted, looking at Adelaide in her trousers and fur busby.

'I simply walked past. He wouldn't dare to stop me. My husband and I are terribly good friends of Lord Raglan's.' She looked them up and down. 'I must say, you two look ridiculous.'

This made Lucy and Adelaide laugh anew, partly with the relief of having achieved their aim and avoiding separation from their husbands. Charlie and Bill arrived later and congratulated them on the success of the ruse.

The crossing to the Crimean peninsula was only supposed to take around thirty-six hours and they decided to keep a low profile and eat in their cabins rather than in the officers' dining hall. However, the ship was almost instantly becalmed in the waters of the Black Sea. It was twelve days before Lucy saw the coast of the Crimean peninsula, an ominous, shadowy vision through torrential gusts of diagonal rain.

PART THREE

Chapter Nine

15th September 1854

The Pimlico Charitable Hospital was situated near Westminster Cathedral and every day Dorothea's driver took them on a route that passed the Palace of Westminster, still in the process of being rebuilt after a disastrous fire in 1834. Heaps of bricks were stacked in Whitehall, where builders always seemed to be standing around smoking and passing the time of day, reluctant to shift aside to let a carriage pass. From their accents it was clear many were Irish, refugees from the Great Famine that had recently swept that land and decimated the population. Dorothea often looked at them out of her carriage window, singled out one man in particular and wondered about his story: whether he had been able to bring his family over, or if he was here alone and attempting to send back money to his loved ones. The busy streets of London must feel very strange to these peasants who had earned their living from the soil until their potato crop failed catastrophically.

Dorothea was kept very busy at the hospital. Her role was to chat with patients, read to them and try to raise their spirits, but she was fascinated to learn the basics of wound dressing, and assisting doctors in blistering, cupping and blood-letting. Although it was not usual practice for ladies, the matron, Miss Alcock, realised that Dorothea was competent and allowed her to help with medical care, and she had rapidly become one of the most knowledgeable of the nursing staff. The patients were all destitute folk who required a letter from the charity commission guaranteeing their good character before they were admitted, so as to weed out the drunkards and criminal classes.

On her ward there was great interest in the progress of the war and Dorothea often read the newspaper to her patients, just as she had for Mr Peters. They cheered at the news that their brave boys had arrived in the Turkish lands then became frustrated at the delays in engaging in battle, wanting to crush the Russkies as soon as possible. In the final week of July, reports began to appear in *The Times* about a cholera outbreak amongst the troops at Varna. Dorothea followed the movements of the 8th Hussars with special interest and knew they were there. At first there was a short paragraph mentioning four deaths, then there were another six, most in the French camp, but by the second week of August it was reported that five hundred had died and Dorothea became seriously alarmed.

At breakfast the next day, she saw her father was reading reports from Varna and couldn't help asking the news about the cholera. 'I'm so terribly anxious about Lucy!' she said. 'We've had no word about how she is or whether she's affected by the outbreak.'

Her father looked up, surprised. 'But she is very well! I have received a letter from her.'

Dorothea was astonished. 'What? A letter? Are you sure?' She thought for a moment that he had imagined it. Since Lucy had left he was increasingly prone to believing his own flights of imagination and she had become convinced that the mental infirmity of old age had affected his reasoning.

'Of course I'm sure. I read it myself. I have it in my study.'

'Why on earth did you not tell me?'

Mr Gray returned to his reading. 'It didn't occur to me, I suppose. The letter was addressed to me.'

A wave of anger and hurt flushed Dorothea's cheeks but she bit back a rebuke. Despite her certainty that he was senile, it was hard not to get cross with her father sometimes; she was still furious with him for giving his consent for Lucy and Charlie's marriage. Dorothea had given him many strong reasons against the match and still he had agreed to it. He had always liked Lucy better; that was the honest truth. Perhaps it was because she reminded him of his late wife, or maybe because she was so pretty and blonde and far more adorable than plain, dutiful Dorothea with her dull brown locks and sharp features.

These days she found herself irritated by her father's hypochondria. Every day he had some new symptom he wanted her to ask the hospital physicians about: a painful toenail, a slight rash on his chest, or difficulty with his bowel movements. She knew this was most likely a symptom of his senility, but found it hard to empathise. He was only in his mid-fifties. Surely, if he but tried, he could pull himself together?

'Might I see the letter?' Dorothea asked, her voice a little tetchy, and he sent Henderson to fetch it from his study with lengthy explanations as to its precise location.

When she at last held it in her hands, she read it rapidly. Lucy wrote gaily of the female friends she had made on the ship; she had always possessed a facility for female friendship, with her outgoing nature and lively conversation. Even as a child, whenever there was a guest in the house Lucy would be nearby, asking questions and charming them with her pretty manners. She loved to be in company. It cheered Dorothea to read the letter until she checked the date and realised that it had been written three months previously when their ship stopped off in Malta, long before the cholera outbreak.

'Did you reply?' she asked, but her father shook his head. His mouth was full of buttered roll so she had to wait for his reply.

'I didn't know where to write,' he said, wiping buttery crumbs from his lips.

Poor Lucy! She must think they had both abandoned her. Dorothea had not written again after the impassioned letter she sent on the eve of their departure had received no reply, but now she decided to try once more. She had no idea if the letter would get through to Varna but she could at least attempt to reach her sister.

'My dear Lucy,' she wrote. 'Father and I think of you constantly and pray for your good health. We have read of the cholera affecting our troops and are anxious to know you are safe.' She advised her to avoid foul, stuffy atmospheres or handling the bodily fluids of infected patients, then added more tips such as cooking fruit before eating it and drinking plenty of water to avoiding overheating in the warm weather. 'I will ask at the hospital about the treatments they use for those who fall ill, and will write again anon. But of course prevention is by far the best course.' In the last paragraph she sent her warmest regards to Charlie, and said she wished them both well. 'Please take care of yourself,' she wrote, closing her eyes in silent prayer that Lucy would be spared.

She sent Henderson to post the letter, addressed care of the 8th Hussars, and instantly felt a wave of relief that communication was once again opened between them, albeit one-sided. Perhaps she would write every week so that Lucy would receive regular correspondence from home. Even if she chose not to reply, she would know that Dorothea still loved her and was thinking of her.

As chance would have it, a letter from Lucy arrived just a few days later, crossing hers in the post. Yet again it was addressed to their father but this time he showed it to Dorothea at once. She could read her sister's anxiety between the lines and felt an acute pang of missing her. It was clear that Lucy wanted advice from her. 'If there should be some medicines available in London both to prevent and to cure this dreaded cholera, I would be most grateful if you could procure supplies and send them over. The doctors here seem at a loss,' she wrote.

At the hospital the following day, Dorothea asked Miss Alcock, her ward matron, for advice and was told that the physicians in Pimlico Hospital sometimes gave opium for the pain, but they no longer believed in the use of calomel, a purgative. The best thing was to keep patients hydrated with sips of water and cool their heads until the fever passed. The sister told her that there was currently an outbreak in Soho and they were refusing to take any patients from the area for fear of it spreading within the hospital.

'What is the mortality rate?' Dorothea asked, and wished she hadn't when Miss Alcock replied that it seemed as high as twelve per cent in some areas. Pray God it did not kill twelve per cent of the army in Varna. Pray God Lucy was safe.

Normally the physicians didn't deign to speak with the nurses. However, that afternoon, Mr Clarence, a particularly amiable young physician, came to visit the acute cases and on his way out, Dorothea was bold enough to accost him and ask his views on cholera prevention and treatment.

'It's interesting you should ask,' he said, 'as I was discussing it this very morning with Mr John Snow, a colleague at University College. He has analysed the Soho outbreak with great rigour and become convinced that every single sufferer had drunk water from the pump at the corner of Broad Street and Cambridge Street. He has long believed cholera is not an airborne disease; otherwise it would surely affect the lungs in the first instance. I can see his point there.' He paused to ensure she was following.

Dorothea frowned. 'Whereas it affects the digestive system, so that points to the cause being something ingested?'

'Precisely.' He nodded eagerly. 'Mr Snow persuaded the Board of Guardians of the parish to remove the handle, thus making the pump unusable and, lo and behold, cases of cholera infection dropped away rapidly. His own analysis of the water found white particles of unknown origin. Of course, much more research is required but it seems to me *prima facie* evidence for a waterborne illness. It could also be borne by contaminated foods, I imagine, especially those in which water is used during preparation.'

Dorothea was alarmed. 'My sister is in Varna with the troops. What advice should I send?'

'Instruct her to boil all water before use. And if infection occurs, keep the patient hydrated with sips of cooled boiled water. That's all that is being done with the Soho victims and so far the recovery rate is much improved on previous outbreaks.'

Dorothea was horrified: in her previous letter she had advised Lucy to drink lots of water, not considering that their supplies might be contaminated. If only the new telegraph line the army was constructing were ready, she could have sent a telegram to warn her. She hurried home as soon as she could and wrote with all the advice she had gathered, then she ended the letter with an emotional plea from the heart.

'Lucy, please at least consider coming back on the next available ship. I hear the army is moving north to the Crimean peninsula and an ex-soldier in my hospital last winter, a very sweet man, told me that wives will only drain supplies and get in the way.' She commended Lucy for her bravery so far but said: 'Now the real battles with big guns will begin, it is no place for a lady. It says in *The Times* that the war will be over in a matter of weeks, then Captain Harvington will be following you home. Please consider my suggestion and be assured that Father and I would welcome you with open arms.'

Dorothea read and re-read the letter, making revisions to the tone so that she could not be accused of being patronising (a word that had passed Lucy's lips several times during their bitter argument), then she made a fair copy and sent Henderson to post it.

From that moment on, her first thought when she got back from the hospital each day was to ask if another letter had arrived from overseas. But weeks went by and there was no word. Had Lucy succumbed to cholera? Was she dead already? Dorothea had no way of finding out and the waiting was intolerable. While working at the hospital, or spending evenings at home, her impetuous, warm-hearted, adorable little sister was always at the forefront of her thoughts.

Chapter Ten

A reporter for *The Times* newspaper, a plain-speaking Irishman called W.H. Russell, was living close to the troops in Varna and he sent back dispatches that described conditions as he saw them. Dorothea followed the news stories with mounting anxiety. Russell informed the British public that over a thousand men had died from cholera, diarrhoea and dysentery before a single shot was fired and that medical facilities were scandalously inadequate. Instantly there was an outcry, with government ministers scurrying around looking for someone to blame and worthy gentlemen writing to the papers asking what could be done.

On the 9th October, six months since Lucy had embarked, Mr Russell's story in *The Times* told of the army's 'glorious victory' at the Battle of Alma but said there were few surgeons and no hospitals so those requiring anything more than a simple battlefield dressing must sail south to Constantinople aboard what he described as 'fetid ships'. He wrote there was insufficient linen for bandages and that conditions were those of 'humane barbarity', with some injured men waiting forty-eight hours or more for treatment. Soldiers' wives who had accompanied the troops were helping to look after the less seriously wounded, but officers' wives had been encouraged to stay at Varna or Constantinople. Dorothea had no idea where Lucy might be; only that she was far from home and in mortal danger.

Her fear increased as the autumn air turned chilly and she thought of Lucy out there with only her summer wardrobe and some evening gowns. Should she send some warmer clothes, perhaps a coat? Or would they get lost along the way? It was dark when she left the hospital each evening, underlining the changing of the season. Most of her time was spent at work or at home with her father, but she sometimes went with her friend Emily Goodland, the sister of William, to hear concerts given by the Royal Philharmonic Society at Exeter Hall or to view the paintings in the Royal Academy of Art in Trafalgar Square. She often discussed her worries about Lucy with her friend. One chilly October evening Emily mentioned she had heard that a Miss Florence Nightingale, who was superintendent at the Institute for the Care of Sick Gentlewomen in Harley Street, had been asked by the government to take a small party of nurses out to the Turkish lands to see what could be done to relieve the suffering of the wounded.

'Perhaps you could ask one of Miss Nightingale's party to look out for Lucy?' she suggested. 'They could pass on a message if they see her.'

Dorothea's heart leapt. 'I am a great admirer of Miss Nightingale's. Do you know which nurses she will take?'

'I'm not sure,' Emily replied, 'but I did hear that she wants mature women with nursing experience.' She looked at Dorothea with a peculiar expression. 'Why? You wouldn't consider volunteering, would you?'

Instantly, Dorothea felt she should, and not just so that she could look for Lucy. Something else tugged at her heart. This was her chance to see a little more of the world and make a difference to it. She had no illusions about the awful injuries she might have to treat in a battlefield hospital; she had dressed some terrible wounds sustained by the men building the new railways, who got crushed by hefty metal rails, had limbs mangled in unfamiliar machinery and were severely burned when boilers unexpectedly exploded. She knew she could cope with virtually anything after that. She could be useful in Crimea; she knew she could.

'Yes, I would. Do you know how one should apply to be amongst the party?'

'I don't know any more than I told you. I assumed you would feel your ties at home would prevent you from making such a trip.'

'On the contrary, I should be most interested in finding out about it.'

She sensed Emily disapproved but could not work out why. Maybe it was because her friend didn't entirely approve of her working in a hospital. They could be dangerous places, and many of the nurses she worked alongside were rough women who drank on duty and treated patients with disdain. Most lady volunteers didn't so much as soil their begloved hands, but Dorothea loved to learn about medicine and often shocked Emily with her tales of procedures she had carried out.

Next morning, she rose early and skipped breakfast in order to make enquiries about the party of nurses going to the Crimea. Her matron, Miss Alcock, found out on her behalf that the final interviews were taking place that very morning at 49 Belgrave Square, the house of the Minister for War, Sidney Herbert, so Dorothea rushed straight there.

A line of chairs was set out in the grand entrance hall and she was invited to take a seat. No one else was there when she arrived but as she waited, an Irishwoman who looked to be in her fifties or sixties came in and sat with a groan, one hand clutching her lower back. They greeted each other but did not have a chance to make conversation before Dorothea was called in to an adjacent room. At a long table sat four women, who were introduced as Mrs Herbert (wife of the minister), Mrs Bracebridge and Miss Stanley (both friends of Miss Nightingale) and Miss Parthenope Nightingale (Florence's sister).

'What experience could you bring to our party?' Mrs Bracebridge asked.

Dorothea explained about her work, and told them that she knew all about wound dressing and care of fevers.

'How did you come to learn of such things?' She peered at Dorothea as if reassessing her.

Dorothea coloured, then said that her matron, Miss Alcock, had encouraged her to learn.

It seemed Mrs Bracebridge knew Miss Alcock and they conversed for a while about that decent soul. Her manner warmed somewhat and Dorothea gained confidence.

'Before I started work in the hospital, I spent years nursing my mother through breast cancer and other complaints that arose from her condition.' Dorothea hurried on so as not to dwell on this. 'The experience gave me a keen insight into care of the dying.'

'What age are you?' Miss Stanley asked in a friendly tone. Dorothea told her and she wrote it on a sheet of paper. 'Are you married?' she continued, and when Dorothea said she was not, she asked, 'Do you hope to marry?'

'No, I do not,' Dorothea answered truthfully. Any such hopes she might once have harboured had long been extinguished.

'Good,' Miss Stanley nodded. 'Women who intend to find a husband among the wounded soldiers are no use to us. Worse than useless, in fact. There must be no fraternising of any sort with the patients.'

'I understand. Of course not.'

'How many years have you been a nurse?' Miss Nightingale asked, and Dorothea said she'd spent six years nursing her mother, then another five working at the Pimlico hospital.

'What is your religion?'

'Church of England.'

'Who will care for your father if you are chosen to come on our expedition?' Mrs Herbert took over. 'Do you have siblings?'

'My father has servants to care for his physical needs, and is quite content with the company of his butler. I'm sure he will manage perfectly well without me.' Dorothea paused. 'My only sibling, my sister Lucy, is already out East; she accompanied her officer husband. I am concerned because we do not hear from her regularly and she was in Varna during the cholera outbreak. Perhaps I would be able to reunite with her at the same time as helping ...' Her voice tailed off as she saw the looks the women were exchanging.

Mrs Bracebridge pursed her lips. 'We are not here to help families be reunited. The women we choose must be totally dedicated to nursing injured soldiers and will probably never set foot outside the hospital ... I'm afraid you are not suitable.'

Dorothea panicked: 'I only meant that perhaps while I am working out there I might hear word of my sister. I certainly would not shirk my ward duties to look for her. I have never missed a day since I started volunteering in Pimlico. You can ask Miss Alcock; I'm sure she will tell you I am utterly dedicated.'

'All the same, your mind would be on family matters. I'm afraid we must say no, Miss Gray. Now, if you don't mind we have other candidates waiting to be seen.'

'Please reconsider,' Dorothea begged, struggling to stop herself bursting into tears. 'I should never have mentioned my sister. Of course it is unlikely I would see her amongst all the thousands of people out there. I want to nurse, to relieve suffering and to serve my country.'

Mrs Bracebridge was immovable. 'Send in the next candidate please, Miss Stanley.'

Miss Stanley, the youngest of the four interviewers, stood and moved to the door, opening it and holding it for Dorothea to pass.

As Dorothea rose, she gazed from one face to the next, desperately looking for a sign of sympathy, a weakening of resolve, but their minds were made up. She wasn't going.

She was distraught during the carriage ride along Birdcage Walk to the hospital. The trees had turned golden brown almost overnight, and falling leaves swirled high in the air carried on fierce gusts of wind. If only she hadn't mentioned Lucy. What a fool she was.

She confided in Miss Alcock, who sent a personal note to Mrs Bracebridge arguing Dorothea's case and her hopes were raised once more. But the reply came back promptly that they had received 617 applications, many of them from highly qualified women, and had already chosen the nurses they were taking.

Dorothea wept as she read in *The Times* of Florence Nightingale's band of thirty-eight women setting off to Paris on the 23rd October then overland to Marseilles and on by ship to Scutari. Her one chance of leading a life of some value was lost. Instead it was back to reading to patients, dressing their wounds and helping them to eat their meals in the same old London wards, then the stultifying atmosphere of evenings spent with her father in a house that was too big for them, where her footsteps echoed and everything reminded her of the absence of Lucy and the emptiness in her heart.

PART FOUR

Chapter Eleven

14th September 1854

At sunset, the ship carrying the Hussars and their wives anchored off the Crimean coast by a long sandy bay near a town called Evpatoria. The water was filled with ships and landing craft stretching in all directions, each with multi-coloured lamps decorating their masts as if they had arrived for a festival. Wind whistled through the rigging, causing a clanking sound. Onshore, the French were busily setting up camp; it seemed they were always first. The beach was deserted but in the distance Lucy could see the outlines of the town's buildings against the darkening sky. What would the inhabitants think of this mass invasion? There was as yet, thankfully, no sign of any resistance.

Charlie and Bill attended an officers' briefing in the dining hall then came down with the news that men were to disembark first. Women were strongly advised to stay on the ship but if they must come ashore with their husbands, they should bring only what they could comfortably carry, since there was a long march ahead and no one to help them. Men had been ordered to carry nothing but their weapons and three days' rations. Lucy looked in alarm at her trunk and bulging bags. There was no way she could manage them herself. Adelaide had just one bag and was keen to follow her husband, and Lucy was determined to go wherever her friend went. She guessed Fanny Duberly must have more luggage than average so she knocked on her cabin door to ask what she planned to do.

'My horse has not yet arrived from Varna,' Mrs Duberly told her when Lucy asked if she planned to disembark, 'and I am certainly not going to march on foot. I have been quite unwell these last days, and my servant Connell died just last night after a long struggle with fever.' She looked grey, with pinched cheeks and pale lips, and wore a white nightgown that had seen better days.

'I am so sorry. Is there anything I can do to help?'

'I rather doubt it; not unless you have medical training.' Her tone was unfriendly.

'Will you stay on this ship?' Lucy asked, thinking perhaps she could leave some of her luggage behind in that case.

'I believe I am being transferred to the *Shooting Star* tomorrow as this vessel has to make another journey. Once my horse arrives, I will ride ashore daily to catch up with the troops.'

'I will see you then perhaps. I am planning to go ashore today.'

Mrs Duberly looked her up and down with disdain. 'You think you are up to it, do you? You don't seem the hardy sort to me. Well, good luck to you.'

Further along the corridor, Lucy bumped into Captain Henry Duberly, Fanny's husband, and offered condolences on the death of their servant. He was more courteous than his wife and when Lucy asked if she might leave behind some belongings to be transferred to the *Shooting Star*, he promised to arrange it personally.

'Leave them in your cabin,' he said, brushing away her thanks. 'It's no trouble at all.'

Now all she must do was decide what to take with her. Adelaide suggested she bring her warmest clothing as the night air was becoming chilly although the days were still hot, so she chose a heavier gown of forest-green wool with a floral pattern on the edge of the flounces, her brown boots and a green cashmere cloak, and left behind the eveningwear.

As they prepared to disembark the following morning, the wind picked up, the sea became choppy and heavy clouds scudded in front of the sun. Light drizzle began to fall as Lucy and Adelaide were ferried by rowing boat onto a sandy beach crowded with red-coated soldiers carrying rifles and bayonets, and dozens of fully-laden horses and carts. There was no sign of their husbands and no shelter so after trying fruitlessly to find someone to ask what they must do, Lucy and Adelaide began to march alongside the troops heading for the first night's encampment. They each clutched their one bag and an army-issue blanket, hooded cloaks wrapped around them against the increasing downpour. They had brought some rations of black bread and salt meat from the ship, so they ate as they walked and drank water from wooden flagons.

The men came to a halt on a barren plain and began to set down their weapons, but there was no sign of any tents and Lucy and Adelaide asked a passing captain where they should rest.

'You must find shelter where you can, Ma'am. The tents have not yet come ashore.'

'Do you know where our husbands might be? They're with the Hussars.'

He shrugged. 'I'm afraid I don't have that information. It's possible they have been sent ahead on reconnaissance.'

Lucy felt a quiver of panic. No one was looking out for them. They had been warned this might be the case but the reality was terrifying. It seemed they were to sleep out of doors in a hostile land, where Russians might arrive to kill them in their bedding rolls if the elements had not first given them a fatal chill.

'The French camp was erected last night,' Adelaide protested. 'They are preparing dinner at this very moment, while we must survive on cold rations in the open air.'

'I am sorry, Ma'am.'

Adelaide shook her head crossly. 'We must make the best of it then.'

Some folk were fashioning improvised shelters out of brushwood, but Lucy and Adelaide found a wagon that appeared to have been abandoned, and placed their blankets and bags underneath to lay claim to it. Adelaide tried to start a small fire in a sheltered spot by a bush but it sparked then fizzled out, creating a column of smoke but no heat. When darkness fell they crawled under the wagon and wrapped themselves in their blankets, using their bags as pillows, but the noise of the rain pounding on the wood and the groans of those who had failed to find any shelter combined to make sleep fitful. It was the most uncomfortable experience of her life, but Lucy told herself she could put up with it for one night. She must.

When the bugles sounded at daybreak, they emerged stiff, cold and bedraggled. The rain had eased enough to strike a fire from some kindling Adelaide had thought to place beneath the wagon to dry out. Being able to boil water and brew tea made them feel a little more human. Mid-morning, Charlie came riding up and Lucy screamed with delight. He leapt from his horse and wrapped his arms around her, lifting her face to his.

'Look at you! A night on the road and you are as beautiful as ever. I'm so proud of you, my adorable wife.'

She felt like bursting into tears, telling him how scared she had been and begging him not to leave her again, but she swallowed the words. She was an army wife now and must not swamp him with her fears. 'Will you be staying with us tonight?'

'I think it's unlikely, my dear. My men are riding ahead to establish where the Russians are holed up and I must be on hand for them to report to. Bill is in the same position. But you two seem fine on your own. As soon as we can, we will return.'

'Must you leave straight away? Is there no time for some tea?'

He shook his head with a regretful smile, then gave her a lingering kiss on the lips. 'I can't wait to lie with you again,' he whispered. 'We must be patient. Remember that I adore you.' With that he leapt onto his horse, saluted them and rode off. Adelaide had been hanging back to give them some privacy but now she called after him, 'Tell Bill I am well and miss him dearly.'

Some of the tents arrived later that day and a couple of soldiers took pity on Lucy and Adelaide and erected one for them. For the next two days they stayed in camp, with occasional visits from Charlie or Bill to reassure them, until on the morning of the 19th September they were told to pack for the long march south towards Sevastopol, where the Russians were at last to be defeated. A vast column formed, with French troops to their right and Turkish bringing up the rear, and Lucy listened with interest to the babble of languages being spoken as these men from quite different backgrounds joined cause against a common enemy. Amongst the British ranks, everyone's mood was lifted by the music of the regimental bands playing patriotic classics such as, 'Cheer, boys, cheer'. It was hard for the women to keep pace with the marchers as their boots slipped on rough scree and their long gowns became entangled in thorny bushes. Lucy and Adelaide found the Turkish troops starting to overtake them. Two dark-complexioned Turks – men of whom Lucy would normally have felt nervous even though they were allies – took pity and carried their bags for a while, until their commanding officer shouted something and they handed them back apologetically.

Lucy's limbs ached and a blister on her right heel became more and more inflamed as the day wore on, but at least she was not afraid of ambush by Russian troops with so many soldiers around them. There was general grumbling, with many wondering why they had not landed closer to Sevastopol and attacked immediately, but Adelaide assured Lucy that Lord Raglan and the French commanders must have some clever plan in mind.

In the afternoon they reached a stream and stopped to drink. Lucy removed her boot to bathe her poor heel in the cool water. A whisper went round and, looking in the direction others were peering, she saw the hazy shape of a gathering of people on a ridge ahead.

'Are these … are they Russians?' she asked a nearby soldier and he confirmed they were.

A thrill of fear ran through Lucy and she clutched Adelaide's hand.

'I hope we'll get a chance to fight them,' the soldier said. 'The cowards have been retreating but I hear they are encamped just a mile ahead at the River Alma and we plan to attack them there.'

Now the troops had reached this point, it seemed inhumane, outlandish even, to Lucy that the men around her were going to attempt to kill those who stood on a distant ridge. Could they not sit down and talk through their differences, as women would have done? But she didn't voice her thoughts, not even to Adelaide. She was an army wife and this was what armies did.

Charlie and Bill returned that evening and Charlie brought out a bottle of porter he had purloined from somewhere. The ladies accepted a glass each, as did Bill, and Charlie entertained them with stories of the rivalries between the Earl of Lucan and the Earl of Cardigan, who were brothers-in-law yet hated each other vehemently.

'What is the source of their quarrel?' Adelaide asked.

'Cardigan thinks Lucan doesn't treat his sister well enough,' Charlie replied. 'Marriages can bring out the worst in families.' He caught Lucy's eye and winked. 'It's rather alarming that our commanders don't get along but one can only hope it won't affect their judgement.'

At that moment a messenger came to summon Charlie; Major Dodds wished to have a word about plans for the morning. Adelaide went into the tent to prepare for bed, leaving Lucy and Bill chatting by the fireside. Emboldened by the porter, she took the opportunity to ask about Charlie's family.

'Adelaide tells me you have met the Harvingtons.'

'Yes, on a few occasions.'

'What manner of people are his parents? His two brothers?' She was curious to hear everything, since Charlie would never speak of them.

Bill paused. 'I didn't know them well. His father is a stern, rather old-fashioned man.'

'I hope when we return from war, I might meet them and we will be able to repair the rift that has distanced them.'

Bill poked the embers of the fire warily. 'Charlie has not told you of the tragic circumstances of the rift?'

'No, not really! At least, all he told me was that it involved an argument over a debt. What happened? Pray tell.' She watched him eagerly.

'It is for him to tell you. I'm sure he will one day, but for now all you must do is give him as much love as you possibly can, because he needs it and he deserves it. Fate has dealt him a cruel blow in the past. But I have observed you, Lucy, and I think you have the right mixture of qualities to be an excellent wife for him. I'm so glad he met you.'

She was rendered momentarily speechless by this puzzling outpouring. 'Thank you. I hope I will do my best. But ...'

There was no time for further questions as Charlie rushed back with news: 'Four a.m., Bill. You and I are on the right flank.'

A shiver went down Lucy's spine.

This was it.

The two men spoke head to head for a few minutes, serious, professional. She rose and went into the tent to prepare for bed. When Charlie came, they lay with their arms round each other, faces close, but she knew his thoughts were elsewhere – as were hers. Her heart was pounding with the knowledge that next day he must fight and there was a chance he might not return. How did any wife cope with this? All she could do was breathe slowly and remember that he was Lucky Charlie who did not catch cholera when all around him were falling sick. He may have had a difficult past but now he had her and she would look after him. She breathed in his scent to memorise it and clung to his warm flesh, as if trying to imprint it on her own.

Their husbands rode off at the crack of dawn. Lucy could still feel Charlie's hurried last kiss on her lips, and wondered if she would ever have a chance to kiss him again. As she and Adelaide made tea they were uncharacteristically silent.

Some women were climbing to a ridge from which they could view the battle so Lucy and Adelaide followed. From the top they were close enough to see the main Russian encampment just across the River Alma, close enough to make out smoke from their fires drifting into the air. It was eerie to think of them sleeping in their tents and heating food, just as in the British camp, perhaps some of them also accompanied by their wives. Yet soon they must be attacked and driven back; soon they must be killed.

The British, French and Turkish armies had superiority in numbers but the Russian army was on a raised plateau and they'd had time to dig in their gun emplacements. Suddenly Lucy was deafened by a wall of noise: explosions from big guns and the pop-popping sound of small guns mingling with the eerie sound of the bagpipes played by some regimental bands. The fighting had started. Dust rose in the air blurring individual forms and Lucy wondered how the men could tell who was friend or foe. She was horrified to see bodies fallen face down in the river and to realise they must be dead. The Russians appeared to be advancing down the hill, and suddenly her heart was filled with such fear for Charlie that she could no longer watch. Sick to her stomach and over-whelmed with the awfulness of the scene before her, she turned and hurried down the hill to sit on her own, hands covering her face. She'd thought she could cope but nothing in her upbringing had prepared her for witnessing such carnage. After a while Adelaide joined her, reassuring her that already the British and French appeared to be prevailing.

Back at camp, Adelaide decided to occupy herself by cooking and somehow turned their dried pork rations and some herbs picked in the undergrowth into a fragrant stew.

'Won't you try some?' she asked.

'I feel too sick,' Lucy said. 'I'll wait until the men return and I can breathe easy again.'

She considered asking if Adelaide knew about the tragedy in Charlie's life that Bill had alluded to – those two seemed so close they must have discussed it – but it hardly seemed the right time with their husbands in battle facing a deadly foe. Besides, she felt embarrassed that Charlie had not told her himself. Instead she asked Adelaide about her children, knowing she always enjoyed talking about Martha and Archie.

But as Adelaide spoke, Lucy realised she was only half-listening. Her brain focused on the booming of the big guns in the distance and her constant churning fear for Charlie.

Suddenly, at around four-thirty in the afternoon, the gunfire ceased. They looked from one to the other. Half an hour later the first souls came down from the ridge to announce victory for the allies, and Adelaide and Lucy hugged each other. Lucy found another bottle of porter in Charlie's bedding roll and poured them each a small glass to toast the troops. Men began to trickle back to camp, weary and dirty. The wounded were carried on the shoulders of their comrades, since no ambulance carts and insufficient stretchers had been brought along. The women went to offer sips of water and words of comfort while they waited for a doctor.

Charlie arrived around eight in the evening, and Lucy dashed up to him, almost pulling him from Merlin in her joy. Her chest had been tight with fear all day but now at last she could breathe easily. With him he brought a ladies' parasol of black lace over ivory silk, a wickerwork picnic basket and a bottle of wine he had found abandoned on the Russian side.

'Their wives were watching behind the lines,' he said. 'It was a day out for them.'

'Where is Bill?' Adelaide asked, her voice tight with nerves.

Charlie grinned reassuringly. 'He was helping to round up prisoners but should be back before too long. Shall we open the wine now or do you want to wait for him?'

They agreed it was fairest to wait. An hour went past, then another. Finally Charlie offered to ride out and see what was keeping Bill.

Half an hour later, they looked up to see Charlie galloping across the field towards them. He leapt from his horse, eyes wide with shock and his whole body shaking. 'I'm s— so sorry.'

Adelaide screamed and clapped her hand to her mouth.

Charlie struggled to speak: 'One of the prisoners had a pistol and when Bill tried to disarm him he was sh-shot through the h-head.' He broke down and sobbed so hard the last words were virtually indistinct: 'He died instantly.' Adelaide's legs buckled and she sank to the earth with a cry, her face buried in her hands. Charlie leaned his face into his horse's flank, his body trembling with violent sobs, and Lucy looked from one to the other, so shocked she couldn't react. Bill had gone. He wasn't coming back, although he'd been the picture of health when he rode out that morning. It was unfathomable. What about his children? What about Adelaide?

Lucy realised she must comfort her friend but what should she do? Charlie had fallen to pieces. If only Dorothea were there. She must comfort people who'd lost their husbands all the time. She would know what was needed, but Lucy didn't have the first idea.

Chapter Twelve

Charlie arranged for Bill's body to be brought to a quiet spot amongst some bushes on the edge of the camp, where Adelaide kept vigil by his side all night long. Lucy and Charlie took turns to sit with her as she grieved. Sometimes she muttered prayers, at others whispered to Bill under her breath while stroking his face or holding his hand. Someone had arranged his fur busby on his head to hide the fact that part of his skull had been blown away. Adelaide wouldn't accept any tea and barely said a word to either Lucy or Charlie, but focused all her attention on the man lying on the ground. As night went on, a purple stain seeped down into his face, which swelled until he was barely recognisable, while his limbs stiffened awkwardly, but he was still her husband, the man who played at being a big bear while their children clambered over him.

Charlie was in tears much of the time. How would he cope without the steady presence of Bill, who had been such a close friend? Only the previous evening they'd all been chatting by the fire. Somehow Lucy had expected there would be an inkling of impending death, such as they'd had with her mother, but Bill was full of life one moment and gone the next. Her heart ached for him, for Adelaide, Martha and Archie. And sometimes a selfish thought passed through her mind: *Thank God it wasn't Charlie.*

Towards morning, Adelaide began to go through Bill's pockets, removing personal items, and she gave a little cry when she found a letter addressed to her in an inside pocket.

'What can this be?' she asked and opened it with trembling hands. Soon tears were streaming down her cheeks unchecked, and when she finished reading, she held the letter to her lips and kissed it tenderly before handing it to Lucy.

'My most precious darling,' it said, 'I am writing these few lines, lines that I hope you will never read, in case fate is against us and our time together on this earth is now at an end. The memories of our blissful life together fill my thoughts and I feel grateful to God for giving us the great passion and intimacy we have shared. Without you, my life would have been humdrum and ordinary; with you I scaled the very highest peaks of love, and count myself the most fortunate man who ever lived. Not only did God give us each other but he rewarded us for our long patience with two miraculous children, on whom I have doted so dearly. You are the most admirable mother, the most magnificent woman that ever I encountered, and I know I leave our offspring safe in your hands. Cherish them for me, talk to them of me from time to time, and tell them that I died to make their futures safer. I will be with you, Adelaide, watching as you hum while sewing, while you gaze out the window at the tall trees swishing in our garden, while you read to our children. You and I shall meet again, of that I have no doubt, but first I wish you will not mourn too bitterly. Devote your boundless energy and strength to raising our little ones so that I may live through them. I adore you, now and for always, Bill.'

'It is his last gift to you,' Lucy said, handing it back, her voice catching. 'It's beautiful.'

Adelaide wiped her eyes. 'And now I must do as he asks. First I will bury him with as much dignity as we can achieve in this foreign land, then I will sail home to my children.' She grabbed Lucy's arm. 'Come with me. You have seen enough now to know we made a mistake. We shouldn't be here. There is no accommodation for women and there is not enough food to go around. You could be more help to Charlie sending him packages from back home. This is a place for men to fight.'

Lucy was stricken. The truth of Adelaide's words was clear. But how could she leave Charlie, knowing he might suffer the same fate as Bill and there would be no one to stand vigil, no one to bury him with dignity? And if he lived, how could she leave him to return each night to a cold bed and dry army rations, with no woman to make tea or wash his clothes? And yet, she did not know how she would manage without Adelaide. The thought of leaving with her was enormously tempting.

'I will talk to Charlie,' she promised and Adelaide nodded, adding: 'I would much appreciate your company on the voyage.'

When she told Charlie of her friend's suggestion he broke down in tears.

'Lucy, darling, please don't go. How could I manage without you?' He clung to her, distraught. 'Am I to lose my best friend and my wife as well, one day after the next?'

His tears surprised her, but she knew he was overcome with grief about Bill's death. 'Of course not. I just thought I could be of use to Adelaide …'

'Please don't abandon me. Things will be easier for you when we establish a new camp. There will be proper washing facilities and decent food, and you will make new friends to take Adelaide's place. Besides, we will only be in Crimea at most a few more weeks.'

His plea was so impassioned that Lucy couldn't help but agree, despite her strong misgivings.

'Of course I will stay. I am your wife and my place is by your side.'

The funeral was held in light drizzle beneath overcast skies. A bugler played the haunting 'Last Post' as Bill's body was wrapped in a sheet and lowered into a hastily dug grave. Adelaide had placed in his arms the coloured drawings their children had sent and a lock cut from her own hair. She laid his bayonet alongside him, and turned away so as not to see the soil thrown on top.

'Now I must go home.' She clutched Charlie's arm. 'Please will you make arrangements for me to get on the next ship? I must reach my children as soon as the Royal Navy can possibly carry me.'

He promised to do what he could.

While Adelaide packed her bag, Lucy penned a quick letter for her father, telling him of her whereabouts and about the victory at Alma but omitting mention of Bill's death. 'I miss you terribly, Papa,' she wrote at the end, her chest tight with homesickness. She missed Dorothea too; what she wouldn't give to see her sister again, despite their quarrel! She knew she was going to feel bereft without Adelaide's calm, sensible presence and realised in a flash of understanding that she had provided security, like a substitute sister.

Though Adelaide was distressed when Lucy broke the news she would stay, she said she would ensure that the letter was delivered as soon as she got back, which she hoped would be well before Christmas. A wagon full of wounded men was leaving for Evpatoria and she was to ride with them to meet her ship so their tearful farewells were rushed. Charlie stood with his arm firmly around Lucy's waist, as if fearful she might change her mind and jump on board at the last moment. She hoped he would stay to be company for her, but as soon as the wagon had gone he rode off to check on his men, who were out on patrol, and Lucy was left completely alone.

She wandered over to the cookhouse to find Mrs Williams chatting to Mrs Jenkins and some women Lucy had never met. Mrs Williams made the introductions and Lucy tried to spark a conversation. 'I hope you ladies won't mind me intruding. I'm happy to help with laundry or cooking, or any chores you are doing,' she said. 'I hate to be alone.'

'You could always go and live on board ship. I thought that's what the officers' wives were doing,' remarked Mrs Jenkins, unsmiling.

'I want to be with my husband and if that means living in a tent, so be it. I've managed so far, with only a few mishaps.' She told them the story of the leeches, laughing at herself; her horror at those creatures now seemed as nothing compared to what had followed.

'We'll be on the move tomorrow,' Mrs Williams told her. 'We're going to camp on a plain outside Sevastopol. It'll be a long march. Is your blister quite healed?'

Lucy was touched that she remembered her mentioning it. 'Not quite, but I will apply fresh dressings. I hope you ladies won't mind if I walk with you? I promise to keep up.'

'Soak your heel in strong tea tonight,' Mrs Williams suggested. 'That will help. I'll call by your tent in the morning.'

The march, a distance of around forty miles, took three days to complete. The women sang to raise their spirits, and Lucy surprised them by singing some popular show tunes, including 'Lay a garland' and 'Rol al lu, rol al lay'.

'I thought it was all symphonies and arias with you aristocratic types,' Mrs Jenkins said.

Lucy laughed. 'My father was a furniture merchant so we are not remotely aristocratic. My mother was fond of all types of music. She took me to the music-hall a few times, and she always sang around the house.'

Mrs Jenkins made a face but seemed appeased and the women stopped to listen whenever Lucy struck up a new song. Her voice was easy on the ear, they agreed.

As they walked, they passed through farmland which had been deserted by its Russian and Tartar owners and they grabbed any produce they could carry: late-season grapes, peaches and pears from the orchards, and beets, potatoes and corn from the fields. This seemed fair enough but Lucy didn't accompany the women when they broke into abandoned houses and stole silver salvers, porcelain ornaments and bottles of wine or champagne. Food was one thing but taking someone else's property seemed wrong, even in wartime.

She missed Adelaide terribly. They came from similar backgrounds and had the same sensibilities. She had become in some ways like a sensible elder sister, a version of Dorothea but one who did not criticise her the whole time. Now she was gone, Lucy's thoughts turned increasingly to her sister. There had been no response to her letters sent from Malta or Varna, but she supposed it must be difficult to locate individuals when they were on the move. She hoped a letter would come once they struck camp. Surely it would.

After three days of walking, which left Lucy's feet blistered so badly that she often took off her boots and stockings and tramped barefoot on the earth, they reached a plain from which they could see the rooftops of the town of Sevastopol and in the distance, the sea. Just over a ridge was a wide stretch of land that was to become the new British camp; supplies would arrive via the nearby port of Balaklava. Each company was allocated an area and their tents were erected in long rows. The temperature was dropping every night, and Lucy quickly sought out Henry Duberly to ask for her trunk to be delivered from the *Shooting Star*. Mrs Williams told her she was wasting her time. An attack against Sevastopol was due any day and after that they could all go home but Lucy was grateful when the trunk appeared because she had in it some beige calf's leather shoes that were gentle on the feet. At last she could arrange all the little items she had brought with her: her tin bath for washing, her mother's beloved silk bedspread, a little painting of blue flowers, some cooking pots, cutlery and china plates. The familiarity of her possessions in this otherwise foreign landscape was comforting. There was a general store in the nearby village of Kadikoi where she was able to purchase basic foodstuffs at inflated prices. Charlie kept his pay in a locked wooden box in case of pilfering but gave her some whenever she asked.

His mood had been flat since Bill died. Lucy suggested that he set up a card game some evening, but he preferred to sit by the fire outside their tent, eating his dinner, drinking a few tots of rum, and then falling into bed. They made love, but it was perfunctory and lacking in the passion he had previously shown. His talk was of the commanders' frustrating delay in ordering the attack on Sevastopol and the impossibility of fully encircling the port, meaning that supplies would still be able to get in even though it was besieged.

'What is Raglan thinking of? How can we possibly prevail from this position?'

Lucy had no suggestions to offer, except to repeat what Mrs Williams had said about an imminent attack, and to remind him that the British army was the greatest in the world and must soon triumph. This was the kind of conversation he used to have with Bill and she knew he felt the loss of his friend greatly. When she asked him how long he thought they would be camped there, he shrugged gloomily and said, 'It's anyone's guess.'

Once their camps were set up the French and British artillery began bombarding the Russian positions outside the town, with explosions that sounded like thunder and made the ground shake. The Russians fired shells back but Charlie reassured Lucy their camp was out of range and she had nothing to fear so long as she didn't stray any closer. Still she was anxious with each blast and glanced around as if expecting Russian troops to appear on the horizon with bayonets raised.

Before daybreak on the morning of 25th October, they awoke to a rumpus outside the tent.

'The Turks are fleeing their lines,' someone called. 'The bloody cowards!' Charlie dressed hurriedly and saddled his horse.

'The Russians are attacking Balaklava,' someone else yelled. 'They'll encircle us.'

Lucy just had time to cry, 'Be careful, dear,' as Charlie mounted his horse and called his men to arms.

Mrs Williams hurried past and over her shoulder called, 'Come with us, Mrs Harvington. We can watch from Sapoune Heights.'

Lucy did not want a view of the battle but neither did she want to be left on her own, so she tagged along, nerves knotting her insides. They found a crowd already on the Heights. Lord Raglan himself, distinctive in his red jacket and oversized epaulettes, held court in the centre of a group of officers with field glasses. Fanny Duberly was with them, and Lucy called a greeting but she stared straight through her, cutting her. Some distance away, several dozen soldiers' wives huddled together, gazing towards Balaklava. Lucy didn't know what was going on, or even which groups were British in the chaotic scene below. Soon they could hear gunfire and explosions and smell the acrid scent of gunpowder.

Mrs Williams nudged her. 'See that red line? That's the Sutherland Highlanders. The Turks might have run for the hills – wouldn't you know it! – but the Russkies'll never get through them Scotsmen.'

'Is that not a line of Russians advancing towards them?' Lucy asked.

'It is, but they'll hold all the same.'

Just when it seemed as though the Highlanders might be overwhelmed, a British cavalry brigade rode in to relieve them. 'Are the Hussars among them?' Lucy asked.

'No, that's the Heavy Brigade,' she was told.

Lucy felt dizzy with nerves as she watched the fierce clashes from afar. It seemed to her she could hear the individual yells and groans of the men, and the clash of steel on steel, but in reality the only audible sound was the loud booming of the shells and the crack of gunfire.

'They're stealing our big guns from the redoubts,' one of the officers called to Lord Raglan. 'Damn cheek. Someone should stop them.'

'It will have to be the Light Brigade,' Raglan said, pointing to a group to their left, and Lucy followed his gaze, guessing that might be where Charlie was.

'Do you think the Hussars are with the Light Brigade just now?' she asked Mrs Williams.

'Should be. They're being held in the north valley. I'd have used them before now if I was in charge.' She had opinions on everything and Lucy wouldn't have been surprised had she marched over to share them with Lord Raglan.

The firing died down, but it appeared as if no one on the battlefield knew what to do next. Suddenly, one of the officers cried, 'By Gawd, what's Cardigan doing? He's heading down the north valley. The order was to go to Causeway Heights.'

Lucy noticed the commanders' consternation first then looked in the direction he indicated and saw the mounted Light Brigade advancing slowly down the furthest valley. Suddenly they broke into a gallop, just as the Russian guns on the surrounding hills began to explode in great flashes of fire and thunder. It was impossible to make out what was

110

going on: smoke billowed in clouds, and the noise was beyond deafening, but soon the men of the Light Brigade began to fall from their horses, not in their ones or twos but in their dozens. The horses fell too.

Everyone on Sapoune Heights was silent and Lucy bit her lip so hard it bled. It was awful to watch this slaughter and be so powerless. The stunned silence was broken as one of the officers burst into tears, followed by another. Two men clutched each other and sobbed like children.

'What's going on?' Lucy asked, petrified.

'It must be a mistake. They're lambs to the slaughter,' said a woman Lucy had never met.

'Are the 8th Hussars definitely there?'

Her question hung in the air. More men fell, and riderless horses bolted in panic. The Russian cavalrymen appeared to turn their own horses away from the battlefield and their ranks fell into disarray. Perhaps that had been the plan all along but it seemed a perilous strategy.

'Cardigan is through; he's made it,' one man with field glasses called.

They watched as more riders reached the end of the valley, hesitated, then turned to ride back towards the Sapoune Heights. Why would they return? None of it made sense. Lucy was rooted to the spot, shivering, scarcely daring to breathe, until she heard someone cry, 'Here they are!' Far down to their left, horsemen were limping towards them in ones and twos. A few spectators started cheering. Instinctively, Lucy bolted as fast as she could down the slope towards the point where the survivors were gathering. Other women ran too. It was further than she'd thought and she was panting and exhausted when she reached the spot and started scanning each blood-smeared, smoke-blackened rider who arrived, desperate for sight of her husband.

'He's Lucky Charlie,' she told herself, weaving amongst the terrified horses. 'He'll be fine.' Lucy repeated the words as a prayer. It felt like forever but must have been less than an hour before she found him, his busby in his hands. He jumped from his horse to embrace her and her eyes darted from head to toe, looking for wounds. He seemed unharmed.

'Go back to camp, Lucy,' he told her gruffly. 'I don't want you here. I have to help the men who have fallen, then I'll return as soon as I can.'

She clung to him, pleading, 'Please don't go out there again. There are too many guns.' Her ears were still ringing from the sound of them.

'It's safe now. Just go!' He sounded fierce.

Back at camp, Lucy crawled into their tent and poured herself a glass of dark rum from Charlie's bottle. It burned her throat, easing some of the tightness in her chest, and when she had drained it she poured another. Tears came, for all the men who had perished, for Bill and Adelaide – and for herself as well. She had watched dozens – perhaps hundreds – of men meet their deaths and all of them had been loved by someone: there was so much heartbreak to come. She poured a third glass of rum, which made her feel sick but at least took the edge off her misery. She would have drunk more but for the knowledge Charlie would want some when he got back and it was their last bottle.

She was asleep when he crawled into the tent but he lay down beside her and squeezed her breasts, then lifted her petticoats and made love to her with fierce urgency. He pounded hard inside her, without any whispered endearments, but she didn't mind. She knew he was relieving the horror of the day. It was almost as if he was making love to her in order to prove they were still alive.

Chapter Thirteen

The morning after the Battle of Balaklava a head count was taken. Two officers and nineteen men of the 8th Hussars had been killed, twenty wounded and eight presumed to be taken prisoner. A sombre mood settled on camp, reflected in cold, gusty and squally weather. When Charlie went out to an officers' briefing in the morning, Lucy made her way to the cookhouse.

'We don't need your help,' Mrs Jenkins told her coldly.

Lucy was taken aback. 'I know I'm not very efficient. In the time it takes me to peel one potato you can rustle up a tasty stew. But I am very keen to be involved so please try to find some menial task, if only to humour me.'

Mrs Jenkins looked around at the other women. Their faces were unfriendly, their arms crossed.

'Where is Mrs Williams?' Lucy peered round, looking for her.

'Her husband Stan's injured so she's at his bedside ... wherever that might be.'

'I'm so sorry to hear that!' Lucy gasped.

'The powers that be don't seem to have thought about the fact men might get injured out here. But I s'pose we shouldn't

113

say such things in front of a *captain's* wife in case it gets passed back.' The tone was unpleasantly sarcastic.

'I'm sorry if it makes you uncomfortable to have a captain's wife among you. I promise that nothing I hear when I'm with you women is ever repeated to my husband. You can speak freely.' She gave a nervous smile, puzzled by their attitude.

'No one cares what your husband thinks,' another woman chipped in. 'He's a lousy stinking meater.'

'A what?' Lucy gasped. She'd never heard the term.

'It means coward,' another explained, looking uncomfortable.

Lucy turned to Mrs Jenkins for an explanation. 'They're saying that Charlie didn't ride with the Light Brigade during the charge,' Mrs Jenkins said quietly, holding Lucy's gaze. 'Lizzie Williams' husband and loads of others say he claimed to have some problem with his stirrups when they all trotted out. He hung back trying to fix them, then only rejoined the Hussars when they rode out of the valley again all shot to pieces.'

'I don't believe it. I'm sure you're mistaken,' Lucy cried, her cheeks pink.

'Ask your husband. I think you'll find we're right. Lizzie Williams says she wants nothing more to do with either of you.'

'I can't …' Lucy was baffled. 'I'm sure it is not true. Please don't judge him until you've heard both sides.'

'Well, he's hardly going to admit it, is he? Your Charlie, the meater. Fine gentleman you've chosen there.'

Lucy stared at them for a moment then turned to hurry back to her tent, her heart beating hard. An image flashed through her mind of Charlie riding up after the battle without a hair out of place. The other men had torn, bloodied uniforms and terrorised horses but he and Merlin had seemed fine. All day, the scenes of battle played on her mind. Surely he must have some reasonable explanation; perhaps he had been given different orders from the rest.

That evening at the cookhouse she held her head high, avoiding the gaze of the women who had confronted her, simply picking up two bowls of stew. She and Charlie ate inside their tent with blankets pulled round their shoulders against the chill, then he poured his usual tumbler of rum.

'Is there any word on the total casualties from the battle yesterday?' she asked.

'Officially there are six hundred and fifteen missing but it's not yet clear whether they have been killed or taken prisoner. There are many bodies that can't be identified.' He shuddered.

'It's all so awful. Did you know when you received the order that you would be riding out in range of the Russian guns?' She watched him out of the corner of her eye. 'I don't know how you could force yourself to do it. I'm sure I couldn't.'

Charlie looked up sharply, narrowed his eyes and chose his words before speaking. 'Lucan queried the order but Nolan confirmed it. It seems our commanders may have been at cross purposes but a soldier is trained to obey, not to question.'

'It must be hard when every instinct is telling you to turn away, when you don't have faith in the powers that be …'

'Must we discuss this, Lucy? Do you have any idea how distressing it is for me when so many good friends have been lost? I played cards with these men. Percy – you remember, the one with the champion beetle in Varna – is gone. Cecil is gone. You'll forgive me if I don't feel like talking about it but would rather enjoy a little respite during my off-duty hours.' It was the first time Charlie had spoken critically to her.

'Of course, my love. I'm sorry.' She couldn't tell him of the rumour going round about him, or the consequence that she no longer had a single friend in camp and would be utterly alone during the long hours when he was riding out on duty. She was sure they must be wrong. He was a captain in Her Majesty's army, so he had to be brave. There must have been some misunderstanding – but if he refused to talk about it, how could she explain his side to the women?

Charlie drained the bottle of rum, instructing her to buy another at Kadikoi in the morning, then he fell onto their bed and was soon in a restless sleep. He turned on one side then the other, meaning that Lucy could not settle, and then he began to mumble 'Susanna' with the same intense longing she had heard in Varna. Lucy pressed her hands against her ears to blot out the sound. It was as if she were lying with a man who was a stranger to her, a man who was in love with someone else. She had thought she knew Charlie inside out, but really there was much she knew nothing about.

Chapter Fourteen

Ten days after the trauma of Balaklava, the Russians attacked
again at a place called Inkerman, a few miles north of the
British camp. Once again, it was a surprise attack in the
hours before dawn and men were summoned by insistent
bugles. Charlie leapt from his bed and began automatically
to pull on his uniform, then his legs seemed to give way and
he slumped, his hands shaking.

'What is it, dear?' Lucy asked, alarmed.

Charlie's eyes were wide, his skin chalk-white and his
brow clammy. He stared at her but couldn't speak and she
could hear he was breathing in quick, short pants. 'I ... I ...
cannot ...' he stammered.

'Let me pull on your boots,' she chivvied and crouched
at his feet, but he shrank from her touch, clutching his chest.

'My heart ... it's beating too hard,' he gasped. 'I think it
will fail.'

'I'll try to find a doctor.' She jumped to her feet.

'No!' His agonised cry rang out and she stared at him. 'I
m-must rest.'

Lucy calculated quickly. She couldn't have him accused of
desertion, so she must somehow prove that he was ill. There

was a man several tents away who was quarantined with dysentery. Thinking fast, Lucy rushed down and retrieved his bedpan from outside the tent flap, careful to avoid contact with the contents, then placed it prominently by their tent instead. Next, she rushed to the spot where the Hussars were congregating, preparing to ride out, and told an officer that Charlie had been up all night with fever and digestive symptoms, and that she feared it might be cholera or typhus. The officer agreed to pass a message to Major Dodds.

The camp was emptying as all men fit for duty made their way to battle and she saw the women from the cookhouse hurrying to find a vantage point from which to watch the fighting, pulling on coats against the morning chill. The shuddering boom of shelling felt close by and Charlie jumped with each explosion, his eyes glazed; in fact, he did seem ill.

Lucy made some tea, adding a spoonful of sugar from the fast-dwindling stock she had brought from London, then she lay beside him and stroked his head, murmuring, 'There, there; just rest, my dear,' until he fell asleep. She looked down at his sleeping face and felt very afraid. She had put her safety entirely in this man's hands. He was her husband, nine years her senior, and he was supposed to look after her, not the other way around. As he lay there, a new frown line between his brows, Lucy remembered Dorothea's words: 'You hardly know each other ... wait till after the war and see if you still feel the same way.' If only she had listened. She missed Dorothea terribly. Oh, to be at home with her safe, wise, sensible sister now. She could be writing letters to Charlie from the comfort of the morning room, instead of sitting alone on this cold, damp plain.

But then she remembered Bill's words: 'Give him as much love as you possibly can, because he needs it and he deserves it.' Charlie was alone in the world apart from her, and that

118

thought helped her to summon her love for him again. He needed her and she would be there for him.

He was sleeping soundly, so after a while she went out to walk around the camp. Already, wounded men were trickling back, some walking and others carried on stretchers. The army hadn't yet managed to get ambulance carts to the British camp and no one knew where the injured were to be treated. Lucy knew nothing of nursing but she brewed a large pot of tea in the cookhouse and took cups of it to the men.

'Where are you hit?' she asked. 'Have you seen a doctor yet? I'm sure one will be here soon.' The men seemed resigned to their fates. At least they were alive, although she could tell several were in agonising pain.

She got into conversation with one young Scotsman who had a severe leg wound. She could see his knee bone through the shattered, bloody flesh. Someone had tied a tourniquet above the hole but Lucy guessed he was likely to lose the leg – if he were to survive at all. It was said the odds were not in favour of amputees. She felt sick looking at the leg so focused on his face instead.

'Are you married?' she asked.

'Naw, I live with my ma in Clydebank,' he said. 'I wish she was here right now. When I was a nipper, if a big boy hit me she would charge straight out into the street and box his ears. Once when a schoolteacher caned me she marched down to the school and had a shouting match with him, then she hit him over the head with her umbrella. I wonder what she would do to the Russkie who shot up ma leg?' He chuckled. 'He wouldnae know what hit 'im.'

Lucy laughed out loud. 'What about your father? Is she fierce with him too?'

'Oh, aye, she keeps him in line. There's never been any doubt who's the boss in oor hoose.'

'Is she a large woman?'

It was the Scotsman's turn to laugh. 'Tiny! She's only about four foot six, but with a voice like a ship's foghorn and a personality to match. Bless her …' He was thoughtful for a moment. 'I wonder, Ma'am, if it's not too much to ask, could I dictate a letter and you could write it down? I'm not sure I can write just now an' anyways, I've no paper.'

'Of course,' Lucy agreed, and rushed back to her tent for supplies.

'Dear Ma,' the soldier began, and Lucy wrote the words in her neatest hand. 'I've been shot up and am waiting for them to take me to a hospital ship bound for Scutari. It's my leg that's hit. I doubt I'll be fighting again so maybe once I'm well enough they'll ship me home, which is a good thing as the winter is coming and I don't fancy being out here much longer. Hope the weather is fair in Clydebank. Give my best to Pa and to my sisters. Your ever-loving son, Iain.' He gave her the address and she promised to see it was sent straight away. She wondered if he had any inkling that he might not recover from this wound. He didn't appear to. Perhaps it was best. When a stretcher-bearer came, he learned they were taking him to Kamiesch in a French ambulance since there were no British ones to be had. He would sail out on a French ship.

'How do you say "thank you" in French?' he asked Lucy, and she told him: '*Merci*.'

'Sounds as though I'm asking for mercy. I suppose I am.' He held out his hand to shake hers then closed his eyes as they carried him away. Lucy watched him go, praying silently that he would make it back to his fierce, diminutive mother.

She comforted several other men that day, but Iain was the one who stuck in her mind for his ability to laugh while seriously, perhaps mortally wounded. That struck her as unbelievably brave.

120

When she returned to their tent, Charlie was lying on his back staring into space. She gave him some tea and he drank it, but he refused food and didn't want to talk. He seemed pale and dazed, for all the world as if he had genuinely suffered a bout of cholera and was slowly coming back to health.

'Spend another day or two resting,' she urged him, thinking that it would appear more convincing to his comrades than a rapid recovery. 'You don't seem yourself yet.'

That evening when Lucy went to the cookhouse, she only picked up one bowl of stew. 'This is for me. Charlie's still poorly,' she announced to the group present. She didn't look at any of the women directly because she didn't want to see the suspicion she imagined on their faces. Let them whisper behind her back if they wanted to. She would not fuel their malicious talk.

Charlie managed a few mouthfuls and Lucy ate the rest, then they lay together, faces close, and in a whisper she asked him if he was feeling better.

'A little,' he replied.

'Bill's death hit you hard. I miss his calm presence, but for you it must be ten times worse because he was your trusted colleague as well as your friend.'

'He was like a brother. Closer than a brother.' Charlie closed his eyes. 'He was certainly a better man than either of my real brothers.'

'Tell me, is there a chance that you might make peace with your brothers one day?' Lucy spoke tentatively. It hardly seemed an appropriate time to be asking, but for once this subdued Charlie seemed prepared to speak of personal matters.

'No.'

'Surely, when they know what you have been through out here, your family will feel sympathy?'

Charlie shook his head. 'Never. They never will.'

'But why?' She was exasperated. 'Why would they cast you off forever because of a little debt?'

He sighed hard, his breath brushing her cheek. 'It was a gambling debt and my father hates gambling … But it wasn't just that. I drank too much. And I seduced the daughter of a friend of my father's …'

Lucy flushed: 'You *seduced* her?' She felt a sharp stab of jealousy. 'What do you mean?' Her imagination flew away with itself. Had there been a child? Why had he abandoned her? Did he love her still?

'I led her to believe I might marry her and then … couldn't. All in all I was a dissolute rake and they'd had enough of me. Father bought my commission in the army to keep me out of trouble. Oh God, if only …' He sounded on the verge of tears and turned to muffle his face in the pillow.

Reassured there was no threat from another woman, Lucy spoke gently. 'Bill said that a tragedy led to your argument with your family. He said you would tell me when you were ready.'

Charlie made a choking noise. 'I couldn't bear you to think ill of me. I would rather die than lose you. You must know that.'

'There is nothing you can tell me that would make me leave you. *Nothing*. I know you are sometimes carried away by high spirits, and I know that sometimes you are scared, but you are a good man and I love you with all my heart.'

There was a long pause and when Charlie spoke his words were muffled by the pillow. He couldn't look at her. 'It was five years ago, but to me it's still like yesterday. I took home Tempest, my horse before Merlin, who was a glorious bay. A beautiful creature. As soon as she saw her, Susanna wanted to ride her – she was a decent horsewoman – but I said only if I ride with you, holding on to you, because she can be skittish.'

That name: Susanna. Lucy's cheeks burned at the thought of Charlie sitting on horseback with this woman.

'And once we were both on his back, trotting down the paddock, nothing would do but she wanted us to canter. And so we cantered and then she urged me to gallop. And I agreed because I wanted her to be impressed with my new posting as a Hussars captain and to show off this spirited new horse of mine.'

Lucy rubbed his shoulder, trying to speed him up so she could know the worst.

'There was a gate in front of us and Tempest ran at it, then refused. I landed on my shoulder – dislocated it – but Susanna landed on her head and her neck broke. It just snapped, and she was dead. Oh God, I loved her so much. She meant everything to me.' Charlie sobbed.

Lucy's heart raced. It was hard to hear him say that of another.

'They wouldn't even let me go to her funeral. I wasn't allowed to say goodbye.'

'It's awful but it was not your fault! Such accidents happen with horses. I myself broke my wrist in a fall when I was younger.'

His voice lowered to a whisper. 'It was the last straw. After Susanna died Father told me I was no longer their son. I had to leave home forthwith.'

'No one stood by you?' Lucy was astonished. 'Not your brothers, your mother?'

'Only Bill. He spent night after night talking to me, forcing me to carry on. Without him, I should certainly have killed myself.'

'Oh, please don't say that. I know you loved Susanna and it was a shocking, heartbreaking experience but you must make the most of your own life. She would want you to.' Lucy tried to form a picture of her predecessor in her mind's eye: it could have been Susanna camping in that soggy field rather than her, had she not died so suddenly and tragically. Would she have fared any better?

'Charlie, listen to me: you were not to blame. It sounds as though she was too impetuous and you both got carried away in the moment. If anything, the fault was more hers.'

'But Susanna was only seven.'

Lucy froze. 'What do you mean?'

'Susanna, my beloved sister, was only seven when she died. When I killed her.'

'I thought … I assumed you were talking about the lady who was the daughter of your father's friend.' She stumbled, lost for words, the full horror of the incident just beginning to dawn on her.

'That lady could never look at me again after Susanna's death. I saw a look in her eyes such as I now see in yours: disgust.'

'No, Charlie, no!' She bent to kiss him hard on the lips. 'I misunderstood – that's all. I didn't know you had a sister; you never said.' She wrapped her arms around him, struggling to find the right words. 'If anything, I love you more knowing that you have endured such a cruel loss.' She held him and stroked his hair. 'Pray, tell me about Susanna. What manner of girl was she?'

'I can't talk about her. I simply can't.'

Lucy wanted to probe further, but Charlie refused to say more.

'You know the truth now and I would rather we never spoke of it again.'

Lucy was left with dozens of questions. Inside she was deeply shocked. The revelation was worse than anything she had imagined. Charlie's family would never forgive him – she saw that now – and he would never forgive himself either. It would forever cast a shadow over his life – over *their* lives.

Chapter Fifteen

Some autumn days were oppressively hot, with sharp sun glinting like diamonds; others were chill, drizzly and damp, with heavy, purply-grey clouds like bruises blotting out the sun. On hot days, Lucy washed their clothes and hung their bedding to air, in an attempt to dispel the musty odour and get rid of the creeping mould that invaded their possessions. She ventured to the cookhouses of neighbouring companies, trying to strike up friendships, but the cool reception made her wonder if word of Charlie's cowardice had spread. She was lonely and yearned for a friend, just one, but none were forthcoming no matter how much she tried to make cheerful conversation. Charlie went back to his duties but he was withdrawn and spoke little.

The provisions Lucy had brought were running low and the army rations of a pound of biscuit (or a pound and a half of bread) and a pound of dry or fresh meat per man sometimes did not materialise. She knew there were difficulties in getting supplies through Balaklava and that the shelves were bare at the general store in Kadikoi, but she overheard some women saying that it was possible to buy basic supplies in Balaklava harbour. Lucy decided to make the trip herself and begged a lift on an army wagon, which took her across the plains and down into a steep little harbour, much smaller than she had expected. It was just one row of shops and houses fronting onto a harbour packed with ships stretching five or six deep off each wharf, a forest of masts bobbing. In the first shop she managed to buy some potatoes and a small bag of sugar; in another she purchased two carrots. As she emerged, Fanny Duberly was saddling her horse in the road, wearing smart green and beige plaid riding attire. Lucy looked at her directly and said, 'Good day,' in a loud voice, forcing Mrs Duberly to return the greeting.

'Will you ride up to the camp today?' Lucy asked. She did not much care for Mrs Duberly but was so lonely she would have endeavoured to engage any lady she met in conversation that morning.

'Perhaps. First of all I plan to ride to that Genoese fort on the clifftop. They say the view is magnificent.' Lucy turned and saw a tiny ruin overlooking the bay.

'It certainly looks pretty. How is your accommodation on the ship, Mrs Duberly? I trust you are comfortable?'

'Indeed, I can't complain. Of course the cabins are rather cramped but we dine exceedingly well. Last night there was *foie gras* and duck, served with rather a fine Bordeaux.' She finished strapping on her side-saddle and climbed onto the horse by first mounting the sea wall. 'I wish you good day, Mrs Harvington.'

Mrs Duberly clicked her tongue, pulled on the reins and rode off without once asking after Lucy. Her behaviour was insufferably rude but since none of the soldiers' wives were talking to Lucy, she was grateful for the slightest human interaction.

That evening there was no meat available and as she and Charlie dined on mashed potatoes and boiled carrots, she thought of the luxurious fare being enjoyed by Mrs Duberly and the officers on their ships. Whoever was responsible for supplies was getting their priorities wrong because the soldiers were becoming weaker and soon would be in no condition to fight. Why could they not establish a reliable supply chain? She'd heard the French dined well in Kamiesch. It seemed they were better organised for this war in virtually every respect, while conditions in the British camp grew more challenging by the day.

On the night of 12th November a fierce storm blew up. Lucy and Charlie lay awake watching flashes of lightning through the canvas and listening to the pelting of rain and the lashing of the wind. It grew stronger and tugged insistently at the tent until around three in the morning, the pegs on one side lifted and the entire structure flipped over, leaving them exposed to the elements. Charlie leapt to his feet and pulled the tent back but he had no mallet to hammer in the pegs. Using a cooking pot, he banged them in as firmly as he could, but the repair lasted less than a minute before coming loose again. Looking around, Lucy saw they weren't alone. Some tents had been lifted clean into the air and men were chasing them across the camp. Hardly any were still standing. After struggling fruitlessly to re-erect theirs, Charlie suggested they simply wrap the tent around themselves for some protection from the rain. However, as soon as they settled down a corner would lift and the whole tent would strain to fly away. Lucy was sodden right through her undergarments, her hair was soaked and she had never felt more demoralised in her life.

It seemed like the final straw, but in fact conditions just continued to deteriorate, with each day bringing some fresh challenge. Charlie managed to re-secure the tent but from then on it leaked through one of the seams no matter how hard Lucy tried to patch it, and they often woke to find themselves lying in a puddle of cold water. The army ration of coal was reduced and any trees in the vicinity had long since been chopped down for firewood, so Lucy could no longer light a fire during the day. She saved their precious supplies to make tea and a warm meal when Charlie came off duty, and the rest of the time she huddled in blankets, never truly getting warm or dry. She thought with longing of her extra-warm, cherry-red winter coat and her fur hat and muff: she hadn't brought them as she hadn't expected to be here in winter. She wrote another letter, this time directly to Dorothea, begging that she send out warm clothing, listing the items she would particularly like to receive, but she no longer had faith that letters were getting through. Either that, or Dorothea had abandoned her – a thought too painful to consider.

When Lucy next begged a lift down to Balaklava, hoping to purchase fuel, she found the shops bare. The stormy weather had whipped the sea into a thick yellow foam and the village street was a river of mud and filth. She walked right to the end of the row, and suddenly noticed what looked like a red British army tunic in the water. She went closer, curious about the way it was bobbing in the surf, then a wave pushed it towards her and she realised it was a body. A human body. A short scream burst from her lungs and she sat on a wall, worried she might faint. The soldier was clearly dead, his head beneath the surface: why was no one recovering his body? Had standards slipped so low? Everyone deserved respectful treatment after death.

When she felt calm enough to walk again, Lucy headed back to the village entrance, where she knew the harbourmaster's office was situated, and went in to inform him of the body. He was a small, bespectacled man, who looked up from a pile of papers.

'What's that you say? Well, he's hardly the first. I'll send someone to fish him out.'

'I couldn't tell which regiment he was from. Will you inform his commanding officer? There sh ... should be a funeral ...' She still felt shaky from the discovery.

He gave her a shrewd look. 'Yes, you're right, there should be. Well, we'll see what can be done.'

'But how do you think he got there?' Her voice rose. 'He couldn't have been shot by the Russians, could he?'

The harbourmaster opened his mouth to say something, then thought better of it. 'I expect he fell off one of the cliffs and got washed round on the current. There are some tall cliffs hereabouts.'

'It's such a waste! Well, if I can be of any assistance ... I'm going back to the camp now and could take word.'

'I suspect identification will require a little longer than that. Depends how long the poor chap has been in there. Don't you worry; I'll deal with it. Now, is there anything else I can do for you?'

Lucy hesitated. 'I don't suppose you know where I might find some fuel? Our ration of coal has run out ... Is there anywhere I could try?'

'We haven't had a delivery of coal since before the storm. But tell you what ...' He rose from his chair and went into a room behind, emerging some minutes later hauling a sack full of coal. 'You take this. I don't like to see a lady going cold.'

Lucy's eyes filled at his kindness. It was the first time in weeks that anyone had been kind to her. 'Are you sure? Please allow me to pay for it.'

'I wouldn't dream of it, Ma'am. Now, if you'd care to sit here for five minutes, I will arrange a lift back to the camp for you. We can't have you carrying that sack all on your own.'

He left her in the office and she looked around. There was a mirror on one wall and she caught a glimpse of herself, her cheeks hollow, nose red from the cold, blue-grey shadows under her eyes, and hair an unspeakable bird's nest. How could he tell she was a lady? Not by her appearance, that was certain.

On his return, he hauled the sack of coal out to a wagon about to leave for the British camp, and helped her to climb on board. Lucy was overwhelmed, thanking him effusively until the poor man seemed embarrassed.

'Not at all. Please drop in next time you are passing.'

Back at camp, she extracted a heap of coal for her own use then took the rest to the women congregated in the cookhouse, inviting them to share it amongst themselves. They regarded her suspiciously.

'Please take it. We are all in the same situation here,' she said, and gave a weak smile before leaving them to divide the fuel.

Later, she decided not to tell Charlie about the soldier floating in the ocean, but she described the harbourmaster's generosity and showed him the pile of coal. He barely listened and made no comment, sunk in such gloomy spirits that it was hard to communicate with him. When he returned from duty the first thing he did was pour himself a large drink. He had run out of army rum but purchased a spirit called arak from a contact in the Turkish camp. It was a clear liquid that turned cloudy white with the addition of a few drops of water. Lucy took a sip and found it vile but Charlie had developed a worrying taste for it. Whereas rum had usually lifted his spirits and made him sociable, even garrulous, the arak seemed to make him morose.

'I don't know how you can drink that stuff,' she teased. 'To me it tastes of aniseed drops and I've never been able to bear them.'

He said nothing but she persevered, trying to keep her tone light and carefree.

'Mint humbugs are your favourite, are they not? Remember the day in Warwick when nothing would do but we toured the shops till we found some? That was just before our wedding.'

Charlie was polishing his buckles and didn't comment.

'Do you think the attack on Sevastopol will be soon? Has Major Dodds said anything?'

'I have no idea.'

'Surely they must attack before winter sets in? The temperature drops by a degree every night. We can't survive out here in tents, can we? ... I hear the French have been building huts.'

'What a shame you didn't marry a Frenchman then.'

'Goodness, Charlie!' she exclaimed. 'You are in a low mood tonight. Why don't you organise a card game? I'm sure you could put together a four for whist.'

He wasn't interested. 'It's too cold for cards.'

Lucy wondered if he was embarrassed in front of his men because they knew of his not riding out at Balaklava. Perhaps that's why he no longer socialised. She longed to chat after a day spent alone and friendless but he wasn't in the mood for conversation. There was a growing chasm between them and she had no idea how to breach it.

In bed, she snuggled close, hoping to tempt him to make love. There had been no passion since the night of the Battle of Balaklava, and Lucy hoped that if she could seduce him it might bring back some of their old intimacy; but when she tried, he rolled over and lay with his back to her, pretending to be asleep. She knew he was depressed; he must be as worried as she was but instead of sharing his worries, he had retreated inside his shell. How could she give him the love he so badly needed when he closed himself off to her? If only she were more experienced as a wife, she could have found a way to coax him back but instead she could

131

feel the strength of their marriage slipping away a little more every day.

In her head, she sometimes had conversations with Dorothea in which she told her she had been right, that it had transpired she and Charlie had not known each other well enough to marry, and that she should not have accompanied him to war. Who could have guessed that such blissful happiness as they had known in the early months of the year could have vanished by its end, to be replaced by this impenetrable distance?

Chapter Sixteen

Charlie's squadron was put on night patrol to try and prevent Russians smuggling food or arms into the city under cover of dark. November had turned to December and it was clear that Sevastopol would be besieged through the winter and that the British army were somehow to survive in their tents without sufficient food or fuel. He left camp at eleven in the evening and didn't get back till seven the following morning. There was frost in the air that made the ground sparkle and he returned half-frozen, his moustache crusted with ice. Lucy had to sit him by the fire wrapped in blankets with cups of tea or broth to thaw him before he could go to sleep. Without him, she slept with all their blankets and coats piled on top of her, yet still she could never get warm. It was a penetrating cold, a cold that felt dangerous, as if it could sap the life out of her if she didn't keep resisting it.

When she ventured to the cookhouse, everyone she met had sunk into low spirits. They did what was necessary to stay alive – they ate, they drank, they sat by their fires huddled in blankets – but that was all. Most stopped washing because the water was too icy-cold to contemplate splashing it on your skin. Women started wearing their husbands' spare trousers underneath their skirts and Lucy joined them, piling on all the clothes she could while still being able to move.

One day the *Times* reporter Mr Russell came to their part of the camp, walked along the row of tents, and stopped in front of Lucy. She recognised him for his Irish accent, his curly dark hair under a blue peaked hat, and his bushy beard and moustache (Lord Raglan forbade the soldiers from growing beards).

'Good day, Ma'am. I'm Mr Russell of *The Times*. And you?'

'Mrs Lucy Harvington.'

'I apologise for disturbing you but I'm writing a piece about the mood in the camp and wondered if I might ask you a few questions?'

'All right.' She couldn't see any harm in it.

'Tell me, how would you describe morale at present?'

Lucy stared at him, puzzled he could ask such a thing. 'Morale? I don't think that comes into it. We're just doing our best to stay alive.'

'But don't you feel patriotic? Surely you support the army in its necessary mission?' His pencil was poised over a notebook and as his dark, honest eyes met hers, she felt drawn to frankness.

'It feels as though the army high command have abandoned us. There's not enough food, fuel or warm clothing to go around, and it seems we are expected to survive a Crimean winter in tents. No one understands why we are in this dreadful position when we were told Sevastopol would be taken in weeks and the war would be over by Christmas. What went wrong? I simply don't know why we are still here.' Her anger and frustration burst out in a passionate diatribe, and Mr Russell scribbled down her words. 'My husband is on night patrol and returns each morning frozen solid, unable to speak for the cold that has locked his jaw. We had the first dusting of snow last night and all know this is only a mild foretaste of the severity of winter to come. Why do we not at least have huts with stoves, as the French do? Why are we not served nutritious hot food? It's insufferable. Something must be done.'

Mr Russell raised his eyebrows. 'That's quite a speech, Ma'am, and I'm sure our readers would be shocked to hear it. Perhaps you will help to spur the powers that be to take action. Tell me, what is your husband's name?'

'Captain Harvington of the 8th Hussars. But these views are mine, not his. You won't say it was him, will you?'

'Of course not. I'll attribute the views to *Mrs* Harvington. I'm very grateful to you.'

Lucy never saw the article in *The Times* but she knew it had been published because Major Dodds reprimanded Charlie for the sentiments expressed.

'That's not fair!' Lucy cried. 'I expressly said they were my views and not yours.'

Charlie was too weary to argue the point. 'Lord Raglan ordered us not to talk to Russell as his portraits of the war are too negative. You are my wife and therefore my responsibility.' He turned away and the next words were spoken over his shoulder. 'Are you really so thoughtless and stupid? I rather hoped to feel I had your support at this time, yet instead it seems you have stabbed me in the back.'

Fired with the injustice of the accusation, Lucy pounded her fist on his arm. 'Charlie, don't say that. I didn't know about Lord Raglan's orders.'

He turned and stared coldly, as if she were a stranger he wished to have nothing more to do with. There was not a glimmer of affection in his eyes.

'Please forgive me!' she cried, scared by his demeanour. 'I'm sorry.'

His eyes narrowed and he said bitterly: 'Sometimes sorry is not enough. I should know that better than anyone.' He walked off to tend his horse without giving her a chance to reply.

Early in the morning of 24th December, Lucy was roused from a dream: it was Christmas in Russell Square and the rest of the family had bought gifts but Lucy had nothing to give; she was rushing around trying to make presents out of a potato, some salt pork and a piece of coal but was conscious they were shoddy substitutes for the prettily wrapped gifts the others had piled by the fireside. Suddenly she remembered the ship in the bottle Charlie had bought her in Istanbul; perhaps it would do for Dorothea. Her mother hovered on the fringes of the dream, present but out of sight. Lucy wanted to ask her advice about something but she couldn't remember what it was.

'Mrs Harvington! Are you awake?' A voice called from outside the tent.

She opened her eyes. 'Yes, who is it?'

'Second Lieutenant Cole, Ma'am. I must talk with you, Ma'am.'

Suddenly she was alert. She rose hurriedly, adjusted the outdoor clothing in which she slept, and peeled back the tent flap. She could tell before the man spoke that something had happened to Charlie.

'I'm afraid it's bad news, Ma'am … Captain Harvington has been shot by a sniper near the Malakhov.'

Lucy knew the Malakhov was a heavily reinforced Russian redoubt just west of Sevastopol. 'Can you take me to him? Let me pull on my boots.' She turned to look for them, blood rushing in her ears.

The second lieutenant cleared his throat. 'I'm so sorry, Ma'am.'

The message was there in his lowered eyes, his embarrassment. He didn't need to say the words; in fact, Lucy would rather he didn't. Since Bill died she'd feared this moment might come. Now she must force herself to be as brave and dignified as Adelaide had been, even though her legs had turned to water.

'I would like you to take me to him, please. I want to see my husband.'

Chapter Seventeen

There was a thin layer of snow on the ground, like icing sugar on a cake, and sharp white sun glinted off spurs and buckles. Lucy had brought some blankets and a flagon of water, but apart from those practicalities she kept her mind deliberately blank. She wouldn't allow herself to think until she could see Charlie and then she would do whatever had to be done, one step at a time.

They rode to Cathcart's Hill, some distance behind the British camp, and as they approached she could see a small group of men gathered. Major Dodds came to help her from her horse, visibly distressed; 'I'm so sorry, Mrs Harvington. He was a fine officer and a great friend.'

She didn't reply, too busy peering around to see where Charlie was; and then she realised the shape on the ground wrapped in a sheet must be him. She crouched, peeled the sheet from his face and gave a little cry. He looked peaceful, as if sleeping, and as handsome as the day she had first seen him at the Pendleburys'. She touched his cheek and whispered, 'I'm here, darling. It's Lucy.'

Major Dodds cleared his throat. 'We plan to bury him up here with the other officers. Of course, you'll want time to say your goodbyes ...'

'Where was he shot?' She couldn't see any marks on his head.

'He took three shots to the body, Ma'am.' She didn't recognise the speaker, but guessed he was a member of Charlie's squadron. 'I don't understand what happened. We knew Russian snipers had their guns trained on that point where the trail emerges from behind some rocks. I suppose Captain Harvington forgot in that split second because he rode out and stopped his horse there, looking towards the Malakhov. That's when they got him.'

'Is his horse injured?' She knew he wouldn't have wanted anything to happen to Merlin.

'He's unhurt, Ma'am.'

She nodded, pleased for that small mercy. 'May I be alone with my husband?'

Major Dodds consulted his pocket watch. 'We'll come back at noon for the funeral.'

'That's too soon.'

He frowned. 'Let's say three o'clock then, before the light fades and the temperature drops. Can I get you anything, Mrs Harvington? Please let us fetch a lady friend to sit with you.'

She shook her head, impatient for them to be gone so she could hold a vigil for Charlie the way Adelaide had for Bill. As soon as the men were a distance away, she began to whisper to him. 'My darling, I love you so much. Our first months of married life were the happiest of my life. I know things have been difficult in Crimea but we would have survived and gone on to live such a good life together.' As she spoke, she stroked the contours of his face, committing every detail to memory. She bent to kiss him and could still detect the scent of arak mingled with the odour of his body. She unwrapped the sheet and now she could see where the bullets had exploded into his flesh. There was a gaping wound just under his ribcage, one in his right shoulder and another lower down in his belly.

'Oh Charlie, where are you, my love?' The aching emptiness of his absence yawned in front of her. They would never kiss again, never make love again. She yearned to talk to him and know he could still hear. Perhaps he had left a letter for her, as Bill had for Adelaide – that would be something at least. She began to search his pockets, not caring that her cloak was being stained red from his blood. She removed his silver pocket watch from his vest pocket, took a few coins, a key and a handkerchief from one trouser pocket and, from the other, a flask. She opened the flask and although it was empty, the pungent odour of arak was evident; Charlie had been drinking on duty. 'You silly man,' she whispered affectionately. But her eyes filled with tears when she realised there was no letter, no final message. After the row the previous evening, she longed to hear him tell her one last time how much he loved her. Now she would never hear his voice again.

In the lining of his vest pocket, her fingers detected a tiny fold of card. She pulled it out, her fingers clumsy with cold. Inside there was a lock of blonde hair, similar in colour to hers, perhaps a shade paler. The words on the card read, in Charlie's handwriting, 'Susanna Harvington, 2nd May 1842– 6th June 1849'. Suddenly the little girl who had died felt real to her. She could imagine her excitement when her big brother came home with his grand army horse, the mane neatly plaited and stirrups gleaming. For the first time she felt the enormity of Charlie's loss, a jagged, gaping wound that would never have healed.

She lay on the ground beside him, wrapping the blankets tightly around them, and she hugged him as tightly as she could so that his blood soaked into her clothing and smeared her face and hands. She snuggled up close, her head on his shoulder and lifted his arm onto her waist, holding it around her, its weight like a final hug. And then she remembered that as he left the previous evening, he had kissed her briefly on the lips and murmured, 'Forgive me.' She had been drowsy and got the impression he was apologising for his distance of late. But perhaps he had already decided he was about to die. Why hadn't she replied? How she wished she had whispered to him, 'There's nothing to forgive. I love you with all my heart.' She'd been silent because she was tired and still hurt by his earlier harshness; she could never have known these would be his final words to her.

Major Dodds came back sooner than she'd expected. 'It's time,' he said, clearly embarrassed at the sight of her, all bloody and emotional.

She wanted to scream '*No, don't take him!*' She had no likeness of him; how would she remember his dear face? But already he didn't look like himself; already she could tell some intrinsic part of him had gone. The sun was setting and she couldn't ask these men to work in the dark. She gave Charlie one final lingering kiss on his cold lips, slipped Susanna's lock of hair into the pocket by his heart, then rose and lifted the blankets. A soldier wrapped the sheet carefully around his body then they carried him over to a place where she saw a shallow grave had already been dug. The 'Last Post' was played as they lowered him into the ground and Lucy just felt numb, as if this were happening to someone else, yet at the same time her heart thumped so hard in her chest that she could almost hear it. She realised she hadn't cried yet. What must these men think of her, to be dry-eyed at her husband's funeral?

She stayed to watch as they shovelled earth and rocks on top of him, then Major Dodds offered to accompany her back to the camp. 'I am here to help, Mrs Harvington. Let me know what services I can perform for you.'

141

'I'm not ready to go back to camp,' she said, her mind made up. 'I will stay here a while longer.'

'I don't think that's wise, Ma'am. The temperature is dropping fast.'

The sun had already sunk below the horizon and just a pink glow remained in the western sky.

'I'm not ready to leave him. Perhaps you could tether a horse for me to return later?'

Major Dodds didn't want to agree but neither did he wish to argue with a grieving widow. She could see the arguments playing out in his head, before eventually he gave his consent and ordered a soldier to tether a horse nearby. He gave her some biscuits from his ration, and topped up her flagon of water from his own, then patted her shoulder and warned her not to tarry long.

As soon as they left and the hill was in darkness, Lucy could feel Charlie's spirit with her. 'Hello again, my darling,' she said. She wrapped the blankets tight around herself then lay down on top of his grave. 'It's nearly our first Christmas as husband and wife. I couldn't let you spend it alone.' Adelaide had kept overnight vigil with Bill and she would do no less. Besides, she had no idea what she would do when she left him: there was no woman friend at the camp to offer support, her family appeared to have disowned her and she could not expect a welcome from Charlie's. For the last year her entire life had been centred on this man who now lay a foot below her.

Lucy dozed for a while but awoke shivering convulsively as the vicious cold penetrated to her core. Her fingers and toes were stiff and sore when she wriggled them. She could hear the horse stomping and blowing. The poor creature must be freezing. She rose and went over to stroke its nose then untied the reins to set it free.

'Go on!' She slapped its rump. 'Go back to camp. It's not fair for you to freeze out here.'

The horse hesitated then, when she slapped it again, turned and galloped off. Now she was truly alone. She took out the pocket watch and realised it was almost midnight. As the minute hand slipped onto twelve she spoke to Charlie again: 'Merry Christmas, my very own sweetheart. I hope you know that I love you tonight more than I've ever loved you.'

She wrapped herself in the blankets again and lay down on his grave to sleep.

PART FIVE

Chapter Eighteen

14th November 1854

London was unseasonably cold that autumn, with fog obscuring the view of the Cathedral from the windows of Pimlico Hospital. The Soho cholera epidemic had passed but Dorothea's ward was crammed with patients suffering acute lung disorders, so her working days were spent to the sound of hacking coughs, wheezing chests and the expectoration of dirty yellow phlegm.

At home, her father had backache and issued petulant orders from his armchair. Dorothea applied mustard poultices and tried to be sympathetic but she noticed that when he thought no one was watching he managed to walk to the sherry decanter on the sideboard without any sign of discomfort.

Still she read *The Times* every day, following the progress of the war avidly, and like other readers she was horrified by Mr Russell's reports of the Battle of Balaklava and the charge of the Light Brigade, which appeared in the paper on 14th November: 'a more fearful spectacle was never witnessed than by those who ... beheld their heroic countrymen rushing to the arms of sudden death'. She knew the 8th Hussars were part of the Light Brigade – a term that none outside the military had been familiar with until recent months, but which was now part of the national vocabulary. Had Charlie led his squadron down the northern valley amidst Russian guns? If so, had he survived? The odds weren't good. According to Mr Russell, 118 had been killed and 127 wounded out of just 670 men.

She continued to write to Lucy once a week but there had been no replies. They'd heard nothing from her since the anxious letter from Varna asking advice on cholera. Dorothea became increasingly fearful and even began to scheme about sailing out there to rescue her little sister. How would she go about such a thing and how much would it cost? But the problem remained that she didn't actually know where Lucy was. She pored over the globe in her father's study, calculating the distance between Constantinople, Varna and Crimea. If she travelled East, how would she ever find Lucy? And still she clung to the hope that the war would be over soon. Everyone had said at the outset they'd be home by Christmas, but that was beginning to look wildly optimistic and Mr Russell's forecasts were gloomy. Winter was setting in and it seemed unlikely the allies could take the well-defended port of Sevastopol before spring.

A week after the report of Balaklava, Dorothea was skimming the newspaper when her eye was caught by a short paragraph saying that Florence Nightingale's friend Mary Stanley was leading another delegation of nurses to Constantinople. Dorothea still kicked herself that she had thrown away her chance to accompany Miss Nightingale last time, through her own thoughtless words. If only she could have a second chance she was determined to prove herself worthy.

First of all, she asked her matron, Miss Alcock, to write to Miss Stanley recommending strongly that Dorothea should be included in the party. By return, Miss Alcock received a note suggesting that Dorothea should write to Mrs Sidney Herbert, the wife of the Minister for War. Dorothea lost no time in applying, listing her surgical experience and adding that she was available to leave at very short notice. This exchange of letters took place over the space of two days and she felt a frisson of excitement and at the same time gut-clenching anxiety that she might be turned down yet again. It was hard to concentrate on work while keeping an eye on the ward door for a messenger who might bring a reply.

A week passed without any news and then on the 30th November a letter came from Mrs Herbert herself asking if Dorothea would care to present herself at her Belgrave Square house that very day. Dorothea was beside herself with nerves as her carriage drew up, trying to predict all the interview questions that might be directed at her. She had already decided to claim that, contrary to any impression she may have given last time, she was not planning to seek out her sister. She mustn't fall into that trap.

In fact, there was no interview this time. Mrs Herbert welcomed Dorothea into a vast drawing room where she was bemused as they measured her for boots, galoshes and a woollen cape. She was then sent across to Miss Stanley's house nearby and given two shapeless blue gowns, which would be her nursing uniform and should be worn with an apron and cap, which she was expected to supply herself.

'I'm so glad you can join us, my dear,' Miss Stanley smiled, and Dorothea wasn't sure if she remembered their previous encounter. 'We are more necessary than ever, given news from the Crimea. Did Mrs Herbert tell you the departure date?'

Dorothea shook her head, scarcely daring to believe she really was going this time.

'Tomorrow evening you must attend a meeting at Mrs Herbert's house, where we will have the honour of being addressed by her husband, the Minister for War, and the following morning we catch the train for Folkestone. There is much to be done.'

Dorothea left with her new uniform and stood for a few moments in the street, gathering her thoughts. Her life had changed immeasurably in the last hour and she knew it would never be the same again. She wrapped her arms around herself to steady her nerves, as if giving herself a hug.

The next twenty-four hours were a whirlwind of farewells – to her matron and the patients at Pimlico, to her friend Emily, and, most importantly, to her father.

'Who will look out for me?' her father asked, in a querulous tone.

'Henderson will do everything to ensure your comfort, Papa. He has even promised to give up his afternoon off until my return so you will never be left unattended.'

'But why must you go?'

Dorothea explained again, knowing that her father would have forgotten by dinnertime. His eyes stared blankly, his short-term memory all but destroyed, and his logic that of a four-year-old child. She sometimes wondered if some disease of the brain were responsible rather than just the ravages of old age but had never heard of a cure. All they could do was look to his immediate comfort, something Henderson managed with more patience than she could muster.

Miss Stanley had said they were only to take one box and a small bag apiece, so Dorothea packed with great care. She took a full kit of medical essentials, several spare aprons and caps, her warmest undergarments and nightwear, needles and thread, some writing paper and envelopes. There was no room for eveningwear and she took just one day dress, imagining she would spend most of her time in uniform.

Mr Sidney Herbert was boyish-looking, with large brown eyes and a sweep of wavy hair across his forehead, but in his address he was every inch the statesman. He warned them to expect hardship and discomfort but said that they were representatives of their country and must be obedient at all times. There was a long legal agreement to sign: they agreed to devote their time to nursing the sick and wounded of the British army under the direction of the Superintendent of Hospitals (in other words, Miss Nightingale) and that the wages would range from ten to twenty-five shillings a week depending on age and experience.

As he spoke, Dorothea looked surreptitiously at the other women in the room. There were over thirty of them, almost all older than her, and roughly half were nuns. Before long she hoped to have made new friends amongst them. She looked forward to that.

When she got home, it was after nine o'clock but she noticed a lamp was lit in the drawing room and Henderson told her she had a visitor. She removed her cloak and entered the room to find Mr Goodland pacing in front of the fire-place. Her first reaction was alarm.

'Mr Goodland! Are you all right? Has something happened to Emily?'

He frowned. 'Forgive me for calling so late, Miss Gray. Emily is well but she gave me some news this evening that I felt I must … I have to talk to you about.'

'Pray, sit down.' Dorothea had a sense of foreboding. 'Shall I call for tea?'

'What I have to say will not take long.' He remained standing, but Dorothea sat down to steady herself. There was a long pause while he mustered his words. 'I understand that you intend to travel to the Turkish lands to nurse with Miss Nightingale's ladies. I am here to ask you not to go.'

She was startled: 'I'm afraid the arrangements are already made and I leave tomorrow morning. I'm sorry I did not have time to come to your chambers to bid you farewell but there has been much to do.'

'All the same, Miss Gray, I ask you to cancel your plans and consider staying here and marrying me. You must be aware that I have long admired you, both for your intelligence and the sweetness of your character. You would make the ideal wife for a man such as myself. I would see that you want for nothing ...' His face reddened at her shocked expression. 'Surely you cannot be surprised? You must have been aware of my intentions.'

'No, I swear; not at all.' She felt awkward; in fact, she had wondered at first whether his thoughts ran in this direction but had dismissed it when he gave no indications of romantic interest.

'All this time I have visited you every Sunday. Earlier this year you trusted me to perform a service for you in writing a letter on a most important family matter. I felt sure you knew ...'

'Genuinely, I had no idea, or else I would have ...' Dorothea's heart was beating hard. How could she let him down gently? 'Mr Goodland, you have been a most excellent friend to my family and I am grateful for your attentions, but my feelings for you are simply that – friendship.'

He cleared his throat. 'Perhaps you need time to think about my offer. That would be perfectly understandable.'

'There is no time, since I leave tomorrow. I am determined to seize this opportunity to take care of our brave soldiers. The disappointment when I was not selected for Miss Nightingale's original band of nurses has merely strengthened my resolve. I am sorry, Mr Goodland. I am flattered, of course, but I must decline your offer.' She folded her hands in her lap to stop them shaking.

She could tell from the scowl and the stiff set of his shoulders that he was cross. 'If you feel you must go, we will have to see how things stand upon your return. I cannot leave my offer open unconditionally but if I have not found another wife by then, perhaps we can discuss this matter again.'

Dorothea almost gasped at his audacity. His attitude almost seemed to imply that this proposal was an act of charity and she should consider herself lucky. 'I urge you to seek another wife, sir, as I have no intention of becoming Mrs Goodland, either now or in the future.'

He snorted with anger, seeming about to say something else then thought better of it. 'In that case, I must bid you goodnight, Miss Gray.'

She stood to see him out but he strode ahead of her and slammed the door to the hall behind him. Instead of going after him she sat down to calm her nerves.

She knew she was making the right decision. She couldn't imagine herself as the wife to such a dry, stilted man. They had so little in common that conversation was an effort and there was a pomposity about him she found unpleasant. Even though it seemed likely to be the only marriage proposal she would ever receive, it was better to be happy and single than unhappily wed. She hoped Emily would not be cross with her for spurning her brother; she would write to explain.

Next morning when her driver dropped her at London Bridge station to catch the Folkestone train, Dorothea was brimming with anticipation and had already put the awkward scene of the previous evening to the back of her mind. She beamed at her fellow travellers and couldn't wait for the train to start moving away from the platform. Every mile she travelled was a mile closer to Lucy, and to a new, more fulfilling life.

Chapter Nineteen

Dorothea had never gone further than Bath before and she marvelled at the sights along the way: the bustling Gare du Nord in Paris, full of the excited babble of French travellers; the steamer down the Rhône, which sat fog-bound for two hours before the sun burned through and made the land glow vivid green; the lines of poplars marking the waysides, which she knew had been planted by Emperor Napoleon; the noisy port of Marseilles where huge cargo ships were being loaded and unloaded; Mount Stromboli, like a mountain of fire against the blackness of the water; and the glorious port of Piraeus where they were allowed ashore for a few hours to see the impressive archaeological ruins. Their ship, the *Egyptus*, rolled around in the water and Dorothea frequently felt nauseous, but she found that walking in the bracing air on deck usually settled her stomach.

Soon she had chatted to many of the women in their party but the one to whom she felt most drawn was Elizabeth Davis, a plain-speaking Welshwoman of sixty-five years of age, who had led a life of considerable adventure. She could talk a blue streak and soon Dorothea had learned her history. Miss Davis had left home at the age of fourteen and worked in service for families who took her all over Britain and Europe. That's how in 1815 she came to be in Belgium at the time of the Battle of Waterloo. She became engaged to a Liverpool ship's captain but he tragically drowned two days before their wedding. Thereafter she travelled the world as nanny to the children of another sea captain, going to the West Indies, India, Australia and South America. On her return she trained as a nurse at Guy's Hospital in London and had volunteered to come to the Crimea as soon as she heard of the need for nurses.

'I don't like the sound of Florence Nightingale,' she told Dorothea, with narrowed eyes. 'I haven't met her but I judge people on their names, and I don't like hers.'

Dorothea laughed. 'Have I passed the name test?'

'You'll do,' Elizabeth said, straight-faced. 'You don't have airs and graces at least. We'll find out later about your capabilities as a nurse. There are a few in this party who look like Mrs Gamp.'

Dorothea chuckled. Mrs Gamp was a caricature of a nurse in Charles Dickens' novel *Martin Chuzzlewit*, a drunken creature entirely lacking in morals. 'Mr Dickens did us no favours there. I'm sure many people formed their opinion of nurses from his portrait.'

'The shame is that I've met a good many nurses who could have been his model. I'm sure you have as well. Tell me, what led you to volunteer to come out here?'

Dorothea confided in her about Lucy; there was plenty of time to tell the story of their quarrel over Lucy's hasty marriage, and Elizabeth tut-tutted when she heard Charlie was estranged from his family. Dorothea told of the two letters they'd received, the last one from Varna at the height of the cholera epidemic and nothing since.

'You would have had notification from the army if she had succumbed to illness,' Elizabeth assured her. 'They write letters to the families.'

Dorothea had thought of this. 'But Charlie is her family now. Perhaps he omitted to inform us. Relations between us are hardly cordial.'

'You would have heard if she died,' Elizabeth repeated firmly. 'I'll do my best to help you find her. She's out there somewhere.'

They arrived in Constantinople at sunset on the 18th December and Dorothea's first sight of the mosques and minarets was like an illustration from *Arabian Nights*, with black silhouettes against an orange sky. The party expected to be taken straight to the Barracks Hospital in Scutari, where reports said there were three thousand men lying wounded, but instead they were kept on board ship for a night and could only gaze across at the flickering gas lamps on shore and listen to the sounds of boatmen calling to each other in foreign dialect. When they awoke at dawn, they were told they were being accommodated in the Hôtel d'Angleterre on the European side of the Bosphorus while details were worked out. As they were rowed to shore, Dorothea was disappointed that heavy grey cloud obscured the view. They bombarded Mary Stanley with questions: 'Why are we here? What is this place? When can we start nursing?'

'Miss Nightingale is not yet ready for us,' came the reply from a rather flustered Miss Stanley. 'Rooms have not been prepared. You'll find it very pleasant in the Hôtel d'Angleterre, I'm sure. Some officers' wives are staying here already and they have nothing but praise for the hospitality.'

Dorothea's ears pricked up. Might Lucy be in their hotel? How wonderful that would be. While the party clustered in reception waiting for rooms to be allocated, she asked the receptionist whether they had a guest named Mrs Lucy Harvington but was disappointed to be told no one of that name had stayed there.

Elizabeth was sympathetic. 'Life is never that straightforward. We'll talk to the officers' wives and I expect one of them will lead us to your Lucy.'

The hotel was very smart, easily up to European standards, and the women were told they were permitted to walk in the adjacent gardens, which belonged to the British Embassy. After they had left their bags in their rooms, Dorothea and Elizabeth went outside to stretch their legs. Despite the clouds, the weather was much warmer than at home, and it was enjoyable walking in the embassy garden where, despite the lateness of the season, they still had roses and geraniums in bloom. It was laid out like an English garden but the echoing call to prayer that rang out as they walked was a reminder that they were far from home.

They came upon three Englishwomen sitting on a bench and Elizabeth introduced them, asking, 'Are you by any chance the wives of army officers?'

'Yes, indeed.'

'Were you with your husbands in Varna?' Dorothea asked, and they said yes, that they had been left behind when the soldiers sailed for Crimea in September, then just a month ago, they were transported to the hotel here, which made a welcome change from the very poor conditions further north.

'I wonder if you might know my sister, Lucy Harvington, whose husband is a captain with the 8th Hussars?' Dorothea's voice was full of hope, but it was instantly dashed as all three glanced at each other and shook their heads.

'I'm sorry. We got to know most of the officers' wives who stayed behind in Varna and I'm certain she wasn't among them. But several managed to find a place on a ship and sail to Crimea last September, so she could be there.'

'Unless she went with the soldiers' wives to Scutari,' another suggested. 'Some were left there on the way out and didn't even make it to Varna; others returned there after the

157

army left Varna. I heard they all stay in the vicinity of the hospital Miss Nightingale has created in Selimiye Barracks.'

'Yes, she could be there,' the first woman said. 'That would explain why we didn't come across her.'

Dorothea turned from one to the other: Lucy could be in Varna, Scutari or Crimea, and of the three, Scutari seemed the safest. Oh, if only she were there! The women promised to ask around among their acquaintances and let Dorothea know if anyone had met Lucy.

'Will you stay here long?' Elizabeth asked them.

'As long as the war lasts, I imagine,' the first woman smiled. 'You'll find it's really rather pleasant – much nicer than a winter at home. And if our husbands get leave, they may be able to sail down and visit us.'

Elizabeth pulled at Dorothea's arm to urge her to walk on, so she said her goodbyes, thanking them for their time.

'It's "really rather pleasant",' Elizabeth mocked as soon as they were out of earshot. 'What does she think this is? Royal Ascot?'

Dorothea agreed that the women's attitudes seemed rather cavalier for wartime, but she speculated that their relaxed air covered up a deep-seated anxiety about their husbands' welfare. Treating it as a restful break was simply a way of coping.

'I think you are too generous,' Elizabeth grumbled, but she left it at that.

At dinner that evening, they once again asked Miss Stanley when they would be proceeding to the hospital to start work. She seemed uncertain: 'Miss Nightingale has a lot on her plate and can't spare the time to show us the ropes. It may be that we will be based at another hospital in Constantinople, perhaps the General Hospital nearby, or maybe the new one at Koulali; at any rate I promise you will be working soon, ladies.'

Dorothea was frustrated by the delay. Rumours soon spread about the reasons for it: 'I heard Miss Nightingale says she doesn't want any more nurses, that she already has enough,' said one woman. 'She's not keen on nurses she didn't choose herself,' said another. 'She and Miss Stanley have fallen out over it.' Yet another blamed religious prejudice: 'She doesn't like the fact there are so many Roman Catholics among us; she's afraid we'll try to convert the patients instead of curing them.'

The nurses felt angry to have come all that way only to be left sitting idle, but for Dorothea it meant she had a chance to start looking for Lucy and she began exploring the neighbourhood around the hotel. Every time she turned a corner and came upon a group of officers' wives, she felt a surge of hope, only for it to be dashed. Once she thought she saw Lucy's blonde hair up ahead, but when she overtook the lady in question, she was at least twenty years too old. Lucy kept appearing as an unspeaking figure in her dreams but on the horizon, too far away to reach. It was Christmas, a time for families to be together, but Dorothea spent Christmas Day with a group of nurses she had only known a few weeks, eating mince pies sent by the British ambassador's wife and playing whist. They could hear sounds of music and revelry from the embassy next door, where a ball was being held, but none of their party was invited.

Dorothea left the company at one point to speak to the hotel receptionist.

'Would it be possible to arrange transport to take me to the Barracks Hospital in Scutari tomorrow? First thing, please.'

Chapter Twenty

Dorothea assumed that the hotel receptionist would order a carriage for her, like the Hansom cabs one could hail in London. She was astonished when she was led to the waterside where the Bosphorus divided the city, and saw waiting for her a rather precarious-looking ten-foot-long caïque.

'Is this how I'm to travel to the hospital?' she asked.

The receptionist bowed. 'Yes, Ma'am. It is on the other shore. Permit me to help you aboard.'

Dorothea felt a twinge of anxiety as he helped her step into the wooden caïque with blue paint peeling from its sides, and she lowered herself carefully onto some cushions in the stern, just above the water level. The Bosphorus was choppy and they bobbed on the waves.

'How long will it take to get there?' she asked the stocky sailor manning the sails. It seemed he didn't speak English so she called after the receptionist, who had a rapid exchange in Turkish with the sailor before replying, 'About twenty minutes. Enjoy your trip, Ma'am.'

The sailor leapt around, angling the sails to catch the wind, and soon they were speeding out into the centre of the wide channel that separated the city of Constantinople into two halves. He yelled furiously at the proprietors of other caïques who got in their way and zigzagged round the huge ships, giving them a wide berth. It was chilly out there, despite the bright sunshine, and Dorothea was glad of her warm winter coat, bonnet and muffler. She hadn't mentioned her trip to Miss Davis, who would almost certainly have wanted to accompany her. If she were to find Lucy, she wanted them to be alone so they could sit and tell each other everything that had happened since their last meeting. It only occurred to her once they were on the water that she should have mentioned her whereabouts in case an accident befell her. Too late now.

About halfway across, when they had not been mowed down by any huge international vessels, Dorothea decided she was in safe hands and began to enjoy the view. The sun peeped from behind clouds, illuminating the golden domes of mosques and the white marble of palaces along the shores. She felt very brave to be undertaking this trip on her own, in a foreign land, but a sense of purpose drove her. Perhaps, at the end of the day, she would be returning with Lucy reclining beside her on the cushions at the back of the caïque.

A tower stood on a rock just off the Asiatic shore and Dorothea assumed it was some kind of lighthouse. The sailor pointed at an imposing white stone building with a terracotta roof and four corner turrets sitting up a wooded slope and announced, 'Selimiye Kişlasi.' Dorothea hoped that was Turkish for 'barracks hospital' and that there had not been some fearful misunderstanding; she had been very clear with the receptionist. The caïque pulled in to a jetty at the foot of the slope, from which she could see a trail winding steeply upwards. The captain took her hand and helped her onto the jetty, indicating in sign language that he would remain there until she returned.

She began to walk up the rough-hewn path, her boots slithering in mud. The carcass of a black dog lay on its side, its fur matted, eyes pecked out of their sockets and flies buzzing around. She gave it a wide berth. A crumpled newspaper fluttered in the breeze, and just behind it a mound of faeces had attracted a swarm of buzzing insects. This was obviously not a path used by everyday tourists, which one would hope would be a little more gentrified. She could cope, of course – London streets could be just as bad – but when she saw a rat covered in fleas that glistened like a shiny moving coat, she shuddered and walked faster.

As she approached the barracks building, Dorothea saw a nun in a black habit by one of the entrances and hurried over.

'Good morning! Do you speak English?'

'Yes?' The nun was carrying an armful of linen and seemed in a hurry.

'I'm told the wives of English soldiers who were left behind at Varna have been brought here and I'm trying to locate someone. I wonder if you could tell me where they might be found?'

The nun looked at Dorothea's coat, her hair, her bonnet, and clearly recognised a lady of good breeding. 'They're living in the cellars beneath this building – round that way.' She pointed. 'But I don't think you want to be going there. It's not very savoury. Some have regrettably fallen into bad ways.'

'I'm grateful to you.' Dorothea nodded her thanks. She wasn't going to let anyone put her off once she'd come all this way so she headed in the direction indicated. It was only then the breeze turned in her direction, and brought a stench of rotten, decomposing flesh and drains blocked with days-old sewage. The Thames often stank with the effluent from slaughterhouses and the overflowing of cesspits fed by household lavatories, but it was as nothing compared to the foulness of this smell, which caught in her throat and made

162

Dorothea gag. She lifted her muffler to cover her mouth and nose before continuing round behind the building.

Towards the back, she saw some filthy children sitting on the steps down to a dark cellar doorway. She greeted them but they just stared at her and didn't move aside, forcing her to push past them and tread on the very edge of the stairs. There were no windows in the cellar and it took her eyes a few moments to become accustomed to the gloom. She could hear sounds of human life – murmuring, heavy breathing, snoring – but still it came as a shock to find quite how many creatures were crowded into that dank basement in conditions of complete squalor. Just near her feet, two women sat on the ground sharing a bottle of some kind of alcoholic liquor. They stared up with curiosity but were obviously inebriated so she didn't stop to question them. Other women were in various states of undress, and she didn't feel it would be proper to address them. She pulled the muffler tight, worried about catching a disease from the foul air, and stepped further into the room. Now she could see there were perhaps forty or fifty souls here, all crammed together, sleeping on blankets on the ground.

She stopped by one woman who appeared relatively sober. 'Excuse me, I'm sorry to trouble you but I wonder if I might ask you some questions?' The woman shrugged consent, or at least didn't refuse.

'I'm trying to find my sister Mrs Lucy Harvington, who travelled to Varna with the 8th Hussars. Might you know her?'

'Nope, never 'eard of 'er.'

'Were you at Varna?'

'Yeah, before the bloody army abandoned us here.'

'Are they not looking after you?' Dorothea frowned.

The woman snorted. 'Does it look as though they are looking after us? What d'you think?' She gestured around the room.

'You must complain,' Dorothea insisted. 'Talk to Miss Nightingale. Someone must have been charged with your wellbeing.'

The woman laughed harshly. 'Yeah, we'll have a chat with Miss Nightingale ...' – she spat on the floor – 'if only she will let us through the doors of her nice clean hospital. What d'ya think the chances are?'

'I'm sure the army would arrange transport home if you asked for it.'

'Yeah, and what do you suggest we do there? Set up a flower-arranging society? Chat to our servants about what's for dinner? We ain't got no money, milady.'

Dorothea took a step back. She didn't know what advice to offer. 'I'm sorry for your troubles. I would be *most grateful* if you could ask around about my sister.' She emphasised the words 'most grateful' to imply there might be a small reward. 'If anyone has heard of the whereabouts of Mrs Lucy Harvington, please ask them to contact me at the Hôtel d'Angleterre.'

There was general laughter and someone mimicked her accent: 'Oh yes, the Oh-tell Dongle Terr, we'll be sure to let her know.' This provoked more laughter from those in the vicinity and Dorothea began to feel alarmed.

'Thank you very much, ladies,' she said as she stepped over extended legs, trying to avoid standing on anyone's ragged possessions on her way to the entrance.

'Ladies!' the sarcastic cry echoed, causing more raucous laughter.

Dorothea hurried up the steps, her heart beating hard. Lucy would never stay in a place like this, would she? Even if the army abandoned her, she had sufficient eloquence to complain to someone and insist they find her suitable accommodation. She couldn't understand why these women had let themselves go so badly. She supposed that soldiers' wives tended to be rough sorts without much education or breeding, but surely they were used to better than this?

Dorothea hesitated outside the cellar, wondering whether to abandon the search, but another doorway beckoned further up the incline. She would simply peer inside to see if the situation was the same. When she reached it, she saw a corridor with several rooms leading off and she stepped in for a look. She couldn't see anyone sitting on the floor but she could hear footsteps close by, and headed towards them. A shadow passed in front of her and she called out, 'Excuse me' but there was no reply. The corridor curved to the right and she decided she would simply glance around that bend then head for the exit. Suddenly two men appeared, blocking her path.

'I do apologise,' Dorothea said, automatically polite, shrinking against the wall to let them pass. They were dark-haired and swarthy, and they stank of cheap alcohol. One said something to the other in a language she couldn't make out, but she was pretty sure was not Turkish. Scared now, Dorothea turned to leave then all of a sudden one of the men shoved her in the back so hard that she fell face-down on the floor with a thump. She started to scream but a filthy hand pressed over her mouth and she felt a man lower his weight onto her back. There was no time to think; she struggled with all her might to get free but she was pinned down. Her arms were bent beneath her. Did they want money? She had some coins in her reticule and tried to yank it free, but then she felt the men lifting her petticoats and she kicked her legs hard in desperation. *No! Stop this now!* She tried to bite the hand covering her mouth but couldn't get her teeth around it. Two hands gripped her ankles, forcing them apart, and another one began to fumble with her drawers. She struggled with renewed vigour, tears stinging her eyes, and managed to free an arm, with which she repeatedly pummelled the leg of the man lying on top of her. He didn't seem to notice. Against the two of them she had no chance.

They found the seam where her drawers separated and she felt fingers probing her private parts, where she had never been touched before, causing a stinging sensation. Tears began to stream down her face and her whole body trembled. The fingers poked hard at her, seeking entrance, and she squeezed her eyes tight, clenching her fists against the pain. *Surely this was not happening to her? It couldn't be. She must be dreaming.* The fight left her and she slipped into a state of deep shock. Perhaps she was about to be murdered. Perhaps these were the last moments of her life. *She would never see dear Lucy again.*

She came round to scratching sensations below, as if the man's fingernails were untrimmed, as if he were clawing at her like an animal. He uttered what sounded like a swear word, and the other grunted. They seemed annoyed about something. Suddenly the hand was removed from her mouth, the weight lifted from her back and the men appeared to be leaving. She heard the clatter of a couple of coins landing on the ground just by her face, then their voices receding. The whole incident had lasted no more than a few minutes.

Dorothea lay waiting till she was sure they had gone then sat up and yanked at her drawers and petticoats to cover her modesty. One stocking had a hole at the knee but she could darn that later. She glanced around to see if anyone had been watching but there wasn't a soul in sight. She wiped her eyes with a lace handkerchief and blew her nose into it, then stood up, finding her legs shaky. She pulled her coat tightly around her, adjusted her bonnet, and staggered out into the daylight.

The children still sat on the steps further down and didn't look up as she passed. She marched back along the front of the building, keeping her eyes focused straight ahead. She hurried down the steps to the waterside, past the flea-ridden rat and the dead dog and to her great relief the caïque she had arrived in was still there, secured to the jetty. The sailor was smoking but he flicked his cigarette into the water and took her hand to help her climb on board.

'Hôtel d'Angleterre, please,' she said in a trembling voice as she sat down, and he began to prepare the sails.

All the way back she ignored the pain between her legs, didn't allow herself to think about what had just happened. She couldn't bear to. Most of the time she simply stared at the murky green water. Maybe if she could manage not to think about it for long enough, she could simply pretend it had never happened.

Chapter Twenty-one

Dorothea hurried up the stairs to her hotel room and locked the door behind her, then sat on the edge of the bed and rummaged in her medical kit for a bottle of smelling salts. She inhaled deeply and the ammonia made her sneeze before she felt the familiar increase in heart rate. At least the salts helped to clear the revolting smell of the cellars from her nostrils.

When she felt well enough, she stripped to her undergarments and began to wash herself in a basin of cold water. She could have asked one of the hotel maids to draw her a hot bath but she didn't want to see anyone, not yet. Between her legs there were scratches and the whole area was inflamed from its rough handling. After careful washing she applied some turpentine oil, which stung so smartly it brought tears to her eyes. She'd heard that prostitutes used mercury to prevent diseases such as syphilis and gonorrhoea but she hadn't brought any with her.

Once she had finished washing, Dorothea pulled on her nightgown and climbed into bed. The sheets were soft and cool and she closed her eyes hoping for the oblivion of sleep, but instead she began to shiver. She pulled her coat on top for warmth and lay in a cocoon listening to the far-off murmur of ladies' voices in the gardens and some Turkish maids talking in the corridor. She was so stupid, coming to this foreign land with her naïve English assumptions. She'd imagined that the soldiers' wives would simply be staying in another hotel, where she could make enquiries for Lucy at reception. It hadn't occurred to her they would be reduced to such dire circumstances, or that foreign men would make certain assumptions about her simply because she was found there. She had lived a protected life to date, but all her old ideas would have to be discarded in this radically different situation.

There was a knock on the door and Dorothea cowered under the covers until she heard the voice of Elizabeth Davis: 'Are you all right, dear?'

It would be good to see a friend. Dorothea climbed out of bed and unlocked the door to let her in.

'I've been feeling rather unwell today,' she explained, her voice trembling. 'I'm sure I just need some rest.' She sat on the bed.

Elizabeth took in her pallor and placed a hand on her forehead. 'You feel rather hot. Lie down and let me take your pulse.' She frowned and declared the pulse to be weak and erratic. 'Is your digestion disturbed?' Dorothea said not, but admitted she had been feeling a little dizzy. 'Any coughing?' Dorothea shook her head. Elizabeth bent to listen to her chest, then asked if there was a rash, or any pain. Again, Dorothea told her there was not, although it was a lie as her private parts were still throbbing.

'I think perhaps it is a nervous exhaustion brought on by worry about my sister. No doubt a day in bed will cure me.'

Elizabeth was concerned by her high temperature, though, and a slight inflammation she detected in the neck. Dorothea was once again shivering and Elizabeth tucked the covers tightly around her. 'You're sure there is no sore throat or headache?'

'Perhaps a mild headache but nothing that sleep won't cure.' She closed her eyes, suddenly exhausted with the effort of conversation.

'You rest, my dear. I'm going to ask the kitchen to prepare some lemonade and I'll return later to see if your temperature has dropped.' She glanced at Dorothea's open medical kit. 'Between us we have a cornucopia of medicines, at least.'

When Elizabeth returned, she brought another nurse, Kate Anderson, and a bowl of warm arrowroot mixed with port wine as well as a tall glass of cool sweet lemonade, which Dorothea sipped gratefully.

Kate examined her and sponged her brow with cool water. 'I don't think it's scarlet fever,' she said, and Dorothea confirmed she had already survived a bout in childhood. 'They have malaria in these parts.'

'I don't feel feverish. Please … I can feed myself.' Kate had lifted a spoonful of arrowroot towards her lips.

'If you're sure.' Kate gave her the spoon and watched as she swallowed the glutinous mixture.

'I'm feeling much recovered. It's been most kind of the two of you, but I think if you don't mind that I need to be on my own, to rest.'

When they were finally persuaded to leave, Dorothea lay with grim thoughts swirling round her brain. If the men had given her a disease down below, surely she would not feel feverish so soon? She wasn't sure whether sexual congress had taken place or not – could it have? She hadn't bled, and she'd heard the rupture of the hymen caused bleeding. Either way she felt deeply ashamed. What if she had conceived a baby? She didn't even know the nationality of the men, hadn't recognised the tongue they spoke. They were simply ruddy-skinned sailors from a foreign land who thought she was for sale, as no doubt many of the other women living in those basements were.

Dorothea stayed in bed for the next four days, in a state of shock and misery. Was she permanently damaged by what they had done to her? At home she might have confided in Miss Alcock, but she felt she did not know her new companions well enough and so she kept it to herself. And all the time she felt sick with fear that Lucy might have met a similar fate – or worse.

Elizabeth and Kate brought her light meals of soup and boiled chicken along with news from the world outside. One day, they were taken to visit a nearby naval hospital and returned with some of the men's clothes to launder and repair. Dorothea offered to help so her friends brought a bundle of garments to her room, where they sat sewing companionably. Stitching seams and darning holes helped to occupy Dorothea's mind while she recovered from her ordeal.

Miss Stanley had continued to negotiate with Miss Nightingale about the employment of the nurses she had transported to Constantinople and at last, after two weeks in the Hôtel d'Angleterre, they were told they would be taken to the Barracks Hospital at Scutari the following Sunday. Dorothea flushed at the news and her heart beat faster, but she told herself she must go. It was the reason she had come to the Turkish lands. This time she would be with a group of women and there would be safety in numbers. Her fever had lifted, she no longer felt pain down below, and she yearned to keep busy, so she insisted she was well enough to accompany the party.

They sailed from the same jetty but in a much larger boat, with room below deck for the women, all forty of them, to shelter from a light shower that caused a stunning rainbow to arc across the Bosphorus from west to east. She had not told anyone of her previous visit so had to pretend to share the women's revulsion at the dead dog still lying on the path, and at the stench, even more vile than she had remembered, which met them as they approached the hospital. Dorothea didn't glance in the direction of the cellars, resolved not to be afraid. It crossed her mind to worry that her attackers might appear and recognise her, might even accost her, but she reassured herself that they had hardly seen her face. Thank heavens for small mercies.

Instead of being taken to meet Miss Nightingale, the party were shown by a nun to some rooms in a tower at the corner of a quadrangle where they would sleep twelve to a room, and where their luggage could be left. There were beds but no chairs or tables and just matting on the floor. The nun explained the brown basin was for washing, the wooden bucket held clean water and the tin pail was for dirty water, and she showed them where to empty their bedpans.

The foul smell was still in evidence but was not as strong indoors. The nun informed them that nurses were not permitted to leave the building, and Dorothea was greatly relieved. Each was given a sash with the words, 'Scutari Hospital' embroidered in red thread to wear over their uniforms, signifying their right to be there.

Mrs Bracebridge, whom Dorothea remembered from her initial interview, appeared and requested that some volunteers go with her to help in the linen room, so Dorothea stepped forward. There was no sign of recognition; Mrs Bracebridge turned briskly and led them down a long corridor and up a flight of stairs to a large room that was packed almost from floor to ceiling with what looked like dirty old rags.

'These were sent by the British public after Miss Nightingale complained we did not have enough bandages. As you can see, most are unusable, but your task is to salvage the fabric that will do, wash it and cut bandages from it.'

'When might we see some patients?' Elizabeth Davis asked.

Mrs Bracebridge seemed surprised. 'I doubt you will see any patients. Miss Nightingale is very careful in her selection of nurses. If you should have cause to go onto one of the wards, note that you must not under any circumstances talk to the men. It is quite forbidden.'

'That's ridiculous!' Miss Davis had no fear of authority and always seemed to be the one who spoke up for their party. 'Those poor boys are far from home, they're injured and in pain, and talking to a motherly British woman would bring them much-needed comfort. What sort of a rule would forbid that?'

Mrs Bracebridge glared at her. 'It's a rule which if you break it will result in you being shipped home straight away, that's what. Dinner is at seven in the dining hall. Carry on, ladies.'

When she'd gone, the women glanced at each other and burst into a fit of giggles.

'I've met her sort before,' Kate Anderson said. 'The ones who think themselves superior in intellect to the rest of us, when it is far from the truth.'

'I hear Miss Nightingale is something of an autocrat,' another nurse butted in. 'She has already sent home two nurses who went out with a male orderly to see the sights, and came back with the slightest hint of alcohol on their breath.'

'It's said she doesn't like those who spout religion at the bedside,' Elizabeth Davis remarked. 'I can agree that were I lying in pain with a festering wound the last thing I should wish would be someone praying over me. However, our party includes nuns of both Anglican and Roman Catholic persuasion. Must they keep their prayers to themselves in Miss Nightingale's wards?'

'It's probably for the best,' Kate Anderson answered. 'She doesn't sound like the kind of person you can reason with.'

Dorothea didn't agree but didn't say so. From everything she had read in the press she had formed a very favourable opinion of Miss Nightingale. It seemed she was a woman who was not afraid to speak up in order to get her own way, and that was a rare quality. Doctors could be high-handed and autocratic in Dorothea's experience, yet somehow they bowed to the will of this indomitable force of nature. She might make enemies amongst politicians and bureaucrats but it was said that the wounded soldiers adored her and spoke of her almost as a ministering angel who patrolled the wards at night with her lantern. Dorothea was dying to meet her and would have liked nothing more than to engage her in conversation about modern medical practice. If only they could be friends.

At dinner that evening, she sat by a nurse who had travelled out with the first group last November, who told her of the squalor in the barracks when they arrived: 'They say there was a rotting corpse of a Russian soldier in Miss Nightingale's own room, and vermin everywhere. The first thing we did was scrub the entire hospital area from floor to ceiling, then we washed the men as well, cutting their hair to get rid of the lice and getting the authorities to supply clean shirts for all. She's a hard taskmistress but she certainly gets results.'

It was two days later when Dorothea first set eyes on Miss Nightingale. A small party of women swept past her in a corridor and Mrs Bracebridge caught Dorothea's arm.

'Come with us. We need some help carrying supplies.'

Dorothea tagged along behind, noting that there was a male orderly in the group and he was holding a sturdy iron bar. They walked across the quadrangle to another corner of the building then up a staircase to a wooden door. Mrs Bracebridge tried the door then turned to a tall woman with short-cropped brown hair and said, 'It's locked, Miss Nightingale.'

With a start Dorothea realised this was the famous heroine of whom she had read in the newspapers.

'I thought so,' Miss Nightingale said. 'Joseph – if you wouldn't mind.'

She stepped back and watched as the orderly began to force the door with his iron bar. She was slender, Dorothea noted, with intelligent eyes, and her hair had a rich auburn hue. Miss Nightingale noticed her watching and the eyes swept over her briefly.

Once the door was open, she marched inside and began to issue orders: 'Joseph, you take that crate of port wine. Selina, look for scissors; we desperately need more scissors. You,' – she pointed at Dorothea – 'take that box of soda crystals and follow the others.'

Dorothea had lifted the box and turned to leave when a grey-haired gentleman in uniform stormed up. 'Miss Nightingale, not again! What do you think you are doing? This is a British government store and you have no right to break into it.'

'I have every right when I am treating soldiers fighting for the British army. Do not attempt to obstruct us, Mr Wreford.'

A fierce argument ensued but whilst berating him, Miss Nightingale waved a hand indicating that Dorothea and the others should continue to remove the goods, and so they did.

'Why must she fight for essential supplies?' Dorothea asked another nurse as they made their way back to the wards.

'It's been like this all along. The officials here do not seem to think nurses are necessary and have tried to thwart Miss Nightingale at every turn. Fortunately she is well able to cope with them and if they become too bothersome she merely complains to Mr Herbert, the war minister, who is a close friend. She is quite indomitable.'

Dorothea grinned. Miss Nightingale was very well-spoken and obviously from a good family, but she had no compunction about speaking her mind in the face of authority. Back home in decent society she could not have been in the company of men without a chaperone, but here she could give as good as she got when dealing with bureaucrats. Dorothea wondered briefly what Miss Nightingale would have done had she been attacked by two ruffians in a cellar and imagined the ferocity with which she would have responded. If only Dorothea had managed to fight harder; despite her determination to forget, she was plagued by the memory of the assault, and the guilt and fear that accompanied it, the feeling that she had given in too easily.

There was no doubt that Miss Nightingale had greatly improved circumstances in the Barracks Hospital, having had it scrubbed from top to bottom, and throwing open windows to let in fresh air, but still the corridors that served as wards seemed grim. When she glanced in, Dorothea was shocked to see long rows of men with only a narrow space between them, most looking half-dead; every morning bodies wrapped only in sheets were carried out by orderlies for the mass burials that took place in the nearby graveyard at one o'clock daily. She was itching to be allowed onto the wards to help, but days went by when her group were merely tasked with rolling bandages, mopping floors, or mending.

Among the nurses, Miss Nightingale was the main topic of conversation and opinion was divided on her merits. As they ate their evening meal – generally coarse bread, rancid butter, sinewy meat and tea without milk – they grumbled non-stop about their famous superintendent.

'She has sumptuous three-course meals using gifts sent by the British public. There's a store cupboard full of food intended for wounded men that finds its way into her belly instead.'

'In my opinion, she's not much of a nurse. She's got no time for dressings but you can't keep her away from the operating theatre. I heard she knows more about amputations than many a surgeon.'

'Don't you think it's hypocritical that she bans us from the wards after eight of an evening to avoid the risk of any sexual contact in the hours of darkness, but she doesn't hesitate to sail around herself, with no concern for her own reputation?'

On the positive side, Dorothea heard that Miss Nightingale sat long into the night writing letters to government officials agitating for further supplies to be sent, and to the mothers of every single soldier who died at the hospital. Her critics found her lacking in empathy and overly self-important, but Dorothea could well imagine how much a grieving mother would treasure a letter from her. Back in Britain she had become the most famous figurehead of the war, in the way that commanders such as Wellington or Nelson had been in previous wars. Her letters to newspapers swayed public opinion and forced politicians to accede to her demands or face an outcry.

One morning as she made her way to the laundry room, Dorothea realised a ship must have arrived with more wounded soldiers from Crimea as stretcher after stretcher was being carried to the wards. The men were in a shocking state: filthy, with bloody bandages falling off their wounds, eyes staring wide from pain and shock. They stank of vomit and the distinctive rotten-apple scent of gangrene. There were so many – fifty, sixty, seventy – that it would take Miss Nightingale's staff hours before they reached each one and Dorothea instinctively followed the procession to see if she could help. In the wards where the men were being set down, every nurse was worked off her feet and after a brief hesitation, Dorothea crouched by the patient nearest to her. He had dressings on a shoulder and a leg wound and was semiconscious. She pulled back the leg dressing carefully and nearly retched at the sight beneath: dozens of tiny white maggots were wriggling within the wound. Bile rose in her throat. This dressing could not have been changed for days, giving the flies time to lay their eggs and for said eggs to hatch.

Dorothea went to the nurses' store, found a basin and a pair of tweezers, then returned to extract the creatures one by one. She lost count of the number of maggots she removed but her basin was almost full by the time she had them all. She took the basin to a nearby kitchen and poured boiling water over them to make sure they perished, then returned to dress her patient's leg with lint and oilskin. His shoulder did not have an open wound but was dislocated, the bone sticking out at an awkward angle, and she was able to arrange a sling to support it so it would not cause so much discomfort. She washed him and pulled on a clean bedshirt then tucked a blanket around, whispering that a doctor would see him presently. He mumbled something and she held her ear close to his lips. He repeated the word: 'Mother.' Dorothea wasn't sure whether he was asking for his mother or he thought *she* was his mother, but she patted his hand kindly and said 'Yes, you are safe now,' before turning her attention to the next patient.

This one was a young lad, and he was tearful: 'I'm going to die, and my father and mother did love me so,' he sobbed. He had lost his left arm and right hand, and was greatly emaciated since no one had thought to feed him and he could not feed himself. His back was covered with bedsores where he had lain untended on the ship. The wounds were still clean, at least, so Dorothea reassured him.

'Be brave, and you will see your parents again.' She fed him a spoonful of cod liver oil and a spoonful of lemon juice followed by some beef tea and arrowroot mixed with egg and milk for sustenance. After that she cleaned and dressed the sores, and by the time she finished he seemed calmer. A full stomach always helped, in her experience.

In all, she had worked on eight patients before she was spotted. Mrs Bracebridge stormed over to challenge her: 'What on earth do you think you are doing?'

Dorothea explained that she couldn't bear to see these men wait any longer for attention. It was clear no one had looked at their wounds since they were treated on the front line, probably at least a week earlier.

'Well,' Mrs Bracebridge sniffed, 'you can be sure Miss Nightingale will hear of this.'

She didn't ask her to stop, though, so Dorothea carried on working until dinner hour. At the meal that evening, Elizabeth Davis introduced her to Mrs Eliza Roberts, a stern-looking nurse who before the war had been a sister at St Thomas' Hospital in London for twenty-three years.

Elizabeth seemed excited: 'Mrs Roberts tells me that she heard three officers' wives of the 8th Hussars went to Crimea with the troops. One of them was a Mrs Fanny Duberly, wife of the quartermaster. She doesn't know the names of the others but it seems likely your sister was among them.'

Dorothea clasped her hand to her mouth, before recovering her wits enough to say: 'How good to meet you, Mrs Roberts. I wonder, what was the source of your information, and when did you come by it?'

'Dr White of the 8th Hussars happened to mention it when he was down here collecting supplies for the army hospitals they are establishing in Crimea. That was just before Christmas.'

'Did he say anything about the other two women? Their ages, perhaps, or their appearance?'

'Yes … He mentioned that one of them was very young; far too young to be travelling with the army, in his opinion. And blonde. I'm sure he said she was blonde.'

'That's Lucy!' Dorothea didn't know whether to feel relieved that Lucy had survived the cholera outbreak in Varna, or alarmed that she was now up on the front line of the war. Her overwhelming feeling was relief, though. She was narrowing down the search, getting closer to finding her sister every day. With any luck they would soon be reunited. 'Thank you so much. I'm very grateful to you for sharing this information.'

'There is also bad news,' Mrs Roberts said. 'Miss Nightingale would like to see you in her rooms at ten o'clock this evening. She wants to have a word.'

Dorothea knocked on the door of the room in the north-west tower that Miss Nightingale had made her base, and entered on a sharp command of, 'Come in.' A concertina-style Turkish *fanoos* cast a glow around the bare walls, and there was a bed in one corner. Miss Nightingale dipped her quill pen into an inkpot and carried on writing furiously, so Dorothea stood waiting. There was nowhere to sit down and no such invitation was issued.

Miss Nightingale finished her letter and blew on the ink before placing it to one side. 'Miss Gray?' she asked, and Dorothea affirmed that she was. 'I understand you were treating patients today, although you have not been authorised to work in this hospital. Explain yourself.'

She was staring directly at Dorothea, her eyes black as coal in the lamplight and her gaze unwavering. Dorothea returned the stare and decided to speak her mind. 'There were men lying on stretchers at my feet, their wounds festering under grimy, blood-soaked bandages and their suffering apparent to all. Since I learned how to care for the sick, it has never been my habit to walk past anyone in need of my skills. I think we have a responsibility to help where we can, and today I saw that your nurses were stretched to the utmost so I stepped in, simply to clean wounds and wash the patients. I cannot believe that you, or any other experienced nurse, would not have done the same in my situation.' Dorothea surprised herself with the passion of this speech; it was not in her nature to argue in that way, but she felt her case very strongly.

For a moment, she thought a slight smile curled Miss Nightingale's lips but her words were neither amused nor tolerant. 'I cannot have my authority questioned and my rules flouted in this hospital. I'm afraid I am going to have to ask you to leave.'

Dorothea had not been expecting that. She gasped in utter shock. 'What do you mean? Where do you expect me to go?'

'I'll see you get on a ship back to England as soon as possible.'

'No!' The word burst from her lips, almost a shout. 'I won't go back. There are men here who need my help. I am a good nurse, Miss Nightingale, and I can ease their suffering and perhaps, God willing, save lives.' She was devastated to have made such a poor impression on the woman she so admired. How could she prove herself if she were not to be given a chance? An idea occurred to her: 'If you don't want me here, which is of course your prerogative, I beg you to send me to Crimea, where the soldiers are sustaining their injuries. By the time they reach Scutari they are much weakened and gangrene has often set in, but if I am allowed to care for them within hours of them being injured I know I can make a difference. I hear they are establishing hospitals up there. Could I not work in Crimea, Miss Nightingale? Please will you send me?'

Miss Nightingale picked up her pen and tapped the end on the desk for several seconds, considering. 'As it happens, I have received a request from Lord Raglan to send eight nurses to the hospital in Balaklava. But I would be doing him no favours if I sent him someone quite so insubordinate.'

'Please send me,' Dorothea begged. 'I promise I will obey orders to the letter. You don't know me, Miss Nightingale, but I am a volunteer at the Pimlico Charitable Hospital and have glowing references from my matron there. I can show them to you.'

'Come over here, Miss Gray.' Dorothea walked towards her. 'Let me smell your breath.' Dorothea opened her mouth and Miss Nightingale sniffed loudly, then asked, 'You did not have wine or brandy with your dinner tonight?' Each nurse was allowed one glass of either during the evening.

'I don't like to drink,' she answered truthfully.

'You have probably heard that I am a great believer in cleanliness. Tell me, Miss Gray: what is your opinion?'

Dorothea decided a little flattery would not go amiss. 'I have always sought to make the wards where I work clean and tidy, with plenty of fresh air, and I was pleased to see you have done the same here. I have heard of the appalling conditions when you arrived and think it is miraculous that you have achieved such a remarkable transformation in such a short time.'

'And yet they die. We are losing one in two of the soldiers who come here.' She seemed sad, the cares of her position weighing heavy.

'I'm sure that's because of the delay in the start of treatment. If they can be nursed in Crimea until they are strong enough for the journey to Scutari, I'm convinced the death rate would fall drastically.'

Miss Nightingale gave a deep sigh. 'Perhaps that's so. Well, I suppose I will send you to Balaklava,' – Dorothea drew in her breath sharply – 'but first of all you must understand that you will no longer be under my protection.'

'I understand,' Dorothea said, unable to stop a grin spreading across her face.

'The party will sail on the *Melbourne* on the 23rd January, the day after tomorrow. See if you can stay out of trouble until then.' She picked up her pen and a fresh sheet of paper and it was obvious to Dorothea that her interview was over.

She hesitated. 'Thank you so much, Miss Nightingale. I hoped to have this opportunity to tell you how much I admire all you are doing ...' She tailed off, as Miss Nightingale did not appear to be listening.

'That will be all,' she said. 'Shut the door on your way out.'

Dorothea left the room but stopped outside in the corridor to cover her face with her hands, momentarily overcome with emotion. She was on her way to Lucy. She couldn't wait to get to Crimea so the two of them could be together, so they could be close again, the way they were when Lucy was a little girl, long before Charlie Harvington came on the scene.

Chapter Twenty-two

25th January 1855

As the *Melbourne* approached the Crimean coast, its passengers could have no doubt they were getting close to the war. Distant explosions rumbled like thunder and smoke spiralled into the air from a town Dorothea was told was Sevastopol, the place the British and French armies were besieging. Her chest felt tight with nerves: would she be up to the huge challenges ahead? She hoped not to betray the trust Miss Nightingale had placed in her but those explosions sounded very alarming.

There were eight nurses and two surgeons in their party, all of them very affable. Elizabeth Davis had managed to wangle a place in the group and before they reached Balaklava she had extracted the life story of each travelling companion and told them of her own colourful background. For some reason that was never explained, they were not allowed to moor in Balaklava until the following Thursday and the days hung heavy as they listened to the shelling but could do nothing to help its victims. For Dorothea, it was particular agony to be stuck at sea, knowing that Lucy could be just a mile or so away.

They eventually docked in Balaklava, scraping between dozens of other moored vessels, to find a hamlet lined by rows of derelict cottages that seemed little more than a rubbish tip, a sea of mud, ice and dead, frozen-stiff horses with rictus grins and staring eyes. It was snowing lightly and there were few people in sight. Elizabeth trudged off to ask at the harbourmaster's office for directions to the hospital while the others stood on the quay by their luggage, and soon the chill was eating into their marrow. Dorothea thought it seemed a godforsaken place.

Elizabeth returned with a man leading two mules; seemingly this was the most practical method of transport on slippery ground. He tied their luggage to the animals with practised ease but indicated they would all have to walk. Slipping and sliding, they tramped up a steep hill to the top of the cliffs, from where it was but a short distance through the hamlet to Balaklava General Hospital.

Dorothea had been expecting something similar to the Barracks Hospital but perhaps a little smaller; instead they were taken to two parallel rows of buildings on a hillside which, even at a glance, were in a poor state of repair, with at least one of them lacking a roof and several others missing windows. Piles of rubble indicated walls that had collapsed altogether. Alongside there were a couple of windswept tents, a house made out of stone and four wooden huts, which appeared to be still in the process of erection.

'Is this it?' one of the surgeons asked, his tone expressing a gloom that was shared by all. At least it didn't have the putrid stench of the Scutari hospital, but wispy snowflakes were swirling in the wind and the ground was hard with frost, so it would have been preferable to find the walls and roofs intact. They left their luggage just inside one of the entrances and made their way down a corridor, trying to find someone to whom they could report their presence.

The first person they saw was a doctor, and when he heard these were the nurses he had been promised he gave a great sigh.

'I don't suppose you could start immediately? We have almost four hundred patients and only a handful of staff.'

Elizabeth grumbled to Dorothea that a cup of tea and a wash might have been nice but they slipped off their outdoor clothing and pulled on aprons and caps.

Dorothea was shown to a ward in which men lay on rows of bunks with no mattresses, just a scratchy grey blanket beneath them and an old brown rug on top, their coats serving as pillows. As at Scutari, the beds were jammed so close together there was scarcely room to move between them. She stopped at the first bed and asked the occupant how he was feeling.

'It's me toes,' he said. 'Got so painful I couldn't walk. I came here three days ago and someone put on a dressing but I've not seen a doctor since.'

Dorothea unwound the dressing carefully, bracing herself for more maggots. The final turn of lint came off and, to her utter horror, two of the man's toes came with it, like withered slugs. The remaining ones were swollen and blackened with frostbite. He didn't have any feeling in his foot so didn't seem to realise what had happened. She managed not to convey her shock but wrapped the lost toes in the old bandage for disposal and cleaned the rest of the foot. She checked the left foot and it was also frostbitten, although not quite as severely.

'When can I get out of here, Sister?' he asked. 'They need me back at the front. I'm the best sharpshooter in my company.'

She decided not to tell him he would have to practise walking with fewer toes; she would leave that to the doctor. Instead she spoke cheerfully: 'I'm going to apply mustard poultices to your feet to encourage the blood supply – always assuming I can find mustard here. It's an old family remedy that works wonders. I'll return shortly.'

She asked the way to the store cupboard and after some rummaging, found what she was looking for: flour, grease and mustard powder. In London, she used this remedy for a variety of ailments from gout to bronchitis, and as relief for her father's sore back. It warmed the flesh and seemed to promote healing. She mixed equal quantities of flour and mustard with water to make a paste which she applied to the inside of her cloth then she gently smeared grease on the patient's swollen feet before wrapping a poultice tightly around each.

'I'm lucky it's nothing more serious than frostbite,' he told her. 'I've lost dozens of friends. We've dug into trenches facing out towards the Russian redoubts, and shells come crashing down when you least expect it. No man ever knows when his number might be up.'

'You rest now and I'll ask the doctor to come and have a look at your toes.' She smiled, and was about to proceed to the next bed when she saw a tiny black dot moving on the rug that covered him. She pinched the louse between thumb and finger and it was only then she realised the whole bed was crawling with them. As she watched, one scuttled across the man's forehead. He was obviously so used to the itching sensation that he didn't react.

'Would you like me to shave you later?' she asked, and he agreed gratefully. 'That would be grand, nurse.' She decided she would talk to the other women about boil-washing the blankets and cutting the men's hair. She had caught lice from a patient in Pimlico once and could remember all too well the maddening itch that no amount of scratching could relieve. Every night for weeks she had to comb her hair vigorously, removing the creatures one by one, until all were gone.

The next bed was also crawling with lice, and she had to clean maggots from an arm wound that went deep to the bone; there was no putrefaction so she dressed it carefully, hoping there might be a chance to save the limb. There wasn't a lack of will; there simply weren't enough medical personnel to care for these men.

Dorothea worked tirelessly until it was too dark to see and her belly was growling with hunger. She followed a food cart across to another building and found the kitchen, where Elizabeth Davis appeared to have appointed herself head chef and was stirring huge copper vats of soup. Elizabeth passed her a bowl of soup and she sat down, her knees feeling as though they wouldn't hold her up a moment longer.

'This is the best I could do by ransacking their store cupboards: potato and onion soup with some wild thyme I found on the hillside. I'll have to go foraging for supplies in the morning.'

'This is simply awful,' Dorothea said, taking a sip. She caught Elizabeth's expression: 'No, I don't mean your soup. I was talking of those poor men, who are in a shocking state of neglect.'

'Well, thank goodness we're here,' Elizabeth replied. 'We'll soon have it all shipshape. Mrs Shaw-Stewart is going to take charge of the laundry, and Miss Langston is working out a duty rota. She seems an efficient type – if rather bossy.' Both of these were ladies who had accompanied them on the voyage from Scutari.

'There's so much to do, it's hard to know where to start.' Dorothea felt overwhelmed by the scale of the challenge, but then she remembered that Florence Nightingale had faced much worse when she first arrived in Scutari. If she could prevail, so could they.

'There's strength in numbers, my dear ...' Elizabeth began, but stopped as a doctor came in and collapsed heavily into a chair as if the very last spark of the day's energy had left him. Elizabeth quickly ladled out some soup and handed it over, and both women regarded him as he took a spoonful. His brown hair was striped with grey and there were deep pouches under his eyes that made him seem older than he probably was.

'Excuse my rudeness, ladies,' he said. 'I'm Dr White. Have you recently arrived?'

'We disembarked today,' Dorothea replied. 'Have you been here long?'

'I've been with the army since Varna, and in the Crimea since September last year. It feels like a lifetime.'

Dorothea remembered that White was the name of the doctor Mrs Roberts had mentioned, the one who had spoken of Lucy. Could there be two of the same name? 'I don't suppose you know Captain Charles Harvington of the 8th Hussars, do you?' she asked. 'My sister Lucy, his wife, is travelling with him.'

Dr White put down his soup bowl, his brow furrowed with compassion. 'I'm so sorry,' he said. 'Captain Harvington died just before Christmas. I'm attached to the 8th Hussars, so I knew him quite well. I believe your sister has sailed home. What a shame you missed her!'

Dorothea stared at him. Tears sprang to her eyes. Of course, the thought had occurred to her that Charlie might have been killed in one of those awful battles she'd read about, but she'd assumed she would have heard the news before now.

'A Russian sniper caught him when he was out on patrol. I hear he died instantly. I'm so sorry for your loss.' He produced a handkerchief and handed it to Dorothea.

It wasn't Charlie she was crying for but poor, dear Lucy. How dreadful to be a widow at the age of eighteen. She had been so much in love and now she must be suffering terribly. Dorothea hoped she'd been supported by the women friends she had mentioned in her letter from Malta, and that she'd had company for the sad voyage home.

'I wonder if you know who looked after her when she received the news? Did anyone accompany her to the ship?'

Dr White did not have any further information but said, 'She must be well on the way now, perhaps safely home already.'

Dorothea hoped he was right. It was best for Lucy to be back in London where she could grieve in peace, with their father for company. Selfishly, she was disappointed that they would not be reunited sooner. To travel all that distance only to miss her was a crying shame. But Dorothea was needed in Crimea. There was no question of turning for home.

Chapter Twenty-three

The women were allocated rooms in an old Russian house adjoining the hospital, with two cots and a coal-burning stove crammed into each. Dorothea and Elizabeth decided to share. They hurried across from the hospital building using a *fanoos* to light their way. Snow was falling harder now, turning the landscape white against a black sky, and the cold was unforgiving. Elizabeth made up her bed and climbed straight into it, bone tired, but Dorothea retrieved a pen and paper from her bag and began to write to Lucy in the lamplight.

'I've just heard the news about Captain Harvington and I'm so desperately sorry,' she wrote. 'He was too young and full of life to be taken, but I hope it is some comfort to know that he died serving his Queen and country.' She said she prayed that Lucy's trip home had been smooth, then explained that she had travelled out to nurse in the Crimea. 'Please write to me care of the Balaklava General Hospital, so that I will know you are safe.' Already Dorothea had decided to stay for the duration of the war. She couldn't do otherwise; these men needed every ounce of her skill and knowledge to ease the appalling situation in which they found themselves.

She extinguished the lamp and lay down to sleep but her thoughts were all with poor Lucy. How had she coped with the crushing pain of the loss? Dorothea remembered her at their mother's funeral, like a broken bird, far too young to have her world collapse. Underneath her sorrow had been a simmering anger at the universe that had allowed her mother to die – and in time, it came to be directed at Dorothea. It hadn't been a logical anger that she could articulate in words. She was cross when Dorothea tried to take a mother's role, but she'd had no choice because at thirteen, Lucy needed a mother. And there was something else: she was cross that Dorothea hadn't been able to save their mother. It was unfair because Dorothea had tried every single technique that modern medicine had to offer. She had read learned papers on cancer, procured the latest drugs and tried every treatment known to man. Anything she could possibly do, she had done – all to no avail. Tears pooled and she cried herself to sleep on her first night in that cold, war-torn land.

In the early hours of the morning, Dorothea awoke from a dream, disturbed by a scratching sensation on her arm. She moved the arm and a dark shape leapt to the floor, landing with a soft thud. There was just enough light to make out a long tail as it disappeared behind her trunk. Dorothea screamed from the depths of her lungs. 'A rat! Elizabeth, there's a rat in here.'

Elizabeth woke, grumbling. 'Where is it?' Dorothea pointed, trembling, whereupon Elizabeth got up to look, only to find it had escaped through a narrow gap between wall and floor.

'Goodness, all that fuss for a little rat. We'll block the hole later.' She poked the embers in the stove then crawled back into bed for a last snooze. But Dorothea knew it hadn't been little; its body had been almost a foot long and its tail the same again. She'd seen rats in London but none that size, and certainly hadn't woken to find them sitting on her arm. It seemed an ill omen. Life here was going to be tough.

When Dorothea and Elizabeth tried to open the door of the Russian house next morning, they had to push hard. Two foot of snow had fallen, blocking their exit, and their ankle-high galoshes were of little use in keeping their feet dry as they hurried across to the hospital. They went first to the kitchen and found an impromptu meeting taking place between the purveyor, Mr Fitzgerald, some hospital orderlies and the other women who had travelled with them.

'We need a system, with each responsible for particular areas,' Miss Langston said. 'Mrs Shaw-Stewart is happy to manage the laundry and I believe you are managing the kitchen, Miss Davis? Now, Mr Fitzgerald, can we give you a list of our immediate requirements? Perhaps you would be so good as to fulfil them.'

He looked flustered, obviously unused to being given orders by a bunch of women but too polite to object: 'I don't know ... it's hard to find fresh food here. And we're completely out of laundry soap.'

'You'll do your best to find more, I'm sure. The shortage of medicines is particularly alarming. All I could find was castor oil and Epsom salts, which would be fine if all our patients need purgatives – but I doubt that's the case. We need some digitalis for heart problems.' She ticked the medicines off on her fingers. 'Quinine and antimony for fever; squills for coughs; ipecacuanha to induce vomiting. And we need more opium. Have I forgotten anything?'

Elizabeth Davis chimed in: 'Perhaps some salep. They grow it in the Turkish lands, and it makes a good sedative drink for those who are anxious.'

Everyone had suggestions based on their own nursing experience and Mr Fitzgerald looked worried. 'You will write this down for me, won't you?'

'Certainly.'

Next, Miss Langston announced she had compiled a rota whereby each of the nurses was responsible for seven wards, with sixteen beds in each, and they would work in twelve-hour shifts with a day off every three weeks. All agreed that was a sensible distribution of responsibility and took note of the designated mealtimes: breakfast at eight, then dinner at noon, tea at five, supper at seven or eight, drinks at ten, and bed around midnight. Dorothea checked the rota and was disappointed to see that she would not have a day off for three weeks. She was anxious to go to the British camp and find some of Lucy's friends – she needed to know exactly what had happened to her sister before she could rest easy – but it would have to wait for now.

After a quick breakfast of coarse bread and tea, Dorothea entered the door of ward seven, the first of the wards she had been charged with looking after. A new patient had arrived during the night with a gunshot wound to the head. There was a hole the size of a threepenny bit in his skull, and it had bled copiously so he was white and weak from blood loss. A surgeon had tried but been unable to retrieve the bullet, which was lodged somewhere within the brain tissue, where it would inevitably spread sepsis. There was little chance of him surviving the next twenty-four hours. Astonishingly, the patient was able to talk to Dorothea, telling her that his name was Donald Leekie and that he was twenty years of age. As she washed him, she asked about his family.

'We're from the North-West, near Lancaster, Sister. Me ma works in a laundry and Pa's down the mine.'

'Do you have brothers and sisters?'

'Oh, aye. There's six of us; I'm the eldest and the youngest is only four. Money's tight so I try to send some home to help out, although it's not easy on army pay, Sister.'

'Would you like to write a letter to your mother?' Dorothea asked. 'I can give you pen and paper.'

'It wouldn't be much use, Sister. I can't write and me ma can't read.'

'I will write the letter for you if you tell me what to say. I'm sure your mother can find someone to read it to her.' Dorothea felt strongly that he should send a last message to bring his mother comfort, so she fetched pen and paper and waited for him to speak.

'Dear Ma,' he said. 'I am in the Crimea. It is very cold here with snow on the ground. I hope you and Da and my brothers and sisters are all well.' He closed his eyes. 'That's it.'

'Are you sure that is all you want to say?' Dorothea urged. 'Will you not tell them that you have been shot?'

He screwed up his nose. 'I wouldn't want them to worry.'

'Nothing else then?'

'Ermm … You could ask Ma to say hello to Mary Burton for me.' He gave a shy smile, which he immediately tried to repress.

'Is she your sweetheart?' Dorothea smiled back.

'I *wish* she were my sweetheart. I always liked her but I never got around to telling her. When I get home the first thing I'm going to do, after seeing Ma, is visit her.'

Dorothea felt her skin prickle with gooseflesh thinking of his lost chance at love. 'Is Mary Burton very pretty?'

'Not really. She's got bad teeth and a round, freckled face, but she is the best-natured girl you're ever likely to meet. I reckon she's a girl as could make a man a good wife.' He smiled his shy smile again.

'Well, I will definitely ask your mother to tell her you said hello. I'll send this letter later today. I have one of my own to send so it is no trouble. If you think of anything you want to add, call me over.'

She carried on with her ward rounds, feeding patients who could not feed themselves, changing dressings, shaving men, administering medicines and poultices, assisting the doctors with cupping, blood-letting and blistering. There were men with pneumonia, scurvy, typhus, dysentery and fever as well as battle wounds and injuries from the debilitating cold, and all appeared malnourished. When they heard she had only left England two months earlier, lots of them asked what the public back home felt about the war.

'They are following every step of it in the newspapers and there is enormous pride in our brave soldiers.' Dorothea was glad to be able to answer truthfully.

'Queen Victoria herself is said to read reports from the front avidly, and every man serving is hailed as a hero.'

'Do they know we don't have winter uniforms, or enough food? Do they know we live in tents in the snow?'

Dorothea assured them that the shortages had been reported, especially by Mr W.H. Russell of *The Times*, and she had no doubt that the necessary supplies would be on their way already. The news they had not been forgotten seemed to cheer the men and almost did more good than medicine.

Every time Dorothea went into ward seven she glanced over at Donald Leekie, who spent the day asleep in a sitting position with his head resting on the wall behind. In the early evening, Dorothea came to feel his forehead and offer food and it was only then she realised he had died where he sat, quietly and without fuss, and that rigor mortis was already setting in.

She fingered the letter in her apron pocket and remembered that he hadn't given her his mother's address. She would get it from his commanding officer. She decided to add a note of her own so that Mary Burton could learn there once had been a soldier who dreamed of making her his wife.

Chapter Twenty-four

The sight of Miss Langston politely haranguing Mr Fitzgerald became a daily one. Despite Dorothea's assurances that news of the shortages of food and medicine had reached Britain before she left, the situation in Balaklava had shown no sign of improving. It often seemed to her that bureaucracy at higher levels got in the way of common sense. In Scutari she had heard of a shipment of cabbages sent to feed the injured soldiers that sat in anchorage for so long that by the time the necessary paperwork was signed they were completely rotten. Men succumbed to the old-fashioned disease of scurvy while a cargo of lime juice intended to prevent it turned mouldy at a mooring in the Bosphorus. It was no wonder that Florence Nightingale had sometimes taken matters into her own hands, Dorothea mused, infuriated on behalf of the fighting men who were being let down. In mid-February, the same kind of muddle occurred in Balaklava harbour. A shipment of supplies arrived and pulled in to port, but the captain refused to unload his cargo because no one had paid him for it. Mr Fitzgerald argued vociferously, enlisting the harbourmaster's help, but the captain was adamant. When this news was relayed to the women, Mrs Shaw-Stewart asked that she be taken to meet the captain and the next thing they knew the cargo was being unloaded.

'What on earth did she do to change his mind?' Dorothea asked Elizabeth, all kinds of ideas flitting through her mind. Threats? Seduction? Both were unthinkable.

Elizabeth chuckled, as if she could read Dorothea's thoughts. 'She wrote him a cheque for the whole lot from her personal bank account. Oh, to be wealthy!'

The shipment contained enough new clothing for each patient to have a fresh outfit. There were jars of preserved fruits from Malta, which would help to treat scurvy, and there were crates of wine and brandy to flavour the arrowroot they fed to the most poorly patients. Dorothea examined the cargo, hoping that there had been ample provisions on the ship that took Lucy home. There had still been no word, although she watched daily for a letter. Elizabeth was busy counting the bottles and storing them with great care to prevent pilfering. She had erected barricades in the store cupboards to exclude rats of both the animal and human variety.

The day after the shipment was delivered, Lord Raglan visited the hospital. He sashayed grandly from ward to ward in his army greatcoat, patting patients on the shoulder with his one arm (the other having been lost at Waterloo) and bellowing, 'Hurry up and get well, good man,' to those who had but hours to live, and, 'Don't waste any of that,' to men who were so hungry they were wolfing down bowls of unflavoured arrowroot.

'Don't stint on the brandy and wine,' he told Dorothea, as if it were his own largesse that had supplied them. 'I am sure our country grudges nothing to such courageous men.' She noted a liverish look about his complexion, a yellow tinge to the eyes, and guessed he didn't stint on brandy and wine himself, although she was sure he chose more refined vintages than those supplied for his men. All told she found him arrogant and insensitive, and she worried that he was too old at sixty-seven years, and too lacking in human insight, to be overall commander of the British troops.

'They're saying if he had been more decisive and ordered the attack on Sevastopol last autumn, the war would have been won outright and he would have saved thousands of lives. He shilly-shallied and the moment was lost. At least that's what I heard.' Elizabeth Davis was a repository of strong opinions, not always plausible, but in this case Dorothea could well believe it.

At last, three weeks after her arrival at the hospital, it was Dorothea's turn for a day off. She'd had Dr White draw her a map showing the whereabouts of the 8th Hussars camp where Lucy and Charlie had stayed, and got Mr Fitzgerald to organise transport for her on a supply wagon. They drove inland for seven miles following the tracks of a new railway that was being built to connect Balaklava with the British camp. So far it had only reached the tiny town of Kadikoi, where she saw navvies at work laying rails, but when it was finished, the wounded would be brought down from battle-field to hospital far more quickly, and supplies could be taken up to the soldiers more easily. After Kadikoi the road deteriorated and the journey was bumpy and slow, trundling up and down hills, until eventually they emerged onto a plain where Dorothea could see rows of tents stretching into the distance. Horses were grazing behind them and people shrouded in blankets huddled around desultory fires. The sky was a leaden grey, the ground marshy from snowmelt, and altogether Dorothea had never seen a more dispiriting place. She found it impossible to imagine her beautiful, well-dressed sister in such surroundings. How did Lucy cope, even before the tragic news of Charlie's death? She felt a pang of love for her.

'This is the British camp, Ma'am,' her driver told her, and he added something else but it was drowned out by a sudden explosion that made the earth shake.

It terrified the wits out of Dorothea and she screamed. 'Should we take cover?'

He shook his head, sucking his teeth. 'The Russkies keep sending shells in our direction but they fall well short of the camp. They're aiming at the men just over that ridge there.'

The fighting seemed devilish close as far as Dorothea was concerned. How awful for the women to listen to those explosions, knowing that any given shell could just have killed one of their menfolk not far away.

'This is the 8th Hussars camp,' her driver told her. 'I'll take you to the cookhouse. That's most likely where the women'll be. I'm heading back in an hour or so but you'll easily catch a lift with someone else. There's wagons going back and forth all day long.'

When they came to a halt, Dorothea clambered down and smiled at the five ragged women who were sitting round a fire with a bubbling pot hung over it. They looked up at her smart coat and hat with suspicion.

'My name's Dorothea Gray,' she said. 'I'm the sister of Lucy Harvington, the wife of Captain Harvington. You knew her, I expect?'

They looked at each other and one replied, 'Yes, what of it?'

Dorothea was surprised at the lack of friendliness. Lucy had described these women as 'salt of the earth' types. 'I came out here hoping to meet my sister but I understand I am too late. I wonder if you could tell me how she was when she left? Did any of you see her after the news of her husband's death?'

Again the women looked at each other. 'I didn't – did you?' Each woman shrugged and shook her head.

'We just heard that Captain Harvington was dead and then she was gone. She didn't come to say goodbye or nothing.'

Dorothea addressed her: 'I'm sorry, I didn't catch your name.'
'Mrs Jenkins.'

Dorothea felt uncomfortable hovering above them but was reluctant to sit on the wet ground. 'Perhaps you can tell me who were her particular friends? I'd be most grateful if you could direct me to them.'

Mrs Jenkins sighed, as if the question were an imposition on her valuable time. 'Well, there was Captain Cresswell's wife, a nice lady, but she left last September or October after her husband died. Then she got on all right with Mrs Williams, but she's gone down to Scutari to nurse her Stan.'

'So who comforted Lucy when she had the news of Captain Harvington's death? Was anyone with her at the funeral?'

Another woman spoke. 'Major Dodds would have been there. He and Captain Harvington were friendly. But I don't know who else.'

'And you didn't see Lucy while she was packing for the voyage home?'

Mrs Jenkins hesitated, a sly look on her face. 'Well, that's the thing. She didn't actually take her stuff with her. Just upped and went without it. We reckon she must have been so distraught she couldn't bear to look at it.'

Dorothea felt her chest tighten with alarm. 'She left her belongings? How very odd! I wonder if you might know what has happened to them?'

Mrs Jenkins got to her feet reluctantly. 'I don't know the whereabouts of all of them, mind. Just a few things.' She hobbled off down the row of tents. The remaining women busied themselves stirring the cookpot or rearranging their coats without meeting her eye. Dorothea noticed they wore men's trousers underneath their skirts and stout men's boots on their feet.

They waited in silence till Mrs Jenkins returned with her arms full: there was a rectangular wooden box, an old summer bonnet of Lucy's, a lace fan, and a ship in a bottle with a painted scene of Constantinople. She handed over the goods. Dorothea hesitated for a moment then sat down on the grass to examine them. Her coat would have to dry out later.

The box had a brass plate with Charlie's name engraved on it and the lock appeared to have been forced, the wood splintered all around it. Dorothea opened the lid and gasped in surprise when she saw a thick bundle of the letters she had written to Lucy, none of them opened. Why would Lucy not have opened them? Was she still angry about their row? And then in a flash Dorothea understood: they had been stored in a locked box owned by Charlie. He hadn't passed them on to her. Fury rose in her gullet. How unspeakable of him to come between two sisters. What a truly despicable thing to do.

Flicking through the pile of letters she saw they all bore her handwriting, bar one. On the envelope it read, 'To my darling wife'. Dorothea had no compunction in tearing it open and reading it, even once she realised that Charlie had obviously written it for Lucy to find in the event of his death. 'My dearest, I hope you know how deeply I love you and how very proud I am to have called you my wife.' In some ways it felt wrong to read on, but Dorothea couldn't stop herself. 'I regret that we did not have time to bring children into the world, as you would have been the best of mothers,' he wrote. 'I hope that after a suitable period you will remarry and have children with another man, a better man than me. I don't want our tragedy to overshadow your life when you are still so very young.' Dorothea skim-read further down the page. 'You will have found out by now that I withheld your sister's letters from you and I beg you to forgive this action, which I know was wrong.' Dorothea shook her head. *You evil, selfish man*, she thought, with a surge of pure fury. 'I felt especially guilty when you told me how much you longed for word from home, and how sad and bewildered you were not to hear.' If Charlie had been there, Dorothea would have attacked him physically; she felt rage surge around her veins. *How could he have done this? Why?* 'The truth is that I was afraid your sister might still succeed in turning you against me. She might have persuaded you to return to Britain and leave me on my own out here. I wanted us to become the only family each other needed, but I know now it was very wrong of me. You should realise that Dorothea wrote many times and sent many parcels. Usually I opened them and pretended to you that the goods had come from the store, so you did not miss out.' Dorothea read quickly, swallowing her contempt. He thanked Lucy for her love and understanding and finished by saying that it was a godforsaken war, that he should never have brought her there, and that with his last breath he would be praying for her safe return to London and wishing her all the happiness in the world for her future.

Dorothea folded the letter and stuck it back in the envelope, greatly distressed by what she had read. All those months, Lucy must have thought she had been abandoned by her family. If only she had been curious enough to look inside the box – but Charlie probably kept the key on his person. He must have assumed Lucy would find it and open the box after his death, and for some reason she hadn't. Why hadn't she? She guessed he used to keep cash in there as well, and that whoever had forced the lock had pocketed the money. She was livid with Charlie, but she felt guilty too. She should have paid more heed to that letter from Charlie's family warning that he would not make a good husband. She should somehow have forced Lucy to stay in London.

Mrs Jenkins saw Dorothea's distress and misunderstood the reason: 'You can't blame folk if they helped themselves to a few bits and pieces. We're all short here and it's not as if Mrs Harvington needed her clothes any more. She'd gone off without them.'

'No, of course I don't mind,' Dorothea said. 'Lucy would want you to have them. Thank you so much for these few items.' She took out a handkerchief to wipe her nose, determined not to cry in front of these strangers.

'She was a lovely lady,' another of the women said. 'One time she brought us a bag of coal. Everyone was short of coal and she could've kept it to herself but she didn't, she shared. She was a generous sort but too young and too green for a place like this.'

'Yes, she had a lovely nature,' Mrs Jenkins agreed, her previous defensiveness melted by Dorothea's emotional state. 'Can we offer you a cup of coffee? It's not very good coffee, mind. They give us green coffee beans and no grinder to make use of them but we've found a way of pounding them with a stone … Jane, get the lady some coffee.'

Mrs Jenkins appeared to be the boss, because a woman rose to do her bidding.

'You'd probably rather have tea,' Mrs Jenkins continued, 'and so would I. But we ran out of that months ago, along with sugar, and there's never been any milk. We're lucky to get bread or dry biscuits and the occasional stringy bit of meat.'

'Was Lucy going hungry?' Dorothea asked. 'How did she manage? She can't cook.'

Mrs Jenkins chuckled. 'She was all fingers and thumbs in the kitchen but after Mrs Cresswell left she would come and sit with us most days and she peeled a potato or two. She must have a strong constitution because she didn't get the cholera or any of the fevers going round up here in Crimea. Her husband, on the other hand … well, it's not my place to say.'

'You can speak freely with me,' Dorothea said, eyes narrowed at the thought of him. 'How did Captain Harvington cope?'

Mrs Jenkins wrinkled her nose. 'He was a fair-weather soldier: fun to be around when the going was good but as soon as things got hairy he was hiding in the bushes and taking to the bottle. Your sister was the stronger character, for sure.'

It did not surprise Dorothea to hear Charlie had proved a coward, especially now she knew the extent of his selfishness. He was all frivolity and no backbone, she thought bitterly. How could Lucy have fallen for him?

As the woman called Jane handed Dorothea her coffee – a watery greyish drink – she noticed she was wearing one of Lucy's gowns beneath her coat, a shell-pink silk one with cascading skirts and a decorative flounce up the centre of the bodice. 'Why do you think Lucy left her clothes behind?' she asked. 'Did she depart in a great rush?'

Jane quickly wrapped the coat around her to hide the gown. 'I expect she heard there was a ship leaving and she wanted to catch it. No point hanging round here a minute longer than you have to.'

They all nodded and seemed convinced that must have been the reason. Dorothea stayed an hour, asking the women about their experiences in Varna and then here, trying to understand what her sister's life had been like this past nine months. She got the sense there was something they weren't telling her. Why did Lucy not say her goodbyes? Why did she leave both her own and Charlie's possessions behind? It didn't seem right and she felt a knot of worry.

Later, back at the hospital, Dorothea described the scene to Elizabeth Davis. 'They appeared shifty, as though they were hiding something, but I couldn't get them to admit what it was.'

'You must speak to Major Dodds.'

'He was at the front so I left a note for him. I hope he'll reply soon. Something is wrong; I know it.'

Lying in bed that night, Dorothea tried to distract herself from her worry by focusing on the positive things the women had told her. Lucy hadn't been ill in Varna, thank God. She had tried to help with the cooking. But the camp had been so dismal, with no comforts to speak of, and she must have been lonely if Charlie had taken to the bottle. She prayed the women were correct in thinking that Lucy had caught the first ship home. In that case, she should hear from her soon. If she had not, where could she be?

The days passed, and every time Dorothea saw a mail sack arrive, she prayed that it would include a missive telling her of Lucy's safe arrival in London. Her imagination began to run away with her: what if Lucy were stuck in Scutari with no money for the onward voyage? Would she be driven to prostitution? Dorothea couldn't believe this. And then she worried that she might be ill somewhere, or even – unthinkable – that she had perished.

Her fears multiplied when she received a letter from her father saying that Lucy had not returned to the Russell Square house. She saw it was dated 7th February, Lucy's birthday; if Lucy left Crimea straight after Christmas, she should have been home by then. Where was she? Her father said there had been a letter from her just before Christmas, which had been delivered personally by a very charming lady friend of hers named Adelaide Cresswell. Mrs Cresswell, a recent widow, had apparently accepted a glass of negus and stayed for a long conversation, but he had no news of Lucy after that. Dorothea wrote back immediately asking if her father could undertake to obtain Mrs Cresswell's address. Perhaps she might be able to speculate on Lucy's whereabouts.

'Charlie died just before Christmas,' she told Elizabeth. 'That's two months ago. How could it have taken her so long to get back?'

Elizabeth had a suggestion. 'These ships have various disembarkation points. She could be in Malta, or Piraeus, or even Constantinople, waiting for another passage.'

Dorothea shivered at the memory of the soldiers' wives in the cellar at Scutari. She knew Lucy would rather die than sell herself; pray God it hadn't come to that.

Chapter Twenty-five

Dorothea purchased some goods from the hospital store – a jar of preserved fruits, a chicken, some potatoes, a bag of sugar and a tin of tea – and sent them up to the 8th Hussar wives, thanking them for looking after Lucy. As she wrote, it occurred to her to wonder if any of them could read; they had clearly lacked curiosity about the letters in Charlie's box. She signed her name and asked the supply wagon driver to explain the gift was from her.

They were still short of fresh vegetables at the hospital but since the shipment arrived they were far better off than those at the British camp. They at least had clean, lice-free clothes and bedding, and meals three times a day. Elizabeth worked wonders with the ingredients to hand, making jellies from the preserved fruits, and somehow managing to serve a nutritious broth or stew every lunchtime. She had a temper, and any orderlies who got around her barricades and stole food from her larder caught the rough edge of her tongue, but she was good company and most of the medical staff dropped by to listen to the latest gossip when they had time.

'I hear in the Turkish camp they are eating the meat of their dead horses,' she told Dorothea. 'They're nothing but heathens. An orderly told me they cut off the ears of their enemies and pin them on their tents as decoration.'

'The Turkish patients in my ward seem perfect gentlemen,' Dorothea objected. 'If they eat horse meat, it is perhaps because they are starving. Remember that we would be short of provisions had it not been for the recent shipment.'

'The French, on the other hand – they import delicacies such as *foie gras* and champagne.' Elizabeth Davis affected an aristocratic accent.

Dorothea raised an eyebrow, thinking this must be an exaggeration. Elizabeth Davis tended to be critical of any nationality but her own.

'It's true!' she exclaimed, noting Dorothea's scepticism. 'They are sold by the *vivandières*. Have you seen them parading around, thinking they are so special? They're the ones in short red skirts over red trousers, with the blue fitted jackets and wide-brimmed hats. Mr Russell of *The Times* calls them *hors de combat* and I don't doubt he's right about that.'

Dorothea blushed at the lewd double entendre. She suspected that although her fiancé had died before their wedding, Elizabeth possessed more experience of adult sexual relations than she.

'So was there never a gentleman caller you considered marrying?' she asked, adding a pinch of salt to her broth and stirring.

Dorothea blinked, taken aback by the abrupt change of subject and unused to discussing such personal subjects. 'It was difficult with Mother's illness. I didn't like to invite anyone to the house. I was twenty-six when she passed away and that's when I started nursing.'

'I'm surprised one of the doctors at your Pimlico hospital didn't snap you up.'

Dorothea smiled shyly at the compliment. 'There was one man, a barrister, who called on me for about a year.

He proposed the night before I came out here but I turned him down.'

'What was his name, and how did you meet him?' Elizabeth blew on a spoonful of soup, tasted it and made a face before adding more salt.

'William Goodland. He was the brother of a friend.'

'But you weren't in love with him.' Elizabeth said it as fact.

'When he proposed, I was more surprised than anything else. Our conversation was always awkward and we knew so little of each other that I wondered how he could dream of spending his life with me. We were perfectly cordial, but ...'

'There was no passion,' Elizabeth finished the sentence for her and Dorothea blushed again. She cared for men on her wards and had often seen their most intimate parts, but talk of passion led her thoughts back to those rough men who had attacked her in Scutari. If that was passion, she wanted none of it.

The doctors and nurses at Balaklava Hospital pooled their medical knowledge and invented ingenious remedies to circumvent the lack of supplies. Dorothea found many of the nurses used poultices of their own design. Kate Anderson recommended that the area of the heart be kept warm with a mustard poultice whenever the pulse was weak. Another nurse, Mrs Evans, mixed mustard powder with warmed oil and rubbed it directly onto the stomach and back, but she favoured linseed oil poultices for frostbite. Elizabeth Davis cooked up her own brew of bitter herbs for digestive disorders and made it more palatable by mixing in a little port wine or brandy. 'Back home I use rhubarb but chance would be a fine thing here,' she commented. Many favoured herbal remedies, such as meadowsweet for fever and pennyroyal for gastric complaints, and they had all brought their own supplies in wooden medicine chests similar to Dorothea's.

Kate Anderson arrived in the kitchen one day in some distress, her apron spattered with fresh blood. 'I do wonder about the side effects of chloroform,' she cried, looking shaky. 'I just had a patient who retched so violently when coming round from surgery that the stitches in his belly burst, ripping the flesh around and creating a much greater, more ragged hole than that caused by a Russian bullet. It was horrible.'

'It does take some worse than others, but if you've ever seen an amputation without chloroform, the poor man biting down on a rag against the excruciating agony, then there's no going back ...' Mrs Evans was the speaker, but all the older nurses nodded in agreement.

'They have such pounding headaches from the chloroform. You can see in their eyes how foul the pain.'

'I think the trick is to administer as little as possible. Two or three drops at most,' Elizabeth Davis said.

'Isn't it good to feel we women are so useful here?' Kate asked, and there was a general murmur of agreement and nodding of heads.

'You can always give opium for the headaches,' Mrs Evans contributed. 'Most of 'em ask for it.'

'But it can prove fatal if the constitution is already weak,' Dorothea volunteered. 'It doesn't work for all. And I worry about those who become dependent on it.'

She told them of a patient named Captain Roderick Lethbridge, who arrived at the hospital on foot complaining of severe stomach pain. 'Help me!' he yelled so loudly that the entire ward awoke from their slumbers, and he bent double, leaning against a wall. 'Bring me opium,' he demanded of Dorothea, grabbing her arm.

'Have you been shot?' she asked, and he shook his head, grimacing. 'We should wait for the doctor to examine you. What brought on this illness?'

'Damn you, I've had it before and the doctor always gives

me opium. He said the stomach is ulcerated and pain relief is the only course.'

As Dorothea led him to a bed she smelled arak, the local spirit, on his breath. A fug of it permeated his clothing. 'Will you change yourself into a nightshirt?' she asked. 'I'll fetch you a clean one.'

'For God's sake, woman, I can't stay here. I'm needed back on the line. Just get me some opium NOW.'

His pupils were tiny pinpricks and he was sweating profusely, although his skin was cool to the touch. Dorothea took his pulse and was alarmed at its unsteadiness. 'Let me find a doctor.'

'Be quick about it. I haven't got all day.' He was a most unpleasant character, she decided, but even the worst sorts deserved care.

She walked the corridors until she spotted the kindly Dr White doing a round in ward nine. She hurried up and as soon as she told him the name of the patient he nodded. 'He's an opium addict. Since your friend Miss Davis barricaded the store cupboards, he hasn't been able to top up his supplies.'

Dorothea was astonished. 'But he's a captain, in charge of a hundred men. And he stinks of alcohol.'

'He probably drank alcohol when he ran out of opium but found it was a poor substitute, so he came here.'

'Do you think he is pretending to have stomach pains? He is certainly making a lot of noise about it.'

Dr White shook his head. 'No, I expect he's genuinely in agony as his system craves more of the drug. How much stock do we have?'

'I believe there is plenty for our needs. A consignment arrived last week.'

'In that case, give Captain Lethbridge half a bottle and tell him to take nine drops of tincture in a glass of water. As you know, the normal dose is ten. You could also dose him with Miss Davis's bitters, for their laxative effect – but leave out the port wine.'

'Should I recommend bed rest?'

'No, send him back out. When he comes here again, as he assuredly will, give him a smaller amount and tell him to reduce the dose to eight drops. It's for his own good, although I doubt he will see it that way.'

Four days after Dorothea's visit to the 8th Hussars' camp, Major Dodds called at the hospital to speak to her, in response to the letter she had left for him. She was overwhelmed with relief when he poked his head round the door of her ward and introduced himself. He was a tall, slender man with a decorative squiggle of moustache and curly locks like a girl's.

'Thank you so much for taking the time to see me,' she said, and walked out into the hallway to talk in private with him.

'Not at all,' he replied. 'I can't tell you how deeply saddened I was by Charlie's death. I miss him every day. He was a good friend.'

Dorothea wondered if Charlie had told him about her, the sister-in-law who tried to prevent his wedding? If so, nothing in Major Dodds' manner gave it away. 'I am anxious to hear how my sister fared after receiving news of his death. She has not yet arrived back in London and I'm worried.'

'Lucy was very calm,' he replied. 'I don't believe I saw her shed a tear, but she wanted to sit vigil with Charlie, and after we buried him she refused to leave the graveside. I did my best to persuade her, of course, but was forced to return to camp on urgent business. We left her with a horse so she could make her own way back. I'm sorry, but I didn't see her after that.'

Dorothea pursed her lips. Lucy had never been a confident rider. 'And the horse?'

'It was in camp the following morning. I assume she came back in the dead of night then got a lift down to Balaklava for the first ship out of here. I'm told she left most of her possessions but perhaps that's because she couldn't carry them.'

'Is it possible the horse could have thrown her and she lay injured and undiscovered?' She felt a surge of anger that no one had cared enough to check she was safe.

Major Dodds was adamant this could not have been the case. 'The track between the camp and our officers' graveyard on Cathcart's Hill is a very well-trodden one, I'm sorry to say. I suggest you ask the Balaklava harbourmaster, who will most likely have a record of finding her a berth that morning. Your sister is a memorable lady.'

'What day was this?' Dorothea would need a date to check the harbour records.

'I thought you knew. It was the night of 23rd December when Charlie was shot and his burial was on the 24th. On Christmas Day, there was a service at the chaplain's room in Balaklava, where we prayed for his soul, and I know she was not present at that. I sent someone to tell her about it but she was nowhere to be found.'

'I suppose you are too busy to look after every grieving widow,' Dorothea said, somewhat sharply, outraged that no one had raised the alarm at this point.

'Yes, I am,' Dodds said, seeming oblivious to her scorn. 'But I am sure you will find your sister is safe and well and has simply found herself on a slow boat with many stops along the way.'

Poor Lucy, all alone on Christmas Day, when Dorothea was eating mince pies at a hotel in Constantinople, just across the Black Sea. It was agonising to think they had been so close, and yet so far apart.

The harbourmaster knew Lucy from Dorothea's description, but could not be of any assistance in locating her either:

'I certainly did not find her a berth on Christmas Day. Only a couple of smaller boats went out. The next day ...' He checked a large leather-bound ledger, running his finger along each line as he read it. 'Yes, the *Agamemnon* and the *Nonpareil* left port bound for Constantinople. I suppose she could have got on one of them without me noticing. I don't have eyes in the back of my head. But I can't think why she would not have come to me if she were seeking passage. We had made each other's acquaintance some weeks earlier.'

Dorothea panicked at this. If Lucy had not left Crimea, where was she? She rushed back to the hospital kitchen and burst in.

'Elizabeth, what shall I do? My sister didn't board a ship after her husband's death. She has not been seen for months.' She sat down, trembling, her mind leaping through the possibilities, each more terrifying than the last. 'Is there a friend no one knows of with whom she is sheltering? Is she dead, her body lying abandoned for wild animals to feast on? Has she been taken prisoner by the Russians? Where do they keep their prisoners? Elizabeth, what shall I *do*?'

For once, Elizabeth didn't have any answers.

While Dorothea agonised over what to try next in the search for her sister, her days were filled with work on the wards. There were no major offensives in February or March, but still men were being wounded by shelling and rifle fire, as well as struck down by sickness. Dorothea's patients weren't just British: some French, Turkish, Maltese and Croatians lay in her wards, and in one corner there were three Russian prisoners. She communicated with them as best she could, using improvised sign language with those who spoke no English, and always made sure to ask if they had seen a pretty blonde English lady, but none had. Spring began to show its face in the fields outside: tiny wildflowers pushed up their heads and unfurled to display white, yellow, pink and blue petals; new types of bird call were heard as migrants passed overhead; and the weather swung from chilly one day to temperate the next.

On a day in mid-March, the door to one of Dorothea's wards was pushed open and a large, dark-skinned woman walked in wearing a bright yellow dress, blue bonnet and red hair ribbons. Her hips were almost as broad as the doorway and she had a deep, fleshy cleavage. Every bit of her dripped with jewellery: glittery necklaces, dangling earrings, clinking bracelets, jewelled clips in her hair, and a large gold brooch on her breast. She was wheeling a rickety trolley and called in a loud voice with a West Indies accent: 'Tea, coffee, lemonade, cakes. Anyone for refreshments?'

The soldiers couldn't believe their eyes and neither could Dorothea. She approached the woman but before she could ask who she was, a brown bejewelled hand was thrust out to clasp hers and the woman's face crinkled into a smile like sunshine. 'Mary Seacole, late arrived from Jamaica by way of London and Constantinople. Now, my dear, you must tell me which patients are not well enough to sample my wares. I wouldn't want to harm any of these pore, sufferin' boys. Here – try one of my sponge cakes; they're light as clouds, if I say so myself.'

Dorothea took the proffered cake as she introduced herself, and asked, 'What is your business in the Crimea?'

'I'm opening a hostelry at Kadikoi. Got me some Turkish carpenters working on the building right now and we'll open in a coupla weeks. Thought I'd come and offer some of these boys a sample in the meantime.' She glanced round to see several of them waving hands in the air to attract her attention, keen for a change from Elizabeth's worthy soups and stews. 'You don't mind, do you? Everything's goin' free for today, and tomorrow I'll only charge those as can afford it.'

Dorothea couldn't resist biting into her sponge cake, and found it light and flavourful, with a hint of vanilla. 'I don't see why not. But how on earth did you make these? There is no butter to be had in Balaklava.'

'I'll give you the recipe, dear. Some of my formulae are a carefully guarded secret but not this one, which relies primarily on egg whites.' She winked and turned to push her trolley to the first bed, her huge yellow-clad behind swaying.

Dorothea tried to stay nearby as Mrs Seacole circled the wards dispensing cakes and drinks. The effect of her extravagant appearance and cheerful nature was almost as uplifting as the treats. 'I'm a doctress myself, as well as a hotelier,' she told Dorothea. 'I hastened over from Jamaica after I heard about the cholera hitting the troops, because I have some infallible treatments for cholera based on long experience. Have you any cases?'

'Not since I've been here,' Dorothea said. 'I arrived at the end of January.'

'You want to watch when the weather gets warmer. That disease can raise its ugly head out of nowhere.'

Dorothea told her the latest research in London indicated that the illness was carried in infected water and Mary nodded: 'That's as may be. But I can't believe folks are still prescribing opium, which blocks the gut, instead of purging the toxins.'

'You are an advocate of purgatives?'

'Why, of course I am. Purging and rehydration at the same time. I used my remedies to treat British soldiers in Jamaica during the outbreak of '52 an' I believe in all modesty I know more about curing the cholera than anyone else in the world.'

Dorothea was curious about her methods. 'I'd be most interested to compare notes with you some time.'

'Come to my hotel, the British Hotel, by the railway sidings at Kadikoi. We'll be open Thursday next, if I keep bawlin' loud enough at those Turkish Johnnies. Come be my first guest.'

Dorothea didn't make it to the opening day but the following week, she visited the British Hotel along with Elizabeth Davis, thinking it might be a good place to ask around for sightings of Lucy. At first sight it was a ramshackle hut made from planks of wood and sheets of iron held together with odd pieces of rope. Inside there was a counter backed by shelves full of goods, and some tables and chairs were set out. Delicious smells permeated: coffee, lemons, home baking, cinnamon, and some strong herbal aromas that were harder to identify. Mary Seacole came bustling out to greet them from behind the counter.

'Miss Gray, it's an honour.' She led them to a table as Dorothea introduced Elizabeth. 'What can I get you good ladies? I have meat pies, mulled claret and rice pudding, or lemonade and sponge cakes?'

Both Elizabeth and Dorothea opted for a meat pie and a cup of tea. Mary sat down to chat with them while her assistant, whom she called 'Jew Johnny', heated the pies. She explained the struggles she had had to open this place: how the British commanders refused her permission to set up closer to the front, how the local Tartars pilfered every single thing that was not tied down, how hard it was to keep rats out of her storeroom, but how glad she was that she had employed Turkish workers. 'These boys are starving. They have no supplies coming in. Nothing. The shortages of food at the British camp are as nothing compared to what the Turks are going through. Everyone is so darned mean about those boys, saying they are cowards and talking 'gainst them. I thought we were here to protect them from the Russians but it sure don't look that way on the ground ...'

When the warmed pies arrived she left them to eat in peace, and Elizabeth and Dorothea marvelled at the tasty flavours. They were sure they could detect cinnamon and there was a kick of a hotter spice as well. The meat had been cooked for hours and was more succulent than anything they had eaten since leaving England.

As they dined, a woman in a smart plaid riding jacket and skirt arrived on horseback, dismounted and tied up her animal. 'I'll have tea and two of your sponge cakes,' she called, taking a seat two tables away from them.

She glanced briefly at Dorothea and Elizabeth, and Elizabeth introduced herself, forcing the woman to do the same: 'Fanny Duberly,' she said coldly, without extending her hand. 'My husband is Quartermaster of the 8th Hussars.'

Dorothea leaned forward. 'Did you know my sister? Mrs Lucy Harvington, wife of Captain Charlie Harvington?'

Mrs Duberly sniffed. 'I made her acquaintance but I didn't know her well, of course. We mixed in quite different circles.'

Dorothea ignored the apparent snub. 'I'm anxious that she seems to have vanished after Charlie's death. No one knows where she is. I wonder if you have seen her since Christmas Eve?'

Mrs Duberly shook her head firmly. 'She simply took off without saying goodbye to any of us. Of course I don't stay in the camp,' she added. 'I have a yacht near Lord Raglan's. In fact, I'm dining with him tonight.'

Elizabeth turned her head so Mrs Duberly couldn't see her rolling her eyes.

'Do you have any idea where Lucy could be?' Dorothea persisted. 'I'm really most worried about her.'

Mrs Duberly tutted and turned away for a moment, as if making a decision. 'I'm sorry to say this, Miss Gray, but from my knowledge of your sister I would not be surprised to hear that she has already found herself a new husband. She was a most flirtatious girl, who dressed quite inappropriately for the environment here and turned the heads of several of the men. My own husband Henry was seduced by her wiles and ended up going to a lot of trouble to ship her luggage around the peninsula and have it delivered to her. She struck me as the kind of woman who will always find some man to look after her, one way or another.'

Dorothea rose, every instinct urging her to slap Mrs Duberly across the face. She had never slapped anyone before but that's because she had never heard anyone insulting her sister. Elizabeth grabbed her skirt and stopped her from committing violence, but answered on her behalf.

'You should keep a better eye on that husband of yours. It's little wonder he's running around doing favours for the first pretty girl to come along if the alternative is looking at your sour face all the time.'

Mrs Duberly was rendered speechless by the insult and Mary Seacole bustled out from behind the counter to restore calm. 'Ladies, may I offer you all a glass of warmed ruby wine?'

Fanny Duberly rose with a swish of her skirts. 'No thank you, Mrs Seacole. I will come back another time when the company is more convivial.' She knocked over a chair on her way out but didn't stop to pick it up.

Dorothea and Elizabeth stared at each other wide-eyed. 'Have you ever heard the like?' Elizabeth commented. 'Such rudeness!'

'Lucy is not at all like that,' Dorothea rushed to explain. 'She is gregarious but she would never flirt with another woman's husband. Never.'

'Some folks just have strange ways about them. I get all sorts in here,' Mary Seacole soothed, pouring out two glasses of ruby wine. Dorothea quietly slipped hers to Elizabeth when their hostess was not looking, with the result that she became rather more talkative than usual, and a little less steady on her feet.

*

April began and the days grew warm and sunny but they brought Dorothea no further letters from home. She wrote to Miss Nightingale at the Barracks Hospital describing her sister and beseeching her to ask her staff if anyone had seen such a lady, but a terse reply came back saying that Dorothea should be aware there was no time to search for missing relatives. She thought of Lucy every morning when she woke, and every night when she went to bed, her heart aching with worry for her poor sister, but in between there was little time to think of anything apart from her work. She knew she needed to go looking for Lucy but she had an obligation to her patients – and where would she even start? On optimistic days Dorothea hoped that Lucy would simply turn up with news of an adventure to explain her disappearance; but on pessimistic days, she began to prepare herself for the worst.

Rumours spread that the army were to launch a major attack on Sevastopol within the week. Work had been proceeding on a new hospital in Balaklava, close to the ruins of the clifftop Genoese fort, where the operating theatres would be situated. Patients requiring surgery after battle would be taken there, while the General Hospital would treat all the other sick and injured. Miss Langston asked amongst the nurses if anyone was willing to work in the operating theatre and when Dorothea said she was, she was told curtly she should report for work there the very next day.

Chapter Twenty-six

When Dorothea arrived at the Castle Hospital – a row of prefabricated huts built along the clifftop overlooking Balaklava harbour – she was immediately questioned about her experience by four different doctors. Looking around, she saw the hospital was well-supplied with new beds and mattresses and more linen than they could possibly use – all sent by well-meaning members of the British public. There were patients of many nationalities, some of them muleteers who had hoped to make a profit from the war and had been injured in the fighting, others recruits from different regions of the vast Ottoman Empire, as well as British and French soldiers. Each doctor was in charge of two or three huts, and they all seemed keen for her to work with them, but it was a tall, ginger-whiskered Scotsman called Mr Crawford who prevailed.

'What languages do you speak?' he asked in his lilting brogue.

'French, and a smattering of Italian,' she replied. She had learned them from her governess.

'No Scots? Will we need a translator then?' he twinkled.

Dorothea smiled: 'I can just about discern your meaning so I'm sure we'll get by.'

'Good! Now, I have my professional peculiarities and like nurses who will humour me. I require my instruments to be rinsed in boiled water between patients.' He showed her the gleaming set of tools he had brought with him, neatly arranged in a wooden case with a blue satin lining. 'And at the end of the working day, I like the operating table to be washed down and the floor mopped clean. Does this put you off working with me?'

Dorothea admitted she had not assisted in an operating theatre before, but added: 'I attended a lecture on the subject of cleanliness and it sounded convincing to me. The idea of mingling one man's blood with that of the next seems to me rather grim. Certainly if I were to be operated upon, I should not wish it.'

He continued: 'I like to work quickly, not in order to set any national records but so I can give the patient a minimal amount of chloroform. An above-the-knee amputation should take no more than seven minutes if we understand each other's ways. I hope you will not faint on me. I've got no time for fainters.'

Dorothea promised she would endeavour not to faint, adding that in her work so far she had proved to have a strong stomach.

'In my Edinburgh hospital, the survival rate of my patients is over sixty per cent, but out here so far it is under forty, because the injuries are so very severe. I will need your help to raise it, and I will require superlative post-operative care. So long as you don't consider it impertinent, I'd like you to accompany me on a ward round so I can check your dressing skills.'

Dorothea was surprised and at first she felt rather patronised, but they walked together round one ward, discussing the injuries presented, and she liked the way he bantered with the patients. 'I know your type: you'd do anything to get off sentry duty,' he joked with one lad of seventeen years who had lost his right arm. 'You came here for a rest, did you?' he asked another with a nasty head wound. She changed the dressings on half a dozen patients under Mr Crawford's scrutiny, following his instructions on the position of strapping here and the application of a poultice there. She told him of her horror at finding wounds crawling with maggots when soldiers arrived in Scutari, and he surprised her by saying that wasn't necessarily a bad thing.

'Repulsive as they may be, maggots can debride rotting tissue without injuring the healthy. In some cases they may prevent the onset of gangrene.'

Dorothea wrinkled her nose. 'I hope you will not require me to introduce them to wounds.'

He thought about it for some seconds: 'It's not a crazy idea, but I suppose it would be generally unpopular with you faint-hearted nurses. Let's see if we can make a difference by more conventional methods.'

'It takes all sorts,' Elizabeth twinkled when she and Dorothea exchanged notes at the end of the day. She was still working at the General Hospital so they did not see each other until they went to bed. 'I had a doctor once who made me clip his fingernails and trim his eyebrows. They do have their little ways.'

Elizabeth had some worrying news to impart: the warm weather had brought a resurgence of cholera and three cases had been admitted to the hospital. They were being kept in isolation, but no one gave them much chance of survival.

Dorothea had a pang of worry about Lucy. Was she safe from cholera wherever she was? 'We should purchase some of Mary Seacole's cholera remedy,' she suggested. 'If her baking skills are anything to go by, it could be miraculous.'

Elizabeth agreed to pass on the suggestion, and added she would buy a bottle for the two of them so it would be on hand in case they should succumb.

On the 9th April, the long-awaited attack on Sevastopol started. Huge numbers of shells rained down, filling the air with smoke and thunder, and everyone at Castle Hospital braced themselves to receive trainloads of wounded. Two hospital ships were moored and provisioned at Balaklava to transport those who needed long-term convalescence to Scutari. The grumbling about Lord Raglan's shortcomings as a commander continued, and Mr Crawford was one of the critics: 'Everyone knew the date on which the bombardment would start; the common soldier was even writing home to his mother about it. There is no doubt the Russians had been informed and their batteries and earthworks well secured,' he opined. 'This attack is a reckless waste of lives.'

Wounded men trickled in. Most injuries were as a result of recoil from the big guns or accidental fire from their own side. Dorothea was nervous assisting at her first operation with Mr Crawford. She hoped she would not let him down by becoming nauseous or faint when his knife cut into flesh, but in fact she found she could stay clear-headed by focusing on what needed to be done. She thought about the instruments rather than the incision, about the patient rather than what was being done to them.

Mr Crawford's instructions were clear and precise. Three patients needed shell fragments or bullets removed from their flesh, and Dorothea held out a basin to receive them, then threaded the needle with silkworm suture for Mr Crawford to close the wounds again. His freckled hands were quick and skilful. At their first leg amputation, she poured two drops of chloroform onto a rag and held it over the terrified soldier's mouth, murmuring words of comfort as he drifted into unconsciousness. At Mr Crawford's request, she passed him his long, thin knife, which he used to slice through the flesh below the knee, then his bone saw so he could cut through the tibia and fibula. The grinding noise was rather grim but Dorothea focused on soaking up the blood that was pumping from the femoral artery and soon the lower limb was detached. Mr Crawford had left a long flap of skin to fold over the wound and finished it with neat, sure stitches, checking his handiwork from all sides before calling for porters to carry the man to a ward. Dorothea breathed a sigh of relief: she had got through an amputation without faltering, and now she was sure she would do fine as a surgical nurse.

She was by the soldier's side when he came round later, queasy from the chloroform but anxious to know how the operation had gone.

'Am I going to make it, Sister?' he asked.

It was always a difficult question to answer because she didn't like to give false hope, but in this instance she answered, 'Don't worry, you're in good hands. And the leg is only lost below the knee so it will be easier for you to walk again.' She gave him some opium for the pain, mopped his brow with a cool cloth and tucked the blanket round him.

As the opium took effect, he became a little delirious, asking, 'Can't I have a kiss, Maude? Go on, just a little one on the lips,' before drifting off to sleep.

Next morning, as Dorothea changed his dressing, she couldn't resist teasing him: 'So who is this Maude? And is she often so forward as to kiss you?'

The poor lad blushed crimson to the roots of his hair and mumbled apologies.

Dorothea was pleased to note that Mr Crawford's handiwork had been successful: the stump had stopped oozing and there was no sign of infection. It would have been hard to work so intensively with a surgeon whose work she did not respect.

*

Towards the end of April, Dorothea was working in one of the Castle Hospital huts when the door opened and a party of three fashionably dressed ladies in riding gear entered. Dorothea blinked, wondering if she was hallucinating. They wore tight-fitting velvet jackets with peplums, full silk-taffeta riding skirts and plumed hats in sprigged maroon, forest green and golden bronze, as if on a day trip to Royal Ascot.

Dorothea approached the party and a man, who appeared to be some kind of tour guide, stepped forwards. 'Good afternoon,' he said, bowing slightly. 'I'm showing these ladies some of the sights of the Crimean War and wondered if you would mind us looking round your hospital?'

Before she could reply, one of the ladies interrupted: 'We've just ridden along the valley where the valiant Light Brigade charged and it's full of the most beautiful wildflowers, as if they've sprung from the blood of the men killed there. It was most moving.'

'And we walked along a redoubt and looked over into Sevastopol,' another joined in gaily. 'It was such fun, but shortly after we passed the Russians started firing. They only just missed us!'

'You don't mind if we look around the wards and chat to some of the patients, do you?' the man asked again.

Mr Crawford had entered the hut and overheard their exchange. 'I'd appreciate it if you would stick with Nurse Gray,'

227

he said. 'She will direct you to patients who are sufficiently well for a visit. Some are too poorly for any …' – he hesitated, choosing his words carefully – 'additional excitement.'

Dorothea was disgusted by the festive air of the group and would have banned their visit entirely, left to her own devices. Did they not realise there were men in the room who were dying? Was death to become a spectator sport? But Mr Crawford had said she must guide them around, and so she did, with veiled resentment.

First she introduced the ladies to a gunner who'd had eleven shards of shrapnel removed from his back, so he had to lie on his stomach while the wounds healed; he twisted his head to smile up at them. Next they met an infantryman who had lost a hand while cleaning his Minié rifle. And then she took them to a patient with a deep thigh wound that had succumbed to gangrene. She removed the dressing so they could see the blackish-green putrefying flesh and experience the rotting smell of the thick, oozing pus; they had said they wanted to see the sights of the war, after all.

There was a shriek and one of the ladies fainted, fortunately being caught by their guide before hitting the floor. Dorothea fetched a chair and some smelling salts to revive her and as she administered them, she caught a glint of amusement in Mr Crawford's eyes. The touring party hurried out soon afterwards, and he came over for a word.

'Of all the patients on the ward, it was interesting you should choose to introduce them to our gangrene patient. I imagine, like me, that you were finding the frivolity of the lady tourist rather hard to stomach.'

'It was my first experience. I didn't know that such a thing existed. Had you encountered them before?'

'I've met several parties of lady tourists, who have sailed out here on their yachts to view the sights. Did you hear there is now a racetrack behind the British camp where you can bet on your horse of choice, or enjoy a lavish picnic? I think it might require one of the lady tourists to be shot for them to show more respect for the fact that this is a war. Perhaps I shall arrange it.'

His expression was resigned as he turned away, but Dorothea was in a bad temper about the lady tourists all morning.

One evening in early May, Dorothea's heart leapt when a messenger brought her a letter from her father. She skimmed the first page in which he whined about the pain in his back, saying that Henderson was quite incapable of administering a poultice correctly and asking if Dorothea would please hurry home. Poor Papa; she missed him. Now they were so far apart she even sympathised with his hypochondria. He gave her Adelaide Cresswell's address, as she had requested, and only mentioned in a postscript that Lucy had still not arrived in London. It was clear he did not appreciate the situation as he wrote, 'Please ask her to hurry up, because I require her company.'

It was now more than four months since Lucy had last been seen and Dorothea felt sick with anxiety every time she thought of her. She could picture her so clearly – laughing at the antics of the squirrels in Russell Square, or singing a beautiful melody – and it seemed impossible she could be dead. Lucy was too young, too full of vigour. But if not, had she been taken prisoner by the Russians? How would they treat their captives? If she was being held inside the besieged town of Sevastopol, she must be starving. Did they have hospitals in the city? Fresh water? Was she being abused by her captors? Dorothea lay awake at night, endlessly going over the possibilities and trying to come up with a plan to find her, but there seemed little she could do except wait till the war's end then renew her search.

She got up at first light and wrote to Adelaide Cresswell, introducing herself and asking if she could think of anyone to whom Lucy had become attached during her time overseas, someone to whom she might have fled after Charlie's death. It seemed a long shot, but for the time being it was the only one she had left.

Chapter Twenty-seven

5th May 1855

An important visitor arrived in Balaklava that spring: Miss Florence Nightingale, no less, had decided to visit the battle-field outposts and try to impose the rigorous standards she had introduced in Scutari. Elizabeth Davis told Dorothea that a Sanitary Commission had been sent to Scutari by the new Prime Minister, Lord Palmerston, to investigate the extremely high fatality rate in the hospital. They had found the barracks building was sited on top of a festering cesspit, that excrement was seeping into the water supply and that one of the drains was blocked by a decomposing horse carcass. Miss Nightingale had sought to keep the wards clean and fresh, but every time she opened a window poisonous vapours were creeping in. Suddenly Dorothea had a vivid recollection of the vile smell of the cellars at the Barracks Hospital, and she shuddered.

'And now Miss Nightingale has come to Crimea to impose the Sanitary Commission's recommendations on us,' Elizabeth continued. 'I've already had her poking around in my kitchen asking questions about the provisions. She brought a French chef to advise us on providing a more varied diet for the men. Ridiculous! The menu is as varied as it could possibly be, given the ingredients we have to work with.' She snorted and clattered the poker she was using to stir the embers in the stove in their room.

Later that day, Miss Nightingale breezed into Dorothea's ward at the Castle Hospital, a brief nod her only acknowledgement they had met before, and there was no mention of the letter Dorothea had written to her about Lucy. She was followed by Mrs Roberts, who was making notes in a little book. Dorothea watched, annoyed, as Miss Nightingale began her own ward round without so much as a by your leave. At each bed she bent to ask the occupant how he was feeling, to check the wound dressing and the cleanliness of the bedding. She called Dorothea across to one bed where a smear of fresh blood had oozed through a dressing onto the sheet and insisted that the sheet be changed straight away. Dorothea bit her tongue and complied, although as far as she was aware Miss Nightingale had no official jurisdiction in Crimea.

'How do you manage without a proper kitchen at this hospital?' she asked. 'Surely meals are cold before they are served to these poor men?'

Dorothea assured her that porters were capable of bringing up food from the General Hospital very quickly, while still perfectly warm, but Miss Nightingale was looking for areas she could improve and decided this was one. A new kitchen must be built at the Castle Hospital. Dorothea knew Elizabeth would be furious. Miss Nightingale also visited their medicine supply cupboard along with Mr Fitzgerald and reeled off a list of remedies she felt were missing. 'There's no sulphuric acid! How on earth do you manage without it? And I don't see any senna pods.'

Mr Fitzgerald meekly wrote a list, promising to see what he could do.

'No, don't *see*, Mr Fitzgerald. Just *do*!'

She turned her piercing gaze on Dorothea. 'Nurse Gray, do you write to the mothers of the men who die?'

'I try,' Dorothea faltered. 'But it's not always possible. Some are without identification and never regain consciousness, while others pass through quickly on their way elsewhere. But I was much taken with the example you set in Scutari and have endeavoured when I can to write a letter for the soldier, if he is able to dictate one, or to contact his family directly when he is not. We have very little time ...' She tailed off, realising that Miss Nightingale's attention had already shifted to the organisation of the linen cupboard.

'Miss Nightingale, before you go ... I wonder if you were able to ask if anyone has seen my sister in Scutari? She has been missing for almost six months and I'm most anxious about her.'

The dark eyes turned on her and Dorothea thought she saw a flash of compassion, just for an instant, but the words were formal: 'I'm surprised at you, Nurse Gray. You must surely realise the impossibility of me taking time to find one individual in the midst of all this suffering.'

Dorothea nodded, downcast, and Miss Nightingale strode out to the corridor, followed by her entourage. Mr Crawford and another surgeon were hiding round a corner but they fled as the party advanced, keen to avoid an introduction to the irksome visitor. The patients were anxious to meet her, though, and beamed after a visit as if it had been Queen Victoria herself at their bedside. Dorothea eavesdropped on a few conversations and was impressed by the way Miss Nightingale listened carefully to each soldier's story, asking questions about his family and how he came to be in the army. She had the talent of making each one feel as though he mattered.

She may have been popular with the patients, but the same certainly could not be said for the staff. Dorothea and

Elizabeth now slept in a newly built hut on the hillside and every night when Dorothea returned, she had fresh complaints about Miss Nightingale, who had completely changed the kitchen arrangements and rearranged the stores so that nothing could be found any more. She complained that Miss Nightingale had made an almighty fuss after spotting a rat outside a pantry, and Elizabeth had remarked that it was *by design* she kept the rats outside rather than inside the food store.

'If she had seen all the rats when I arrived here, nesting in the pantry they were. Their babes were being born in the vats of flour that were used to make the men's bread. Since I set up my traps and barricades there has not been a single instance of a rat found in our store cupboards, not one, and she makes a huge hurly-burly about seeing one in the corridor outside. Pah!' She was shaking with rage. 'Someone had better get that woman out of here or I won't be responsible for my actions.'

It wasn't some*one* but some*thing* that incapacitated Miss Nightingale: eight days after her arrival in Balaklava she succumbed to a fever and collapsed. She was carried in a litter to one of the huts at the Castle Hospital and attended by the Principal Medical Officer, Dr Arthur Anderson, who said it was among the worst cases of Crimean fever he had come across. This was a strange illness they had encountered on the peninsula in which normal fever symptoms were accompanied by nosebleeds, black stools and a painfully swollen liver. Mrs Roberts took charge of nursing the famous patient but Dorothea offered to relieve her for a few hours at a time when she wanted to rest. Mrs Roberts was reluctant to leave the hut so they had another bed delivered, in which she could sleep while Dorothea sat cooling Miss Nightingale's skin with damp cloths and dripping water through her lips to keep her hydrated. Her hair had been shaved to cool the brain but still her skin was burning to the touch and she moaned and raved like one demented.

'There is a phantom, a Persian phantom,' she mumbled, tossing her head from side to side. 'It's too much money. Tell them not to do it.' She suddenly gripped Dorothea's hand in a fierce hold. 'You *must* stop them.'

Dorothea agreed she would stop them.

'There are three principles. Three. Are you sure you know what you are doing?' Miss Nightingale raised her head from the pillow and glared at her, still gripping her hand.

'I understand. Three principles,' Dorothea repeated. 'Now please try to rest.'

It was alarming to see this titan quite so gravely ill. The soldiers idolised her and the British public had more or less sanctified her; it would be a massive blow to morale if she should die.

Word of Miss Nightingale's illness spread. One day Mary Seacole came trundling into Dorothea's ward, bringing with her the aroma of sweetmeats and freshly baked bread that seemed to hang around her person.

'I've brought Miss Nightingale a bottle of my fever potion. They won't take it from the likes of me but p'rhaps you can give it to her?' She smiled broadly, showing off her pearly teeth.

'I doubt Mrs Roberts will give it to her unless you are able to tell me what it contains,' Dorothea said, peering at the reddish-brown liquid. 'She is very protective, as if Miss Nightingale is her own child.'

'It's a remedy I've taken myself on many occasions and prescribed to hundreds. It has never failed to cure fever.'

'Even so, she will want more reassurance.'

Mary was reluctant but at last she gave Dorothea a list of her ingredients: pomegranate rind boiled with powdered cinnamon, guava fruit and shavings of bitter bark from the dogwood tree. 'I can't get the dogwood bark or guava here

235

so this precious elixir is a bottle I brought with me from Jamaica. Give Miss Nightingale half a glass every four hours and I guarantee the fever will break within a day.'

Dorothea decided had it been her she would have taken the potion, which sounded innocuous at least, but Mrs Roberts refused outright.

'Miss Nightingale did not visit the British Hotel as she heard of its reputation for rowdiness. Fresh pies and cakes for the troops is one thing, but too much ruby wine is quite another. Mrs Seacole is a bartender, not a physician, although I hear she tries to masquerade as a healer. I know I speak for Miss Nightingale in refusing her remedy.'

Mrs Roberts proved a formidable door-keeper and Dorothea was delighted when Fanny Duberly, who had come to offer her best wishes, was refused admittance. Mrs Roberts also tried to refuse Lord Raglan but was forced to admit him when his rank and position was emphasised. By that stage, Dorothea knew that Miss Nightingale had turned the corner. The fever had passed, as had the hallucinations, but she was still so weak she couldn't have summoned the strength to get out of bed. It was going to be some time before she was capable of returning to work.

On the 5th June, a litter carried Britain's national heroine down to the harbour and she set sail for Scutari, where she promised to rest as much as possible until her health fully returned. The date of her departure was not chosen at random: the 6th June marked the commencement of the next major British and French attack on Sevastopol, so Miss Nightingale's ship pulled out of Balaklava just in time to avoid the onslaught.

Throughout the 6th and 7th June, Dorothea was by Mr Crawford's side as casualties were brought by train and then by litter to the Castle Hospital. Patients on stretchers were left on the path outside to be carried in by porters as soon as the previous operation was completed. Soldiers who died during surgery were taken out the back way for burial, while those still under the effects of chloroform were taken to a ward to recover consciousness.

They worked steadily, using the systems they had developed over the previous two months. Dorothea kept a pot of water on the boil to dip the instruments into between patients, using a large pair of tongs. She had to judge precisely how long she could leave them so that they would be cleansed of the last patient's blood but Mr Crawford would not burn his hand when he came to use them again minutes later. She changed the blades on his ebony-handled amputation knives and sharpened his bone saw, checking that the forceps, bullet extractor and bone nippers were all in their correct places. She talked softly to each patient as she put the chloroform rag over his mouth and nose, saying, 'Breathe deeply, this will make you sleepy.' Outside, the shelling continued, but they existed in a bubble where the only thing that mattered was the patient they were operating on. Casualties tailed off as the light faded in the evenings and they returned to their rooms for a few hours' sleep before starting again the following morning.

On the 8th June, the British and French armies broke out of their trenches and charged towards the enemy, causing the casualty rate to multiply within hours. Normal systems soon broke down as the flow of wounded increased and twice that morning patients were brought to the operating table and given chloroform before anyone except a porter had checked if they actually needed an operation. Mr Crawford asked Dorothea if she would step outside when each new trainload of wounded arrived to assess the incoming patients, and select the ones most in need of surgery who might have a chance of living through it. As the queues grew ever longer, stretching the length of the hospital, she was daunted by the enormity of her task.

'Use your best judgement,' Mr Crawford told her, in his calm, measured way. 'That's all any of us can do.'

It was a position of great trust and she had to put emotion to one side. There was no point in prioritising the gentle-faced young lad who had taken a shell in the stomach and was injured so badly that the slippery coils of his intestine were spilling out. He whispered to her, 'Please, Ma'am, please,' while clutching her hand with all his fading strength but she knew he had lost too much blood and would certainly have died on the operating table. She grabbed an orderly and asked him to administer opium then wash and shave the boy while keeping his wound covered so he could not look down and see it.

'What's the point in washing him? He's dying anyway,' the orderly said, and Dorothea felt like slapping him.

'Just hope that some day someone does the same for you!' she snapped. 'And stay with him. Keep him company. Try to put yourself in his position.'

There was an officer with his face shot off. His right eye socket was empty, the flesh of the cheeks shattered so the underlying bone was visible, and the mouth just a gaping hole. She gave instructions on how his wounds should be bandaged but knew there was nothing anyone could do to restore his features. Only time would tell if his face would heal into any semblance of a normal countenance. He must have been in excruciating pain but kept thanking her, over and over again, like a well-bred gentleman at a garden party, only adding, 'Won't I think of my friends the Russians when-ever I look in a looking-glass!'

One young soldier gave her his money and pocket watch, making her promise to get them to his brother, who was in the Lancashire Fusiliers, if he should die. She took them but told him she fully expected to hand them back the following morning after he'd had a good night's rest and a warm meal.

For surgery, Dorothea chose soldiers with bullets embedded in flesh, legs torn half away, or great gashes in arms or chest, clean wounds that Mr Crawford would have a chance of closing before gangrene set in. Where limbs were bleeding profusely, she applied tourniquets so they would not die of blood loss before reaching the operating table.

'I am playing God,' she realised, and found herself praying for His guidance in a way she had not prayed since her youth.

When she had assessed each newly arrived batch of injured soldiers and given directions as to their care, Dorothea returned to the theatre to assist Mr Crawford. His face and hair were splattered with blood, his tweed suit drenched in it, but he worked without stopping, giving his entire attention to the patient on the table in front of him. Sawing through bone took great physical strength and the veins on his neck stood out with the effort but he didn't once stop to rest between patients, so neither did Dorothea. The summer heat made the smells more intense – the metallic scent of blood, the acrid odour of men who had not washed in days, the sweet whiff of chloroform – and caused perspiration to drip down their faces as they worked.

Towards evening, Elizabeth Davis brought them bowls of broth and set them on a side table, but by the time Dorothea got round to taking a spoonful it was cool and unappetising. She had never been squeamish but cleaning all the flesh and sinew and blood on the table and on the floor around it stifled hunger. The squeaky noise of sawing, the slipperiness of blood, the salty taste of perspiration on her lips put her off. No matter how hard she scrubbed her nails, it still felt as if there were scraps of human tissue stuck there. How could she eat with those hands?

As the light faded, Dorothea lit white *fanoos* lanterns and positioned them around the operating table, with her left hand holding one directly above the patient while continuing to pass instruments to Mr Crawford with her right. Before long it made her arm ache but she tried to hold it steady.

'Are there many more left outside?' Mr Crawford asked around midnight.

'Twelve,' she replied. 'Just twelve.' The sound of shelling had died down. There was no news from the battlefield apart from occasional shocked comments from the men, which made little sense to Dorothea: 'We've taken the Quarries, but there are too many in the Redan'; 'The Zouaves have the Mamelon but were driven back from the Malakhov'; and the despairing, 'How can the Russkies have so much fight left in them?'

Rather than waste time going back to their rooms, Dorothea fetched blankets and Mr Crawford slept on the ground outside while she made herself a bed in a store cupboard. She snatched a few hours' sleep then as dawn broke, she rose, washed her face and hands, and went back to the operating tent where she found a queue of stretchers had already formed and Mr Crawford was at his post.

'You must be tired,' she said. The previous day, he had operated for twenty hours.

'Not really,' he replied. 'When there is work to be done, I find a fuel in my veins that keeps me alert. If they could bottle and sell it, it would be more popular than whisky.'

Dorothea agreed. She didn't feel tired, didn't feel hungry or thirsty. She felt she had never used her brain so fully as she did now, trying to do her best for each and every patient to give them a chance of survival.

'And the lack of regular meals is probably rather good for me,' Mr Crawford continued, patting his belly. He wasn't exactly corpulent but the buttons strained somewhat on his grey striped waistcoat.

Dorothea tactfully refrained from comment.

Towards dusk on the 9th June, the trainloads of injured stopped arriving. Dorothea stepped outside to find there were no patients waiting for surgery. She walked round the back of the huts to see if a porter had mistakenly left anyone there, then wandered over to look out at the view over the sea. Suddenly she came upon a shallow pit full of bodies, blackened in the sun. At a rough guess there were perhaps twenty of them. Some were staring hideously. Arms and legs were tangled in each other, a few reaching out as if trying in vain to escape. She staggered backwards and gave a little scream. These men should have been wrapped in sheets and stored in a dignified fashion before prompt burial. Already she could detect the pungent scent of flesh starting to decompose. She supposed the sheer volume of casualties had overwhelmed the system but no one should suffer this indignity after death.

Some movement make her look upwards and high in the sky she saw dark shapes circling. As she watched, a vulture dived at speed and landed on one of the bodies, where it began pecking at the eyes.

'Get off!' Dorothea screamed, her voice shrill with hysteria, her arms flapping uselessly. 'GET OFF!'

Mr Crawford hurried out the back of the operating theatre to see the cause of the commotion. He picked up a stone and hurled it at the bird, causing it to lift into the air, then he grasped Dorothea's arm.

'You shouldn't be here,' he urged. 'Go back inside while I get an orderly to cover this pit.'

When he returned, she was still badly shaken and he suggested, 'Let's go to the General Hospital for dinner, or whatever meal Miss Davis might be serving. It's about time we had some sustenance.'

As they walked he made conversation about the war, and she suspected it was in an attempt to take her mind off the horror of the mass grave.

'The Russians still seem determined to hold their town. In wartime sieges, the aim is to starve the population but I hear the citizens of Sevastopol receive supplies by sea. Raglan has bungled every opportunity and it's commonly thought he's gone senile.' This was a familiar theme in his conversation. 'Did you hear he refers to the French as the enemy, as if we were back at Waterloo?'

Dorothea didn't respond, thinking that if Lucy was being held prisoner in Sevastopol, she was glad to think they were getting supplies.

'Will you stay if the war is lengthy?' he asked. 'Or must you return to your family at some point?'

'I'll stay as long as the war lasts.' For a moment Dorothea was tempted to confide in him about Lucy but decided against it; she didn't want to impose on their professional relationship or make him feel he had to offer assistance.

'Good.' Mr Crawford nodded. 'Me too.'

In the kitchen at the General Hospital they found Elizabeth Davis running at full stretch, doling out platefuls of rabbit stew to all and sundry. Somehow Dorothea managed to eat, despite her head being full of images of those awful blackened corpses.

After they had dined Mr Crawford walked her to her room. 'It's been a difficult day,' he said. 'I hope you are able to forget the sights you have seen and sleep soundly.'

She thought it touching that he was so concerned for her wellbeing and said, 'Thank you. I'll see you in the morning.'

She dozed for a few hours but was disturbed when Elizabeth came to bed around one o'clock and began snoring

242

gently. Dorothea couldn't get back to sleep and a restlessness made her open the door and walk outside in her nightgown into the balmy night air. The black sky was speckled with more stars than she had ever seen before, and she wondered if Lucy might be looking up at them as well. They were like the souls of the men who had died, twinkling brightly in heaven. She had witnessed sights that would haunt her to the grave but at the same time, she had never felt so fully alive.

PART SIX

Chapter Twenty-eight

25th December 1854

Early on Christmas morning, on a hill north of Sevastopol, the sun crept over the horizon, making the frost glisten, but the air temperature remained below freezing. Not a sound could be heard: no birdsong, no human voices or snuffling animals, no shelling, not even a breath of wind. It was a long time since Lucy had moved and she drifted in and out of consciousness, no longer feeling the knife-like cold slicing through her. She wasn't thinking about anything except staying with Charlie. How could she leave him alone in this frozen earth? It would be too cruel. She didn't intend to die with him but at the same time she couldn't think what she would do without him, and so she continued to lie on his grave in a fuzzy state, somewhere between life and death.

In the ear closest to the ground she became aware of a rumbling from deep within the soil. It got louder and now she could feel a vibration travelling through her cheek, like the rattling you heard on a railway track long before the train came into sight. She didn't move but she listened as it became a clattering sound, getting closer and closer.

'*Aman Allahım! Bu ne?*'

It was a male voice, but she couldn't understand what was being said. Next, Lucy felt her shoulders lifted from the ground and opened her eyes to see a man with caramel skin wearing a black fur hat. He exclaimed again then, still holding her with one arm, slipped off his heavy greatcoat and wrapped it around her. He sat down on the ground, cradling her in his lap, and began to rub her arms vigorously.

'Are you English?' he asked softly, his words clear but with a foreign accent, and she nodded. He squeezed his arms tightly around her, trying to transmit some of his body warmth into her. '*Sizi böyle burada nasıl bıraktılar?*' he murmured to himself.

He fished in one pocket of his greatcoat and removed a small leather flagon, unscrewed the top and held it to her lips: 'Drink.'

The liquid had a strong flavour; it didn't taste alcoholic but it was warming. There was ginger in it, she guessed, and the sweetness of some kind of fruit. She could feel it beginning to revive her.

'What are you doing out here? Have you been here all night?'

She tried to talk but her jaw was frozen stiff and wouldn't move. She opened her mouth wide and stretched her lips to loosen them. He held the flask for her to drink again, and she blinked. 'My husband is here,' she managed to mumble at last.

The stranger stared at her with concern through irises so dark they were almost black. 'Your husband would not want you to join him in the grave. This is not India.'

Tears pricked her eyes and she looked away.

'Let me take you back to your camp, where your friends can look after you. You need to warm yourself by a fire, eat some hot food ...'

She shook her head and cried 'No!' with such vehemence he looked puzzled. She expanded: 'I can't go back there. I want to stay here.' Her words were slurred because her tongue, lips and jaw were so numb.

'You will die if you stay here, and I am not going to let that happen. In five minutes we are leaving.'

Lucy opened her mouth to argue, but was suddenly overwhelmed by an upwelling of emotion brought on by this unexpected kindness from a stranger. Tears began slowly at first but soon they were gushing down her cheeks, her nose dripping, her chest aching with the effort of gasping for breath. Her whole body shook with the release of pent-up grief. Instead of trying to stop her, the stranger held her tightly and rubbed her back through the greatcoat. She could smell a slightly fusty scent about him, which was not unpleasant.

'You must have loved him very much,' he said. His dark eyes were full of compassion, almost as if her grief pained him as well.

She realised that in fact she had only known Charlie for a year but it had been the most wonderful year of her short, otherwise uneventful life, and the thought of all she had lost made her cry even harder.

'I'm afraid I do not have a handkerchief,' he apologised, so she fumbled in the folds of her gown and managed to find one of her own.

When the sobbing began to abate, the man stood and lifted her in his arms, still wrapped up in his coat. She saw he had a horse nearby.

'Please. I don't want to go back to the British camp,' she panicked. She wasn't ready to face the hostile women who had called her husband a meater, who might hint that he'd been responsible for his own demise.

'Very well. I know a place close by where you can get warm and rest a while. Would you like to go there?'

For a moment, Lucy wondered if he was planning to kidnap her and sell her to the white slave trade but almost immediately she dismissed the thought. Her instinct was that he seemed a good man; besides, he had offered to take her to the British camp if she wanted.

'Yes, please,' she whispered.

He put his hands around her waist and lifted her onto the horse's back, then mounted, before pulling her around so that she was sitting in front of him, safely enclosed in his arms. *This must have been how Charlie held Susanna*, she thought.

'Forgive me that I don't have a side-saddle. I hope you are not uncomfortable.' He kicked his heels and the horse began to move.

She closed her eyes as they cantered across the bleak Crimean landscape in the pale light of dawn. It felt wrong to leave Charlie's body in that cold grave, but if she kept him firmly in her thoughts, she hoped somehow he would sense it and understand.

They rode for some miles without speaking. Sunlight was creeping slowly across the land but there were no signs of life except the stark outlines of trees against a grey sky. At least it wasn't snowing. She began to feel guilty that her rescuer would be freezing since she still wore his coat, but he showed no sign of it as he focused on driving the horse forward as fast as he could while holding her securely.

After twenty minutes or so they rode through a gateway and he helped her to dismount in front of a sturdy white stone house, two storeys high. She assumed it must be his family home and wondered if his wife would be there, but when he pushed open the door, still supporting her with his other arm, she saw that all the furniture was covered in dustsheets.

'This is a *dacha* belonging to a wealthy Russian family,' he told her. 'They abandoned it last year when fighting came to the area.'

When she realised they were alone in the house Lucy became alarmed. What did he plan to do with her? She shrank against a wall. She would not be able to run or even struggle if he tried to have his way with her, so weakened was she by the cold. How foolish she was to have come here with this foreign stranger! What on earth had she been thinking?

'I will make a fire in the bedroom upstairs so that you can rest awhile,' he said.

He disappeared through a doorway and came back with an armful of logs, which he carried up the sweeping staircase.

Lucy backed into a corner and stood, trembling. She supposed she should run and hide, but she wouldn't get far. Her legs were weak and her toes were on fire with a stabbing pain. What should she do? Her brain wouldn't work properly, befuddled with shock and grief and cold.

The man came down the stairs again, keeping a respectful distance. 'My name is Murad bin Ahmed. I am an officer in the Ottoman army, responsible for finding provisions for the troops. And you?'

'Mrs Lucy Harvington,' she told him, her voice wobbly with nerves. 'I came out here with my husband Charlie, a cavalry captain.'

He nodded. 'Mrs Harvington, I must return to our camp now but I suggest you spend the day resting here. There is a little food in the cellar if you are hungry. I found this place while searching for supplies for our men. I'll come this evening and if you are ready to go back to the British camp I will take you then.'

Lucy felt a fresh wave of panic. Was she to be left alone in a strange house in the midst of this country at war? 'What if someone comes?'

'The house is very remote. I've been a few times and have never been disturbed. But if it would make you feel safer, I'll leave my pistol. Did your husband ever show you how to fire one?' Lucy shook her head. He produced an old-fashioned duelling pistol with a pearl handle and came a step closer to show it to her. 'It's loaded so you just have to un-cock it, point it and pull this trigger. It will fire a distance of up to thirty feet. But I am convinced you will not need it.' She did not extend her hand, so he placed it on a side table.

He moved towards the door, as if to leave. 'The bedroom is on the left at the top of the stairs.'

Suddenly she realised that she was still wearing his coat around her shoulders. She shrugged it off and rubbed her arms, shivering in the chill.

'I think you will be warm enough upstairs,' he said with a bow. 'Until later, Mrs Harvington.' He picked up his coat and walked out, leaving her all alone.

Lucy looked around at the high-ceilinged hallway and the curve of the stairs. She picked up the pistol and held it close by her side as she began to climb the stairs, knees trembling. She had to cling to the banister for support and stop to rest several times, but she was drawn upwards by the sound of a fire crackling and the comforting scent of woodsmoke.

In the bedroom there was a large, canopied bed. Light was slanting through shutters that covered floor-length windows along one wall. On another wall, pale rectangles showed where paintings had once hung. A mahogany bureau stood just inside the room and by crouching and getting her weight behind it, Lucy managed to shove it in front of the bedroom door as a barricade. She placed the pistol under a pillow then climbed beneath the burnt-orange quilt which covered the bed. An overwhelming weariness descended and she was asleep within moments.

When Lucy woke, sun was streaming through the shutters. Her first thoughts were for Charlie and she sobbed harshly for everything she had lost. Her eyes, her skin, her heart – everything felt raw from the trauma of the previous day and night. She pulled Charlie's watch from her pocket for the comfort of holding something of his, and saw it was midday. Her feet were swollen and painfully red so she sat up and rubbed them vigorously. After a while she got up to hobble across the room and open the shutters. Outside there was a wide vista: a cultivated garden with a lawn, ornamental trees and what looked like a vegetable patch, and then, in the distance, a glint of grey sea. She couldn't see another habitation, and there were no boats on the water.

She shoved the bureau aside and wandered out onto the landing, which had several doors leading off it: more bedrooms, with the beds made up but all decorations removed from walls and surfaces, and a room with a claw-footed bathtub in the centre. She glanced in a mirror hanging on one wall and was shocked to see how pale and thin she looked, her cheeks almost hollow. The months of poor diet had taken their toll, as had the deathly cold of the previous night. *I hope you can't see me, Charlie,* she thought. *I look such a fright.*

Tentatively, she crept down the stairs, half-expecting to be challenged despite Murad's assurances. She found a dining room with an elaborate chandelier hanging over the centre of a mahogany table that would seat at least twelve, then a drawing room with dustsheets covering the familiar shapes of chairs and tables. Lucy opened the drawing-room shutters and saw the same garden view but now she noticed there was a well to one side, and a loveseat beneath an arbour. It must be glorious to sit there in summer with a loved one.

She continued her exploration and found a library of leather-bound books with Russian lettering on the spines, then she walked down a corridor to a large kitchen area with a sink and a grate where a cooking pot could be

252

suspended over a fire. She remembered Murad saying there were some supplies in the cellar and found a doorway with steps leading down. It was dark, so first she located a lantern on a shelf and found matches in a cupboard.

At the foot of the steps she held the lantern aloft and saw shelves of ceramic containers with labels on them in Russian. There was a crate of wrinkled potatoes with sprouts poking out and she squeezed one, wondering if they might be edible. A basketful of apples was a lucky find and she bit into one, her stomach gurgling as the sweet juice awakened her hunger. She opened a container at random and inside there was a white substance, probably a type of flour. The next one was almost empty but there were traces of sugar on the bottom. She licked a finger and dipped it in the residue then sucked off the delicious sweetness, the first sugar she had tasted for many months. It was Christmas Day, she remembered; the previous Christmas Charlie had visited her at home and they had laughed merrily as they fed each other sweet treats, watched by a disapproving Dorothea. She closed her eyes to try and relive the memory but it felt like another lifetime, lived long ago. In the remaining canisters, she found grains and some dried herbs she could not identify. If only she had learned to cook. At one end of the cellar she found a pile of logs chopped for firewood and picked up a few so she could light a fire in the kitchen grate.

Next, she ventured out into the garden to draw some water from the well. The first time she lowered the bucket it hit against a layer of ice on the surface. She found a heavy stone and hurled it in to break the ice, then was able to draw two bucketfuls of water: one to heat over the fire to enable her to wash, and the other to boil some wrinkled potatoes. She looked around the garden; even with the sun already lowering towards a wintry horizon, it was beautiful, and so remote there was no other dwelling in any direction. A tiny bird that looked like a type of sparrow hopped across the frozen grass in a futile search for food.

After washing and eating, Lucy continued her exploration of the ground floor. She opened the double doors of the main room at the front of the house and gave a little shriek to see the familiar shape of a pianoforte hidden beneath a dustsheet. She pulled it back to reveal a box grand piano with ornate scrolls on the carved legs and a curlicued music stand. It was a stunning instrument that had been meticulously cared for, with not a mark on the polished wood surfaces. Lucy played middle C and the tone was clear, the tuning pitch perfect, so she played a few chords and trills, then paused to see if anyone had overheard. The only sound was the wind in the trees, so she played some more.

'Listen to this, Charlie,' she said out loud. 'The first music I've heard in months.' She realised she had been talking to him in her head all day, although barely conscious of it. Everything she looked at, she imagined him looking at with her. She knew he would be proud of her for getting water, lighting a fire and preparing a small meal. And now she had a pianoforte too.

She sat on the stool and began to play a Chopin *Nocturne*, opus number 9 in E-flat major. Charlie had particularly liked it. The clarity of the notes, the joyful trills and its sheer familiarity brought goosebumps to her arms and tears pooled in her eyes, but she didn't stop playing. Somehow the music was releasing a great tension in her ribs and making her feel like herself again. When she finished, she let the tears roll down her cheeks. 'That was for you, darling,' Lucy whispered.

The light had almost faded so she lit a lantern, wondering what she would do when the oil ran out. Might there be more somewhere in this wonderful house? So far it had provided everything she needed. She walked round again, getting used to the layout of the rooms, the shadowy corners and the way the floorboards creaked as if the house was welcoming her – or as if Charlie was there too. Was that crazy thinking? In one cupboard she found ladies' toiletries, including a silver filigree scent bottle. She opened it and sniffed the perfume, which was sweetly floral, like jasmine mixed with something more darkly exotic. She dabbed a little on her wrists then continued her tour, taking the measure of the house, getting to know it.

She was in front of the fire in the kitchen when she heard the front door opening and Murad calling her name. She hesitated before walking out into the hall, still a little wary of him.

'I brought you some bread,' he said, holding it out. 'It's only half a loaf. I'm sorry I could not bring more.'

'Don't worry, I'm not hungry. I found food in the cellar.' She wrapped her arms around her shoulders defensively.

'But you need to build your strength. I insist you eat the bread.'

She felt tears coming to her eyes at the thought that this stranger was trying to look after her. He looked frozen to the bone yet he had ridden all this way.

'Come in to sit by the fire,' she gestured. 'I'll eat a little of your bread if you will have the rest.'

He agreed so readily and wolfed down the bread so rapidly that she realised he was starving. She fetched him an apple from the cellar and he ate that too.

After they had finished he regarded her seriously. 'Are you ready for me to take you back to the British camp? Your friends will be worried.'

Lucy shook her head. 'I can't go back. I'm not ready. I wondered if I might stay here a while longer? Until I feel stronger.' She hadn't thought through the idea beforehand; the words just came out, but once she had uttered them they seemed to make sense.

'Here? On your own?' His brow furrowed and she could tell he thought her a madwoman. Perhaps she was.

'It's peaceful here. I need some time to reflect before I undertake the long voyage back to Britain.'

Murad got up and walked to the window, staring out into the darkness as he thought through her request. 'There is not enough food in the cellar to keep you. I've already taken all the dried meat and fish.'

'I assure you, I eat very little.'

He was thinking out loud. 'I could bring you something from time to time but our troops are desperately short of food. If only I could tell your friends at the British camp where you are, perhaps they would send supplies.'

'No. I don't want you to … Please don't tell anyone I'm here. There's no need for you to feel responsible for me. I intend to live very quietly.' The more she spoke, the better the plan seemed. She felt the house was a sanctuary. Besides, she could still feel close to Charlie here, only a few miles from his grave. Once she left, she might not have that strong sense of his presence any more. When she got back to London, Dorothea would probably say it was all for the best that Charlie had died, and she couldn't bear to hear that.

Murad wasn't happy with the idea, but he accepted that he was not going to change her mind and turned to practicalities: he carried more firewood and matches up to the bedroom for her, he located extra lanterns and a supply of oil, some candles and candlesticks, and he found a cupboard with spare blankets for the bed.

'I must go back to my camp now. I will try to come tomorrow. Keep the pistol nearby.'

'Don't worry. I'll be fine. Thank you.'

She couldn't wait for him to leave so that she could reclaim the house as her own again. Hers and Charlie's.

Chapter Twenty-nine

Next morning, Lucy explored the garden. She was not a knowledgeable gardener and couldn't identify the rows of plants from their leafy tops but she found an old spade and, using all her strength, managed to dig up a few specimens from the frozen earth: there were embryonic carrots, scrawny onions and some potatoes and beets that appeared edible. She gathered just enough to last the day, cleaned them and boiled them together into a kind of soup. She couldn't find any salt and the flavour was watery and insipid, but at least it filled her stomach and there was plenty left for later.

Next she heated several potfuls of water, carried them upstairs and laboriously filled the bath. She undressed and climbed in, closing her eyes and surrendering to the womb-like warmth, so relaxed that she almost fell asleep. But when she opened her eyes she saw the water had turned red from Charlie's blood, which had dried in her hair. It was strange and sad to lie there soaking in blood from his veins and she shed a few tears before pulling herself together. More water had to be boiled and carried up the stairs so she could rinse herself clean. Of course, the owners of the house had servants to fill their baths – there were some small servants' rooms behind the kitchen – but she had to do it herself and it all took time.

Lucy only had the gown on her back – the blue wool one she'd worn when they sailed from Plymouth the previous April – and her blue jacket and bonnet. She searched through cupboards and couldn't find any women's clothing but she came across a heavy outdoor cloak of thick black wool. She wrapped it tightly around herself while she washed her clothes and hung them near the bedroom fire to dry. The cloak was cosy, and felt appropriate as it was the closest she had to mourning clothes. In London she would have been dressed head to toe in black.

The light was fading by the time she sat down at the pianoforte to play. She knew many pieces by heart and skipped from Handel to Beethoven, Bach to Haydn, but mostly she played her favourite Mozart piano sonatas, Mendelssohn's *Songs Without Words* or Chopin's *Nocturnes*. The *Nocturnes* had special significance for her because Chopin had passed away in the same month as her mother; he was thirty-nine, her mother forty-six, both of them too young to die.

While Lucy kept busy, her sadness was held at bay but it hit her full force when she went to bed that evening. If only she had brought her mother's bedspread instead of leaving it behind in camp, where it would probably be trampled into the mud. She yearned for Charlie with a pain that was physical, wrapping her arms tightly around a pillow and sobbing till her head was pounding. '*I want you,*' she cried. '*Come back to me, I need you. How could you leave me?*' And for the first time she admitted that in her core there was a part of her that was angry with him. If only he had been braver. If only he had stayed.

Murad came a couple of days later, by which time she had decided to trust him. If he were planning to manhandle her, he would have done so by now, but he seemed a quiet, gentle man.

'You look much recovered,' he said. 'I feared when I first saw you that I was too late to save your life, yet two days later your complexion is glowing and you seem rested.'

'I like it here. The solitude agrees with me. Thank you for bringing me.' They were sitting in the drawing room, where she had removed the dust covers to find Empire-style chairs and settees in rich rose-coloured brocade and ivy-green damask, with elaborate gold carved arms and legs. 'I am taking good care of the house for its owners, so I hope they would not mind.'

'We are all forced to do things in wartime that would never happen in normal life. I could not be sitting talking with you if we were in my home town in Turkey.'

'Not even if we were introduced by friends at a social gathering and there were others present?'

'No, I can't talk with any women except my female relatives.'

She wondered how Turkish men ever found wives in that case. 'At home in London, I would not be seen in society for two years while mourning my husband. I suppose that's what I'm doing here in this house: observing a period of mourning.'

'It is understandable. In my religion, the mourning is shorter – just four months and ten days, and after that a woman is permitted to remarry.'

Lucy shuddered at the thought of being with any man except Charlie. She couldn't imagine feeling such love for anyone again. It was impossible. Murad watched her, his dark eyes seeming wise. She looked at his hand, resting on the arm of the chair, with its dark, foreign skin, and noted he had especially long fingers and clean nails. How did he manage to keep his nails clean in an army camp? Charlie's had always had dirt engrained beneath them and his palms were rough from tending the horses. Although Murad spoke good English he looked nothing like an Englishman and she was conscious she looked nothing like a Turkish lady.

'I was told that Turkish men do not like to be in the presence of a woman who is not veiled,' Lucy said. 'Would you like me to find some piece of fabric to wear on my head when you are here?'

He smiled and shook his head. 'It doesn't matter. I understand you are of a different culture and it is not your way.'

'I'm sure that in your culture, as in mine, we would be forbidden from being alone in a house together.'

'I will be sure not to tell anyone.' Murad gave her a quick, complicit smile.

She thought that the only person who would chide her was Dorothea – dear, wonderful, overbearing Dorothea. 'I have some soup prepared in the kitchen,' she told him. 'It's not very good but you are welcome to share it with me.'

She rose and he followed eagerly, watching as she heated the soup over the fire then ladled out bowlfuls, which they ate at the kitchen table.

'You must not feel an obligation to look after me just because you found me,' she told him. 'I can manage on my own.'

He regarded her with his dark eyes. 'But I am worried about you. What will your family and friends be thinking?'

'My family no longer want anything to do with me,' she said, and explained about the rift caused by her marriage. 'I've had no word from my father or my sister since I left England last April, although I have written several times.'

'Letters often go missing in wartime.'

'Possibly, but my friend Adelaide received several letters at every camp we stayed in. Why should I have none? I could understand if one or two went missing – but all of them?' There was a tightness in her throat. She still couldn't comprehend how Dorothea could have abandoned her so completely. The bonds formed during eighteen years of family life must have meant very little for her to cast them off so easily. It was strange, because usually her anger was short-lived.

'And this friend, Adelaide? Could you not go to her now?'

'She is in England. I have no friends in Crimea … Only you!' Lucy gave a weak smile.

He bowed his head. 'I hope I will prove worthy of the honour. But still I am alarmed that you have not informed anyone of your whereabouts.'

'Believe me, there is no one for me to inform. At least … I suppose I will write to my family in due course …' She supposed she must go home to London eventually but for now she had decided to be on her own, to grieve in peace.

After he left that evening, Lucy realised she had asked nothing of his own life. She didn't know his background, or whether he was married or had children. She was selfishly wrapped up in her own problems and really it was most impolite. On his next visit, a few days later, she asked her questions.

'My family live in a small town called Smyrna on the Aegean coast of Turkey, the Asian side,' he told her.

'What is your father's line of business?'

'My father is dead. He died when I was thirteen,' he said, and Lucy interrupted.

'Is that so? My mother died when I was the exact same age. Were you very close? My mother and I were exceedingly close.'

'Yes, I loved my father very much. As the only son I had to look after my mother and sisters after his death, although my Uncle Cemal helped. He's the one who paid for my commission in the army. He also insisted that I learned English, because it is the international language of business.'

'Your English is flawless. Tell me, what will you do after the war? Will you remain in the army?'

Murad shook his head emphatically. 'My uncle has a business supplying fish to shops and restaurants. I expect to work there and perhaps become a partner one day. I must earn enough money to support my sisters until they marry, and to pay their dowries. It's going to be expensive,' – he grimaced comically – 'as there are four of them.'

What a burden for him, Lucy thought. 'Few families pay dowries in England now.'

'In Turkey, it is a matter of pride. The *çeyiz* – that's what we call it – will include goods for the marital home, clothing, jewellery and money. If the family of the new husband is not happy with the dowry offered, they can call off the wedding.'

Lucy had been looking for a tactful opening to ask about his own marital status and now she said, 'I expect you will receive a substantial dowry from your own wife.'

Suddenly he seemed embarrassed, looking at the ground as he answered. 'I cannot marry until my sisters are settled, and until I am earning enough to support a wife and family.'

'Of course not, no.' She wished she hadn't asked as it seemed to make him uncomfortable. Soon afterwards he announced he had to leave and she hoped it wasn't because he wished to escape her line of questioning.

'Is there anything you need?' he asked. 'I can't promise to find it but I can try.'

'No, thank you. I have everything I need right here.'

Lucy felt a sense of peace descend when he had gone. She wanted the house to herself, to enjoy its spacious calm. As a child, she had been very sociable and had never liked solitude. She read few books because she would rather be in the kitchen making conversation with the cook, or in her mother's room chatting about clothes and parties, or in the drawing room quizzing Dorothea on medical matters. But now she loved the stillness and silence because they let her feel close to Charlie. She could talk to him in her head

262

and feel that he could hear. Perhaps he was watching over her as she wandered round this Russian family's house – Murad had told her it was called a *dacha*, a word she liked very much. She didn't feel lonely in the *dacha*. Solitude was her choice.

Chapter Thirty

Lucy didn't count how long she had been at the *dacha* but she observed the gradual loosening of winter's grip, the ripening of new vegetables in the garden she tended every morning, and the stealthy unfurling of leaves on the trees. In the afternoons she kept herself busy looking after the house: dusting surfaces and washing windows, beating rugs and cushions, even climbing on a chair perched atop a table to run a feather duster over the chandeliers, as she had seen their maid do at home. Every evening she played the pianoforte, grateful for the musical memory that allowed her to recall so many pieces. Activity kept her sadness at bay, for a while at least.

One evening when Murad visited, she noticed he was scratching furiously at his neck and asked if he was all right.

'I apologise,' he said, shamefaced. 'Tiny insects – I don't know what you call them – lay their eggs in our clothing and it seems impossible to get rid of them, no matter how I try.'

'They must be lice. Some had them in the British camp. Do you not have women to wash your clothes?'

'We do our laundry ourselves, apart from the highest-ranking officers. Some are more fastidious than others.' He made a face and smiled.

'Please let me wash your clothes for you,' Lucy offered. 'I found soda crystals and carbolic soap in the cellar, which I'm sure will do the trick.' He seemed about to refuse, so she added, '*Please.* I am looking for ways of occupying my time gainfully.'

Murad was reluctant but eventually agreed and next time he visited he wore his spare uniform and brought the affected jacket and trousers. When Lucy looked closely she could see the minuscule black creatures crawling around in the seams and stepped back instinctively, hoping they would not leap across to her own clothing or hair.

She was about to drop his jacket into a sinkful of boiling water when she noted a shape in one of the pockets and pulled out a little book bound in green leather. Inside there were pages and pages of elaborate pencil drawings: images of plants, birds, jugs, mosques with minarets, all formed from curly patterns. One image showed a sea of whorls in which swam strange sea creatures. The skill was extraordinary. Had Murad drawn these with his own hand? She put the book to one side to return to him.

The most effective treatment for lice, she discovered, was to boil the garments in a big pot on the stove then scrub them with carbolic soap. No insect could survive that treatment. Finally she heated the heavy iron over the grate and pressed his uniform into shape on the kitchen table.

When Murad returned, he seemed overwhelmed by her endeavours, expressing his gratitude over and over, to the point where she urged him to stop.

'I found this book,' she told him, holding it out. 'You didn't tell me you were an artist.'

He shook his head bashfully. 'I am no artist. Others are much more proficient, but I enjoy the pastime. It is a type of calligraphy in which all the images are formed from Arabic letters and in combination they have special meanings. They would normally be done in coloured inks but I have none with me. Really, these are but rough scribbles.'

'And yet I can see you are very talented. They're beautiful.' As they ate their meal, she looked at Murad anew: he was an artist as well as an army officer. His art was of a strange foreign kind she had never encountered but no less skilful for that.

Before he left she asked, 'Might I not wash your bedding as well? And perhaps I could do washing for some of your fellow officers? Please give me some way to repay your kindness and feel that I am not totally useless in this area at war.'

He protested: 'Laundry is not a job for a lady. What of your beautiful hands?'

She waggled her slender fingers in the air. 'To worry about my hands in wartime would be vanity indeed. Believe me, I care not for such things any more.'

She was glad when she had work to occupy her: the mornings were for gardening, the afternoons for laundry or cleaning, and the evenings at the pianoforte. It was good to be busy. She liked the routine, which kept her occupied but allowed thoughts of Charlie to come and go with her shifting mood. Often she dwelled on Susanna and the shocking accident that had destroyed his family. She could picture how it had happened, could see his bravado leading him to foolish extremes as he strove to entertain his beloved little sister. It was stupid but it was not evil, and it seemed desperately wrong that his grief and guilt should be compounded by banishment from the arms of his parents and brothers. She wished with all her heart Charlie had told her sooner, so she could have convinced him that her love for him did not diminish one iota when she heard the truth. She had handled his confession badly because of her confusion over the identity of Susanna, and he hadn't let her speak of it again. If he believed she loved him less, perhaps it was one of the factors that had led him to give up hope. Lucy wished she had been more tender during those last awful weeks as the cold set in. If she had shown him unfailing love and unquestioning support, perhaps she could have persuaded him to stay alive.

Most days she carried her sadness around, like an extra-heavy greatcoat that weighed her down and made it difficult to move. Occasionally the sight of a rabbit sniffing the grass with twitching nose, a pretty bunch of snowdrops hiding under a bush, or a particularly exhilarating passage in a sonata would lift the weight for a while and make her feel a whiff of something that resembled contentment. But more often her throat was tight with grief and tears were never far away. Was this what Adelaide was experiencing back in England? She was lucky to have Bill's children; all Lucy had left of Charlie was his pocket watch and a year's-worth of fading memories.

One day she heard the front door open and emerged from the kitchen to find Murad staggering in with a teenage boy in his arms. His head was bandaged, his leg in a splint, and as Murad laid him on a settee in the drawing room he stared at Lucy with a look she recognised; it was terror, the same look she had seen on Charlie's face the morning he wouldn't go to battle with his company. The boy's eyes weren't focused on his surroundings, but instead were wide with horror at some scene in his mind that obviously felt more real to him than the damask cushions he lay upon.

'I found him lying in a daze outside the Turkish camp at Kamara. He hasn't spoken to me yet so I don't know his name but he certainly doesn't seem fit to return to his company. I imagine he is only about thirteen or fourteen, so he must have lied to enlist.'

Lucy tried to think of something practical she could do to help. 'I'll get you both some soup.'

She had at last discovered a small pot of salt and was experimenting with the dried herbs from the cellar so her soups had become slightly more palatable, but when she placed a bowl on the table in front of the boy, he jumped at the clattering sound and wouldn't touch it. She lifted a spoonful towards him and he shrank, seeming petrified of her.

'I think he has been caught in shellfire,' Murad explained. 'It rattles the brain inside the skull. I've seen grown men in the same state. But he is so young … I wondered if he might stay here with you for a short while, just until he recovers his wits?'

Lucy didn't want company, particularly not a stranger, but it would have been cruel to refuse this poor child, so she said, 'Yes, of course. He can take one of the other bedrooms.'

Murad moved round so he was within the boy's line of vision, crouched down and spoke softly to him in Turkish. He pointed at Lucy and was obviously explaining that he would be safe here. All his movements were slow and gentle but even so, the boy jumped at the slightest gesture in his direction. He was deeply traumatised.

'I know little of nursing,' Lucy worried. 'What care does he need? Should I cut up a sheet to make fresh bandages?'

'Leave him alone for now. You can see how scared he is. I will carry him upstairs to a bedroom but after that I think you should let him be. If he comes into the kitchen when you are eating, you could offer him some food. But if he wants to be alone, leave him.'

Lucy watched Murad's serious, compassionate expression and realised how clever he was. Of course, he must be intelligent to speak English so fluently but this level of intuition required a refined brain. She agreed to proceed as he suggested.

Once Murad left and the boy was in bed, she went to the pianoforte. Usually she played the first piece that came into her head but knowing the boy would be able to hear her, she sat for a while considering the choice. Nothing too cheerful; it had to be calming and beautiful. At last she picked Beethoven's *Moonlight Sonata*; its steady rhythm always spoke to her of the slow inevitable passing of time, the infinite nature of the sky full of stars, of matters much greater than the small concerns of human beings. There was no noise from upstairs but she hoped he took it for what it was: a little piece of good in the world as an antidote to the horror of war.

Chapter Thirty-one

For a few days, the boy did not venture from his bedroom. Lucy left bowls of soup at his door and was pleased to see they were being drunk, as the empty bowl and spoon were left for her to collect. She worried that his chamber pot must be getting rather full; there was an outside latrine around the side of the house, hidden from view, where she emptied her own pot, but she did not like to offer to take his. And then, one morning, he emerged from the kitchen door while she was in the garden weeding the vegetable patch, with the black cloak wrapped around her. She waved but did not try to approach him, only watching out of the corner of her eye as he explored. He limped past the well towards the servants' wing alongside the kitchen, then back to the little courtyard that lay beneath the sitting room's picture windows, and down through a stretch of pretty flower gardens. The house had been designed to take advantage of the sea views, with tall arched windows set into the whitewashed walls on both levels. The boy went down to the far end of the garden where a steep rocky slope dropped to the water's edge, and disappeared from view.

When Lucy went in to the kitchen to make her daily soup, he remained outside for a while then she heard him creeping upstairs again.

The next day she saw him round the side of the house and guessed he had discovered the latrine. She noted that he no longer wore the bandage on his head. That evening Lucy heard a shuffling movement in the hall while she was playing the pianoforte and sensed he was standing listening, but she did not motion him to come in and sit down. Everything must be on his terms. She told Murad of the progress when he came by.

'I didn't know you played the piano,' he said, surprised. 'I wonder … might I ask you to play something for me?'

Lucy tried to think of a piece he would like and chose the first of Mendelssohn's *Songs Without Words*, opus 19, number 1 in E-major. It had a slightly melancholy but resigned air that perfectly suited her mood. Murad sat on a chair just behind her where he could see her fingers moving on the keys, and once again the boy stood in the hall. When she finished, Murad didn't speak for a while.

'Did you like it?' she asked. 'I am especially partial to Mendelssohn but perhaps you would prefer something else? I'm afraid I don't know any Turkish music.'

'That was the most beautiful music I have ever heard.' He seemed overcome, almost speechless with emotion. 'It is music for all time, for any place. You have the most exquisite talent.'

'I didn't write it!' she exclaimed in case he had misunderstood.

'No, but the expression you bring to the playing … every note was perfect.'

'Good. I'm glad you liked it. I shall play something for you every time you come to thank you for your kindness towards me. I think our friend' – she gestured towards the hall – 'enjoys listening as well.'

The following day, while she boiled up soup in the kitchen, the door opened and the boy came in and sat on a chair at the opposite side of the room. Lucy turned and smiled at him. She hadn't had a chance to look at his face properly before and now she saw that his skin was several shades paler than Murad's and he was very thin. He had not yet started to grow whiskers so she imagined Murad was right in guessing he was around thirteen or fourteen. There was a gash on the side of his head over his right ear but it appeared at a glance to be healing well.

When the soup was ready, she put a bowl on the table for him and he pressed his hands together in a gesture of thanks and began to eat. She sat down on the opposite side of the table and did the same. When they finished, he took both bowls to the sink and rinsed them. It felt odd not to talk, so Lucy put a hand on her breastbone and said, 'Lucy' then pointed at him, questioning. It was a step too far, though; he shook his head and ran away.

Later that day she heard him down in the cellar where the provisions were stored, and then she heard a rhythmic thumping coming from the kitchen. She decided to steer clear as she didn't want to risk scaring him again, so she went into the garden to wander in the dusk, listening to the birds tweet insistently as they expended their final energy of the day.

When the air got cold, she walked back into the house and a delicious aroma reached her nostrils. She opened the kitchen door and there in the centre of the table was a freshly baked loaf of bread. The boy was at the sink washing up. He produced a knife and cut a hunk of steaming bread and pushed it towards her. *Quid pro quo.* As she took a bite, tears came to Lucy's eyes. It was like the smell of the kitchen at home where their cook, Mrs Dunstan, baked bread. A wave of homesickness crashed over her. She missed Mrs Dunstan. She missed Papa. More than anything, she missed Dorothea. She didn't want the boy to think she didn't appreciate his effort so she licked her lips and said, 'Mmm.' Indeed it was very good. He seemed pleased that she liked it and watched as she gobbled down the whole piece.

'Thank you,' she said, smiling and nodding.

He put his hand on his chest and uttered the first word he had said since his arrival: 'Emir.'

'Emir,' Lucy repeated, with a burst of pleasure. She had been starting to worry he'd been struck dumb by his injuries. Now she realised it wasn't that; he had just been waiting until he was sure he was safe.

The structure of Lucy's days changed once she had a companion. Every morning Emir made bread for breakfast and they sat together at table, teaching each other words from their respective languages: 'bread' was '*ekmek*'; 'table' was '*masa*'; 'garden' was '*bahçe*'; pianoforte was '*piyano*'. Emir seemed determined to contribute to the household and found a fishing line with which he was very successful at catching fish (*balık*) from the rocks at the shoreline. He helped in the garden, took turns at scrubbing the laundry and he did his share of cleaning as well. Lucy was astonished at his resourcefulness; she hadn't even noticed there was an oven in the kitchen before he arrived. She liked to watch him kneading the dough, just as Mrs Dunstan had, and loved eating the bread as soon as it had cooled enough not to burn the mouth.

Murad was astonished when next he came to visit and they presented him with a proper meal of fish, vegetables and bread. Lucy guessed from the eagerness with which he wolfed it down that it was the first food he'd eaten for some time.

'That was delicious. Thank you both,' he said in English and then in Turkish. 'It always does me good to come here and escape from the madness.'

'What is happening in the war?' Lucy wasn't sure she wanted to know, but the question slipped out anyhow.

'It's the same old shelling and sniper fire across the lines. No progress either way. Sometimes I think we will be here for years, because each side has dug trenches and redoubts from which they cannot be budged.' He seemed exhausted and careworn. 'I came here to fight for my country, so that we will not be overrun by Russians trampling on our precious Ottoman heritage, but it is hard to keep sight of those aims now. Most men simply focus on staying alive.'

'Tell me about your home town,' she asked. 'Smyrna, I think you called it?'

'Yes. It is an ancient city on the Aegean coast where people of many different cultures live: Greeks, Turks, Jews, Mamluks, each in their own neighbourhoods. There is a large harbour, and surrounding the town in every direction there are orchards of fruit trees that are covered in blossom in spring.'

'Is it hot there?'

'In summer, yes; much hotter than here. Winter is pleasantly mild and there is still plenty of sunshine.'

'It sounds wonderful.' She smiled. Murad seemed happy talking of his home. Unlike her, he had a future to look forward to.

Emir asked him something and after a brief exchange in Turkish, Murad told Lucy: 'It's Emir's birthday today. He's sixteen. He doesn't look it, does he?'

Lucy smiled and clapped her hands in congratulation. 'What date is it?' she asked. When Murad told her it was 20th March 1855 she realised that her own nineteenth birthday had passed without her noticing. It was over a year since she and Charlie had married, and eleven months since they had left British soil. Sadness descended as she thought back to the excitement of that day when they embraced in their tiny cabin and he told her that he was the happiest man in the world.

Murad and Emir had another exchange in Turkish then Murad translated for Lucy: 'Emir was asking if he should go back to his company now but I suggested he stay here to recuperate a while longer, if that's acceptable to you.'

'I would be happy for him to stay. He must remain longer, as he is teaching me Turkish.' To demonstrate, she said, 'Ismim Lucy', meaning, 'my name is Lucy.'

When she went to the music room to play piano for them that evening, she chose Mozart's piano sonata number 11 in A-minor, otherwise known as 'The Turkish March', and she could tell it lifted Murad's spirits. Music could do that: it had always had a powerful influence on her own mood but it had never held as much importance for her as it did now in the *dacha*, where it was the medicine helping to heal her broken heart.

A few nights later, Lucy awoke to the sound of men's voices in the house. She heard them calling to each other and then there was a crash. For a moment, she froze, terrified: who could it be? Were they Russian soldiers, or the Tartar bands that she had been told roamed the countryside scavenging for food? She got up and pulled on the wool cloak, grabbed the pistol from beneath her bed, then opened the door to the landing. Her hand was shaking and she pointed the pistol downwards in case it should accidentally discharge. She soon realised Emir had gone ahead of her because she could hear him arguing with the intruders in the kitchen: that meant they must be Turkish. She continued softly down the stairs and Emir emerged to meet her.

'Turkish,' he said. 'Hungry.' He pointed to his mouth.

'Give them some bread and soup,' Lucy told him. 'How many are there?' She held up her fingers: two? Three?

He held up four fingers. There wasn't sufficient to feed four men but they could share what there was.

'Sleep?' Emir asked.

It was the middle of the night, so it seemed churlish to ask the men to leave. Besides, they might well refuse. While they were eating in the kitchen, Lucy put the dustsheets back on the sofas in the drawing room and brought down some blankets so the men could sleep there. There were two spare bedrooms but she didn't want them on the same floor as her, didn't want them getting comfortable and deciding to stay longer than one night. She pushed the mahogany bureau in front of her bedroom door, but still she found it difficult to get back to sleep.

Next morning she lay in bed listening as Emir spoke to them and then the door banged. She waited until she heard their horses galloping away before descending.

'Why were they here?' she asked. She had found that Emir understood simple sentences in English, which was more than she did in Turkish.

'Army ...' he said then motioned running away. 'Home.'

They were deserters. She supposed they would try to make their way back to Turkey now. That was a relief because it meant they were unlikely to return, but still her sense of security in the remote *dacha* was shaken. If she had been on her own, without Emir to translate, anything could have happened. Probably they had not seen a woman for a long time. Maybe they would have treated her like one of those women for sale who hung around the edges of army camps looking for customers. They could even have killed her and taken over the *dacha* for themselves. Somehow Emir had handled the situation with a maturity beyond his years and everything had turned out well. She was very grateful.

'You must stay here. I need you,' she told him, using sign language to underline her meaning.

He seemed pleased: 'Yes.'

The intrusion of the outside world had the effect of making Lucy start to think about what she would do once the war was over. The owners of the *dacha* would presumably return, so it was impossible for her to stay there, much as she would have liked to. In the end there would be nothing else to do but sail home to Britain, to Dorothea and her father. She hoped they would not repudiate her when she arrived on the doorstep. It was hard to understand how they could have forgotten her. Her father, her mother, her childhood, all were distant memories from a far-off place but she forced herself to look back and think about the history of the gulf that separated them.

Of course, it was all rooted in her mother's illness and Dorothea guarding the door to the sick room as if she alone were the rightful daughter. She had been the only one at their mother's deathbed and had organised the funeral without consultation. It was Lucy's misfortune to have been born to elderly parents, her mother in her thirties and her father in his forties when she arrived, so they were not able to care for her as younger parents might. That's why Dorothea had stepped in, no doubt thinking she was acting for the best. If only she had married and had an independent life of her own, she might not have been so domineering.

Suddenly Lucy thought of Mr Goodland, the barrister who used to visit every Sunday. Had he been a suitor? His conversation had been interminably dull, and physically he was unprepossessing, so the thought had never occurred to her. But why else did he visit so often? Was he planning to propose to Dorothea? What would her answer be? It occurred to Lucy how little she knew of her sister's life. She'd always written her off as a dry old stick, without any of their mother's charm, but perhaps she had secrets of her own.

For the first time, Lucy wondered if something could have happened to her father or Dorothea to account for their silence. Had her father died and Dorothea had not wanted to send the news in a letter? Or had Dorothea married and was too busy with her new household to write? Perhaps they had both moved home and Lucy's letters had not reached them. If she returned and they were not at the same address, how would she find them? It was less than a year since she and Charlie set sail on the *Shooting Star*, but everything had changed and she felt like a different person. She *couldn't* go back to living in that dreary house in Russell Square as if she had never met Charlie, never been married or widowed, never been to war. But at the same time she couldn't think of any alternatives.

Next time Murad visited, she told him about the deserters who had come in the night, and how skilfully Emir had managed the situation. 'Why would they desert?' she asked. 'Does your army not flog deserters?'

'They are starving,' he replied bluntly. 'Our soldiers are lucky if they get one small meal a day and men cannot continue indefinitely on empty stomachs.'

'I thought it was your job to find food for them?'

'Precisely. Except there is none to be found. The British and French have adequate supplies but they will not share them with us, and our sultan expects us to live off the land.'

He looked worn out and Lucy guessed he worked tirelessly to feed his men and felt the lack of sustenance as a personal failure. 'Why won't the British and the French share? You are our allies. We have a common cause.'

'I was sure you would have heard: the Turkish soldiers are seen as cowards after they abandoned the redoubts at

Balaklava. It's most unfair as they were simply obeying orders to regroup, but the perception has become common. I think it is also because our skin is darker than yours, so we are not seen as equals. This combination of scornful treatment and starvation has led many hundreds to desert.'

Lucy thought back to her naïve excitement on the way out East and realised how much she had changed since then. 'It is a war that quickly stripped any illusions. We British thought our army invincible after the triumph over Napoleon at Waterloo but it seems no one in charge had the foresight to plan for this campaign. There were no hospitals, hardly any medical supplies and not enough food and fuel for the men. British soldiers became very disillusioned as winter set in ... I ...' She found she wanted to tell him about Charlie's death, but at the same time she didn't want to be disloyal.

Murad sensed she wanted to say something and waited while she wrestled with her conscience.

'I think my husband's ... Charlie's death was deliberate.' Tears began to gather as she said the words out loud. 'He halted his horse at a position where he had been told Russian guns were aimed. I don't know how he could leave me ...' With that, she broke down. There was relief in having voiced her suspicion at last, but misery as well. Putting it into words made it real.

Murad spoke gently. 'You may be right and you may not. All I know is that last winter a lot of British soldiers took their own lives. The war reached stalemate after the horror of the first battles, and the cold and the lack of food eroded morale. I heard of dozens of men who killed themselves.'

Suddenly Lucy remembered the dead soldier in the sea at Balaklava, whom the harbourmaster told her had probably fallen off the cliffs.

Murad continued: 'In the Ottoman ranks there are high rates of desertion because men are close enough to get home but I can understand why an Englishman would be overcome by despair and see death as the only way out. If this is what your husband did, it doesn't mean he loved you any less. I can imagine he was trying to save you, thinking that you would never leave him and would only go home to safety if he were no longer around.' He looked straight into her eyes. 'Do not be angry with him. Think of all the happy memories from your marriage. That is what he would want.'

Lucy had never met such a sensitive and understanding man before, and she stared at him gratefully. Their eyes remained locked for perhaps a little too long.

Chapter Thirty-two

The warm spring weather brought new crops to the garden at the *dacha*: peas, asparagus and spinach, cherries and apricots. There was so much that Lucy was able to set some aside for Murad to take back to his starving men, and Emir always had several extra fish to send. Their stock of flour was running low but Emir found a coarser, darker grain in the stores, which he called *çavdar*, and he began making his bread from that. It was like the black bread they had eaten in Varna but Emir kneaded his dough on the kitchen table rather than the ground so at least it did not have grit in it.

As April turned to May, Murad explained to Lucy that from the 18th of the month, he and Emir would be observing Ramadan. It meant that they could not eat or drink during the hours of daylight but would wait until the sun went down. 'It is a special time of prayer and purification for all Muslims,' he told her.

Lucy knew they were both Muslim. She had become used to Emir quietly absenting himself to pray five times a day. He washed first then went to his own room from where she heard him murmuring the ritual words. But she hadn't known about Ramadan or guessed that Murad was devout.

'Is it not hard to work all day without breaking your fast? I am sure I should find it difficult.'

'For me, the worst thing is the thirst. But it is a time that brings us closer to our God and that is worth far more than any physical discomfort.'

Lucy was interested: 'Your god is Muhammad, is he not?'

'No, Allah is the only god. Muhammad, peace be upon him, was a prophet who came to earth to explain the teachings of Allah.' He told her that the angel Jibril had appeared to Muhammad regularly and during these visitations transmitted to him the words that make up the holy book called the Qu'ran, a book intended to touch the human heart and explain the higher purpose behind everything in the universe. 'Christians portray us as barbarous, superstitious heathens but in fact being a Muslim is about devoting your life to love and obedience to the will of Allah.'

Murad described to her the glories of Islamic art and architecture, the learnedness of their scholars and doctors, their firmly held belief in looking after the poorest in society.

'Why do your women wear veils?' she asked. 'It seems odd not to see the expressions on their faces.'

'The Qu'ran tells us that women should lower their gaze and not display their beauty except to their closest male relatives. But I think you would find that the expressions are all too clear from the eyes alone. My mother can convey every thought in her head with a subtle inflection of the eyes.' He laughed, but there was sadness in his expression.

'You miss her.'

'Yes, we are very close. She is a woman with a great spirit.'

Lucy worried that he and Emir must secretly look down on her for her lack of modesty: to be alone in a house with two unmarried men would create a scandal in Victorian England and must be even more reprehensible under Islam.

But Murad assured her that their religion instructed them not to judge others; only Allah had the right to pass judgement.

The more she heard, the more she thought it sounded a very humane faith, with much in common with the Christianity on which she had been raised. It seemed to inspire more devotion than her religion, though. These men prayed five times a day without fail, while she had not prayed once, not properly, since she had been living in the *dacha*. Her faith had been shaken by her experiences of late. The Christian church saw suicide as a mortal sin and she worried that Charlie might not be admitted to heaven. It was hard to love a god who condemned a man to hell simply because his burden was too heavy to carry on living. If Lucy were at home, she would have talked to their vicar about it but out here she simply didn't dwell on it. It was too painful.

At the beginning of June, Murad warned Lucy and Emir that a major offensive was planned and that he would not be able to return to the *dacha* for some time. The allies were planning to take Sevastopol at long last and drive the Russians out of Crimea. The Ottoman Empire would never be safe while they could launch battleships from Crimean ports. Emir asked if he should return to fight with his company. They had a rapid conversation in Turkish and Lucy gathered that Murad was asking him to stay there and look after her. She was grateful for his thoughtfulness. It would have been terrifying to be on her own during a battle.

They knew when the onslaught had begun as the sky filled with smoke, blotting out the sun. In the garden she could sometimes detect the familiar smell of gunpowder and the distant booming of the shells. It made her very anxious. What if the Russians won and took them all prisoner? Even if the allies won, it would be disastrous for her as she would be forced to leave the serenity of the *dacha* for an uncertain future. And as the days went by, another fear began to grow: what if Murad was killed? Would his wits be sharp on the battlefield when he could not eat to keep his strength up during daylight hours?

She used the pianoforte to calm her nerves, choosing tranquil melodies such as Schumann's *Kinderszehen* and Chopin's *Nocturnes*. Emir stuck close by and she guessed he was nervous too, although he did not admit it.

Ramadan ended on the 16th June and still Murad had not returned. She counted the days since he had last been there: three weeks, nearly four. The shelling could no longer be heard and the smoke had cleared. Where was he, she asked Emir, and he replied, 'Busy. Many things to do. He will come soon.' But she could see the doubt in his eyes.

On the 24th June it was six months since Charlie had died and the anniversary prompted Lucy to re-examine her emotions. The bitterest stage of the grief had passed. She no longer felt as though she was wearing an extra-heavy great-coat that weighed her down; she no longer sobbed in bed until her head ached. Instead she felt sadness for the waste of poor Charlie's life. He had possessed a genuine talent for entertaining others and was in his way a generous soul. In peacetime they could have been happy together. He would have been a lovely father to their children. She could picture him wrestling on the lawn, playing tricks to make the little ones laugh, but careful not to be too exuberant, always mindful of what happened to his darling sister. It was sad, but she accepted her loss.

She credited the change in her feelings to the conversation with Murad in which he explained why Charlie might have killed himself. Of course he didn't know the whole story but it had been a huge weight off her mind to explain that she thought it was suicide and not have Murad pass judgement. She remembered him saying that Muslims were not supposed to judge. If only she could believe that Charlie was now in heaven, freed from all the cares of the world: a Christian heaven or a Muslim heaven – or perhaps they were the same thing.

Finally, on 30th June, Murad arrived. It was the middle of the afternoon and Lucy and Emir were working in the garden. When she saw him, relief flooded her: he was walking, his limbs were intact. Lucy jumped to her feet, ran across the lawn and threw her arms around him, hugging him tightly. As she pulled away, she saw she had embarrassed him as he shuffled backwards and could not meet her eyes.

'Forgive me,' she apologised, realising she had crossed a line. 'I was just so happy to see you. Come and sit down. Pray, tell us what has happened.'

Emir came to join them and listened to Murad talking in English, only occasionally asking for clarification in his own language. Murad told them that French troops had taken the defensive structure called the Mamelon but there had been huge losses in the attempt to capture the Malakhov and the Redan and they had to retreat. Hundreds were killed outright and thousands more wounded. He had been involved in scouring the battlefield for survivors and had seen terrible carnage.

'I saw a French soldier going to the aid of a wounded Russian, only for the Russian to pull out a pistol and shoot him between the eyes.' He shook his head rapidly as if to erase the memory. 'I saw men looting corpses, stealing their boots and going through their pockets. There were worse things, which I would not mention in front of a lady ... but I also saw great humanity. There is an incredibly brave Jamaican lady called Mary Seacole who has set up a hotel in Kadikoi to cater for the troops. The men love her so much, they call her Mother. As I worked on the battlefield, she was treating wounded men, entirely oblivious to the dangers and undeterred by the horror. She gave me a cake she had baked and I saved it till after sunset, when it was much appreciated.' He smiled. 'There are no medical supplies in the Turkish camp so I had to take patients to the hospitals in Balaklava, where there were queues of men waiting for a doctor's attention. And Mother Seacole was there again with her cakes and remedies, spreading cheer even amongst those who seemed certain to die.'

'Is Mother Seacole dark-skinned?' Lucy asked.

'Yes, darker than me, although not as dark as some people I have seen from the Caribbean.'

'What happens now?' she wondered. 'If the troops have not taken Sevastopol, does the war just continue as before?'

Murad shrugged. 'There seems no solution as the city is so well guarded. And I have another piece of news: your British commander Lord Raglan died yesterday of fever. I do not know who will succeed him but I hope it is someone with a wise head.'

Murad stayed to eat a meal with them before galloping back to the Turkish camp at Kamara. That night Lucy lay in bed filled with relief that he was uninjured. It had been wonderful to see him again. She realised she had missed him desperately during the long separation: missed his calmness and quiet wisdom, his gentleness and his emotional nature, the way his eyes often filled with tears as he listened to her playing the pianoforte. In a sudden burst of clarity, Lucy realised something that, once it had entered her head, could not be ignored: she had fallen in love with Murad.

And yet it was impossible. She knew it was impossible. She was still in mourning for her husband; widows should mourn their husbands for a full two years before returning to society, even widows like her who had been married less than a year. She had passed the Islamic mourning period but was nowhere near fulfilling the British one. Besides, Murad was so traditional that he flinched if her hand accidentally brushed his and he had shrunk back in horror when she embraced him earlier. The differences between them were too great, their expectations too far apart for any romance to ensue.

Besides, she had not had the slightest inkling that he liked her that way. Charlie had pursued her from the start, bombarding her with gifts and compliments, and bowling her over with his charm. By contrast, Murad had been reserved and gentlemanly throughout their acquaintanceship. After the war he would go home and marry a nice Muslim girl. He most certainly was not interested in taking a lover; it was probably against his religion. She must forget her feelings and continue to treat him as a kind man who had aided her in her hour of need. Any other thoughts must be put firmly out of mind.

Chapter Thirty-three

Summer arrived with an intense, punishing heat and swarms of little black flies that nipped the skin, making it impossible for Lucy to work in the vegetable garden. She stayed indoors, only venturing out to lay laundry on the grass to dry in the sun. She felt happier than she had done for a long time and sang as she wandered round the house: 'Is good,' said Emir the first time he heard her voice, and Murad was very complimentary when she sang a Mozart *lied* for him. 'There is a sweetness to your tone. You are like an angel.'

She laughed: 'How little you know me. My sister Dorothea would tell you I am no angel!'

She sang jaunty show tunes for them and accompanied them with little dances, encouraging them to clap along to the beat. Gradually she began to feel herself again, the Lucy of old, and she liked the feeling. She and Murad sometimes conversed late into the evening before he rode back to the Turkish camp, talking of their lives at home and the vast differences between their two cultures.

Although Lucy felt clearly the impossibility of a relationship between them, her attraction to him grew stronger by the day. Was it genuine love or was she simply grateful to him? There was no doubt that what she had felt for Charlie was true love, so how could she possibly love again so soon? She remembered having feelings for other men of her acquaintance before she met Charlie but these had been shallow and soon passed. Time was the test ... And yet she had spent no time at all with Charlie before they married; she just knew she loved him. Perhaps it had been the sense of his inner sadness, and the way he needed her that made her love him so dearly. With Murad, there was no such sense. He didn't seem to need her at all; on the contrary, she needed him. Everything was confusing; none of it made sense.

One breezy morning in July, when the weather was not as sweltering as it had been of late, Murad arrived at the *dacha* bringing a spare horse.

'You must be tired of seeing the same view every day. I wondered if you might like to visit the Monastery of St George, which is about fourteen miles along the coast from here? I brought a horse with a side-saddle for you.'

Lucy had mixed emotions. It would be wonderful to spend time on her own with him but the *dacha* was her sanctuary and it didn't feel safe to leave, even though Murad assured her the fighting was in a lull and there would not be any danger. She felt guilty about leaving Emir behind but Murad had not invited him. And she had other worries too.

'I am not a confident rider,' she confessed. 'I'll be fine if we can take it slowly.'

He agreed that they would.

'And I do not wish to see anyone from the British camp. Are you sure we won't run into them?' She didn't want to have to explain herself to Mrs Jenkins or Mrs Duberly. Her life now was none of their concern.

'We must ride past Balaklava, which is only seven miles from the British camp, but we can circle the outside of the town to avoid them.'

As Murad helped Lucy onto the horse, she felt ashamed of her blue gown. She had been wearing it for almost seven months now, just washing it when she could, and it was becoming threadbare. The wool was far too heavy for the heat of summer, even though she didn't wear petticoats or a corset any more. If only she had picked up more clothes that December morning when she left the camp, instead of just bringing two blankets. If only she had brought some of Charlie's things as keepsakes. She hadn't known then she would never return.

They rode along the cliffs under a cloudless sky of startling blue. Dense green forest encroached right up to the cliff edge in places and Lucy was grateful for the shade of the trees. She inhaled the giddy scent of pine and felt happiness bubbling inside her, to be here, in such glorious surroundings. Murad stuck close by, keeping the pace at a slow canter, but they didn't talk as they rode, each lost in the experience.

Balaklava seemed bigger than when Lucy was last there, trains chugging along its railway line and many more buildings spreading into the countryside behind. It was bustling with people and wagons even on the outskirts and Lucy tilted her face downwards for fear of being recognised, but no one paid them any attention.

Beyond Balaklava the coast became wilder, with rocky scree and waist-high shrubs stretching out to a point. Just as they reached the edge of the land with only sea beyond, she saw a tiny gold-domed monastery perched precariously on the cliff edge. The track wound down to a yard where there was a two-storey white building and then the shrine itself, and below it, terraces of steep gardens descending to the water.

They pulled up their horses and Murad helped her to dismount.

'What a charming spot!' she exclaimed. Some children were playing a game of tag in the courtyard, shrieking with high spirits, with no thought for the war taking place just a few miles away. She could see some monks in dark brown habits walking into the monastery. 'Are we allowed to explore? These monks won't mind?'

'Yes, of course. The monks are Russian Orthodox but the allies have given them permission to stay and they deliver supplies weekly, because they are caring for children who are refugees of war.'

'Their parents are lost? Oh, the poor mites.' The children seemed perfectly happy, absorbed in their game.

They walked over to the monastery and Murad held the door for her. Inside the white-painted walls were decorated with dozens of bright-coloured paintings of saints with golden halos, and Murad told her these were called icons. The back wall was formed by the rock face itself, and shrines were carved into it. Thin candles flickered and there was a heady smell of incense. A monk nodded to them, and Lucy shivered at the realisation that he was Russian, the enemy they were here to fight. What must that gentle-faced man make of them? She examined the art in silence, imbued with a sense of the ancient holiness of the place.

Out in sunlight again, Murad took her arm to help her down a stony path to the garden. There was a wooden bench in the shade of a cypress tree and they sat and drank from the flagons of water they had brought along. Wildflowers poked out of crevices in the rock: deep red shrubs she did not recognise, tall yellow irises, and sweet-scented violets.

'How far are we from Sevastopol?' Lucy asked, peering along the coast.

'About six miles.'

She was shocked. 'Is that all? I can't hear any shelling.' The only sounds were the buzzing of a bee nearby and the children shrieking further up the hill.

'I think the heat has drained all appetite for fighting. It's clear the Russians are running out of ammunition because they only return one shell for every six sent over by the British and French. But they defend their redoubts so fiercely that too many are killed in any attempt to storm them. I can't see how this war will ever come to an end.'

'You must be anxious to get home to your mother and sisters. I expect you miss them greatly.'

'Yes …' He seemed about to say something else, then stopped.

'I will miss you when we leave here,' she said. 'I'm so grateful for all you have done for me. I would have died without your help, and now I feel revived and renewed. Your friendship has meant so much …'

She turned to look at him and was puzzled to see that he was blushing deeply, too tongue-tied to speak or even meet her eye. She carried on boldly, as if intoxicated by the drowsy heat and the charm of the surroundings.

'I expect it won't be long after your return before your thoughts turn to marriage. I hope you don't think me forward, but I wonder if you have met any girl you might consider?'

Murad stuttered as he replied: 'In my country, our parents and older relatives choose our brides for us. We have a say of course, but as I told you, I am not permitted to speak to women outside the family.' He stood and walked a little distance then came back again. 'I apologise. I am a very shy man and find it difficult to speak of such matters, even when …'

She waited but he couldn't finish his sentence. 'Oh, but you must speak of such matters when you have an opportunity, because who knows what direction life will take next?

Paths cross and then they diverge and if the moment is not seized it may never arise again.'

He was having trouble speaking and she noticed his hands were shaking. 'Do you ... do you think you will ever love another man? I know how much you loved your husband so I wondered ...'

'I should very much like to, because I know the great joy that comes from such a love. Next time I would like to find someone sensitive and thoughtful, someone who loves music, who is caring and good.' Lucy wondered at her own temerity. She was beginning to suspect ... to hope Murad had feelings for her but would he find the courage to express them without her help?

He sat down on the bench then stood up again and turned his back to her, gazing out to sea. Lucy decided to throw caution to the wind. 'Whatever is on your mind, tell me now before the moment is lost,' she said playfully.

He turned to her, his cheeks puce. 'Lucy ... I ... I know this is wrong, and I hope you will not ... the thing is that ... I love you.'

Her heart leapt. 'I love you too,' she said. The abruptness of her answer startled them both. He sat down beside her and they stared at each other in wonder.

'You are sure? You are not just being kind to me? I don't want your gratitude. I love you with all my heart. You are the most beautiful creature I have ever seen, and yet you are strong and capable too.' The words poured out, now he had dared to release them. 'The way you move, the music you play, your voice, your conversation, your courage in this terrible place: I love everything about you but I never hoped ... I thought the love you had for your husband was so great that you would never love another.'

'That's what I thought six months ago – perhaps even three months ago – but my feelings for Charlie have faded to sweet memories. I have felt myself increasingly drawn to you. When you are with me, I marvel at your intelligence and kindness; when you are not with me, I find myself reliving our conversations and wondering if we might possibly belong together.'

Murad picked up her hand and raised it to his lips. She noticed tears sparkling in his eyes. 'But how can this be?' he asked. 'You are an English lady of Christian faith, I am a Muslim man. It is not possible.'

'And yet it is wartime, and everything is different.' Their faces were so close she could feel his breath on her cheek.

'I will never let you down,' he whispered.

'I know you will not,' she replied. 'And neither shall I fail you.'

As they rode back to the *dacha*, Lucy felt as though she were floating on a cloud. *Murad loved her*. The enchanting surroundings of the monastery garden, just six miles distant from a war, had made the experience all the more intense and romantic. She wished the day would never end: there was so much to discuss, so many things to say to each other. She planned the music she would play for him that evening: for moments of high emotion, Beethoven was always the best choice and she decided the Allegretto section in the Piano Sonata no. 17 in D-minor, with its joyful, bubbling excitement, would be fitting.

They found Emir had spent the day fishing in their absence and a feast awaited them. Suddenly starving, Lucy ate with great gusto. The fish was the best she had ever tasted, the bread was especially light, and she was particularly partial to asparagus from the garden. After dinner, she and Murad decided to stroll outside in the cooler air and as they walked he slipped his arm through hers. She could feel the strength in his arm muscles, the light brush of his hip, and she laid her head briefly on his shoulder.

Suddenly they heard the noise of a door slamming violently. Lucy jumped. 'What was that? Are there intruders?'

Murad stared back at the house and shook his head. 'No, it was Emir. I think he is angry.'

'Why would he be?'

He took her chin between his fingers, their faces close. 'Did you not realise that he is a little in love with you as well?'

Lucy was astonished for a second time that day. She had thought of Emir as a child but of course, there were only three years between them. Perhaps it was true. She resolved to be especially kind to him, in a sisterly way.

Chapter Thirty-four

Murad had to get back to the Turkish camp that night but he returned to the *dacha* the following day and Lucy led him into the drawing room, where they sat on the sofa holding hands and talking, gazing into each other's eyes with awe at their new relationship. Lucy loved to touch his skin, which was warm and smooth, the colour of toffee. She knew her hands were rougher than they had been before she began to work as a laundress and gardener, but still he exclaimed over their whiteness and kissed her fingers ardently.

'I wonder if I might ask you something personal?' he asked. 'I have long been concerned for your family. I am sure they must be desperately worried about you despite the disagreement caused by your marriage. They may have heard of Charlie's death and can have no idea what has happened to you, so they will fear the worst. Could you not write to set their minds at rest?'

Lucy hung her head. She had often thought of this, and yet had convinced herself they wouldn't worry, they would just assume there were difficulties with postal deliveries during wartime. Now she saw how selfish she had been. Perhaps in a way she had been punishing them, which was childish and unworthy of her. 'You are right, of course. I let my hurt feelings get in the way of any consideration for them.'

'I do not have writing paper or a pen but can give you some sheets from my calligraphy book and lend you my pencil. If you should feel like writing to them, I will take your letter to Balaklava and see that it is mailed.'

'But what will I tell them? If I confess that I am living in a house in Crimea, they will tell me to come home straight away.' And, she thought to herself, if she told them she had fallen in love with a Turkish man, Dorothea would be speechless. She would lecture that foreigners have different values, so the match could never work. All in all, Lucy knew, she would pour scorn on her love for Murad.

Murad squeezed her hand. 'Just tell them that you are alive.'

'Yes, I'll write,' she agreed, biting her lip. 'I'll do it today.'

In the end, she decided to keep her letter short. 'Dear Papa, dear Dorothea,' she wrote, then paused. 'I hope you are both well. I expect news will have reached you of Charlie's sad death at the hands of a Russian sniper last Christmas. I was too distressed to sail home directly but have been staying in a house in Crimea, leading a peaceful existence well away from the fighting. In this I have been greatly assisted by a very kind Turkish officer named Murad. He is a good man and goes to much trouble to take care of me. I am living off the land, and helping the war effort by laundering clothes for the Turkish troops. It seems I am of some use in this way so I plan to stay until the war's end, when I will travel back to London. If you wish to contact me you can write to the harbourmaster's office in Balaklava, marking your letter for the attention of Murad bin Ahmed, and I will ask him to enquire there from time to time.' She sent best wishes for her father's health and hoped Dorothea continued to enjoy her work at Pimlico Hospital, before finishing, 'I am, as ever, your Lucy.'

She re-read the page and regretted the formal tone, but decided it would have to do as she couldn't take any more sheets from Murad's book. She addressed the back of the sheet and gave it to Murad, who said, 'I will send it on the next ship out. I have also written to my mother and I told her of you.'

'What did you say?' Lucy was momentarily nonplussed.

'Just what an extraordinary lady you are.' He kissed the palm of her hand, making the skin tingle.

While they were talking, Emir had come into the house and stood watching them from the drawing-room doorway. He said something to Murad in Turkish, his voice aggrieved. Murad replied sharply, in a tone Lucy had never heard him use before. Soon they were arguing, Emir sounding very cross and Murad calmer but standing his ground.

'What is going on?' Lucy cried. 'Please don't argue.'

'Don't concern yourself,' Murad replied, before responding to Emir in Turkish again.

Emir punched the door hard and yelled something, then swept his hands in a gesture that seemed to mean, 'Enough! That is the end of it!' He turned and ran up the stairs towards his room. The whole quarrel had taken just a few minutes.

'What was that about?' Lucy asked, anxiously.

Murad gave a big sigh. 'I told him we are in love. He announced he must leave the *dacha* and go back to his company. I argued that it is not fair to leave you on your own, and he said that it is my problem now. I'm sorry, my sweet. He plans to leave tomorrow morning.'

'No! I'll talk to him.' But she couldn't think what she might say to change Emir's mind, except that she would miss him – and perhaps, in the circumstances, that could be awkward.

'I think we had best let him go. I will have to visit you more often so you do not get lonely.' Murad gave a half-smile but looked distracted. She knew his army duties weighed on his mind and did not want to become another problem.

'I will be fine. I managed before you brought Emir here and I will manage once he has gone. But I will talk to him all the same. I don't want bitter feelings to overshadow the companionship we have enjoyed.'

When she went upstairs, the door to Emir's room was closed and she could hear him praying. He didn't come down that evening when she played the piano and he didn't even emerge after Murad left to go back to camp. The following morning Lucy came into the kitchen and found him sitting with a heap of flour on the table in front of him. He smiled at her but he had shadows under his eyes, as if he had not slept well.

'Before I go, I show you how to make bread and catch fish,' he said.

Lucy was touched beyond measure. She hadn't attempted to learn before because that was Emir's contribution and he seemed proud of it but it would be a shame not to have any bread once he had left. 'I'm so sorry it has worked out this way, Emir. I wish you would stay.'

He ignored her. 'Put your flour and yeast like this.' He made a well in the centre of the heap of flour. 'Add a little water and salt.' He showed her how to bring the outsides of the well inwards without letting the water escape, then to add more water and once the dough was the right consistency, how to slap it around, fold it, push and roll it until it was light and silky to the touch. Finally, he lit the oven and shaped the dough on a tray before putting it in to bake, telling her, 'One hour.' She realised he had been estimating the timing whenever he made their bread but she would wind up Charlie's pocket watch and use that.

While the loaf was baking, he took her down towards the rocks, carrying the fishing line. She shuddered when he dug a worm from the soil and attached it to a bent nail on the end of the line. She was certainly not going to do that. He cast out into the waves and when he caught a small fish, he swung it onto the shore and hit it on the head with a stone, where it lay on its side, dead eye staring. Lucy decided she would have to live without fish from now on. She was too squeamish to kill them herself.

'I'm sorry you are going,' she told him. 'I hope you will come and visit me sometimes.'

'Maybe,' he said, but didn't sound convinced.

They returned to the house just as the bread was ready to be pulled from the oven. While they waited for it to cool, Emir went upstairs and collected his few possessions, so he was ready to leave.

'How will you get to the camp?' she asked him as they ate.

'Walk,' he said. 'It is seven miles to Kamara. Not too far.'

'I wish you would change your mind.'

'I cannot. It is time for me to fight again.'

She sighed. 'Please take care.'

She wanted to hug him as he stood to go, but instead she just handed him the remainder of the loaf and some tomatoes and cherries from the garden, which he accepted with a nod. And then he was gone, and she was all alone.

Lucy took the opportunity to wash her clothes and dry them in the sun, and she drew a cool bath for herself. She remembered the first bath she had taken in the *dacha*, when the water had turned red from Charlie's blood, and thought how far she had come from the raw grief of that day. Now she had learned to be self-sufficient and her soul was at peace. She no longer cared for that which had concerned her in London; she lived according to a quite different, more natural agenda. What's more, she had learned to love again, something she had not believed possible just six months ago.

She looked into the room that had been Emir's and saw he had left it impeccably clean. There was no sign he had ever been there. Her own room, by contrast, showed many signs of her occupancy. There was a pile of Russian books from the library, under which she was pressing some flowers. There were some stones with unusual markings she had found on the seashore. She had brought a large mirror out of a store cupboard in the hall and hung it on one wall to help as she did her best to comb and arrange her hair with no other tools except her fingers. And she still kept the pistol under her bed, just in case.

The first day without Emir seemed longer than any other day since she had arrived at the *dacha*. As evening fell, she kept glancing out of the music-room window along the track that led to the house, hoping Murad would come. She prepared some vegetables and the solitary fish Emir had left but didn't feel hungry. She couldn't sit still, couldn't settle to any task. Every noise – the creaking of an old tree, the twitter of birds – made her jump. She sat down to play the piano but couldn't concentrate. Her thoughts were constantly on Murad and she felt a thrill at the thought that they would be alone together. She wanted to kiss him on the lips, to touch his tanned skin and run her fingers through his hair. Would that shock him? Would he push her away?

It was dark by the time she heard horse's hooves and ran outside to watch Murad dismount. Throwing all caution to the wind, she hurled herself into his arms and lifted her face to kiss him on the mouth. At first he held back but before long he was returning her kiss with ardour. His body pressed against hers, causing lust to ripple through Lucy's core.

They went into the house, arms locked around each other, but instead of going to the kitchen for food, their feet led them up the staircase to her bedroom. It wasn't a conscious choice, simply an inevitability. Moonlight streamed through the open shutters as they hurried to undress each other. The buttons of his tunic were stiff and Lucy fumbled.

'Are you sure?' he whispered, stroking the hair back from her face.

'Very sure.'

She pulled her gown over her head and stood in front of him in her silk chemise and drawers. He took off his tunic and shirt, and removed his boots and the sash round his waist, then his trousers. They climbed beneath the bedcovers and she found he was shy; could it be his first time? She placed his hand on her breast, ran her hands over his body and kissed his chest until he shivered. When he was breathing deeply and she could feel his manhood had hardened, she pulled off her chemise to let him see her naked breasts and he groaned and pulled her towards him to kiss them. She let her hand slip down between his legs and soon they could hold back no longer. He climbed on top of her, and gently, so gently, she guided him inside. He gave a cry of longing and lost himself, so passionate and eager that very soon he had spilled his seed.

'I'm sorry,' he cried, ashamed. 'So sorry.'

'There is nothing to be sorry for,' she whispered. 'The night has only just begun.'

Enjoying being the more experienced lover of the two, she pulled off the cover and lay so the moon lit her nakedness, making her skin appear luminous white. Shyness forgotten, Murad let his fingers trail across her nipples, down her belly, inside her thighs, marvelling at the softness and perfection. He bent to kiss her, tasting her skin in places she had never been kissed. He turned her over to explore the hollows behind her knees, the curve of her bottom, the delicate ridge of her spine. He sighed, unable to believe his luck, and soon passion fired him and he slipped inside her again, needing no one to show him the way this time.

All night they made love, unable to rest for long without him inside her. In the early hours of the morning, they slipped down to the kitchen to eat, ravenous with hunger, but then couldn't wait to get back to the bedroom and he entered her as they stood against the kitchen table.

'We must try to sleep,' she whispered once they were back in bed. 'You will be tired tomorrow.'

But when she closed her eyes for a second, she awoke to the sensation of him sliding into her again, pushing deep against her insides, filling her up to overflowing. They tried dozing with him inside her but her muscles moved instinctively because the pleasure was too great to resist, and then he would move in symphony.

As dawn broke, still they were joined, facing each other, her leg curved over his thigh, and he stroked her face with the tip of his finger, tracing her eyebrow, the groove in her top lip, the whorl of her ear, and making tiny thrilling thrusts with his hips. She felt a tension building deep in her womb, ripples of pleasure intensifying, and suddenly her muscles contracted hard around him and she threw herself back with a little cry. She had never experienced that sensation before. It took him by surprise and spurred him to thrust more strongly as her contractions continued until once more his seed burst inside her. How many times was it, she wondered later. Six? Eight?

The sun was rising fast and he groaned. 'I must go. I don't know how I will force myself to leave you but I have no choice.'

'I will only let you go if you promise to come back tonight,' she murmured throatily.

'I promise.' He kissed her full on the mouth then leapt out of bed. Her skin tingled, her lips throbbed and her insides were on fire from his touch. He dressed quickly without taking his eyes off her.

'You are so beautiful,' he sighed. 'I love you more than I ever thought possible.'

'And I love you the same.'

After one last delicious kiss, he sprinted down the stairs and she heard the door close behind him. She lay still, examining the sensations in her body, like nothing she had ever known. It was as if every part of her had changed fundamentally and would never be the same again.

Lucy slept for a few hours and awoke to find her skin still sensitised, the flesh between her legs still swollen with lust. She had no regrets over what she had done. If it had been possible for them to marry soon she would have waited, but this war stretched on with no end in sight and she simply needed to be with Murad. It had felt natural and essential to make love with him. She knew she had stepped far beyond the constraints of English society but war changed your perspectives entirely. She could no longer imagine returning to the staid drawing rooms of London with their strict social etiquette of chaperones, dress codes and calling cards, where there were rules governing every last detail of behaviour. She had stepped into another world.

She rose and washed herself, then dressed and went down to the kitchen to attempt to bake some bread, her cheeks burning as she remembered making love against the table the night before. She followed the method Emir had shown her but somehow her dough became too sloppy and even when she added more *çavdar* it did not have the consistency he had demonstrated. She put it in the oven anyhow and tried to plan what she would feed Murad that evening. All the while her thoughts kept returning to the intensity of their love-making. It had been fun with Charlie; they had often laughed in bed but he had never been able to make her body respond the way it did with Murad. With him it was profound, spiritual almost, a sensation that took her over so completely she could think of nothing but the pounding of her blood, the tingling of her skin. And his skin became hers, so it was as if she could feel what he felt when she touched him. She was glad her two husbands were so different. That made it easier.

She told herself that Murad would be exhausted when he arrived. He'd had no sleep and he had worked all day. She must not expect him to make love to her so ardently ... and yet she knew he would because it was irresistible. As soon as he arrived, they hurried upstairs without words and tore off their clothes, impatient to be lost in each other again. If anything the sensations were more intense, more urgent than before as they explored every part of each other. They ate her tough bread with some fruit, they slept a little, but otherwise they spent the night entwined and enclosed in each other's bodies.

Towards dawn, he whispered: 'I will find a way to spend every night with you, Lucy. I cannot be without you now.'

The words made her glow all over. 'You don't think less of me for making love with you when we are not married?'

He gazed deep into her eyes as he replied: 'But we *are* married. In our hearts we are man and wife. No ceremony could possibly make our love any deeper than this.'

Lucy knew he was right. She felt she could explode with happiness.

The month of August was one long honeymoon during which they walked arm-in-arm in the garden, ate, talked and made love. Every night she learned new ways to please him, and discovered new qualities he possessed.

'Imagine if we had children,' he mused one evening as he ran his fingers through her hair, which she wore loose to her waist at his request. 'I would like them to have golden locks

305

just like yours. When I look at your hair in sunlight there are strands of many different shades, from almost white through to rose-gold and deep sand.'

'And yours is blue-black, like the wing feathers of a magpie. I hope we will have sons who look just like you, with your strong jaw and wise eyes.'

'Perhaps we should have some of each: blonde children and dark children. And we will raise them to speak both English and Turkish.'

'Of course,' she agreed, delighted with the fantasy. 'What kind of house should we live in?'

He grinned: 'Something like my mother's house! It is set on a hill not far from the ocean and has the most wonderful gardens with peach and pomegranate trees. As a boy I used to make myself sick gorging on them.'

'It sounds wonderful.' Her childhood home in Russell Square did not have its own garden, although there was a public square opposite in which she had played as a girl, watched over by Dorothea.

'We would have to get a pianoforte. And you could teach our daughters to play beautiful music.'

She laughed. 'You have to put up with many years of listening to wrong notes and simple tunes repeated over and over before it becomes beautiful. But yes, of course I would teach them.'

'I think you will like the artistry of our culture. Are you familiar with Ottoman carpets? Our ceramics?'

Lucy shook her head. 'The only thing I have heard of is whirling dervishes. Do you have those in your area?'

Murad laughed. 'Yes, we have whirling dervishes. They are men of the Sufi religion, and their dance is an act of devotion. It is quite spectacular to watch.'

They shared memories of occupations they enjoyed in childhood, and she loved the affectionate way he talked of his four sisters, Safiye, Fatma, Halida and Nakiye. 'They are educated women,' he told her, 'and all are very artistic. They embroider, make rugs and paint pretty miniatures. I miss the sound of their laughter; our house is always full of women's laughter.'

'I'd love to meet them,' Lucy said wistfully.

There was an awkward pause. It was all very well to fantasise, but how could any of this become a reality, given the vast cultural divide between them?

'I am allowed to marry a non-Muslim woman if I choose,' Murad said quietly, looking down at his lap.

Lucy's heart leapt. So he would consider marrying her? But could she live in Turkey, in a society where she must wear a veil and live behind closed doors? When would she see Dorothea and her father, never mind her London friends? She would find it hard in a country where women appeared to have much less freedom than she was used to. She did not want to introduce a note of reality to their conversation, so she cried, 'I must learn to speak Turkish! Emir started to teach me, but his English was so much better than my Turkish that we lapsed into communicating in English. Will you be my teacher now?'

'*Seni canımdan çok seviyorum*,' he said with passion. 'That means I love you more than my life.'

Chapter Thirty-five

Murad and Lucy rarely talked about the war. There had been stalemate since the carnage of early June, but on the 17th August, he came to the *dacha* with news of a Russian attack on the French and Sardinian lines. Lucy hadn't even known the Sardinians were amongst the allies, as they had only joined the struggle after she left the British camp.

'The Russians have been soundly defeated,' he told her, 'but I must go back to Chernaia to assist with the wounded.'

'Can I do anything to help?' she asked.

'You are so good.' He kissed her on the lips, stroking her hair. 'I will let you know.'

It was the only night that whole month they did not spend together and Lucy tossed and turned, unable to sleep until he rejoined her the following evening.

'It means the end for the Russians and they must know it,' he told her. 'The allies have bombarded the city so thoroughly it lies in ruins. They have cut off supply lines so the people are starving. The only thing we have not been able to do is capture their well-defended redoubts. I think the end is very near, my darling.'

They looked at each other in consternation. The end of the war would mean the end of their idyll and they had not made plans for the aftermath. 'Did you call by the harbour-master's office today?' Lucy asked. It was a month since they had written to her father and Dorothea and she knew that letters to England generally took two weeks to arrive. If they had written back by return, she should have heard by now.

'Nothing yet. But I am sure we will hear from them any day now.' His mother had written a very sweet letter sending her blessings for her son's friendship with an English lady. Murad smiled as he translated. 'You see? She is a broad-minded woman.' Lucy imagined her as having a gentle character similar to Murad's.

September began and the fierce heat of August cooled by a notch; it was still broiling in direct sun but the minute Lucy stepped into the shade the temperature was fresh and comfortable. She was able to return to gardening in the early mornings when Murad left for the Turkish camp – and not a moment too soon, for weeds were threatening to take over.

When they woke on the morning of the 5th September, they heard a low booming sound. Murad ran to the window.

'It sounds as if there is another offensive. It must be a big one for us to hear it at this distance. I must get to my company.' He was already pulling on his uniform. 'Do not worry if I am unable to return this evening. You know I will get here just as soon as I can.'

He kissed her quickly on the lips and as he hurried to the door she called after him: 'Seni canımdan çok seviyorum.' He turned and blew a kiss.

Lucy rose and dressed then went out into the garden, walking barefoot on the dew. The sound of shelling was even louder now and she could see a huge cloud in the direction of Sevastopol. Suddenly she realised something was missing; usually at this hour the garden was full of birdsong but now it was quiet, as if even the birds knew it was a momentous day.

Of course Lucy hoped for war's end so that no more soldiers would lose their lives, but what would happen to her love affair? If only she could persuade Murad to come to London. It would be hard to return to the petty rules governing polite society but maybe they could create their own circle of free-spirited types of people. They would certainly have more freedom than they would in Smyrna. She wanted to live in her home city, even if her father and Dorothea had disowned her. She hoped they had not, but was impatient for a response to her letter. If only she and Murad could marry and he could find work in London, and visit his family in Smyrna once a year. But what work would he do? How would they survive? If her father still had the furniture business, he could have run that. But she knew in her heart that Murad couldn't be in London. Apart from anything else, he would miss his sisters too much. But Lucy had a sister too. She missed Dorothea, even though she knew her sister would condemn her current lifestyle in the strongest possible terms. There was no perfect solution and it made her anxious to think of the future.

All day long, Lucy kept wandering into the garden, trying to assess what was happening from the level of the sounds of shelling. Had it eased off a little yet, or had the wind simply changed direction? As darkness fell, she had to admit it was as loud as ever and the chances of Murad returning that evening were slim. She ate a small meal then played the pianoforte in an attempt to distract herself from the ache of missing him. In bed she hugged a pillow against her breasts and clamped her legs together until at last she fell asleep.

Next morning as soon as she awoke, she ran to the bedroom window, only to hear the sounds of shelling as fierce as ever. Her spirits sank. The Russians must run out of shells soon. Surely it was not possible to continue at this rate for long? It was horrible to think of all the men being killed and maimed by these explosions, and a tremor of panic gripped her heart in case Murad should be hurt. But he had assured her he would not be sent into battle. His role was to ensure the troops at the front received sustenance, so he worked behind the lines arranging the preparation and transportation of supplies. That's why he could not return until the fighting was over. Combat troops might have some time off when their company was not directly involved in battle, but Murad was never off duty during an offensive.

Lucy understood all this rationally but still she hoped he would slip away that evening. Even if he rode to the *dacha* simply to kiss her then had to leave again immediately, she would have been content. But he did not appear on the evening of the 6th, or the 7th, or the 8th. On the morning of the 9th September, Lucy ran to her bedroom window and leaned out; there was silence. The shelling had stopped. She was so delighted she cheered aloud and hugged herself in delight. It had to mean a victory for the allies. Murad had promised her the Russians no longer had a chance of winning. It must mean they had surrendered.

She cautioned herself that Murad might not return that day. He always helped to collect the wounded from the field and see that they were settled in hospital beds. It might take another day or so but she knew he would come just as soon as he could. The 9th passed, and then the 10th and 11th. There had been no more shelling and the sky was a bright clear blue, although the air was definitely cooling. Lucy's mood plummeted; the only thing that would cheer her would be Murad's return. She kept thinking she heard his horse on the track and rushing to the window of the music room, to find nothing except a tree branch blowing in the wind.

As the days went by, a feeling of dread hung heavy on her. If Murad could possibly have returned, he would have done so; she knew that as surely as she knew anything. She

311

remembered that it had taken over three weeks after the battle in June before he could get away but still she felt sick with worry as she waited and watched the hours and minutes tick by on Charlie's pocket watch. She went through the motions of gardening, cleaning the house, eating, washing, sleeping, but also she spent a lot of time sitting in the garden gazing out to sea, listening for any clue that would help her to understand what had happened.

It was the afternoon of the 16th September when Lucy finally heard a horse's hooves on the track and knew for sure she was not imagining it. She whirled through the house like one possessed, intent only on rushing into Murad's arms. When she opened the door she saw a man dismounting from a horse but knew from the shape it was not Murad. He turned and she saw it was Emir.

'What's happened? Where is Murad?' She tried to read his expression.

'He is hurt. In Sevastopol. He went …'

She interrupted him. 'How is he hurt? He is not dead, is he?'

'Dead, no. But he is hurt.' Emir patted his head.

'You must take me to him. Now.'

'He has gone on a ship to hospital.'

'Which hospital? Where?'

'To Scutari.'

'I must go to Scutari then. Will you help me?'

'Of course.'

She rushed inside to collect her cloak and pull on her petticoats and boots. She had planned to clean and tidy the *dacha* for its owners before she left, to pull the dust covers back on furniture, but there was no time. She left her pressed flowers and stones, and completely forgot about the pistol. Emir waited outside by his horse and when she emerged minutes later, he lifted her onto its back and mounted behind her.

As they rode towards Balaklava, Emir told her what had happened. On the night of the 8th September the Russians had abandoned Sevastopol and Murad had gone in with an advance party to help the wounded they had left behind. According to what Emir had heard, he entered a building damaged by shelling to help a young boy who was trapped there and a piece of masonry fell on his head. He was taken to Balaklava General Hospital, where it was decided he needed long-term nursing and he had been transferred to a ship bound for Scutari. Emir had been looking for him but could not find out what had happened until that very morning when he had been told by another officer, whereupon he hurried straight away to tell Lucy.

She analysed his words, trying to ascertain how seriously Murad was injured. The main thing was that he was alive. He would recover. He must.

They galloped to the port of Balaklava and Lucy asked Emir to pull up by the harbourmaster's office. She dashed inside to find the familiar bespectacled man sitting at his desk, talking to two British officers.

Ignoring the officers, she cried, 'I must get to Scutari on the next boat. It is urgent. Please help me.'

She wasn't sure if he remembered her as the woman to whom he had given a bag of coal the previous winter but he seemed to appreciate her distress.

'The *Belleisle* leaves within the hour,' he said. 'I'll get you a berth on it.'

PART SEVEN

Chapter Thirty-six

Summer 1855

During the hottest months of the year, the mood in the British camp was one of extreme frustration and disillusion. The men continued to fire shells at the Russians then brace themselves for the bone-rattling, ear-shattering explosion as a shell was fired back. They dodged sniper fire while out on patrol and dreaded the next order to advance on the heavily fortified redoubts. It seemed there was no resolution to the war in sight and the horrifying prospect loomed of yet another winter living in tents on that exposed plain. Some soldiers developed nervous complaints as a result of the continual threat of incoming fire combined with the horror of watching their comrades die around them. Dorothea saw men in the General Hospital, staring into the distance, wringing their hands or rocking back and forth; they were unresponsive to the medical staff, who began to call the condition 'trench madness'. Some of those who suffered from it were able to return to duty after a week of rest, while others seemed as though they might never recover.

Dorothea remained at the Castle Hospital, assisting Mr Crawford in the operating theatre and caring for patients after surgery until they were ready to return to the front line or be shipped home. After the Battle of Chernaia in August, she treated a number of Sardinian casualties. They had recently joined the fray, in their smart pale blue uniforms, and were unused to the deafening noise and random chaos of war, so it hit them hard. There were also two Russians whose legs had been amputated and who lay in neighbouring beds, scared to fall asleep in case anyone should attempt to finish them off. Dorothea treated them with especial kindness. The war was not their fault any more than it was hers.

One day, while attempting to communicate with them she realised they spoke a little French, and asked them, '*Comment allez vous aujourd'hui?*'

'What will happen to us?' they wanted to know.

Dorothea hazarded a guess: 'Once you are well enough you will be held as prisoners. Don't be alarmed; you will receive good care.'

This did not seem to reassure them and one asked plaintively if he might be allowed to go home. He had a young daughter, just three years of age, whom he hadn't seen since she was a baby.

'I hope the war will soon be over and we can all go home,' Dorothea replied, then asked: 'Do you have many British prisoners in Sevastopol? I wonder if you have seen an English lady there, young and slender, with blue eyes and blonde hair?'

The Russians looked at each other and shook their heads. 'There are some prisoners,' one replied, 'but we haven't seen them.'

'Do you know where they are kept?'

Again they shook their heads. Dorothea thanked them. She supposed it had only been a remote possibility, but not a day went by when she didn't worry about Lucy.

Over the summer she had entered into a correspondence with Lucy's friend, Adelaide Cresswell, who had replied to

317

Dorothea's letter of enquiry, writing that she was much saddened to hear the news about Charlie. She offered to write to the Harvingtons in case Lucy had made peace and gone to live with them. She wrote candidly that both she and her husband Bill had been concerned about Lucy, as she was so young and green, married to a man who was likeable but – between themselves and not wishing to speak ill of the dead – obviously unsteady. She told Dorothea of Lucy's devoted care while she nursed her husband Bill through cholera in Varna, and of her support when she sat vigil for Bill the night of his death. Dorothea was moved by this; her little sister had obviously grown up. She could hardly bear to think about what poor Lucy must be suffering now.

Towards the end of August, it was clear the allied generals were preparing for another offensive, as trains trundled night and day from Balaklava harbour to the front bearing crates of ammunition and explosives. Mr Crawford grumbled that it looked set to be yet another attack that the Russians knew all about for days in advance. He had as little faith in the new commander General James Simpson as he had had in Lord Raglan. He and Dorothea stockpiled chloroform, boiled silk for sutures, sharpened his knives and bone saw, and prepared themselves as best they could for another wave of injured soldiers. Everyone was on the alert, waiting for the campaign to begin, so it was no surprise when they wakened on the morning of 5th September to feel the ground shaking and to hear a booming noise so loud it was as if the heavens had opened and thunderbolts were shooting down. Soon the smoke cloud was so dense it blotted out the sun. Dorothea hurried up to wait at the Castle Hospital, but all morning no casualties arrived. Word came back that they were shelling Sevastopol first before the advance into the city would begin, and Dorothea was petrified. What if Lucy was there? It was one thing to shell the redoubts but shelling a town full of civilians seemed morally indefensible. There must be women and children, sick and elderly, all of them starving half to death.

Two days passed, the shelling continued and still the allies did not advance. It was eerie living in that atmosphere of constant noise and choking smoke and the patients were anxious and jumpy. Why did the Russians not surrender? Everyone knew they could never win. The besieging armies were now at full strength and hugely outnumbered the troops defending Sevastopol. All they need do was roll out some white flags and everyone could go home to be reunited with their families.

On the 8th September the charge began. The French army quickly seized the Malakhov while the British breached the Redan and the wounded began to flow back to Castle Hospital in their hundreds. There had been hand-to-hand fighting and many had vicious bayonet slashes through their bellies, an agonising wound from which most bled to death. One man's nose was shattered and he was struggling to breathe as blood trickled down the back of his throat. Another's gullet had been cut and he clutched an old rag to the wound trying to stem the bleeding. Everywhere there was blood: Dorothea's uniform was soaked in it and Mr Crawford's face was splattered, with dried blood matting his moustache. They worked grimly all day and through the night, as they had done back in June, until all the patients waiting for surgery had been dealt with. It was almost dawn on the 9th when Dorothea noticed that the shelling had stopped entirely, but she could smell burning.

'What has happened?' she asked one of the porters, and he promised to enquire and report back.

He returned an hour later when Dorothea and Mr Crawford were on the ward, tending their patients: 'The

Russians have abandoned Sevastopol. They set it on fire and crossed a floating bridge to escape to the north of the harbour. Now the soldiers are on boats back to Russia, but it is said there are hundreds of civilians still trapped in the town.'

Dorothea's first thought was for Lucy. 'Can't the army go in and rescue them?'

'They'll need to wait. The fire is burning too fiercely and they are worried the Russians have laid traps.'

'But those left behind will be too weak to move. There may be British prisoners of war. It's inhumane not to assist them.'

Over the succeeding days, Dorothea begged Mr Crawford that they might form part of a party going into Sevastopol to help the injured. He approached the head of the medical unit with their request. Word came on the 13th that they might proceed into Sevastopol as part of a small medical team to administer first aid. Dorothea told no one of her ulterior motive: a secret hope that she might at last find her beloved little sister.

Nothing could have prepared Dorothea for the devastation that met her eyes as she walked into Sevastopol. Not a single building remained undamaged and many were reduced to rubble; they had to climb over piles of it in the streets. The green cupola of the church had been split right down the middle.

Everywhere there were heaps of bodies in different stages of decomposition. The group held handkerchiefs over their noses but still the sweet stench caught the back of the throat.

They wandered aimlessly at first, unsure where to start. Dorothea spotted a man sitting upright, staring straight ahead, and hurried over to see if she could help him. He didn't respond to her enquiries and when she touched his arm, he toppled over, stone dead.

French troops were looting the houses, removing wooden icons, silver samovars, fancy furniture and oil paintings, even stealing from the churches, which didn't seem right. They ran back towards camp with their arms full of treasures, leaping over the dead and wounded who got in their way. It made Mr Crawford very cross and he shook his fist at them, shouting: 'Scoundrels! Stop that at once.'

Dorothea peered through doorways into rooms with no roofs, and down into dark basements where rubble blocked the entrance. Lucy could be anywhere. She simply didn't know where to start looking. She listened for moans that might indicate human life and struggled through debris to find the injured. There was an elderly woman trapped under a wooden beam, a mother and two bruised and terrified toddlers, a young boy with a shattered arm who ran away from them even though Dorothea opened her coat to show her nurse's uniform. In each building, round each corner, she had a moment of wondering – could Lucy be here? – before her hopes were dashed.

The party came upon a hospital building and hastened inside to find the most appalling sights yet: Russian patients had been abandoned by the fleeing troops without food, water or medicine, and they were in a desperate state. Broken bones pierced through raw inflamed flesh; maggots thrived in stinking necrotic wounds; the dead and dying were swollen and bloated, with blackened tongues protruding from their mouths. They had been left to die in agony. Those who could speak called out in Russian, begging for help, pointing to their wounds, pleading for a sip of water.

'We'll have to treat them here,' Mr Crawford said. 'Ambulance carts can't get through the streets. Just do what you can.'

Dorothea started working her way around the first ward, doling out water and opium, and dressing hideous stinking wounds that made her want to retch. She spoke to the patients in a soothing voice, trying to calm them with her tone even if they could not understand what she said.

Suddenly she heard a familiar voice and looked round to see Mary Seacole trundling in with a cart. The smell of freshly baked cakes wafted around the room and heads turned in disbelief.

She waved at Dorothea and began to dispense her goods to any who were capable of eating and drinking: 'Here you are, dear. Sponge cake for you? A meat pie? Some lemonade?' She had bandages and herbal remedies too, including her potion for curing fever, and she applied them skilfully to the poor creatures lying in their beds. Dorothea watched the tender way she cleaned a head wound thick with congealed blood, all the while reassuring the terrified patient in her motherly tones. She seemed a skilful nurse. Mr Crawford raised an eyebrow; he had obviously never visited the British Hotel and did not know what to make of this exotic dark-skinned creature in bright yellow, red and blue, with clanking jewellery and an enormous pillowy bosom. The injured Russians gazed at her as if she were a ghost, or a mirage that could disappear at any moment.

By dusk, the party had worked their way around the hospital but Dorothea had not had time to search for any jails where prisoners might be held. She wanted to continue looking but Mr Crawford pointed out it was not safe to remain in the crumbling ruins of the city after dark. Anything could happen. Dorothea resolved to return to hunt for Lucy the following day, if permission were given. But when she got back to the room she shared with Elizabeth Davis, there was a surprise waiting for her: a letter from her father. She sat on the bed and opened it eagerly. There was a brief note in his messy scrawl saying he had recently received the enclosed correspondence from Lucy.

A sob burst from Dorothea. Lucy was alive! She hadn't realised how tense she had been feeling all day, fearing she might find her sister's body in every basement she had peered into, every hospital ward she visited. But instead here was a letter from her. Dorothea wiped her eyes and began to read, galloping through so fast that she had to go back and read the letter again. Lucy wrote that she was staying in a house in Crimea. Where might it be? She didn't say. Who was this Turkish officer who had protected her? Reading between the lines, Dorothea hoped there had been no impropriety, especially as Lucy was still in mourning. These questions troubled her; but most of all, she was overjoyed to hear that Lucy was alive and yearned to see her, to know for sure that she was safe and well. The letter said to contact her via the harbourmaster's office; perhaps they could be reunited within a matter of days.

Dorothea was too restless to sleep that night and at first light she walked down to the office to speak to the harbourmaster himself.

'Good morning, sir. I have been asked to write to a Turkish officer named Murad bin Ahmed care of this office. Instead I would like to find him and speak with him. Do you have any idea how I might locate him?'

The man removed his spectacles and rubbed his eyes. 'Murad bin Ahmed ... yes, I know him. Speaks good English. He came in several times this last month enquiring after a letter. But I don't think I've laid eyes on him since the fall of Sevastopol. Must be over a week now.'

'Might you know where his company is located?'

'Well, there's a Turkish camp at Kamara, but most of them have been sent to Evpatoria on the west of Crimea. You won't find many left at Kamara. Maybe Mr bin Ahmed has gone west.'

'How far is Evpatoria?'

'My goodness, it must be about fifty miles all told. I don't recommend the journey. There is still sporadic fighting across the peninsula so it's not safe.'

Dorothea walked back to the General Hospital to ask Elizabeth Davis's advice. She knew a lot of people and perhaps she would have a contact in the Turkish camp. First she had to explain that Lucy was staying in a *dacha* with the support of a Turkish officer and Elizabeth's eyes widened.

'A Turk, you say? What is she thinking of?'

Dorothea shrugged. 'I have no idea.'

Elizabeth said she knew a man called Osman Bey who was adjutant to Omar Pasha, the Ottoman commander, and would mention the name Murad bin Ahmed. If he was an officer, Osman might know him. Perhaps they would know Lucy's whereabouts as well.

'You must be happy to find she is well, at least, even if …' Elizabeth didn't finish the sentence. Dorothea remembered Mrs Duberly calling her sister a flirt when they met in the British Hotel. Perhaps Elizabeth was remembering this as well and coming to believe there might be some truth in it.

Dorothea could see that it would be in Lucy's character to jump from one impetuous lover to the next. Mourning would not suit her passionate nature. But Dorothea resolved she would refrain from saying anything critical when they finally met. She had made that mistake once before. This time she would support her sister and try her very hardest to see things from her point of view.

Chapter Thirty-seven

Autumn came suddenly, with a violent thunderstorm followed by weeks of heavy rain that fell day and night without let up. The ground became marshy and it was impossible to dry clothes or bedding properly after they had been washed. There was no more shelling now that Sevastopol had been evacuated but carts brought the Russian wounded across to Balaklava to receive medical care. The wards at the Castle Hospital were full to bursting, with beds lining the corridors as well as crammed together in the wards. Dorothea had wondered whether there might be any resentment between the British wounded and their Russian counterparts but, on the contrary, they were soon playing cards together, sharing their harsh tobacco and chatting to the extent that their language skills permitted. It seemed to be generally accepted that they'd all had a tough time of it.

A message came back to Elizabeth Davis from Osman Bey, saying that he could not be sure of Murad bin Ahmed's whereabouts but it was possible he had gone with Omar Pasha to help relieve the siege of Kars in eastern Turkey. Bey had not heard talk of a Turkish officer offering protection to an English lady but he promised to ask around.

Dorothea was frustrated that there was no way of writing to Murad care of the army. It seemed the Ottomans were much less organised than the English and French armies, with frustratingly little in the way of records to tell them where any individual might be at a given time. She left a note for him in the harbourmaster's office, asking him to contact her urgently at the hospital. She also went to the British Hotel to ask Mrs Seacole's advice, because she knew many Turks personally.

'Oh my dear, how frustrating for you to find your sister is so near yet not be able to contact her. I haven't heard of an English lady staying in a *dacha* but I will ask all my friends.' She added: 'Don't worry about this officer. They're good people, the Turks. They've been given a bad name in this war – all this business of folks calling them cowards and spreading tales that they cut off the ears of their enemies. Well, how many men have you seen in hospital with their ears cut off?'

Dorothea admitted she hadn't seen any.

'I'm sure your sister will be fine. Try not to worry, lovely lady.'

There was nothing else Dorothea could do except wait.

After the siege of Sevastopol ended, the war continued on other fronts but those in the British and French camps knew they were lucky to have survived, unlike so many of their comrades, and an atmosphere of gaiety reigned. Copious supplies of alcohol had been discovered in Sevastopol and drunkenness became endemic in the British camp. Horse races were held whenever the rain eased off, and Dorothea went along with Elizabeth to watch and even to place a small bet, something she would never have dreamed of doing in London. She lost, but enjoyed the camaraderie as everyone cheered themselves hoarse in support of their particular favourites. In the evenings, many gathered at the British Hotel, or anywhere there were a few bottles of hooch and someone with a good singing voice. There were impromptu dances and women were much in demand, as the ratio of men to women was more than a hundred to one. One of Dorothea's colleagues at the Castle Hospital became engaged to a company sergeant of the Royal Artillery and there was a lively party to celebrate. Elizabeth hinted broadly to Dorothea that there were several more romances brewing, as the unmarried women could more or less take their pick, despite being older than would be considered marriageable age back home.

Dorothea's thoughts were never far from Lucy, and she didn't miss a chance to enquire at the harbourmaster's office, but it seemed Murad had not collected her letter. She sent firm instructions to her father to forward any further correspondence, but nothing came throughout the month of October. It was well into November when another letter arrived bearing her father's handwriting. One of the porters brought it to her on the ward and she tore it open then and there. The envelope contained a short note from Lucy saying that Murad had been wounded in the fall of Sevastopol and that she had joined him at the Barracks Hospital in Scutari, where she was by his bedside, nursing him. She did not say what kind of injury he had sustained, or whether he was recovering from it, but Dorothea could tell from the tone that Lucy was distressed. Instantly she decided to go to her.

First of all she asked Miss Langston if she might take a few weeks off to sail to Scutari, promising to return as soon as she could. Miss Langston agreed and sent a porter to enquire at the harbourmaster's office about the next sailing. They were less frequent now than they had been during the fighting but word came back that there was room on a ship departing two days hence.

327

Next, Dorothea went to tell Mr Crawford of her plans and to explain that she would find another nurse to assist him during her absence.

He seemed startled when she explained her reasons: 'But you did not tell me you had a sister. Why have you not mentioned her before?'

She was puzzled. 'It did not seem material to our professional relationship.'

'Hmm ... that's all very well. But what's to be done now?' He seemed quite put out by her news. 'And you will definitely return, you say? But you don't know exactly how long you will be?'

'I'm sorry to inconvenience you like this.'

He tutted, then bit his lip. 'I wonder if you would come outside with me for a moment, Miss Gray. I suppose I must ... I would like to have a word with you in private.'

There was a howling gale blowing outside and although they stood in a porch the rain blew in sideways, soaking them. The sea and sky merged on the horizon into a seething blur of dark grey and despite being the middle of the day it was so dark they could barely see each other.

'Since we have worked together, Miss Gray, I have found you to be a most excellent nurse. You are dedicated and skilled, and I admire your sharp wits and your compassion. Yes, your compassion.'

He paused. Dorothea thought it was out of character for him to speak so warmly without a hint of his Scottish humour, but wished he would hurry up, since she was shivering. She hadn't had time to put on her cloak. 'Thank you. If I need a reference letter to apply for a nursing post on my return, perhaps I might ask you?'

'Well ... That's not ... Of course ...'

Dorothea had never seen him quite so lost for words. 'It's been a pleasure working with you,' she said. 'I have great respect for your surgical skills and have learned a lot from assisting you.'

'Yes, yes. Thank you. But what I wondered was … whether you would consider becoming my wife.'

The noise of the wind increased at just that moment and Dorothea wasn't sure she had heard correctly.

'I beg your pardon?'

'I'd like you to marry me, or at least to consider it. Now I realise this is rather abrupt but in my opinion we get on very well. We share the same values and have respect for each other. I am a few years your senior – I realise that – but I do not as yet have any of the impairments that can afflict the elderly. I have my own house in Edinburgh – rather a good house, with four servants. But we could always get more servants if you felt it necessary …' He stopped, at the expression of total astonishment on Dorothea's face. 'I apologise. I appear to be gabbling. You will, of course, want time to think about this.'

Her heart was beating hard as she tried to compose herself to reply. 'I am very surprised by this proposal, Sir, as you had not given me any indication that your feelings ran in this direction. But I am flattered, of course. I would be most grateful for a little time to think, but I promise I will let you know my answer before I sail for Scutari the day after tomorrow.'

'Yes, of course. That would be most kind.' He nodded. 'Thank you.'

They hesitated, both unsure how to conclude the conversation.

'Perhaps we should go inside out of the rain?' Dorothea suggested.

There was a moment when he leaned towards her and she wondered if he was going to kiss her, then he thought better of it and shook hands with her instead before charging out into the downpour, his boots slithering on the wet ground as he hurried down the hill in the direction of Balaklava. Dorothea stared after him, unable to believe what had just happened. It was the second proposal she had received just as she was on the verge of setting off on a journey. But her feelings this time were quite different than they had been at the last.

Chapter Thirty-eight

For the rest of the day, Dorothea's mind was full of both concern for Lucy and wonder at Mr Crawford's proposal. She found it hard to concentrate and when patients spoke to her she had to ask them to repeat themselves. It wasn't until she was lying in bed that night that she had time to think through her feelings, to sort and assess them.

Mr Crawford hadn't said he loved her; weren't men supposed to say that when they proposed? Of course William Goodland hadn't said he loved her either, but he was a dry old stick who didn't seem capable of high emotion. Mr Crawford, on the other hand, had appeared very emotional, although his words were practical and unromantic. Having watched him under pressure, she knew he had an even temper, and that he was a hard-working, honest man. She liked him. Would it not be a happy life married to such a person? Certainly happier than returning to Russell Square to live with her befuddled father and, after his death, on her own as an old maid. She tried to imagine herself as a surgeon's wife in Edinburgh and felt a warm glow in her core. They could discuss his patients over dinner, and perhaps attend concerts on his evenings off. Dorothea was sure they must have concert halls in Edinburgh. They had never discussed their musical tastes, but didn't everyone like music?

She wondered if this was how Lucy experienced love; or for her was it like the passionate scenes she read of in her romance novels? Should Dorothea be feeling weak-kneed and giddy? She realised she couldn't imagine kissing Mr Crawford: those ginger whiskers would surely tickle her lip but she liked his pale skin sprinkled with freckles. Suddenly, she thought about what it would be like to have marital relations with him and a knot of anxiety formed in her stomach. What if she was no longer a virgin after the attack in Scutari? Mr Crawford was a surgeon: he would be able to tell on their wedding night if her maidenhead was ruptured and would feel she had cheated him. She couldn't possibly marry under false pretences.

Dorothea lay awake most of the night agonising over her dilemma: she must not mislead Mr Crawford by pretending to be a virgin when she may not be. Perhaps it would be best to turn him down; but the minute she thought this, she found she didn't want to. She had successfully relegated the attack in Scutari to the back of her mind but now she faced the dual circumstances of a man wishing to marry her and a return to the place of her misfortune, and the sensation of those two awful men holding her down and poking at her most private parts came back to her with full force. She could remember their smell, of stale sweat and cheap alcohol, the harsh foreign voices, and the throbbing pain in her private parts afterwards. She hoped Lucy was safe and staying well away from those despicable cellars while she nursed her Turkish officer.

In the morning, as Elizabeth Davis lit the fire in their stove, Dorothea decided to confide in her. Elizabeth was a woman of experience who would offer sage advice. At the same time, although she liked to gossip about goings-on in the camp, Dorothea trusted her to be discreet over such a private matter. She began by telling her of Mr Crawford's proposal and Elizabeth chuckled with glee.

'About time too. Anyone with eyes in their head could see he was mooning over you!'

Dorothea was amazed. 'Really? I had no idea. How could you tell?'

'I knew it back when you first started working together. Surgeons don't normally pay any attention to their nurses but he hung on your every word. I'm glad he's finally got round to it. But what are your feelings?'

'He's a good man …'

'Ye-es. He is that.' Elizabeth was watching her closely.

'I think that maybe we could be happy together … But …' Dorothea couldn't think how to explain. 'But I am rather anxious about the wedding night.'

Elizabeth chortled. 'In that case, you are like every other first-time bride that ever lived. But when you see brides all-aglow the morning after the wedding, it's obvious nothing awful has happened to them. Quite the reverse.'

Dorothea summoned her courage: 'Something terrible happened to me when we were in Constantinople. Remember how ill I was? It was the result of being attacked by two foul men.' She felt a sob in her throat as she said the words and paused to compose herself. 'As a result, I am not sure if I am technically still intact.' A tear leaked down her cheek and she wiped it away.

'Oh my dear,' Elizabeth came to sit on her bed and embrace her. 'You should have said. That's simply awful. Where did it happen?'

Dorothea described her trip to Scutari on Boxing Day the previous year. 'It was over so quickly that I could not tell whether penile penetration had occurred or if I have been damaged in some way that Mr Crawford will be able to detect.'

'But my dear, if you were to tell Mr Crawford your story, he would feel only sympathy for your experience.'

'I can't!' It would be too humiliating to tell him about the attack. She would never be able to find the words.

'All right then. Do you remember if you bled afterwards?'

Dorothea shook her head. 'I was very sore but not bleeding.'

'That's a good sign. I'd say you are probably intact. Anyway, in my experience, men cannot tell one way or another. Even a surgeon can be confused because every woman looks different down there.'

'And yet I have heard it is possible to tell. I have tried to examine myself with the aid of a looking-glass but do not know what to look for. I don't suppose you know, do you?'

Elizabeth patted her hand. 'I tell you what ... shall I examine you? That way you can be sure.'

Dorothea coloured. 'I am mortified to ask ...'

'We are both medical people. Think of me as a nurse and yourself as the patient. Let's do it now. I shall light a lantern.'

Dorothea's cheeks were scarlet as she lay back on her bed, lifted her nightgown and parted her knees. She felt shy and exposed as Elizabeth brought the lantern close. 'Just relax now,' she coaxed. Dorothea felt a cool finger moving her drawers aside and touching her delicately. She held her breath. There was a brief pause, then Elizabeth declared, 'Your maidenhead is completely intact. No damage whatsoever. Those men must have failed in their attempts.' She pulled Dorothea's gown over her knees. The examination had taken only a few seconds.

Inadvertent tears trickled down Dorothea's cheeks as she sat up to embrace Elizabeth. 'It's such a weight off my mind. I don't know what I would have done without you.'

334

Elizabeth smiled and patted her shoulder. 'Here's what you can do: stop being a nincompoop and go and tell that lovely Mr Crawford that you accept his proposal!'

Rather than give him his answer at work, Dorothea asked Mr Crawford if they might dine together at the British Hotel that evening. It would enable them to talk in peace, and she thought he might enjoy seeing the renowned Mary Seacole presiding over her establishment. Besides, the food was rather good and it seemed he liked to eat. He searched her face for a clue about her reaction to his proposal, but she merely smiled enigmatically.

That evening she wore the only gown she had brought with her, the brown sprigged muslin. It smelled musty from storage; over the ten months she had been in Crimea she had worn nothing but her nurse's uniform. She and Mr Crawford caught the train to Kadikoi and alighted by the British Hotel, where lanterns were blazing and the babble of talk and laughter drifted out on the night air. Mary was in a bright red décolleté dress, with a wide blue sash and a yellow bonnet, and she greeted Dorothea like an old friend.

'Welcome, my dear. Come, come – the best table is this one in the corner. Are you planning to eat? Let me recommend my Jamaican chicken stew, to warm you on this cold night.'

They both ordered a bowl of the stew. Mr Crawford was nervous, fiddling with the edge of the tablecloth so clumsily that he threatened to capsize the glasses resting upon it.

'Before I answer your very kind proposal, might I ask you a few questions?' Dorothea began.

'Of course. I would expect you to.' He began playing with the cutlery.

'You said yesterday you were some years older than me. I am thirty-two. I wonder if I might ask your age?'

'Forty-one. I hope that's not too old ...'

'Not at all,' she smiled. 'It seems to me a perfectly decent interval ... Now, my elderly father suffers from senility. He lives in London and I have left him with just the servants to look after him, but he expects me to return when the war is over – if he even remembers who I am. I wonder ...'

'He would be welcome to live with us in Edinburgh if that is what you – and he – wish. Or, if he stays in London, you could visit him whenever you like.' Mr Crawford's nerves made him garrulous. 'I very much hope you would enjoy living in Edinburgh but if you find you don't like it, then I could search for a job down south – always assuming they could understand my accent.'

She smiled. 'From all I've heard, Edinburgh sounds most charming, Mr ... Actually, there's one rather important thing you have not yet mentioned to me.'

'And that is... '

'Your Christian name. Although I expect I will find it difficult to call you anything but Mr Crawford.'

'Gordon. Gordon Alastair Crawford. And I know that you are Dorothea.'

'Gordon.' She tried out the name. 'My father is an old-fashioned man, Gordon Crawford, and I think that despite us being substantially more mature than the average engaged couple, he would appreciate it if you would write and ask his permission.'

'But of course. Does that mean you are thinking of accepting my proposal?' He seemed as excited as a young boy with a new toy.

'Yes,' she said, happiness welling inside her so she couldn't stop grinning. 'Yes, I should very much like to marry you.'

He reached over the table and clutched her hand, squeezing her fingers tightly. 'Thank you,' he breathed, gazing into her

eyes as if to check she was being genuine. 'I can't believe …
I am just overjoyed.'

Mary Seacole brought their bowls of stew and Dorothea
suspected she had been watching and waiting for her cue.
She also filled their glasses with a delicious golden cordial,
and they toasted each other.

Mr Crawford continued: 'Now you have agreed, I am
impatient to become your husband as soon as possible. I will
understand if you want to wait until our return home, but
I heard of a colleague getting married at the ambassador's
residence in Constantinople and wondered if you might like
us to do the same? I could meet you there after you have
finished your business with your sister. Possibly we could
even be married before Christmas. But at the same time, I
don't want to rush you.'

Dorothea found it endearing that he talked too much when
he was nervous. 'That sounds perfect,' she smiled. Constantinople
was a breathtaking city and a wedding there would be an
event to cherish forever.

They ate and talked of details. During a lull in the conversation, she said, 'I hope you know I will be a dutiful wife
to you.'

He shook his head. 'From what I know of you, Dorothea,
you have been dutiful all your life. The last thing I want is
to become another duty. I want us to be companions who
travel through life together, making each other happy.'

He took her hand again and enclosed her fingers in his.
It was a wonderful feeling.

PART EIGHT

Chapter Thirty-nine

19th September 1855

Lucy disembarked from the *Belleisle* at a quay on the European side of the Bosphorus and, knowing she was penniless, the captain paid for a caïque to take her to the Barracks Hospital on the Asian side, the same place where she had stayed with Charlie on their arrival in Constantinople. She rushed up the track to the extensive red-roofed building and just inside the doorway she accosted a nun in white habit.

'I'm looking for Murad bin Ahmed, a Turkish officer who was brought here last week.' She was breathless from running.

'Turkish, you say?' She gave Lucy a stern look. 'Are you a relative?'

Lucy made a split-second decision. 'I'm his wife.' She blushed at the lie, but the nun did not appear to notice.

'All right, come with me,' she said, leading the way down a corridor. Over her shoulder she remarked, 'You're very young. Are any family members here with you?'

'No. They're back in England.'

The nun stopped at the door of one ward and asked a question of a nurse, then took Lucy up a flight of stairs to another landing, where she instructed, 'Wait here while I make enquiries.'

Lucy's heart was pounding. She couldn't bear any further delay now she was finally in the same building as Murad. Deep inside there was a hard nugget of fear: what if he was dead? She knew she would fall apart. Suddenly, she felt a wave of dizziness. She crouched on her heels with her head between her knees to avoid fainting.

Instantly the nun was beside her again. 'You poor child! Let me get you a chair.'

'I just want to see Murad,' she whispered, but the nun hadn't heard her as she was fetching a nurse. Together they hauled her into a chair and waved a bottle of smelling salts under her nose. The chemicals stung her nostrils and throat.

'We think we have an idea where your husband is, dear,' the nurse told her. 'I'll take you just as soon as you feel well enough.'

Lucy insisted she was fine, and stood up gingerly. The giddy spell appeared to have passed.

'May God be with you,' the nun said kindly, before taking her leave.

The nurse, who introduced herself as Mrs Roberts, led Lucy along a corridor and up another flight of stairs. She quickly lost her sense of direction in this rambling building of echoing corridors and closed doors. They entered another ward and Mrs Roberts consulted a nurse, then guided Lucy to a bed beneath a tall window. For a second she didn't recognise Murad because his head was swathed in heavy bandaging, his face swollen and his eyes closed, but then she saw it was him, and with a cry she rushed to his side.

'Murad, it's me, Lucy. I'm here,' she whispered urgently, reaching for his hand.

His chest was rising and falling evenly, his expression peaceful but there was no indication he had heard her.

'Murad!' she called a little more loudly, then asked Mrs Roberts, 'Is he asleep?'

Mrs Roberts found a chair for Lucy and dragged it to the bedside, motioning for her to sit down before she replied. 'He has had a nasty knock on the head and has not yet regained consciousness – but you mustn't worry.'

Instantly Lucy burst into tears and Mrs Roberts passed her a handkerchief in a practised gesture. 'After trauma it is good for the brain to rest in order for healing to take place. He is simply at the resting and healing stage.'

Lucy couldn't stop crying. Throughout the journey she had pictured arriving at Murad's bedside to find him weak, perhaps, but overjoyed to see her. She had imagined them kissing and embracing, and her taking over the task of nursing him until he was well enough to be released. Not in all her dreams had she predicted this.

'He may be able to hear you, so whisper cheerful things to him. Let your happy voice tempt him back from the blackness.'

Lucy looked at the blank unresponsiveness of his face and couldn't believe he could hear anything. But at least his breathing was regular, she told herself. That was the main thing; at least he was alive.

When Mrs Roberts left them alone, she tried whispering to him. 'I'm here, darling. Your Lucy. I came to be with you. Hurry up and get well. *Seni canımdan çok seviyorum* – see, I remember the words you taught me. They are true – I love you more than my life.' She told him about Emir coming to fetch her and about the crossing on the hospital ship. 'You must open your eyes soon,' Lucy chided, 'else I shall get lonely.'

Someone brought her a cup of English tea, the first she had tasted in many months, and she was offered a bowl of beef broth, which she declined. Her stomach was tied in knots and she couldn't face food.

As night began to fall, Mrs Roberts returned with an auburn-haired woman she introduced as Miss Nightingale.

'She is superintendent of the hospital,' Mrs Roberts explained in an aside.

'I understand you are married to this Turkish man?' Miss Nightingale said, with steel in her voice. Lucy agreed, eyes lowered. 'In that case, we will find you a room in which to sleep. Do you have any luggage?' She looked Lucy up and down, frowning at her ragamuffin appearance.

'No. In the rush to get here, I brought nothing.'

'Mrs Roberts, could you find Mrs bin Ahmed some fresh clothes? And perhaps some soap and a hairbrush.' She folded her arms firmly. 'Where are your family? You are too young to be alone in such a circumstance. You must write and ask someone to join you.'

'I am fine, I ...'

Miss Nightingale spoke as one who was used to being obeyed. 'Mrs Roberts will supply paper and a pen and I would like you to write this evening. We will mail the letter for you. While you are here, you can assist the nursing staff in caring for your husband and perhaps you can do some mending. In return, we will feed you and give you a roof over your head. Is that clear?'

Lucy agreed, but asked, 'Might I not sleep on the floor by my husband's bedside? I would prefer not to leave in case he wakes in the night.'

'No women are allowed on the wards after eight p.m.' The tone of her voice brooked no argument and Lucy had to concede.

At eight o'clock, when the ward was cleared, one of the nurses took Lucy to a large dining hall where portions of stew were being ladled out, but the smell made her nauseous. She could only manage to nibble a slice of dry bread and drink a glass of brandy. Afterwards, the nurse gave her a *fanoos* lantern and showed her to a small, windowless room with a narrow bed in it. She sat on the bed and wrote the

343

letter she had been asked to write, then climbed under the coven and sobbed herself to sleep, images of Murad's swollen face and bandaged head filling her thoughts. 'Oh please save him, oh please,' she repeated, like a mantra, as she drifted off.

Next morning, there was a knock on the door and a rosy-cheeked woman, who introduced herself as Mrs Bracebridge, walked in with an armful of clothes. There was a fresh set of undergarments and two gowns, one brown and the other violet, neither colours Lucy would have chosen for herself. They looked rather large, but at least they were freshly laundered and she accepted them gratefully. There were some toilet articles as well, and a towel. She washed and dressed then rushed back to Murad's bedside, full of hope that there might have been a change in his condition overnight.

'It's me, Lucy,' she whispered, the tears coming. 'Please wake up. I need you so much. Please. *Seni canımdan çok seviyorum.*'

He breathed in and out at the same even pace, but his eyelids did not so much as flicker.

Murad didn't regain consciousness that day or the next, or for the remainder of the week. Every morning, Lucy took her seat by his bedside, remaining there until eight in the evening, apart from hurried trips to the latrine. She spent long hours memorising every detail of his appearance: the black curl of his eyelashes, a tiny scar on his temple, the lump of his Adam's apple, those fingers that had touched her with such desire ... She found his green leather book and pored over all the fine drawings within, spotting new images within the patterns: lions, musical instruments, ornate buildings. To her eye, he had a prodigious talent.

Mrs Bracebridge brought mending to keep her occupied, saying, 'The devil finds work for idle hands.' Lucy's sewing was sloppy; she had never had the patience for it as a child and now she did not have the concentration, but Mrs Bracebridge overlooked the uneven stitches and roughly knotted threads.

All the nurses urged Lucy to eat. She had no appetite and her already bird-like figure grew skinnier, but Mrs Roberts brought items from the stores to tempt her: jellied fruits, sugared almonds, gingerbread and a local delicacy called Turkish delight. She could usually manage to nibble a sweet treat even if she could not contemplate eating the more filling stews served in the staff dining room. Just the smell of them made her stomach turn.

Many treatments were prescribed for Murad: warm poultices were wrapped around his head and Spanish fly was used to blister the back of his neck to draw out impurities. He did not flinch and it was obvious he could feel no pain. Lucy wasn't sure if that was a good or a bad thing. The nurses showed her how to wash and shave him, and she was glad to take over those duties herself, glad there were services she could perform for him.

It was hard to remain optimistic but Lucy tried, telling herself that God would not be so cruel as to take a husband and a lover from her within a year. No one should have to suffer so much. And then one morning, while she was staring at his face, Murad's eyes suddenly opened and he gazed up at her.

Her first reaction was to scream, making a nurse come rushing over, but immediately afterwards she was filled with overwhelming joy. 'Murad!' she cried, throwing her arms round his neck and kissing him. 'My love, you are back!' Tears streamed down her cheeks.

A little smile curled the corners of his mouth but he did not speak. 'Murad, it's me, your Lucy,' she whispered urgently but his expression did not change, and after just a brief period of consciousness he fell asleep again. Lucy was disappointed but everyone agreed it was a very good sign. Even Miss Nightingale said as much, although she cautioned Lucy not to hope for too much progress straight away.

'He is on the mend,' she pronounced, 'but the healing of the brain cannot be rushed. Keep faith and pray for him.'

There was a grin on Lucy's face all day: Murad was recovering. When Mrs Roberts stopped by and was told the news, she clasped her hands in delight. 'And he's not a moment too soon in rejoining us, is he, my dear?'

'What do you mean?'

'Because of the baby.'

Lucy stared at her blankly.

'You *do* know you're with child, don't you?' She smiled at Lucy's obvious shock. 'We've all known since you arrived, from the nausea and your pallor. Your beloved Murad is going to be a father.'

Lucy had had no idea. She had assumed Murad would take precautions. Wasn't that the man's job? For the time being it was too much to take in. He had to get well again before she could even think about having his baby. They would have to marry now.

She decided she would not celebrate yet; she would wait until they could share the news.

Murad didn't waken again that first day, but the following morning he opened his eyes and smiled at Lucy as she arrived on the ward. She took his hand and kissed it, then whispered in his ear: 'I'm expecting a baby, darling. I've only just found out.' She peered into his eyes for a sign that he had understood and was sure she saw a flicker of recognition. Just a flicker.

The nurses pulled him up to sitting position and gave Lucy a bowl of beef broth to feed him. He let her spoon it between his lips and seemed to relish the flavour, smacking his lips together. 'Would you like some more?' she asked and waited, but there was no response.

'Don't rush him,' a nurse laughed. 'He's only just come round. It will be a while before he talks. One step at a time.'

Still, Lucy was impatient. She held his hand and urged him to squeeze her fingers, but got no response apart from a blank stare. She kissed his lips, trying to discern whether he was kissing her back. She was heartened when a nurse fed him a spoonful of foul-smelling medicine and Murad shuddered and screwed up his face. It seemed his sense of taste was unaffected. She knew he could hear, because he jumped when she dropped a stone darning egg on the floor. And he turned his head to watch movement, so that meant he could see. His brain was working; it just wasn't ready for speech yet.

All that day and all the next, Lucy chattered to Murad about everything that entered her head, seeking signs that he understood her. 'Do you see how poor my sewing is?' She showed him a seam. 'I hope you will not compare my work with your sisters' embroidery.' Miss Nightingale stopped to observe him, peering into his eyes and testing the reflexes in his legs. She pinched the skin on the back of his hand, and said it was a good sign that he grimaced, although he did not pull his hand away.

'I think it might be best if you take him home to his family,' she said. 'He may be more responsive in familiar surroundings. Besides, we need the bed.'

Lucy panicked. How would she get him to Smyrna? She hadn't written to his mother to tell her of Murad's injury because she could not write in Turkish. Their arrival would come as a huge shock. Besides, she didn't have money to pay for the trip.

Miss Nightingale had all the answers: 'If you give me the address, I will write to his mother explaining what has

347

happened to him and what needs to be done for his ongoing care, and I will have someone translate it into Turkish. Perhaps his family will arrange transportation for you. It is hardly the responsibility of the British army, after all.'

Lucy found the address on the letter from his mother, which was in the inside pocket of Murad's uniform tunic, and a note was duly written and dispatched. Just over two weeks later, a messenger arrived with a reply explaining that Murad's uncle had sent a boat to transport them round to Smyrna. The journey would be much safer and more comfortable by sea than attempting to cover the 350 miles overland and would take just two or three days, depending on the wind. All the arrangements were made and the boat, the *Amasra*, was already docked at Scutari awaiting instructions.

Lucy felt fluttery with nerves about leaving the hospital, where they had been so well looked after. How would Murad cope with the journey? How would his family receive her? They must wonder why an Englishwoman accompanied him. She would not be able to communicate with them except in the rudimentary Turkish Emir had taught her, consisting of single words like 'bread' or 'fish'. She wished vehemently she had tried harder to learn the language. And what would they think when they learned she was expecting a baby outside wedlock? They would judge very ill of her, to be sure.

'It's natural to be nervous about meeting your new mother-in-law,' Mrs Roberts told her, 'but she will be grateful to you for looking after her son following his injury. And she will be delighted about her impending grandchild. Every mother yearns for grandchildren. I guarantee all will work out for the best.'

Lucy's nerve failed her momentarily and she asked, 'Can't I just stay here?'

Mrs Roberts lowered her voice: 'There is a cholera outbreak in the hospital. You must protect Murad, as he

348

is not strong enough to survive infection.' She spoke at normal volume again: 'Besides, I expect he will recover much faster in his own surroundings. Miss Nightingale is right about that.'

And so, on 8th November, Lucy packed up the clothes she had been given and donned a white head veil Mrs Roberts had suggested she wear for the journey, just so the Turkish sailors would treat her with respect. Murad was transferred to a stretcher and carried across the lawn then down the rocky trail towards a quay, where the *Amasra* waited.

Chapter Forty

All through the journey down the Bosphorus, across the Sea of Marmara, through the Dardanelles then round the rocky coast of western Turkey, Lucy was sick to her stomach. Murad lay in a cabin below deck but when she spent more than half an hour with him, the stale air and the rocking motion of the ship made her retch convulsively and she had to rush up to the fresher air on deck. The captain gave her a drink made of ginger, which helped a little, but all in all it was a miserable journey. Murad seemed uncomfortable too, spending most of the time asleep but often screwing up his face as if having bad dreams.

As the ship pulled in to the busy port of Smyrna, Lucy felt faint with worry about the reception she might expect. A messenger was sent ashore to ask the family to dispatch a coach, and Lucy washed her face and arranged her veil neatly, making sure Murad was clean and presentable. He tended to dribble so she used a handkerchief to wipe his mouth, and she straightened the bandage around his head, which had slid down over one eye.

As Murad's stretcher was lifted off the ship, Lucy looked around her. There were several dozen tall-masted ships in the harbour, bobbing on iridescent blue-green water with sunbeams twinkling on the surface. White-painted buildings were clustered at the foot of a hill, pierced with minarets and domes, and on the hilltop there was an old castle. Trees surrounded the town, their foliage like plush green velvet draped over the rocky shores. It seemed a pretty place.

As they drove slowly through the narrow streets to avoid jolting Murad, Lucy formed an impression of tall white buildings, plump cats sunning themselves on walls, and a sense of wealth. The houses and gardens were well-kept and there was no sign of beggars. Within ten minutes, they were pulling into a driveway and, rigid with nerves, Lucy wiped Murad's mouth again.

As soon as they drew to a halt, she heard footsteps running towards the coach and the door was flung open. A Turkish woman in a veil looked inside then extended a hand to help Lucy climb down.

'Wel-come!' she cried, in a heavy foreign accent, her voice full of emotion. Lucy was enveloped in a cloud of exotic scent, her face pressed against a pink and gold silk gown. She looked up and saw the woman embracing her had Murad's dark, gentle eyes.

Instantly, Lucy knew she was safe.

After greeting Lucy, Murad's mother climbed into the coach and embraced her son. If she was shocked by his appearance, she didn't show it. Perhaps Miss Nightingale's letter had prepared her. A young man dressed in a white tunic and trousers went round to the other side of the coach and took Murad's pulse, lifted his eyelids to check his pupils, then motioned to the driver that they would carry the stretcher into the house together.

Murad's mother's returned to Lucy's side, pointed at herself and said the name, 'Hafza'. She repeated it until she was sure Lucy understood, and Lucy gave her own name the same way.

'Do you speak any English?' Lucy asked, and Hafza shook her head apologetically. Someone must have taught her the word 'welcome' especially for the occasion.

They followed as Murad's stretcher was carried into the house and taken to a room on the ground floor, with huge windows looking out to the garden. Lucy noticed they even had a chair with wheels on it sitting by the bedside, and she looked forward to wheeling him around in it. Murad was lifted into bed for now and opened his eyes to regard them with a docile expression.

'Hello, darling. We're here. At your home. I've met your mother and she is charming. Are you comfortable, my love?' Lucy used a coaxing tone. She was full of hope that being in the bosom of his family, in familiar surroundings, would cure Murad.

There was no reply. His mother spoke to him in Turkish and was met with the same blank gaze. The man in white indicated that he wanted to wash and change Murad and Hafza motioned for Lucy to come with her. She was exhausted after the voyage and glad to share the burden of Murad's care, but at the same time she felt a little possessive. She had learned what he needed and worried that others would not anticipate his needs so well. Would they realise he often choked and could only have liquid foods? Would they wipe his dribble?

Hafza led Lucy up a marble staircase to a room on the first floor and indicated it was to be hers. It was cool and airy, with a low divan bed covered in multi-coloured silk cushions. A little balcony had a view over the gardens, which were every bit as glorious as Murad had described, full of fruit trees, huge flowers creeping over trellises, and a pond with a waterfall. 'It's beautiful,' Lucy said, smiling and extending her arms to encompass the view, and Hafza seemed pleased. Murad's four teenage sisters came to introduce themselves, smiling shyly and trying out phrases in hesitant English.

'How-do-you-do-we-are-pleased-to-meet-you.'

Lucy repeated their names one by one, determined to remember them, and they giggled at her pronunciations.

After they left, Lucy washed then lay on the bed and tried to rest. There were stunning tiles on one wall, patterned with terracotta, blue and green tulips, and she guessed these must be the Iznik tiles for which Smyrna was famous. She traced the intricate patterns drowsily but couldn't sleep. It felt wrong not to be with Murad.

After a while, she rose and wandered out into the corridor, then down the stairs to Murad's room. Hearing a muffled sound, she glanced through the doorway and saw Hafza sitting by her son's bedside, holding his hand and sobbing with abandon, as though her heart had shattered into millions of tiny pieces.

Chapter Forty-one

Although it was mid-November, the weather was warm as an English summer's day. Murad's sisters brought gowns for Lucy to wear, lighter than the heavy serge ones she'd been given in Scutari, in shades of delicate shell pink, lilac and leaf green. Their Eastern fashion was to wear bloomers beneath a trim-waisted dress that fell to just below the knee. Lucy liked the style, although she was self-conscious that it emphasised the slight bump of her belly. If only she had grabbed her corset that morning when she left the *dacha*, she could have disguised her changing shape.

It seemed to be accepted from the start that she was a member of the family, eating meals with them in the large airy dining room, where they sat on cushions around a circular silver tray on the floor and helped themselves from the communal dishes of food. She strolled in the garden with Hafza or Murad's sisters and tried to make conversation in a combination of mime and the few words of Turkish she could remember plus the rudimentary English they had learned. The girls' governess, who came to give them lessons every morning, spoke good English and was able to translate if necessary. When Lucy asked about the strange fruits hanging on the trees, which looked like pinky-brown apples made of wood, the governess was able to tell her they were pomegranates and she cut one open to show the ruby seeds. When an elegant white bird with a long neck waded into the pond in search of fish, the governess told Lucy it was an egret.

Murad's sisters showed her some of his works of calligraphy, in inks of terracotta, amber, jade, deep turquoise, black and gold, and she was moved beyond words at the stunning artistry but at the same time tears pricked her eyes that a man of such talent should for now be so reduced.

While the orderly took over the job of washing, feeding and dressing Murad and massaging his muscles so they did not cramp, Hafza and Lucy took turns to sit by his bedside, whispering to him, urging him to open his eyes. Still he had not spoken but he smiled and seemed pleased when they entered the room. Lucy sang for him, hoping to trigger a response, and Hafza clapped her hands in delight at the sound of her pretty voice. Still Murad had just three expressions: blank, a smile and a grimace when he didn't like something. Lucy kept reminding herself of Miss Nightingale's words that healing of the brain could take time. Patience had never been one of her virtues – Dorothea used to chide her for wanting everything to happen immediately – but she decided that this time she would simply wait as long as it took.

One day as they sat together by his bedside, Hafza turned to Lucy with a gentle smile. She curved her arms together and rocked them as if rocking a baby, then she pointed at Lucy's belly. Lucy blushed deep scarlet. Her secret was exposed.

'Murad?' Hafza asked gently, pointing at him, then back at Lucy's belly.

Lucy screwed up her face, wondering whether to lie, to say it was her late husband's baby, but it didn't seem fair to deny Hafza the right to be a grandmother to her son's child. 'Yes,' she nodded, waiting for the condemnation she knew she deserved.

Hafza considered the news for a while, then she kissed the tips of her fingers and laid them gently on Lucy's stomach. Her eyes filled with tears but she kept smiling. 'Is good,' she said.

Lucy settled into the rhythm of life in the house in Smyrna. No men were admitted, apart from servants, and the women spent their days within the garden walls but they always seemed busy. She admired the charming miniatures painted by Murad's sister Fatma, the cushion covers embroidered by Safiye and the rugs woven by all of them together. They were curious to test their English, asking Lucy about life in London, although seeming horrified to learn that she went out on her own in a carriage to call upon friends and sometimes even walked in the streets from shop to shop, buying gloves or boots.

As November turned to December, Murad appeared to be making slow progress. Many times Lucy sensed he was trying to form a word, moving his lips and forcing sounds from his throat. She strained to listen and asked, 'What is it, my darling?' but frustratingly could not decipher the meaning. She wondered if he were speaking Turkish but Hafza did not seem to understand either. They could sense his moods, though. When he was lifted into the wheelchair and taken out into the garden to sit in the shade of a plane tree, he was obviously more content. Lucy believed he could hear the birdsong and feel the warmth of the sun on his skin, perhaps even smell the fragrant plants. He hated having medical procedures carried out, and sometimes after the doctor had been to bleed him, or after the orderly had washed him and changed his clothes, Murad was out of sorts, thrashing in bed and grimacing. Perhaps he was frustrated at not being able to do anything for himself, Lucy speculated. She could usually calm him by singing for him. He stopped still and appeared to be listening to the sound of her voice. He liked her to stroke his hand and kiss his face, and would gaze at her with a benign expression.

One late afternoon, she was sitting with Murad in the garden. A buzzing insect that looked like a double-bodied wasp was hovering around and she was watching to make sure it did not attempt to sting him. She vaguely heard the bell ring in the background but assumed it would be a delivery of fish. Murad's uncle always sent some of the day's catch for their evening meal.

One of Murad's sisters came running out into the garden to look for her, then shouted something in Turkish over her shoulder. Lucy turned – and could not believe her eyes.

She blinked hard.

There, standing in the doorway, with a bag at her feet, was Dorothea.

For a moment Lucy was so startled she couldn't react. *Was it really her? But how could it be?*

Dorothea walked into the garden, out of place in her dowdy coat and bonnet. She seemed older, strands of grey hair framing her dear, lined face. Lucy was utterly amazed. She leapt to her feet, ran to her and flung her arms round her, crying, 'You came!' Her eyes filled with tears as emotion swept over her. *Dear sweet Dorothea, whom she thought had abandoned her, had travelled across an entire continent to find her.* Heart pounding, Lucy squeezed as hard as she could, burying her face in Dorothea's familiar shoulder, feeling her sister's arms close around her, smelling her skin. Nothing had ever felt as good as this.

'Of course I came.' Dorothea squeezed back then pulled away to examine her, flushed with joy. 'Your face is thinner but it suits you. And your complexion is radiant. Oh Lucy, I've missed you so much! I can't begin to tell you ...'

'How did you get here so quickly? It's wonderful to see you. I've missed you too. Oh please – sit down.' Lucy motioned to a basketwork chair but hung on to Dorothea's hand, not letting go.

Dorothea looked at Murad for the first time and Lucy followed her gaze. 'This is Murad.' She hesitated, trying to decide how to introduce him. 'Perhaps you received my letter about him? What I didn't tell you, but you perhaps guessed, is that we are in love and plan to marry just as soon as he recovers. And we are seeing progress every day.'

She looked defiantly at Dorothea, waiting for signs of disapproval, bracing herself for a lecture, but Dorothea nodded politely at Murad and said, 'Good to meet you, Sir. If my sister loves you then you must be a fine man.' She sank into the chair while Lucy blinked in surprise. 'My goodness, what a journey I've had,' Dorothea continued. 'You will be surprised to hear I have not come from England, as you might think, but was nursing in Balaklava. All these months we have been close to each other without knowing it!'

'You were in Balaklava?' Lucy was baffled.

'Yes, I volunteered as a nurse. I left England a year ago. I was hoping I would encounter you along the way – and now I have!' Dorothea beamed. 'Oh, Lucy, I can't believe we're together at last. I've been so worried. I've been looking everywhere for you. I never gave up.' She turned to regard Murad again. 'I'm sorry about your fiancé's injury. We will talk of this, as I have some experience of head injuries. But if you can see gradual signs of improvement, that is good news.'

'Dorothea, is it really you? I feel as though you have arrived from a different lifetime. So much has happened ...'

Lucy still hadn't let go of her sister's hand. 'I didn't think you would come. You didn't write ...'

'I *did* write. Once I discovered where you were, I wrote to you every week. It was only after I reached Balaklava and came to look for you, I learned that my letters had been ...' She made a snap decision not to tell Lucy the truth for now; she would show her Charlie's last letter when the time was right. '... Misplaced. You had not received them. You must have thought I had abandoned you. And then to lose poor Charlie ...' She squeezed Lucy's hand. 'My goodness, what a dreadful time!'

Tears of self-pity pricked Lucy's eyes but she blinked them away. 'I still can't quite believe you are here. And Father? Is he well?'

'He seems to be. He is bossing Henderson around like a tyrant, I imagine.'

'I've never understood why Henderson puts up with it. There must surely be other posts he could obtain.'

'I suppose they are simply used to each other and don't relish change. I find it hard to be sympathetic with Father's constant complaints, even though I know they are a symptom of his declining wit, but Henderson manages to pretend concern every time.'

Lucy laughed. 'Do you remember when Papa thought he was dying of a stomach cancer and it turned out to be wind?'

Dorothea rolled her eyes and was about to reply when Hafza came into the garden and approached with a welcoming smile.

'*Bu anneniz mi?*' she asked Lucy. *Is this your mother?*

'*Ablam,*' Lucy corrected her quickly. 'My sister. Dorothea, this is Murad's mother Hafza, who has been as kind as a mother to me since I arrived.'

'*Nasılsınız? Memnun oldum,*' Dorothea said, using a greeting she had learned from a Turkish patient, which meant 'How are you? I am pleased.'

Lucy watched them bow their heads to each other and a huge weight lifted off her shoulders. For the first time since she had left England, she felt safe and protected. Dorothea was here and she wasn't cross – although she didn't know about the pregnancy yet. That would be a fresh challenge to her equanimity.

Chapter Forty-two

Hafza moved Halida and Nakiye in order to give Dorothea the bedroom alongside Lucy's. That night, when everyone had gone to bed, Dorothea crept into Lucy's room in her nightgown, hoping for one of the cosy bedtime chats they used to have in the old days, but Lucy was sound asleep, her hair fanned out on the pillow. Dorothea held her candle above her, looking down at that dear face, and felt such a pang of love that it was all she could do not to wake Lucy and cover her cheeks with kisses. After all this time, they were together at last and, what's more, it seemed they were friends. Nothing mattered more than that.

Over the next few days, the sisters talked incessantly, telling each other all that had passed since they last saw each other. There were many surprises. Dorothea explained that she knew Florence Nightingale, that she had even nursed her when she caught fever in the Crimea, and so when she arrived in Scutari looking for Lucy Miss Nightingale was able to provide the address at which to find her. Lucy explained that she had been living in an abandoned *dacha* not far from Balaklava, where Murad had taken her to recover after Charlie died and that love had developed between them that

361

summer. Dorothea told her about meeting the 8th Hussars' wives at the British camp and gave her the ship in a bottle. Lucy narrowed her eyes when she heard about one of the women wearing her shell-pink gown, a particular favourite.

'I left Mama's silk bedspread there. I don't suppose they gave you that,' she asked, then answered her own question: 'No, I thought not.'

Then Dorothea broke her own news: that she had become engaged to a doctor with whom she worked in Balaklava.

'Oh, I'm so glad!' Lucy clapped her hands together. 'A doctor. He must be very clever. I always thought only a clever man would do for you. Is he handsome?'

'Not particularly.' Dorothea shook her head with a faraway smile in her eyes. 'But he is a good man.' She explained their plan to marry at the ambassador's residence in Constantinople, and suggested that perhaps Lucy might attend.

Lucy was excited. 'Maybe we can have a double wedding, if Murad is recovered enough.'

Dorothea smiled. 'Miss Nightingale told me you were already married but I guessed that was probably not the case.'

'Not yet, but as good as ...' Lucy said quickly.

'Mr Crawford and I were hoping to marry around Christmas, which is only a few weeks hence. I think it may take a little longer before Murad is himself again.'

'Yes, I suppose so. I wish there was a way to speed his recovery. You said you had some experience of head injuries. What must we do?'

'I had a patient in London who had been working on the railways when he was struck on the head with a steel girder. At first we thought he was catatonic – that means entirely unresponsive – but a young surgeon told me that such patients can respond to stimuli, particularly things that were familiar to them before the accident. In the case of this patient, we realised he responded to the sound of his pet dog barking, and when we put the dog on his lap he began to move his hand as if to stroke it. We got his wife to wave a candle back and forwards in front of his eyes, to ring bells, sing songs he knew, and later to take him to places and to meet people he was familiar with. It's good to encourage all the senses, of sight, hearing, taste, smell and touch.'

'And he recovered fully?' Lucy was excited.

'Yes, he did. It was miraculous.'

This advice seemed so invaluable that Lucy got the governess to translate it for Hafza and they began to discuss what stimuli might work for Murad. Hafza said he had enjoyed sea bathing as a child, so they decided that the orderly and Murad's uncle would take him to the beach one day. Lucy would have liked to go along, but Hafza said that was not possible, without explaining why.

'He liked to hear me play the pianoforte when we were in the Crimea,' Lucy said, and Hafza immediately ordered a pianoforte, impatient when she was told it would be some weeks before it could be delivered.

His sisters became involved, suggesting favourite foods, toys he had played with as a child, and the scent of the jasmine plant which climbed the walls outside the window of his childhood bedroom. They were excited to be given something positive they could do to help him and everyone had ideas.

'How long do you think it will take?' Lucy asked Dorothea as they strolled in the garden, arm in arm one evening.

'I wish I could give you an answer, Lucy-loo, but I expect every case is different. I'm so sorry. It must be unbearable for you to see the man you love in this helpless condition.'

Lucy hung her head. 'I wish you could meet him properly. I know you'd like him. He's nothing like Charlie: he's quiet and thoughtful and considerate. He saved my life, you know.'

'I love him for that already. And I pray he will recover soon.'

'It's just that I need him back urgently because ...' She couldn't bring herself to say the words. Instead she turned in profile, smoothing her gown so Dorothea could see the swelling of her belly.

Dorothea drew in breath sharply. 'You're with child?'

Lucy nodded tentatively. Was she about to receive a lecture? The Dorothea of old would have lambasted her without mercy. Having intimate relations outside of matrimony was unforgivable by every standard of society, whether in England, Crimea or Turkey. There was a pause and she held her breath but when Dorothea spoke it was of practicalities.

'When is the baby due?'

Lucy shrugged. She didn't know.

'When was your last monthly bleed? I'm guessing from your size the child must have been conceived in the summer.'

'Yes, in July or August,' Lucy said.

'So it is due in April or May. Were you sick in the early months?'

'Very sick. The nausea has only just passed while I have been here.'

'Might I feel your belly?'

Lucy assented, and Dorothea cupped the bulge in her hands, feeling for the head. She had no experience in midwifery but knew the basics. She felt a fluttering sensation just beneath her hand. 'Ah, that's the baby kicking.'

Lucy's eyes widened. 'Are you sure?' For the first time the reality struck that she was carrying Murad's child inside her. Until that moment it had been an abstract notion but the fact there was a living, breathing creature inside her womb, a creature capable of kicking, was a chastening thought.

Dorothea caught the panic in her expression but misread it. 'There is still time to travel back to London for your confinement and hire an experienced midwife. I know just the woman.'

Lucy shook her head. 'You wouldn't believe how ill I was during the journey from Constantinople. I can't possibly sail home. Besides, Hafza knows a midwife and assures me there is nothing to worry about.'

Dorothea did not share her confidence. Over one in twenty births in London caused the death of the mother and she couldn't believe Smyrna would have a better record. Lucy was young and fit but that offered no protection from post-natal haemorrhage and fever. 'Wouldn't you rather have someone who spoke the same language as you while in the grip of labour pains?'

'Yes. I want *you* to be here, Dorothea. Please say you will.' Lucy spoke with passion.

'Of course I will.' She decided she would persuade Mr Crawford to come as well in case surgical intervention was required. She would trust him above all others.

'And will you stay in Smyrna until then?'

Dorothea was torn. She had told Miss Langston she would only be gone a few weeks, but Lucy's due date was still five months away. And she couldn't abandon Gordon for so long when they had only just become engaged. It would be heart-breaking to leave Lucy, especially in her condition, but she knew she would be well cared for in Murad's household. 'I promised to return to Balaklava for the winter, but now I know where you are we can write to each other. And if you need me, I am only a week's sail away. It will be fine, Lucy-loo. You'll see.'

Dorothea suggested they try to involve Murad in the routine of the household rather than leaving him to spend hours in bed, where he risked getting bedsores as well as muscle wastage. From then on, the orderly wheeled him into the dining room to sit with them while they ate. He could still only swallow liquids; if solid food was placed in his mouth he simply let it lie there, as if he had forgotten how to chew. Lucy sat by him and fed him spoonfuls of soup, and it felt as though he was part of the group.

One evening at dinner, Lucy was talking to Dorothea when suddenly Murad lurched forwards in his chair and uttered a noise that sounded like 'Oosh'.

Lucy got pinpricks all up her arms. 'Did you hear that? He's trying to say "Lucy". He wants my attention. What is it, darling?' She leapt up to cup Murad's face in her hands and he smiled at her benignly. 'Don't you think he was saying my name, Dorothea?'

'It certainly sounded like it,' she agreed. 'Perhaps he can understand our conversation and wants to be included.' It did seem a positive sign, and she was glad for Lucy.

But that evening when Murad was back in bed, they heard the orderly calling for help. Lucy and Dorothea rushed into the room to see Murad jerking violently, throwing himself all over the bed, his tongue hanging out and his eyes rolling. Lucy began to wail, terrified that he was dying. Dorothea knew what to do, though. She grabbed a cloth and, holding his chin, forced it into his mouth then she held on to his shoulders, motioning for the orderly to help pin him down. The kicking and jerking continued for some minutes before Murad flopped back onto the bed and appeared to be sound asleep. Dorothea took his pulse and listened to his heart with her ear to his chest, then removed the cloth from his mouth.

'What on earth happened?' Lucy cried, horrified. 'He's never done that before.'

'He had a seizure,' Dorothea explained. 'If it happens again, be sure to put something in his mouth or else he could choke on his tongue ... Don't cry, Lucy. It's quite a common symptom of brain injury. It needn't mean a setback.'

She got up to embrace her sister, stroking her hair. Lucy still shook with sobs. It was too cruel to be given hope with his attempt to say her name, and then have it snatched away again immediately with this horrible seizure.

None of Dorothea's reassurances could calm her that evening but Lucy had a fundamentally optimistic nature and next morning, her good humour had returned. She began spending hours each day coaxing Murad to talk and reporting things she imagined he was saying.

'I know he likes you, Dorothea. He always responds to the sound of your voice.'

'Really?'

'And he loves this lilac gown his sisters gave me,' Lucy smiled, stroking the skirt. 'I can tell he likes the colour. While we were in the *dacha* he only ever saw me in the same old blue gown so the change must be welcome.'

Dorothea worried that she was reading rather more into his very limited responses than they warranted. Lucy continued to believe that Murad's 'Oosh' sound was an attempt to pronounce her name although Dorothea had heard him utter it quite randomly when her sister was nowhere in the vicinity.

It was a balancing act: she did not wish to raise Lucy's hopes too high, but neither did she wish her to sink into despair while she was carrying his child. Perhaps it was best to err on the side of optimism.

Dorothea had written to Gordon telling him of Murad's injury and Lucy's condition, and within ten days there was a reply. He sent great sympathy for the plight of Lucy's fiancé, writing, 'Head injuries can be the luck of the draw. I have seen men make a full recovery from states such as you describe, usually within six months of the accident. After that, in my experience their condition is highly unlikely to improve significantly.' He had little to add to her advice about stimulating Murad in as many ways as possible, merely recommending that his muscles be kept from atrophying with daily stretches and massage, and that they were to guard against sores.

The weather in Balaklava was wet and cold, he wrote, with frost in the mornings, and the nurse who had replaced Dorothea as his assistant in the operating theatre was clumsy and inept: 'However, this is not the main reason I miss you. I find myself constantly wishing to discuss matters with you, from the condition of a patient to the progress of the war, and to hear your wise, considered opinions. I have no experience in writing love letters full of sweet sentiment – rhapsodies comparing eye colour with precious jewels and voices with the trilling of a nightingale, etcetera etcetera – but it is factual to say that I miss you very much simply because I like you being around. There is a space at my side that I wish you occupied.' He said he understood that Dorothea's sister needed her support, but wondered if there was any chance she could still travel to Constantinople for a Christmas wedding. Her father had written with his permission to wed and her consent would make him the happiest man alive.

Dorothea didn't hesitate for one moment. She replied immediately that she would meet him in Constantinople around the 20th or 21st December and would become his wife just as soon as it could be arranged. She sealed the letter then hugged herself, almost unable to contain her happiness. In front of Lucy she would tactfully play down her excitement, so as not to rub salt in the wound, but she felt private joy bubbling inside.

Chapter Forty-three

On the morning of her departure from Smyrna, Dorothea sat with Lucy under an awning in the garden, holding her hands. 'We have not spoken of our argument about Charlie and the rift it caused between us. I am so sorry I interfered in the way I did. Please don't let anything come between us like that again. If we argue, let us express our anger then clear the air – because we are family and we should always support each other.'

Lucy stared at the ground: 'Perhaps you were right. Perhaps I was too hasty to wed ...'

'If you had not married, you would never have had your year of happiness with Charlie. We all know that life can be short. I believe that, had she been around, Mama would have encouraged you to seize your chance at love and it was wrong of me to try to prevent it by such underhanded methods.'

'Charlie was not the man I thought he was,' Lucy said quietly, her eyes focused on an ant that was attempting to push a large crumb over a crack in the paving stone.

Dorothea hesitated. 'Yes, I know.'

Lucy looked up, surprised. 'How did you know?'

Dorothea sighed. 'His wooden box was among the possessions the women in the British camp gave me. It had been broken open and I read the contents. I'm so sorry, Lucy. Would you like to see it?'

She nodded, frowning. Dorothea fetched the box from her luggage and sat nearby while Lucy first of all gasped in astonishment at the pile of unopened envelopes then unfolded and read Charlie's final letter. Tears came to her eyes but she didn't weep. When she finished, she said, 'If only he had told me these things while he was alive. Were it not for the war, I believe we could have been happy. Thank you for bringing this to me. And now, I will have some letters from you to read during your absence. I look forward to it, even if the news is a year out of date.'

'I will return in April,' Dorothea promised. 'Write if you need me sooner and I will come on the first boat.'

When they embraced, it was in a spirit of absolution of past hurts, of real and imagined wrongs. Lucy sobbed as Dorothea's coach pulled away from the house, but inside she knew they were closer than ever and it was the kind of closeness that should, with any luck, last a lifetime.

Dorothea felt strangely nervous and girlish about seeing Gordon again. She checked her appearance several times in a hand mirror and tucked stray hairs inside her bonnet. They had arranged to meet at the British Embassy, in whose gardens she had strolled the previous December when she first arrived in Constantinople. The ambassador, Viscount Stratford de Redcliffe, was so delighted to hear of the marriage of one of the British army's top surgeons with one of its nurses that he and his wife had offered to let them stay in the embassy and hold their wedding ceremony in a state room with a view over the Bosphorus. Dorothea's carriage driver rang the bell and she was ushered in through a grand hall and upstairs to a drawing room, where Gordon sat conversing with a well-dressed woman. He jumped to his feet as Dorothea entered the room and uttered a gasp of pure delight. No one had ever seemed so pleased to see her before and she glowed with happiness as he rushed across the room to greet her. He was taller than she remembered, and more handsome now he had shaved the whiskers that he had of necessity grown in Balaklava. She liked the soft burr of his Scottish accent and the smell of his tweed jacket; she liked the set of his newly exposed chin.

'Dorothea, may I introduce Lady Stratford de Redcliffe, the ambassador's wife? She has kindly agreed to help with the arrangements for our wedding. In fact, I think she has appointed herself official overseer of our nuptials.'

Dorothea shook hands and murmured her thanks.

'My dear, we must find you a suitable dress – I know just the place. And flowers; we must have flowers. I believe Mr Crawford has already purchased a ring but we still need to talk about the wedding supper. We will make a little party of it.'

'You are most kind,' Dorothea said, feeling overwhelmed. It seemed she was in good hands.

She and Gordon were shown to their respective rooms, and before she retired to rest from the journey he handed her two letters that had been delivered to Balaklava in her absence. She sat on the bed to read them. The first was a rambling note from her father, excited that a Mr Livingstone was attempting to travel across the centre of Africa, although he did not remember to ask after her or her sister. She smiled: it was good to know that he still loved his explorers. The second was a rather longer letter from Adelaide Cresswell, which Dorothea read with mounting emotion.

Adelaide wrote that she had received a very curt reply from the Harvington family when she got in touch offering her condolences on Charlie's death. 'I had hoped they might forgive him after death, and was disappointed they had not.' And then she explained to Dorothea the history of the estrangement: 'Charlie made the impetuous decision to take his seven-year-old sister riding on his cavalry horse. There was a terrible accident when they attempted to jump a gate and the girl perished. His father threw Charlie out of the house, disowning him, and my husband Bill encountered him as he arrived back at his army quarters, intent on taking his own life. It took all Bill's powers of persuasion over the next weeks and months to talk him out of it, so deeply did he feel his guilt in the tragedy.'

Adelaide wrote that she felt terribly sad for Charlie. She had known and liked his character, she could see how he could have made such a dreadful error of judgement, but felt everyone should be allowed a second chance. She wrote: 'One of my own siblings was a daredevil and could easily have turned wild if my mother had not kept a firm rein on him. It is my belief that parents bear a responsibility for the way their children turn out.'

Reading her letter, Dorothea agreed. Charlie was a flawed character, but his sin had been one of thoughtlessness rather than evil. She wondered if Lucy knew of this? She had never breathed a word of it, but surely she must. Suddenly she could see why poor, motherless Lucy would be attracted to a man with a tragic past, someone on whom she could lavish all her pent-up love. It must have felt romantic and compelling.

That evening, Dorothea and Gordon dined with the ambassador – a white-haired gentleman who talked mainly to Gordon about politics and the war – and his charming wife. After dinner they were left alone in a drawing room with a blazing fire, where Gordon sipped a glass of brandy while

Dorothea drank tea. She told him about Adelaide's letter, because it was foremost on her mind, and he listened carefully.

'I can understand now why he was so keen to keep Lucy to himself that he hid your letters,' he mused when she had finished. 'He must have lived in fear of losing her, as he had lost the rest of his family.'

'Adelaide says she thinks parents are responsible for their children's characters, to an extent at least. Do you agree?'

He nodded. 'Yes, very much so. My own father taught me the importance of hard work and humour, values I use in my craft to this day. Many others are not so lucky.' He swirled his brandy in the round-bodied glass, and the amber liquid gleamed in the firelight. 'Tell me, have you given any thought to having children?'

Dorothea's cheeks burned. 'Goodness, I'm far too old for that.'

He reached out to take her hand and asked, 'Do you still have your monthly bleed?'

Dorothea blushed even more deeply and could only nod.

'We are medical people,' he twinkled. 'Surely we can talk openly about such matters? I want us to be honest with each other about everything. If you still have monthlies then there is no reason why we could not have a child – if you would like one, that is.'

'Yes, I would … At least, perhaps we can try.' She blushed again, thinking about what 'trying' would entail and, partly to change the focus of the conversation, she mused, 'I wonder what my sister will do if Murad does not recover? She will have a baby and no husband. It is not an easy position.'

'She will have to consider her options very carefully. But if she is in need I would of course be happy for her to live with us in Edinburgh, with or without the child. I know you feel like a mother to her.'

373

'Less so now, I think. She has become independent in the months since last I saw her. I doubt I will have any influence over her decisions, so all I can do is support her – even if I think she is misguided.' Dorothea chuckled. 'Especially then.'

The ceremony took place in early evening of the 23rd December 1855, by a huge window looking down towards the Bosphorus, with the gas lamps of Constantinople twinkling in the darkness. The ambassador's wife had talked Dorothea into wearing an ivory lace gown with pearl buttons, a fashionable hoop skirt and billowing swoops of fabric, much fancier than any gown she had ever owned. She moved carefully, unaccustomed to the weight of the garment. A large cream gardenia bloom was pinned in her hair, along with a filmy ivory veil. Gordon wore a black dress coat and a cream waistcoat, his ginger hair neatly combed and oiled flat in a style she had never seen him with before (and suspected she never would again). A minister conducted the ceremony, with the ambassador and his wife as witnesses, and afterwards they all stood stock still while a daguerreotype was made to capture the scene.

Lady Stratford de Redcliffe had arranged a sumptuous wedding supper of dainty finger sandwiches, light scones and pretty fruit jellies, and an artful cake in the shape of Hagia Sophia, Constantinople's ancient cathedral built in the Byzantine era to which the Muslims had added minarets to convert it to a mosque. It was a true representation of the multi-cultural aspects of the city, she said, and she hoped it would augur well for their English to Scottish union. Gordon managed to persuade Dorothea to drink half a glass of champagne – 'It's my job to corrupt you,' he joked – and she found she liked the sensation of the fizz on her tongue, if not the sour taste.

She felt light-headed all day, as if she were floating. The time sped past and she was glad they would have a daguerreotype to remind them because everything was a blur. All Dorothea knew was that she had never experienced such bliss.

Chapter Forty-four

The winter in Smyrna was pleasantly sunny, with blue skies and a gentle breeze. When rain fell, it usually came at night and Lucy awoke to find the garden refreshed and glistening. Even in January there were flowers in bloom: small dark pink flowers on bushes and yellow ones that resembled buttercups on the ground.

Lucy and Hafza worked hard to find new ways to stimulate Murad's brain healing. Hafza bought oils of sweet jasmine and neroli to perfume his room. The pianoforte was finally delivered and Lucy spent long hours playing his favourite *lieder*, sonatas and nocturnes. They fed him spoonfuls of soups with unusual flavours – salty cheese, spicy lamb, honeyed figs – prepared by the cook. A cat that often roamed in their garden was placed in his lap and Lucy moved his hand along its back in stroking movements. The male orderly and the driver took him to the sea and immersed him in the cool waves but they reported that he grimaced and bellowed, clearly uncomfortable, so the experiment was cut short.

Others helped too. Local medical men came to burn strange herbs in little metal holders placed against his skin; the hot metal left red rings, but Murad bore it patiently. The imam came to pray over him and all his sisters, aunts and cousins visited to sing favourite childhood songs, to laugh and chatter in his company. Murad smiled benignly at them and uttered his forced, guttural sounds.

Every day, Lucy felt she saw a little progress. When she looked into his eyes, she was sure she could see intelligence and often got a sense that she knew what he was thinking. 'You like the breeze from that window, don't you?' she asked, and when she opened the window his expression seemed somehow calmer. 'You are thirsty now,' she guessed and fed him sips of water. She sensed he didn't like one of the doctors who visited; something indistinguishable in his posture seemed to shrink when the man came into the room. And some days, she felt sure he was melancholy and made extra effort to cheer him up. It must be simply awful to be unable to communicate while people fussed around, doing everything for you.

As her belief that he could understand his surroundings grew, Lucy began to talk to him as if he were fully present.

'See how this gown is stretched across my belly now? I shall have to ask your sister Safiye to let it out for me. She's such a talented seamstress. ... The baby's kicking kept me awake last night. Why does he seem to sleep when I am active then wake when I try to rest? I feel sure it is a boy ... Your mother has been so generous. She gave me these earrings last night – look at the sparkle of the sapphires! They are family jewels but she thinks they suit me best because they match my blue eyes.'

Murad blinked.

'You like them, don't you? You think they suit me.' Lucy kissed him passionately on the lips. 'Oh, I wish you would recover so we could go out somewhere together. I'm fed up being stuck in this house with only women for company. I don't understand why they don't get bored, but I suppose it's what they're used to. I should die of boredom, were it not for the fact that I am confined here anyway to look after you and bear our child. Murad, you must try to get well for the baby's birth in spring. After that, we can take our own house and live according to our own rules. Perhaps we could visit London for the summer, so I can see my dear Papa.'

Murad blinked twice and she took that as his agreement with her plan.

He still said 'Oosh' fairly often, and she remained convinced it was an attempt to pronounce her name. One day when the baby was kicking she held his hand to her belly so he could feel the movement. He looked seriously into her eyes and made a sound that was like, 'A–ba' and she was sure he was trying to say 'baba' or the Turkish word 'bebek'. Excitedly, she told Hafza, using a mixture of mime and sign language. Next time she put Murad's hand to her belly, though, he said something quite different. Did he understand about the baby? She was convinced he did.

Hafza let Lucy spend plenty of time on her own with Murad. There was a bell nearby in case she needed to summon help, for example in the event of a fit, but when she was with him no one disturbed them. During those hours she focused hard on trying to communicate and sometimes, despite herself, she got cross with him for not responding. One morning she challenged him.

'Say "Lucy" right now or I will pinch your arm.'

He simply stared at her so she pinched him hard on his forearm. He grimaced but didn't try to move his arm away.

'Now will you say "Lucy"? Or just "Oosh"? If you don't, I will pinch you again.'

He didn't speak and she pinched him a second time. There were two red marks on his skin, just next to each other.

'Oh God,' she cried, instantly stricken with guilt. 'What kind of monster am I?' She rubbed the area, trying to make the marks disappear. How could she do that to a helpless man? The tiny purple bruises that developed were a reproach and she worried that Hafza or the orderly would ask about them, but neither did.

Sometimes when Murad was in his wheelchair, Lucy sat on his lap and pulled his arms around her, covering his face with kisses. He seemed to like that, and it let her pretend for a short while that they were still lovers. One day as she sat on his lap in the garden, she was astonished to feel a stiffening under his loose trousers. She glanced round to check no one was watching from the house then touched it with her hand. It definitely seemed he was responding to her caresses. She looked into his face, questioning. Did he know what she was doing? Did it make him happy? What if they were to make love? Dorothea had said he should have all kinds of stimulation. But no ... she couldn't. It wouldn't be right.

The idea stuck in Lucy's head, though. Whenever they were alone, she stroked between Murad's legs and he usually stiffened at the touch of her hand. What if he was conscious and trapped inside a body that he could no longer move at will and this was the only way he could communicate his love for her? She had to find out. It would be so wonderful to make love with him again, and could even be the spark that was needed to jolt him out of his unresponsive state.

One afternoon Lucy slipped into Murad's room after his nap, dismissed the orderly who had been watching over him and turned the key to lock the door from the inside. She stripped off her gown and climbed into bed alongside Murad, pressing her body against his. He gazed at her blankly. She stroked his back, his chest, his legs and pushed one of her legs between his, then felt for his manhood. It was slightly stiffened. She stroked it, making it harden, and then she clambered on top to sit astride him. She had his manhood in her hand, about to push it inside her when suddenly the expression on his face changed to a grimace and he threw his head back with a bellow: 'Waaaa ...'

Lucy jumped off instantly, horrified: 'It's all right. I'm sorry. I've stopped.'

Straight away his expression was blank again and he lay still, as if nothing had happened. She stood semi-naked in front of him and burst into tears. There was no love in his eyes, no recognition of what she had just tried to do. He was a child and she was an evil woman for attempting to seduce him. The adult response of his body had fooled her briefly but only because she was searching for hope where in fact none existed.

She dressed quickly and ran back to her own room, where she threw herself on the bed sobbing uncontrollably. All those things she had thought were signs of recovery had simply been inanimate instincts. He was no more responding to her than he was to anyone else. The essence of the man she had fallen in love with was gone and all that remained was a living shell. Any hope that he would recover in time for the baby's birth disappeared. He would never be able to marry her. This is how he would remain and she had to think now about what she would do with her own life – and that of their unborn child.

When she came red-eyed to dinner that evening, Murad's mother rose from her cushion and hugged her as tightly as if she were her own daughter. She already knew in her heart what Lucy had finally accepted: that it seemed unlikely her son would get any better than he already was.

Chapter Forty-five

After their wedding Gordon and Dorothea spent two weeks exploring the sights of Constantinople: the extravagant marble palaces that lined the Bosphorus; the mosques with golden domes and superb tiles; the tall wooden houses set on narrow streets where the call to prayer rang out from all directions. They visited the renowned Grand Bazaar and bought a multi-coloured patchwork quilt to warm their marital bed, as well as a sturdy pot-bellied stove to banish the winter chill of Crimea. Dorothea loved the feeling of being a couple now, of making joint decisions and planning their future. She liked to brush lint from her new husband's collar, to plump his pillows, and generally to concern herself with his comfort. They talked constantly, sharing opinions, exploring the other's tastes in music, art, food and literature, and every new revelation was eagerly memorised and stored away.

Their intimacies in the bedroom were loving and tender, and before long Dorothea plucked up the courage to tell Gordon about the attack in Constantinople. As Elizabeth had predicted, he was enormously sympathetic but also berated her, 'Why on earth did you not share this horrendous experience earlier? It makes me sad that you have dealt with this in your usual silent fortitude.'

On their return to Balaklava they were allocated a wooden hut to share and the first thing Dorothea did was to display their wedding daguerreotype, enclosed in a mother-of-pearl case. Elizabeth had been sent home suffering from an injured foot but left them a letter with her address and a gift of a dozen linen napkins, each with a hand-embroidered flower in one corner. Other friends gave presents of food or champagne and Gordon and Dorothea threw a small party at the British Hotel to thank well-wishers.

There had been many changes during the couple of months of Dorothea's absence. New shops, bars and restaurants had sprung up in Kadikoi and Kamiesch, all of them well stocked with provisions from Britain and France. Some bars had gaming tables, others billiards, and a theatre company now put on revues with names such as *To Paris and Back for Five Pounds* and *The Moustache Movement*. Dorothea and Gordon attended the latter, a heavily mannered show in which the leading lady was played by a lieutenant from the 63rd Regiment of Foot, but didn't think much of it. They heard there was a French dancing saloon in Kamara where balls were held every Sunday but that no decent lady could be seen there because they were frequented by the *cantinières*, who throughout the war's course had done nothing to belie their reputation as harlots. The horse racing began again and Dorothea and Gordon attended a few races, placing small bets on them. Everywhere there were tourists now: wandering lost between the huts in camp, spilling out of the bars, and asking anyone who would listen how they could obtain a Russian cap or rifle as a souvenir.

By the end of January, it was clear the war did not have long to run and the boundaries of the Ottoman Empire looked secure once more. The wards at the Castle and General

Hospitals began to empty as soldiers were either dispatched home or returned to their posts. Stories filtered through of conviviality between British and French troops and the small Russian force still camped by the Chernaia river: national songs were sung around campfires, and bottles of liquor were shared. Dorothea was not surprised. She had never seen any signs of animosity towards the few Russian soldiers she had nursed; this war was not about individuals but about the Russian government's expansionism and territorial posturing. Gordon and she agreed that it had all been a waste of innocent lives. There had been no decisive victory but at least Russian military build-up around the Black Sea would be curbed. Was that worth all the blood that had been shed?

On the 31st March 1856, news reached the British camp by telegram that a peace treaty had been signed the day before, and on the 2nd April the guns were fired in celebration. It felt like something of an anti-climax, except that it heralded the start of the mass evacuation of troops from Crimea. The timing was perfect for Dorothea and Gordon. They could supervise the travel arrangements for their remaining patients, take their leave of the friends they had made, pack their possessions, and then depart for Smyrna in time for Dorothea to attend Lucy's confinement.

On the 14th April, Dorothea and Gordon set sail for Constantinople, from where they took another ship bound for Smyrna. The seas were blessedly calm, and the skies filled with flocks of migrating birds. Gordon turned out to be something of an avian expert and taught her to identify storks, cranes, warblers and falcons from their different shapes and patterns of flight.

They arrived at the house in Smyrna on the 22nd of the month to a warm welcome. Hafza had allocated a guest suite for them within the house, even though it meant she and her daughters must remain veiled at all times and the girls must avoid public rooms when Gordon was there. Dorothea introduced Lucy to Gordon and he greeted her fondly, calling her 'sister-in-law'. She tried to respond in friendly fashion but her normal exuberant spirit was clearly subdued, and Dorothea perceived the cause when they went to sit by Murad's bedside. His condition was much worse than it had been the previous December. His eyes no longer seemed focused, his tongue lolled out of his mouth and Lucy reported that the fits had become more frequent. Instantly the professional, Gordon tested his reflexes, moved a candle back and forth in front of his eyes to check his pupils followed the light, and listened to his heartbeat through his wooden stethoscope. Lucy did not ask the prognosis. It seemed she had given up hope.

Dorothea knocked on Lucy's bedroom door as she dressed for dinner and sat on the bed to talk.

'You look well,' she began. 'I think I have never seen you so beautiful.'

'No, I don't. Look at me – I'm grotesque.' Lucy skimmed her hands over her rounded hips and belly. 'Even if I were beautiful there is no one to appreciate it. We are a household of women who never go out, and never receive company. It's the way they live here.'

'That must be hard for someone as sociable as you.'

'I'm going mad. I just wish …' Lucy paused. 'Well, I wish Murad would recover, of course, but if he does not, I almost wish we had never met. Is that awful of me? I find it agony to spend time with him now that I can't see any trace of the man he used to be and I know for certain he would not wish to live like this.' It made her heartsick to remember their conversations about blonde-haired daughters who played piano and black-haired sons to take over his business, a house with pomegranate trees in the garden – all of it impossible now.

384

'That's perfectly natural. It must be awful for you to watch him in this condition. And the lifestyle here is quite different to the one to which you were accustomed in London.'

'Oh, Hafza is terribly kind and the girls try to include me in their activities, but my lack of knowledge of the language hinders true friendship.'

'You have not learned any more Turkish?'

'I don't think I have a gift for languages. I can't decipher the Arabic letters and my memory simply does not retain words. Yesterday Hafza told me the word for pomegranate – and today I have forgotten it again.' She snapped her fingers by her head.

'I've heard being with child can adversely affect the memory,' Dorothea said. 'Once the baby is born, yours may improve.'

'And that's another thing …' Lucy threw her hairbrush on a dresser with a clatter. The words burst out in a rush, as if she had been storing them up for ages. 'I don't even want this baby. I can't face raising it on my own. I still can't believe the man I love – the two men I loved – have gone.' She began to cry, then stopped herself with an effort. 'It's not fair, Dorothea. It's simply not fair.'

Dorothea rose and put her arms round her sister. She didn't know what to say, so just held her close. 'It will get better,' she whispered eventually, although at that moment she couldn't see how.

Lucy's labour pains began in the early hours of the 8th May and she rushed in to Dorothea's room to waken her. The contractions were still mild so they lay side by side on Lucy's bed and dozed fitfully for a few more hours. At six, they sat holding hands on the little balcony of her room and watched the sunrise turning the stone of the garden walls pink. During the morning, the pains built gradually, and Dorothea rubbed

Lucy's back and stroked her brow, speaking soothing words. In the gaps between pains, she read to her from a novel the British ambassador's wife had lent her, *Hard Times* by Mr Charles Dickens. She was more nervous than Lucy, who did not seem to appreciate the dangers of childbirth. It was better that she didn't, but with each labour pain Dorothea felt more alarmed. It seemed to her the baby was in the right position, with the head engaged. Should it get stuck she could call on Mr Crawford to operate, but such surgery had a poor outcome for mothers, with fewer than half surviving an abdominal opening. Pray God it wouldn't come to that.

Hafza arrived, bringing trays of sweetmeats and cool drinks, struggling to contain her excitement. Towards late afternoon, when the contractions became more frequent and painful she summoned a Turkish midwife, a stooped, elderly woman with deep lines scored in her leathery face. She offered a herbal drink, miming that it would speed the labour. 'Is good,' Hafza said in her faltering English. Dorothea smelled it and shrugged, saying she could see no harm in it. Lucy had become fractious and accused them of trying to poison her, but sipped it all the same and seemed calmer afterwards.

Within an hour of taking the herbal drink, Lucy gave a sudden scream and gripped Dorothea's hand so tightly that her wedding ring cut grooves in the adjacent fingers. The baby was moving down the birth canal. Suddenly there was no time to worry about things going wrong. Dorothea put a careful hand between Lucy's legs to feel for the head then gently manoeuvred it down, giving her sister instructions on when to push. Hafza held Lucy's hands and the midwife watched over them, ready to step in if needed, but it all went very smoothly.

Dorothea carefully slid the head out and cleared mucus from the nose and mouth before delivering the rest of the child and holding it up. To her relief, it began to squawk straight away, sounding for all the world like a seagull chick. It was only then that Dorothea looked between the legs and told Lucy, 'It's a boy.'

Hafza was sobbing uncontrollably as the midwife cut the cord and delivered the placenta, and Dorothea was so profoundly moved she found she was trembling. Many times she had helped patients to pass over in death and now she had done the exact opposite, aiding in the safe delivery of a child to life. It was a great privilege, and an experience she knew she would never forget.

The midwife washed the baby and they saw that not only was he a boy, but he was a very Turkish-looking boy, with a shock of fine jet-black hair and deep golden skin. He looked uncannily like a miniature Murad. The midwife swaddled him in a shawl and Hafza held out her arms for her grandson. She held him close and whispered in his ear what sounded like a Muslim prayer, beginning, 'Allahu Akbar! ...' When the recitation was finished she dipped her finger in a little saucer of sweet juice and rubbed it onto the baby's gums. Only then did she offer to hand him to Lucy.

Lucy shook her head: 'I'm exhausted.' She had barely glanced at the child. The midwife offered her another herbal concoction and she drank it without question then lay back and closed her eyes. Dorothea thought she looked much older than her twenty years, and she stroked her hair and kissed her forehead. 'You've done well,' she whispered. 'Thank you for letting me be here.'

Hafza cradled the child, cooing to him, exclaiming over his tiny fingers and toes. She was beside herself with happiness and couldn't sit still, disappearing briefly to fetch Murad's sisters so she could show them their new nephew. The wet nurse she had hired arrived to give him his first feed and he took to the breast immediately, sucking noisily. Given

Lucy's exhaustion, Dorothea suggested in mime that the party move to another room to let her rest, and they filed out, taking the baby with them.

Dorothea sat with Lucy until she was sound asleep, then went to find Gordon. 'I did it!' she grinned, her eyes glistening. 'I was more scared than I thought I would be but somehow I delivered my first baby. Mother and child – a boy – are in good health.'

Gordon kissed her. 'I hope the experience did not disincline you from having a child yourself.'

Dorothea blushed as she said, 'Quite the opposite.' She did not tell him that her monthly bleed was two weeks late. Today was Lucy's day. Her news could come later, once she was completely sure.

Chapter Forty-six

Lucy lay in bed for four days after the delivery, feeling utterly drained. The heat had grown oppressive and she fanned herself with a paper fan, her nightgown damp with sweat and her head aching. She was tetchy with Dorothea, who brought light meals to tempt her appetite and cool drinks to refresh her.

'How can it be so hot when it is only May? How can anyone survive a summer here? There is not a breath of air. Look, there's no movement in the drapes although the window is wide.'

Dorothea spoke soothingly. 'It is a little cooler in the shade in the garden. There's a breeze down by the fountain. When you feel sufficiently recovered to come downstairs I think you will find it very pleasant.'

'I can't possibly rise today. You have no idea of the pain, Dorothea. And I could not sleep last night for the heat. Even in the darkest hours it's like being inside a bread oven.'

'I agree it's baking hot by night as well as by day. I suppose the people here are used to it.' Dorothea lifted the fan and began to fan Lucy.

'And I have been bitten by some flying insects. Look!' She showed two angry red lumps on her wrist and elbow.

'We keep our window closed at night so the insects do not fly in, but I admit it makes the heat more oppressive.'

'Oh Dorothea, I want to go back to England. Can't we just leave? I yearn to see London ... and Papa. I miss Papa. Please take me home.'

'But the child?' Dorothea asked quietly. 'What of the child?'

'I ... I don't know.' Lucy turned and buried her face in the pillow. How was she supposed to make decisions? Her head was all muddled and she couldn't think straight.

The wet nurse fed the baby but Lucy's milk had come in and soaked through her nightclothes, meaning she had to change frequently. She knew she should be taking an interest in the child, who was brought to her two or three times a day, but most of the time he was monopolised by Murad's mother, sisters and aunts. Everyone remarked on his resemblance to Murad and when Lucy held him, she saw it was unquestionable: he had the long lashes, the same chin, the blue-black hair. It didn't feel as though he was hers. It broke her heart to look at the tiny boy who would never know his father. It broke her heart that Murad would never know he had a son.

On the fifth day after giving birth, Lucy rose, bored with the view from her bed and tempted by Dorothea's description of the breeze by the fountain. She washed and dressed in her lightest gown and arranged her hair in a loose knot. It was shortly after luncheon and everyone appeared to be resting in their rooms because she didn't see a soul as she descended the stairs and walked out into the garden. The heat hit her like a hammer blow and the brightness blinded her. Squinting, she hurried towards the fountain, noting the overblown lushness of the huge-headed flowers and their sweet, almost cloying fragrance. Crickets were chirruping noisily and she remembered Murad telling her that the sound was emitted by male crickets trying to attract females. There were obviously many lovelorn insects in the vicinity. She passed beneath an arbour into the area near the fountain where there was a little court-yard shaded by the garden wall, and was startled to see Gordon sitting in a chair, deep in thought. He leapt to his feet.

'Lucy! I'm delighted to see you recovered enough to venture outside. How are you feeling?'

'I'm hot,' she sighed. 'I came in search of relief from this sweltering climate.'

'Pray sit down.' He pulled up a chair for her. 'May I join you, or would you rather be left in peace?'

'Oh, please join me. I am so fed up with the company of women. Everyone is chattering about this miraculous baby I have produced, admiring his every sigh and blink as great accomplishments. I don't speak Turkish, of course, but one can tell that's the only topic of interest to them.'

'I'm rather in agreement with you. Babies are of limited interest at that age.' He smiled. 'So tell me how *you* are – apart from hot, that is.'

'I'm confused.' Lucy felt a sudden welling of tears and blinked them back. 'I'm homesick for London and I miss my Papa, but how can I take the baby away from Hafza? She has lost her son and it would be unspeakably cruel of me to take her grandson as well. But I can't stay here. I simply can't bear it.'

Gordon nodded. 'You have had too much tragedy in your life for one so young. To lose your mother at thirteen, and then two husbands within a year of each other before you are twenty is harsh indeed. Now you are in mourning and must treat yourself with great gentleness.'

Lucy liked the fact he had called Murad a husband. She felt he had been so in all but law. 'You know my circum-stances, Mr Crawford ... Pray, tell me what you think I should do.'

'I can't do that – it is your decision alone – but if you like, we can explore the options.'

Lucy thought how unlike her sister he was; Dorothea never missed a chance to dictate what she should do. And then she realised that she was thinking of the Dorothea of old, the one with whom she had spent her teenage years in London. In fact, her sister had offered no advice on her current predicament, withholding her opinions and simply offering comfort. As a result, Lucy had no idea what to do. She yearned for guidance from someone older and wiser. 'Yes, please. If you will.'

He poured her a glass of mint tea from a teapot that sat on a little mosaic table and topped up his own glass before continuing. 'So the first option is for you to stay here and bring up the child in Turkey amongst his relatives. Arguably that could be the best thing for him, since he could encounter prejudice in Britain because of his colouring and heritage. In Crimea I noticed an insidious and quite unwarranted hostility to the Turkish troops. But, on the other hand, the very quiet life led by Murad's family does not suit what I already know of your character and preferences. So this option has certain drawbacks. Do you agree?'

Lucy spoke passionately: 'I feel as though I have served seven months in gaol – albeit a very beautiful gaol.' She looked around at the carefully tended garden and sighed.

'Option two,' he ticked off on his fingers: 'you could come home and either live with your father in London, should he decide to stay there, or with Dorothea and me in Edinburgh. Or perhaps you could travel between the two as it suits you. That leaves the question of what to do with the baby.' He was watching her expression closely. 'If you bring the child to England, you would not be unique in raising him alone. Many women have lost husbands in this war, and many children are fatherless.

392

Your friend Adelaide, of whom Dorothea told me, is in the same situation.'

Lucy considered this. 'But what kind of life must I lead? That of a lonely widow? I can't imagine that I will ever find love after Murad but at the same time, having known the joys it brings, it is hard to accept I will never experience them again.' She shocked herself by saying this. How could she think this way while Murad lay trapped in a world of his own? Were their situations reversed, she was sure he would be more devoted. She must be a terrible person.

Gordon did not appear shocked but answered in a rational tone: 'It is true there are some gentlemen who would not want to take on a woman with a dark-complexioned child; but equally I am sure there are plenty of good men who would. And you are very beautiful, my dear, so I imagine the chances are fair.'

Lucy screwed her mouth to one side. She could not get used to thinking of herself as a woman with a child, never mind a dark-complexioned one.

Gordon paused before continuing: 'Your third option might be to leave the child here in Smyrna to be raised by Murad's family, at least during its infancy. I expect Hafza would readily agree, and would welcome you whenever you wished to visit. Meanwhile you would be free to make a new life in England as you wished.'

Lucy frowned. 'But what kind of woman would leave behind her own child?'

Gordon selected his words carefully. 'Many of the soldiers' wives who accompanied their husbands to war have not seen their children in two years. Lady Stratford de Redcliffe, the British ambassador's wife, has four children who were raised in England and she has seen them but once or twice a year during the thirteen years they have been based in Constantinople.' Lucy's tears were flowing silently now.

Gordon continued: 'No one who knows your history could condemn you for any decision you make, so long as the child is well cared for.' He offered a handkerchief and Lucy took it and blew her nose hard.

'I want to go home, but it doesn't feel right … I don't know if I could leave my own child. I must think further.'

'Dorothea and I plan to leave next week and you are welcome to accompany us. Before then, I am going to perform an operation on Murad that I hope will relieve the fits he is suffering. With the family governess translating, I explained it to Hafza and she has agreed. Is it all right with you?'

'Of course. If you think it will help. Thank you, Gordon. Thank you so much.'

After their conversation, Lucy felt a welling of excitement. Perhaps there was a way she could return to London and see her Papa. She missed the weather. She missed having a glass of port wine after dinner. She missed her own clothes. Most of all, she missed conversation and friendship. She didn't miss the petty rules of London society, but she had been so lonely in Smyrna, and before that in Crimea, that now she yearned for company.

Thoughts of leaving made her feel more affectionate towards the baby and when the wet nurse brought him to see her later she covered his little face in kisses. He really was rather a dear thing, sucking his fists and gurgling as he squinted up at her. She had agreed with Hafza that they could name him Murad, after his father, but Lucy couldn't bring herself to think of him as that, so instead she nicknamed him 'Mumu'. Little Mumu.

'Aren't you the sweetest little darling?' she cooed, and he frowned as if trying to work out who she was. 'It's Mama. I'm your mama.' He gazed at her, boss-eyed, then hiccupped, surprising himself and making Lucy laugh out loud.

Chapter Forty-seven

Dorothea supervised as Hafza's staff scrubbed a tiled side room on the ground floor and brought in a long wooden table. She cleaned Gordon's instruments in boiling water and donned her nurse's uniform to assist him during the operation on Murad. He planned to carry out a trepanation, a procedure in which a hole is cut in the skull in order to release any noxious vapours or fluids that are pressing upon the brain. It was not without risk but had often achieved good results in patients who suffered repeated seizures.

They had brought some chloroform with them from Crimea and Dorothea administered it, sending Murad to sleep before he was lifted onto the table. She knew some doctors performed trepanation without anaesthesia but they could not risk their patient thrashing around during surgery. As he lay unconscious she looked at his handsome features and tried to imagine the kind of person he had been, this man who had captured her sister's heart, who had produced the extraordinary calligraphy she had shown them. Lucy described him as quiet and gentle, an opposite type to Charlie; Dorothea wished she had had a chance to meet him in better days.

The operation began: first Dorothea shaved Murad's head then Gordon fixed it tightly within a brace and, using a circular tool known as a trephine, began to cut into the top right-hand side of his skull close to the site of the scar caused by his injury. Blood gushed from the wound and Dorothea did her best to mop it so it did not obscure the area in which Gordon was working. He cut round a section of skull about the size of a shilling and removed it with tweezers. Inside, Dorothea saw the bloodied curls and folds of his brain, the mystical organ that scientists believed controlled human thought and personality. Some whitish liquid oozed out, as Gordon had predicted. If only this operation could jolt Murad's brain back to sentience and reason. She knew her husband had promised no such thing but couldn't help but hope.

Gordon cauterised the wound to stop the bleeding and Dorothea cleaned the blood from Murad's face and neck. The plan was to keep this aperture open so any noxious fluids or vapours could be released and the edges would need careful tending till they healed. The orderly carried Murad back to his bed and Dorothea sat by his bedside checking his pulse as he began to come round. When he retched, sickness dribbled down his chin and she had to clear it from his mouth and airway lest he should choke. She showed the orderly how to do it, and also got the governess to translate her instructions on cleaning the wound every day and giving a dose of the medicine Gordon had prescribed. While she was talking, she glanced around to find Murad's eyes had opened and he was gazing directly at her. He appeared able to focus again; that was an encouraging sign. When Gordon came in to check on the patient, he professed himself pleased.

Over the next two days, Dorothea kept a careful watch on Murad's progress and was glad to note that he did not have a single seizure. His vital signs were good, and to her eyes he seemed vaguely aware of what was happening in the room.

'Is it possible that he still has his intelligence of old but has no way of expressing himself since his physical body no longer functions?' Dorothea asked Gordon. 'Would that not be the cruellest of fates?' At least with her father, he seemed to have no knowledge of his decline; he did not remember that once he had been an astute business owner.

'Let me show you something,' Gordon said. He vanished for a minute and came back with a small glass containing some lemon juice. 'You know that while I have been here I have been testing Murad and experimenting in many different ways to ascertain his capabilities and sentience. What you are about to see is but one of the measures I have tried.'

He pulled up a chair alongside the bed and offered Murad a sip of the lemon juice. Murad's lips opened and he drank a mouthful then shuddered and grimaced at the bitter taste. 'You see that? He doesn't like it.'

Dorothea nodded.

Gordon offered Murad another sip from the glass, and once again his mouth opened, he took a drink then grimaced. Gordon paused to let Dorothea consider the conclusion. 'He had no memory that just seconds before he had not liked that taste. Babies of a few months old have better memories. His reactions are all physical instincts. The corners of his mouth often curve upwards, but I wouldn't call it a smile. He doesn't differentiate between his reactions to his mother and to me, a relative stranger. He shudders and struggles when something does not feel nice, but does not shrink from its repetition. Occasionally he makes sounds but I suspect they are caused by wind or lying in an awkward position rather than being within his control. All my tests have proved – to my mind conclusively – that there is no intelligence there. His memories and everything that made him the man he was are gone, and all that remains is the shell he inhabited.'

He passed Dorothea his handkerchief to stem the tears that were leaking from her eyes, then put his arm around her. 'I'm sorry to be so frank but I know you can take the truth.'

'I'm glad you told me. I would have hated to think he was somehow trapped, knowing his fate and unable to affect it. But now I see that was never the case.' She stroked Murad's head, where the hair was already beginning to grow back, before whispering: 'It was such a cruel war.'

Dorothea went up to Lucy's room to report on Murad's progress. She found her sister curled on top of her bed with the baby asleep beside her, her finger gripped in his tiny fist. Lucy listened without responding as Dorothea told her that Murad seemed slightly improved.

'Would you like to see him?' Dorothea asked. 'He is ready for visitors.'

'I can't. I can't bear to see his tongue lolling out of his mouth and eyes rolling like a lunatic, and I don't think he would want me to see him like that.'

'I think you will find him a little better. He no longer rolls his eyes in that distressing way ... But this is not the only matter troubling you, is it? Gordon told me of your talk in the garden and I wondered if you have made a decision about whether to sail with us next week?'

Lucy shook her head. 'I would love to come. I want nothing more than to return to London. But how can I leave my son when I understand what it is to be mother-less? How can I inflict that pain on a child? I know you will say it is different because I was thirteen when I lost my mother and Mumu does not even know me yet. But no one loves a child as much as its mother. Already I can feel that. And he should not grow up without the security of that all-encompassing, immutable love, the kind of love that Mama always had for us.'

Dorothea pulled a chair to Lucy's bedside and sat down. 'If you want to come home and you do not want to be separated from your child, then you must bring him with you.'

'But how will I look after him?' Lucy sat up, her voice rising. 'I have only recently learned how to look after myself. I know nothing of babies.'

Dorothea took her hand and smiled. 'Neither do I, but perhaps we can learn together.'

Lucy blinked. 'What do you mean?'

'I must share with you some news that I have not yet told Mr Crawford. I beg you to keep it to yourself for now but … I believe I am with child.' She grinned. It was the first time she had said the words out loud and she couldn't repress her exhilaration.

'Oh my!' Lucy grabbed her and hugged her tightly. 'Oh, that is wonderful news! Dorothea, I am overjoyed for you.'

'If you bring Mumu to Edinburgh and live with us, our children can grow up together, like siblings. We will hire a nurse for them and in time a governess, and you can fill your days however you wish.'

'But what would Mr Crawford say to this plan?'

'Before I even agreed to marry him, he offered to have you and Papa live with us. I know he would be delighted to welcome you and your son.'

Lucy clapped her hands in glee, then stopped. 'And Hafza? How can I take her grandson away?'

'You will be able to visit regularly now that steamships cross the Mediterranean. She can still be a part of Mumu's life. And his father can see him as well. Do go and visit him, Lucy. I think you will find him at peace.'

*

399

Lucy's last dinner with Hafza and her daughters was a feast of colourful dishes. There was chicken cooked with apricot and almonds; whole fishes baked in salt; bright vegetable mixtures and, for dessert, sweet pastries and ripe fruits. They gave Lucy a gift of a new gown in the Eastern style, in silk the exact shade of a deep pink flower she admired in the garden. For the baby, there were soft blankets and a tiny suit with trousers and tunic in apple-green silk, decorated with embroidered scrollwork. And for Dorothea and Gordon they had some fragrant oils stored in tiny painted glass bottles within a leather travelling kit. Lucy kissed each girl in turn and hugged Hafza, the woman who had become like a mother to her.

'I will return next winter,' she promised. 'You will see Mumu again before he is a year old.'

Hafza gazed at the child, who lay sleeping in his cradle in the corner of the room, and said something in Turkish. Safiye translated: 'She says he is the best gift she has ever received, and that you will always have a home here.'

Lucy dreaded saying goodbye to Murad but when she forced herself to enter his chamber she got a surprise. The shaved head startled her – she hadn't known his beautiful hair must be cut – but his eyes were open and his lips curled into a little smile as she walked in, as if he was pleased to see her.

'My darling,' she explained, holding his hands in hers, trying not to look at the hole in his skull. 'I'm going home for a while with our son but I will return soon. Don't forget me while I am gone. I have loved you so very much. *Seni canımdan çok seviyorum.*'

His expression was blank but he was regarding her calmly. She kissed him on each cheek then on his curled fingers and said, 'God bless you, my sweet man', before standing to leave the room. Outside the door she paused to compose herself.

She heard the orderly bringing him some drink and then she heard Murad's voice saying 'Oosh', quite distinctly, as if he were calling her name.

On the 1st June, the *Espinola* stopped in Constantinople after picking up some returning British troops in Sevastopol. Gordon, Dorothea and Lucy boarded at a wharf to the south of the European side of the city, along with Mumu and the Turkish wet nurse, who would stay with them to feed the baby until Lucy's return to Smyrna. Gordon had paid for a luxurious suite of cabins where they would have every possible comfort. Lucy had fretted about the journey being hazardous for such a young baby, but Gordon reassured her that Mumu was a sturdy boy of robust good health, and that he and Dorothea were on hand should they be needed.

As the ship struck out into the Sea of Marmara, they stood on deck to watch the minarets of the city getting gradually fainter, until they were ghostly black fingers pointing to the dusky pink sky. Someone shouted, 'Look over there!' and they turned to see a couple of dolphins playing in the water, rolling and gliding in their wake.

'Look, Mumu. Look at the pretty fish,' Lucy said, stroking her son's cheek.

Dorothea was on the point of correcting her, telling her that they were dolphins, when she stopped herself. She caught eyes with Gordon and shared a smile.

Dorothea loved the fact they could tell each other's meaning from a single glance. Every day it seemed they grew closer. Suddenly, standing there in the fading light, she felt full to the brim with love. There was the fierce love she felt for her sister, the warm glow of love she felt for Gordon, deepening by the day, the protective love she felt for her poor befuddled father, and the maternal urge she already felt towards the child growing silently within her. The feelings she'd had for some of her patients was love, just as it was for the little dark-complexioned nephew she hoped soon to introduce to her own child.

She expected Gordon to guess her condition any time now. Perhaps he had already, because when they descended the stairs to their cabin he gripped her arm so tightly that she knew, no matter what happened in the future, he would never let her fall.

Historical Note

The Crimean War

One of the immediate triggers for the Crimean War has a certain resonance in the 21st century: an argument over which religious faction should have priority access to Jerusalem's holy sites during festivals. The religions were different – Russia supported Orthodox rights against those of the Catholics, who were backed by France – but the city was a flashpoint 160 years ago, as it is now.

The bigger picture was about the political repercussions as the vast, hugely over-extended Ottoman Empire crumbled. At its height at the end of the 17th century, it encompassed the modern-day countries of the Balkans, from Greece to Hungary, the Caucasus region from the Black Sea to the Caspian Sea, huge swathes of the Middle East, including much of Iraq, Egypt and Saudi Arabia as far south as Somalia, and the North African coast as far west as Morocco. One by one, areas started breaking away, as Greece did after a rebellion in the 1820s, and Russian Tsar Nicholas I hoped to position himself as a 'protector' of the Balkans and of Orthodox Christians throughout the Ottoman Empire. Britain wasn't at all keen on this, suspicious of his motives and anxious to protect her own naval supremacy (and her trade route to India), and France was similarly wary.

For two centuries Russia had been expanding southwards in search of a naval base on the Black Sea which, unlike its Baltic ports, wouldn't freeze over in winter. But once it acquired Ukraine and the Crimean peninsula, and moved south towards the Danube, it was set for a head-to-head conflict with the Ottomans. In October 1853 Ottoman Sultan Abdülmecid I declared war on Russia, confident he could expect British and French backing, and straight away suffered a humiliating defeat when one of his naval squadrons was wiped out by the Russians at the Battle of Sinope and 3,000 Turkish soldiers killed. It was as shocking in its day as Pearl Harbor would be in 1941, with significantly more casualties. British and French ministers prevaricated throughout the winter of 1853–54 trying to clarify their war aims, which in essence were vague and flimsy, based on fear of Russian expansionism and, in the case of Napoleon III, a desire to bolster French prestige and reinforce his grip on power. Ultimatums were issued and finally, in March 1854, Britain and France declared war on Russia and began to muster their troops.

Britain hadn't been at war since 1815, when Wellington's army famously defeated Napoleon I at Waterloo, but a certain military arrogance persisted from those glory days, which reality on the field of battle soon belied. The British commander Lord Raglan, who had fought at Waterloo, was now doddery and indecisive; in fact, he often got confused and thought he was fighting the French rather than the Russians. Little was known about the topography and climate of the regions they sailed to, and there were catalogues of errors from the start. The long delay while the troops camped at Varna in summer 1854 gave the Russians ample opportunity to retreat from the Danube area and fortify Sevastopol

– and also allowed the fierce spread of the cholera epidemic that killed over a thousand men before a shot had been fired. The Zouave troops of North Africa knew to prevent cholera infection by boiling water before drinking it but the fact that the disease was water-borne was only just occurring to John Snow, a physician in London, and did not reach medics at the British or French camps.

The war could have ended after the Russians retreated from the Danube, but this would not have justified the vast expense in transporting so many men out there (the French had 400,000, the British 250,000). Instead, the commanders decided to destroy the Russian Black Sea fleet based at Sevastopol, so as to bring lasting security to the Black Sea area (or at least that was the hope). The embarkation from Varna began, but the British and French high command got cold feet about a full-on attack on Sevastopol and landed at Kalamita Bay, thirty-three miles to the north. There was no resistance at first, and when they finally engaged with Russian troops at the Battle of Alma on 20th September 1854, it was a victory for the allies despite chaos on the field due to lack of clear leadership. Already there were supply problems: heavy clothing and spare supplies had been left behind at Kalamita Bay, ambulance carts had not yet been shipped from Varna, and there were no hospitals in which to treat the wounded.

The Battle of Balaklava, fought on the 25th October 1854, is still much debated by military historians. The Russian attack was initially successful in driving Turkish troops from their redoubts on Causeway Heights, but the second line of defence, the Sutherland Highlanders, would not give way, and when the British Heavy Brigade charged in, the Russians were forced to retreat. However, as they fled they were taking big guns from the captured redoubts and Lord Raglan ordered the Light Brigade to stop them.

Unfortunately, the vague, misleading order was mangled as it passed through a string of five officers (including the rival Lords Cardigan and Lucan) and the Light Brigade charged into the North Valley instead of the South, right into the sights of the Russian artillery. Of the 661 men who rode out that day, 113 were killed, 134 wounded, 45 taken prisoner, and 362 horses were lost as well. However, the Russian cavalry were so spooked by the courage of the British cavalry that they were reluctant to face them again, so some historians think the accidental charge was not without its benefits in the long run.

The Russians tried once more to prevent Sevastopol becoming encircled at the Battle of Inkerman (5th November), which they lost. But winter arrived with a fierce storm on 14th November that sank thirty of the allies' supply ships. It soon became clear that they must besiege Sevastopol through the winter of 1854–55 without adequate shelter, food or medicine. It was a calamity – and one that could so easily have been avoided.

Women in the war

We know about the experiences of women during the Crimean War because so many of them wrote memoirs of their time there: among them *Journal Kept During the Russian War* by Mrs Henry (Fanny) Duberly, in which, as I have reflected in my story, she seems more concerned about her horse than about the soldiers' wives; *The Autobiography of Elizabeth Davis, A Balaclava Nurse*, by the woman I have fictionalised as a friend of Dorothea's; *Nurse Sarah Anne: With Florence Nightingale at Scutari*, by Sarah Anne Terrot, from whom I have 'borrowed' the stories of some patients; and, of course, *Wonderful Adventures of Mrs Seacole in Many Lands*, by the indomitable Mary Seacole. Some doctors also left memoirs, including George Lawson's descriptive *Surgeon in the Crimea*. Florence Nightingale did not write a memoir but her time there is amply documented in her letters, and her views on medical matters are quite clear from her *Notes on Nursing*, published in 1859.

My major characters are inventions but most of the minor ones are historical: Captain Bill Cresswell of the 11th Hussars and his wife Adelaide are genuine (although I changed the circumstances of his death); Mrs Williams and Mrs Blaydes both served as ladies' maids to Mrs Duberly; the women around Florence Nightingale (Mrs Bracebridge, Mrs Roberts et al.) were real people, as were most of the officers mentioned, and the British ambassador Viscount Stratford de Redcliffe and his wife were key figures in the war. I have taken a few historical liberties: for example, there is no record of a woman as young as eighteen accompanying the troops and it is probably unlikely, but I wanted Lucy to be especially vulnerable so allowed myself dramatic licence.

The soldiers' wives and nurses were a hardy bunch, but they were challenged to the extreme in circumstances that were wildly outwith anything they had experienced in Victorian England. Slowly, and with much bungling, by spring 1855 the British army managed to get a supply chain in place for the British camp by building a railway from Balaklava through Kadikoi. They also built an intercontinental electric telegraph network that meant news from the front could be received in London within a few hours instead of days. And photographs were sent back by Roger Fenton, the first-ever war photographer, although there were no action shots because of the long exposure times he needed (some examples of his work are shown below).

Improvements in conditions were partly driven by the reports of W.H. Russell, the first independent war reporter; certainly it was his coverage of the aftermath of the Battle of Alma that led to Florence Nightingale being sent out to Constantinople to take charge of treatment of the wounded. Although the death rate at her hospital in Scutari was far higher than elsewhere, mainly due to its situation on a festering cesspit, she set standards that would revolutionise the nursing profession. Her health was permanently weakened by the bout of fever she caught in Crimea in May 1855, which modern doctors suspect was brucellosis caused by consumption of infected meat or milk, but she continued to be an influential force until old age.

The second year of war
Sevastopol was well-protected by fortifications on Malakhov Hill and a number of forts, including the Mamelon and the Redan. Assaults on these between March and June 1855 led to high numbers of casualties on all sides for absolutely no military gains. In August, the Russians once again attacked Balaklava but were defeated at the Battle of Chernaia, under a force that included Sardinian troops sent by Victor Emmanuel II of Piedmont-Sardinia. (He hoped his involvement would persuade the French to help him to obtain Italian unification, which they duly did.) On 5th September a huge French bombardment led to the long-awaited capture of the Malakhov and the city fell on 9th September, but not before many of its able-bodied citizens had escaped across a 960-metre pontoon bridge to the north side of the harbour, setting the military stores on fire before they left. The allies entered Sevastopol to find the historic city in ruins, and while the French soldiers took to pillaging the treasures, the British quickly found the alcohol stores.

For the regiments that had been besieging Sevastopol, the war was over bar the waiting, but it continued on several other fronts: in Kars (modern-day Armenia), in the

Baltic, and even with a skirmish or two over in the Pacific, while the allies worked out what they wanted in a peace treaty. The terms signed at the Treaty of Paris in March 1856 were that Russia handed back all territory seized from the Ottoman Empire and gave up her claims to be protector of the Empire's Christian subjects, while the Ottoman Sultan promised to respect both his Christian and Muslim subjects. The Crimean peninsula was restored to Russia on the understanding that she would not build military ports there and that warships would no longer sail in the Black Sea. (It wasn't long before the Russians conveniently forgot this clause, and they were at war with the Turks again in 1877.)

The estimates of those killed during the Crimean War are 450,000 Russians, 120,000 Ottomans, 95,000 French, 20,813 British and 2,000 Sardinians – the vast majority of them (80 per cent in the case of the Brits) due to disease and neglect rather than battle wounds. It's a war that should never have happened, and quickly became a byword for military incompetence: what one historian called 'more than two years of fatal blundering in slow motion by inept statesmen'.

A lot was learned from it, as is almost always the case with wars. After-effects included the abolition of the purchase of commissions in the British army in favour of promotion on merit; the institution of professional nursing training and qualifications; many military, engineering and medical advances; the abolition of the monarchy in France in 1870; and it was probably the spark that led to the end of serfdom in Russia and eventually to the Russian Revolution that overthrew the Romanovs in 1917. Some of the Turks, who had played gracious host to the Western allies, became influenced by Western ideas but there was also resentment at the disrespectful treatment they received from the British and French. In every country involved, citizens began to criticise the aristocratic classes who ruled them and ethnic groups across the region began to demand self-government.

The Ottoman Empire continued to decay and it wasn't long before cracks appeared in the fragile peace – cracks that would ultimately rupture and lead in 1914 to the First World War.

The port of Balaklava

Mrs Fanny Duberly (on horseback) with her husband Henry

The town of Balaklava with the General Hospital on the hill to the right

Officers' graves on Cathcart's Hill

A cavalry section of the British camp, looking towards Kadikoi

The cookhouse of the 8th Hussars

Acknowledgements

Eleanor Dryden, my editor, came up with the inspired suggestion that I write about the Crimean War and has made suggestions at several stages of the writing of this novel that I think have greatly improved it – so huge thanks for all your support, Eli! The rest of the Avon team – Victoria Jackson, Claire Power, Paraston Khiaban, Katie Reeves, Kate Watson, Natasha Williams and Charlotte Dolan – are smart, professional lovely women and I always adore working with them. Thanks also to Keshini Naidoo, my sharp-eyed copy-editor, and to Jo Marino, publicist supremo at the aptly named Light Brigade.

Karen Sullivan, now the brave owner of brand-new publishing company Orenda Books, has been my first reader for many years now and she never fails to come back with the wisest insights into my outlines and early drafts. She has developed the knack of telling me tactfully when she doesn't like a character or thinks a plot strand doesn't work, and she is *always* right, *without fail*. I couldn't do it without you, Kar! For this novel, I also had valuable early comments from the fabulous David Boyle and Kirsty Crawford, writers for whom

I have immense admiration, and my truly wonderful agent Vivien Green: I'm so grateful to have such a brilliant team behind me.

Laurette Burton, author of *The Royal Corps of Signals*, and her husband Cedric Burton of the Royal Signals Museum, advised on military ranks in the 1850s. I'm indebted to them for their advice and apologise that I didn't always follow it to the letter when it got in the way of my story.

Necip Berne, a good friend of my family, did the translations into Turkish, for which I am extremely grateful.

My wonderful friend Piers Russell Cobb conferred with his friend, pianist Charles Owen, to advise me on the pieces that a young lady might have played in the 1850s, and I've adopted all their suggestions. Bless you both! There's a Spotify playlist entitled "No Place for a Lady" should you want to listen while you're reading.

I'm extremely grateful to Natasha McEnroe, director of the Florence Nightingale Museum, and her colleague Holly Carter-Chapell for fact-checking the text relating to nursing history, Miss Nightingale and the Barracks Hospital. Their comments were invaluable. The 8th Hussars Museum in Warwick was useful, as was the Old Operating Theatre in London, which made me wince with its collection of Victorian surgical instruments. And I am particularly indebted to Helen Rappaport and Orlando Figes's books on the Crimean War: they are among my favourite historians, both eminently readable and utterly trustworthy.

A special mention to friends at the Hampstead Heath Women's Pond: I swim there year round, and find the changing-room chats with fellow swimmers endlessly inspiring. What a great bunch of women!

And finally, my love and thanks to Karel Bata. It's always useful to get his film-maker's perspective on plot and character – and he also makes me lots of cups of tea.